The Rose Queen

Katie Flynn is the pen name of the much-loved writer, Judy Turner, who published over ninety novels in her lifetime. Judy's unique stories were inspired by hearing family recollections of life in Liverpool during the early twentieth century, and her books went on to sell more than eight million copies. Judy passed away in January 2019, aged 82.

The legacy of Katie Flynn lives on through her daughter, Holly Flynn, who continues to write under the Katie Flynn name. Holly worked as an assistant to her mother for many years and together they co-authored a number of Katie Flynn novels, including *Christmas at Tuppenny Corner*.

Holly lives in the north east of Wales with her husband Simon and their two children. When she's not writing she enjoys walking her two lurchers, Sparky and Snoopy, in the surrounding countryside, and cooking forbidden foods such as pies, cakes and puddings! She looks forward to sharing many more Katie Flynn stories, which she and her mother devised together, with readers in the years to come.

Keep up to date with all her latest news on Facebook: Katie Flynn Author

KATIE FLYNN

The Rose Queen

PENGUIN BOOKS

PENGUIN BOOKS

UK | USA | Canada | Ireland | Australia
India | New Zealand | South Africa

Penguin Books is part of the Penguin Random House group of companies
whose addresses can be found at global.penguinrandomhouse.com

First published in 2022 by Century
Published in Penguin Books 2022
001

Printed and bound in Great Britain by Clays Ltd, Elcograf S.p.A.

The authorised representative in the EEA is Penguin Random House Ireland,
Morrison Chambers, 32 Nassau Street, Dublin D02 YH68

A CIP catalogue record for this book is available from the British Library

ISBN: 978–1–529–15679–9

www.greenpenguin.co.uk

Penguin Random House is committed to a
sustainable future for our business, our readers
and our planet. This book is made from Forest
Stewardship Council® certified paper.

To our daughter Jasmine

Prologue

Cadi sat in front of her bedroom window admiring the lace roses her mother had painstakingly sewn onto her white cotton dress. The Williamses were a coal-mining family, so by no means had they the money to splash out on a new dress or even material, but Cadi's mother Jill, who was an excellent seamstress, had used her skills to make a dress out of sheets that she had bought from a jumble sale. Determined to make sure her daughter's dress was perfect, she had stayed up late every night sewing each delicate stitch by candlelight and hiding any imperfections with the lace roses she had made from old doilies.

The day of the fete had arrived and Jill had pinned her daughter's fair hair into place, so that the crown of roses would sit perfectly when Lady Houghton inaugurated her later that day.

'This is your day, my darling child, and you are going to be the best Rose Queen the people of Rhos have ever seen,' cooed Jill as she stood back to admire her daughter.

1

As Cadi was the youngest of the four siblings *and* the only girl, this date had been marked on the Williamses' calendar for many months, and expectations were high. Especially with her father, Dewi, who couldn't wait to see his daughter take pride of place in the parade.

Alun, the youngest of her three brothers, suddenly appeared from around the side of the curtain that separated Cadi's part of the bedroom from her brothers'. He blew a low whistle. 'Blimey! Who'd've thought such a skinny little wretch could scrub up so well?' He winked at his mother. 'You must have a magic wand hidden somewhere.' He chuckled, before being instructed to 'get out' by both Cadi and her mother.

'He's only teasing, Cadi,' said Jill as she held up a mirror for Cadi to inspect her appearance. 'You know what boys are like.'

Twisting her head from side to side in order to see her hair from all angles, Cadi smiled at her reflection. 'I certainly do, and I hope you see what I mean about needing a room of my own. Alun didn't even call out, Mam – I could've been in my vest and knickers, or even starkers, for all he knew!'

'I don't know what you want us to do, darling, because we can't afford to rent a bigger house.' She looked around the musty-smelling room. 'We can barely afford this one.'

'I don't mean to moan, and I know you and Dad work all the hours you can – the boys too – I just wish …'

'I know, sweetheart, but it won't be for ever,' assured her mother. 'You'll be moved out and married with kiddies of your own one of these days.'

'I'm only fifteen, Mam! I've years ahead of me yet, and I'm not even certain I want kids.' She rolled her eyes. 'Knowing my luck, they'd all be boys.'

A man's voice yelled out to them from the bottom of the stairs; it was her father. 'Are you two going to stay up there all day?'

Jill called back, 'Coming.' She smiled at her daughter, who stood in front of the window, a shaft of sunlight emphasising her silhouette. 'You wait till your father sees you – he'll be that proud.'

She opened the door and they descended the stairs to where Dewi and Cadi's brothers stood waiting. Cadi blushed as her father nodded approvingly. 'By God, we'll have to fight them off with sticks.'

Pleased to see that the rain had eased off and the sun was breaking through the clouds, Cadi started as a familiar voice called out from behind, 'Let's have a look at you then ...'

Beaming, Cadi turned to greet her best friend and neighbour, Poppy Harding. Holding the sides of her skirt, she pulled them out so that Poppy could marvel at the detail of her dress.

'You look beautiful,' breathed Poppy. Stepping forward, she linked her arm through Cadi's. 'We'd best get a move on, there's a lot of folk waiting for their queen to open the fete.'

The Rose Queen Fete was a special day in the Rhos calendar, and everyone who could do so attended. It was a chance for people to let their hair down and forget about work. The girls would wear their finest dresses, and the boys would be on the lookout for a future wife. Deals would be done, new friendships made and old ones strengthened. Cadi would be seen by people from miles around, something that was very unusual when you lived in such a rural area.

Being a mining village, Rhos was normally a rather drab and dowdy place, but today the houses were adorned with bunting, and baskets of flowers hung outside the village hall and local pub.

'They should do things like this more often,' mused Cadi as they passed her old school, which had also been festooned with decorations. 'It really brightens the place up.'

'Stuff like this costs money, and Rhos isn't wealthy, like Wrexham or Chester.'

'Or Liverpool ...' added Cadi.

'Be fair! Liverpool's a big, important city with a huge port; even Wrexham and Chester can't compete with the likes of a city with that kind of status.'

'I know, I'm just saying it would be nice,' said Cadi. She glanced towards Rhos mountain, which loomed in the distance. In some respects she was lucky to live deep in the heart of the countryside, but to Cadi the mines ruined everything. You couldn't escape the coal dust, which seemed to invade every part of daily life, whether you worked down the mine or not; as for the slag heaps, they were a horrible blot that marred the landscape. She said as much to Poppy.

'It's like they say – coal's a dirty old business, which is why I'm amazed your mam's managed to keep that dress so pristine. It's whiter than a cloud. As for the detail,' she gently ran her finger over one of the many roses that adorned the dress, 'your mam's a genius when it comes to her sewing. I reckon she's good

4

enough to work in one of them high-end shops you was on about, last time you came back from Liverpool.'

Cadi nodded knowledgeably. 'Me too – certainly too good to be working for peanuts, but people in Rhos can't afford to pay good money, so Mam ends up burning both ends of the candle to make ends meet.'

'You're very lucky to have someone so talented in your family,' enthused Poppy. 'No one would ever guess your dress had once been used as a sheet. And coal dust aside, how she managed to keep it free from mould, in a house what's riddled with damp, is more than I'll ever know. Hats off to your mam is all I can say.'

'Mam's been wonderful,' agreed Cadi. 'She made a sort of bag with the leftover bits of sheet. Every time she'd finished doing her alterations, she'd pop it in that and tuck it away in the back of her wardrobe.' She gingerly patted her normally unruly bob. 'As for my hair, I've Mam to thank for that too. She's worked so hard, Poppy. I'd never have managed it without her.'

'Mind you, she's had a good muse in you,' said Poppy. 'When I was Rose Queen my poor old mam had the devil's own job making me look half decent.'

A picture of Poppy as Rose Queen entered Cadi's mind. As she was considerably stouter than Cadi, the dress had not been kind.

Cadi shot her friend a reproving glance. 'Don't be so hard on yourself; what with those big blue eyes of yours, and your sleek black hair, you were simply stunning when you were the Rose Queen – everyone said so.'

Poppy squeezed Cadi's arm. 'And that's why you're my best pal, Cadi Williams, cos you always know the right thing to say.'

As they approached the back of the stage, Cadi placed her hand to her tummy, which was fluttering with anticipation. She nodded to a man with a clipboard who had beckoned for her to step forward. She smiled nervously at Poppy. 'Wish me luck.'

Poppy kissed her on the cheek. 'Good luck.'

The crowd of people who had been chattering amongst themselves fell silent as Lady Houghton delicately placed the crown of roses onto Cadi's head, whilst announcing her to be the new Rose Queen. Cadi blushed to the tips of her ears as the crowd erupted into spontaneous applause, and just when she thought she couldn't feel any more embarrassed, a couple of boys in the throng wolf-whistled their approval, causing her colour to deepen.

As the crowd quietened down, Lady Houghton declared the fete open, and people began to drift off to the various stalls.

'So,' said Poppy as she stepped onto the stage beside her friend, 'how does it feel to be the Rose Queen?'

Cadi sighed happily. 'Wonderful. Deep down, I was dreading all the attention, but it's really quite pleasant.'

Poppy laughed. 'Especially when the fellers show their approval, eh?'

Lowering her gaze, Cadi tried to swallow her smile. 'Not necessarily. Besides, it's uncouth.'

'Uncouth my eye!' grinned Poppy. 'I saw your face when them lads whistled.'

'I suppose it's better than the alternative,' said Cadi.

Poppy gently smoothed one of the lace roses on Cadi's dress. 'Your mam's so talented – this is much better than a new dress. I don't know why you ever thought people would poke fun.'

Cadi touched a couple of stray curls, which had escaped their pins and were now hanging just above her jawline. 'Because my dress is made out of sheets, and Cindy Holland's dress was made out of taffeta. Not only that, but you know what my hair can be like: half the time I look like I've been dragged through a hedge backwards. No matter how hard I try to make my curls behave, they have a life of their own. Quite frankly, I'm surprised I didn't wake up with a face full of pimples.'

Poppy gave her friend a wry smile. 'Cindy Holland fell lucky with her dress cos her sister works in the city. As for you breaking out in spots, I've never seen so much as a blemish on them fair cheeks of yours, never mind a pimple.'

'Like I say, it'd be just my luck. Besides, we all know that if summat's going to go wrong, it'll be me that gets it in the neck.'

Poppy furrowed her brow in confusion, until the penny dropped. 'You're not still harping on about that business with Aled Davies, are you?'

Cadi folded her arms across her chest. 'Yes, I jolly well am! That boy tried to run me over in his honking great tractor, and it's not the first time he's tried to hurt me, neither. Remember when he pulled the chair away as I was about to sit down?' She rubbed her coccyx as she recalled the incident.

Poppy hid her smile behind the palm of her hand. Aled Davies was the son of the local farmer, and he was considered by most to be quite the catch. Cadi, however, had him down as a big-head who believed himself better than everyone else, something that she now affirmed.

'I'm glad he's not bothered coming today because he'd probably do something to ruin it for me.' She fell into quiet contemplation before adding, 'Like he always does.'

Poppy gave a shrewd smile. 'I really believe he didn't know you were about to sit down when he took that chair away; he wasn't even looking in your direction – just like when he drove past with the tractor.'

'Balderdash!' snapped Cadi irritably. 'That boy knows exactly what he's doing. He simply feigns ignorance so that he can pretend it was an accident.'

Believing in fairness, Poppy cut Cadi short. 'I was there both times, and the first time, Aled was talking to one of his teachers—'

Cadi cut across her. 'Swot!'

Sighing, Poppy continued, 'With his hand resting on the back of the chair, he had no idea you were about to sit down because he wasn't looking at you, and it was the same when he drove past with the tractor – he was busy looking where he was going and it's just a shame he didn't see the puddle …'

'Puddle?' cried Cadi. 'I'd hardly call manure that's fallen off the back of the muck-spreader a puddle.'

Poppy grimaced. 'At least he stopped to apologise.'

Cadi folded her arms across her chest. 'I never heard Aled apologising, and neither did you. You couldn't have, because he was laughing too hard.'

Poppy turned away as she tried desperately to straighten her face. Poor Cadi had been engulfed in the manure, and unfortunately the overall effect had left her looking rather comical. 'You must admit it was a little bit funny, and you did get the day off school.'

'That's as may be, but it doesn't take away from the fact that Aled's a mean, spoilt, spotty little oik.'

Tutting, Poppy wagged a reproving finger. 'Spotty little oik? That's not like you, Cadi. Besides, he must be getting on for six foot, so I'd hardly describe him as little.'

'He brings out the worst in me,' pouted Cadi. 'It's the way he struts around like he's the cock of the walk.'

Laughing, Poppy shook her head. 'Honestly, Cadi, how your father ever hopes to marry you off to that boy, I'll never know.'

Cadi's eyes widened. 'Me neither! Dad's convinced the pair of us make a good match – as is Aled's father, by all accounts. I thought arranged marriages went out with the Ark, but that's my dad all over, stuck in the past. Mam too, come to that.'

Poppy frowned. 'I wasn't aware they'd arranged your marriage ...'

Cadi grumbled irritably. 'May as flamin' well have done, the way they carry on.' She rolled her eyes. 'Every time Dad talks about Aled, it's to tell me how lucky I am to have a boy like him interested in me. All I can say is: he's a damned funny way of showing it.'

She cast her mind back to the day that the incident with the tractor and the manure had taken place. She had been standing in the parlour of their terraced house, gingerly removing her clothing.

'I'm sure it was an accident, it's as plain as the nose on your face how much that boy likes you,' said Dewi. 'You should count yourself a very lucky girl to have someone of his standing taking an interest in you, it's not like he hasn't got his pick of the crop.'

'If that's how he shows his interest, then he can sodding well pick someone else,' Cadi said as she gathered her manure-ridden clothes into a bundle.

'I'm sure he didn't mean it, luv,' said her mother. 'Your father's right: accidents do happen.'

'But why do they always happen to me?' whined Cadi as she half skipped, half hopped across the earthen floor to the small stove where her mother stood, wooden tongs in hand, waiting to place Cadi's filthy clothes into a large pan of boiling water.

Arching his brow, Cadi's father turned to Arwel, the eldest of his three sons. 'Tell your sister: if a boy picks on a girl, it's only for one reason.'

'So you admit he's picking on me,' said Cadi, her teeth chattering with the cold. 'Well, if he wants my attention, he can find a better way than covering me in—'

'Cadi!' squeaked her mother. 'Mind what you say.' She scowled at her husband and son, who were both laughing raucously. 'Stop encouraging her.'

'She's right though,' chuckled Arwel. 'I can smell her from here.'

Coughing into his hand, Dewi composed himself. 'I've told you before, I've seen the way Aled looks at you when you're all stood waiting for the bus.' He placed a blanket around his daughter's shoulders. 'He can't keep his eyes off you. Quite frankly, that bus could pass him by and he wouldn't notice.'

'Probably hatching his next plan,' muttered Cadi, adding sulkily, 'I don't see why he bothers going to school, considering that he reckons he knows it all already.'

Her mother gave a derisive laugh. 'For goodness' sake, Cadi, the boy offered to help you with your homework because he wanted an excuse to spend time with you.'

'Well, he needn't have bothered,' snapped Cadi. 'I don't need the help of any man – never have, never will.'

Her father rolled his eyes in exasperation. 'I'm surprised you've got the attention of any feller with an attitude like that.'

'Good! Because I don't want the attention of *any* feller, rich or otherwise,' muttered Cadi. She glanced at her mother, who had resumed her sewing beside the table. She loved her mother with all her heart, but she had no desire to end up working from dusk to dawn for little to no money, whilst forever trying to keep her home free from damp and coal dirt, with no heat or hot water, and all because she'd married a miner. No. If that's what marriage brought you, she would rather stay single for the rest of her life.

Now, as she stood up from the gold-painted wooden throne, she held her hand out for Poppy. 'Come on, they'll be announcing the winner of the Most Beautiful Baby competition in a minute, and I have to be there to hand over the prize.'

'You don't even like babies.'

Cadi hastily hushed her friend into silence as they approached the stage being used for the competitions. 'I can always pretend. Besides, I don't mind them if they're not covered in sick and smelling—'

'Like you did, the day Aled drove by,' quipped Poppy.

Shooting her a withering glance from over her shoulder, Cadi forced her lips into a smile as she left her friend to join the mayor.

After the photographer had taken a picture of Cadi handing over the prize to the mother, who was beaming with pride, Cadi returned to Poppy.

'I've got to go and help judge the beauty contest, are you coming?'

'Of course. I don't intend missing out on a single minute of my best pal's special day.'

Cadi linked her arm through Poppy's. 'Pity it's only for one day.'

'That's why you have to make the most of it,' said Poppy, 'and lap up all the attention because, according to me mam, you won't feel like this again until your wedding day.'

'Living where we do, we're lucky we even get that,' conceded Cadi.

In between judging the various competitions the girls managed to visit some of the stalls, trying their hand at both hoopla and the coconut shy; and it was here that Aled finally put in an appearance.

Seeing him standing in line behind her, Cadi took extra care with her aim, determined to be successful, and was annoyed when her last ball refused to make contact with the coconut.

Taking his turn, Aled flashed a smile at Cadi, who was trying to steer Poppy away. 'Going so soon? If you stick around, I can show you how it's done.'

Cadi heaved a withering sigh. 'I'd rather …' She fell silent as they all watched the first coconut fall from its perch.

Aled grinned smugly at her as he juggled his next ball between his hands. 'It's all in the aim.'

Pulling Poppy away, Cadi waited until they were out of earshot before hissing, 'Can he really get any more obnoxious?'

Poppy shrugged. 'It's not his fault he's good at it.'

'But the way he gloats,' insisted Cadi, 'you heard him.'

Poppy look back at Aled with an air of uncertainty. 'Was he gloating or giving advice?'

Cadi rolled her eyes. 'It's the way he does it, like he's showing off.'

Aled had his arms around a young girl as he helped her perfect her aim. 'Perhaps he's just very confident?' hazarded Poppy.

'Cocky,' said Cadi simply, as she turned to follow Poppy's gaze. 'I remember the time he offered to help me with my homework. Mam reckons it was so that he could spend time with me, but she wasn't there when Aled asked. He was really patronising, like I was some sort of dunce who couldn't add two plus two.'

Poppy looked up. 'What homework was this?'

There was a long pause before Cadi finally admitted that it had been her maths homework.

'But you were always dreadful at maths,' said Poppy. 'Same as me. If I were you, I'd've jumped at the chance.'

'If it were anyone else, I probably would've, but not *him* – he only offered to help so that he could lord it over me.'

Seeing Aled standing with his hands in his trouser pockets, laughing at those who missed the coconuts, Poppy spoke thoughtfully. 'I'll grant you he's a bit of a show-off, and he is a little big-headed, but aren't most boys?'

'Not my brothers,' said Cadi.

'But …' Poppy tried to counteract Cadi's comment, but her friend was speaking the truth.

'You always try to see the good in everyone,' said Cadi, 'which is a truly endearing quality, but you're wasting your time when it comes to Aled.'

'I just want everyone to get along,' reasoned Poppy.

'Everyone else does,' said Cadi simply. 'And if Aled ever gets down off that high horse of his, things might be different, but I can't see that happening somehow.'

'People change as they grow up – I'm sure Aled won't be any different.' Poppy looked around the rest of the stalls, some of which were beginning to pack up. 'Come on, we'd best get a move on before everything's gone.'

It was much later that evening when the girls returned to their homes. Reluctantly Cadi had taken the dress off and hung it up in the back of her wardrobe, before she joined her family at the dinner table.

'Your Majesty,' said Alun, making a low bow.

'Tell him to stop being silly, Mam,' snapped Cadi, but everyone, including her mother, was chuckling. She glanced at the faces around the table, all of which were staring at the top of her head. Reaching up, she gently pulled the crown down and handed it to her mother with an embarrassed smile.

'I'll pop a couple of the roses between the pages of the encyclopaedia, as a keepsake,' said Jill.

Alun stifled a chuckle as he took the seat next to Cadi's. 'It's not like any of us is ever going to read it.'

Jill shot her son a withering glance as she carefully placed the roses in the middle of the book. 'Wash your hands, young man, and if you'd done a bit more reading, maybe you wouldn't be working down the pit.'

Dewi gripped his spoon in readiness for the stew that his wife was beginning to dole out. 'Your mam's right, you should listen to her.'

'You've worked down the pit your whole life,' objected Alun.

'Aye, cos I had no choice, but that doesn't mean to say I *like* working down the mines.'

With everyone ready, Dewi said grace, before they all tucked into the hearty fare.

Speaking between mouthfuls, Dewi turned his attention to his daughter. 'Beautiful, you were. I shouldn't be surprised if they didn't ask you to be Rose Queen again next year.'

Cadi beamed proudly. 'You know you can only be Rose Queen once, Dad. That's why I made the most of today.'

'Aye, you're right there, cariad, but look on the bright side: at least you've your wedding to look forward to,' he said as he skewered a chunk of potato with his fork.

Cadi let out a protest. 'Honestly, Dad! You're as bad as Mam. I don't even know if I want to get married, but if I do, it won't be for a long time yet.' *And certainly not to Aled*, she added in the privacy of her mind.

Dewi spoke disparagingly. 'What do you mean: you don't even know? What else are you planning on doing, if you aren't going to get wed?'

Sensing an argument brewing, Jill pointed at the platefuls of food. 'Less talking, more eating.'

Using his fingernail, Dewi picked a piece of mutton out from between his teeth. 'I don't see what's so bad about getting hitched. It's not like you're going to do anything else with your life.'

'Who says?' snapped Cadi irritably. 'I'm not going to work in the bakery for ever. I want more out of life than that. I want to do summat meaningful, a job where I get to call the shots, instead of being told what to do all the time.' Glancing at her mother, she felt a blush bloom on her cheeks. 'Look at Mam! Working all hours, and never any real recognition for her work; she deserves much better, but she won't get that working round here.'

'What do—' Alun began, but Jill had had enough.

'I didn't spend all that time preparing scrag end for it to go cold, so quit your mithering and get on with your supper,' adding as an afterthought, 'For the record, I'm happy with my lot, Cadi Williams. It may not be your cup of tea, but it suits me fine.'

For the next few minutes the room was silent, apart from the sound of spoons and forks scraping against the plates. When they had finished their supper, the men headed down to the pub whilst Cadi helped her mother collect the empty dishes.

'I'm not saying there's anything wrong with what you do, Mam, far from it. It's just not for me. I want a bit of excitement in my life, and a job where people respect me.'

With her hands covered in soapsuds, her mother itched her forehead with the back of her hand. 'Has all this come about because of today?'

'Not entirely, no. I've always known I wanted more out of life. I suppose you could say today simply con-firmed it.'

Jill passed her daughter a plate to dry. 'I admire your gumption, but I think you may have difficulty finding what you're searching for.'

'I don't expect to be treated like a queen every day,' said Cadi, 'but I do want to feel like I matter, and I liked it when people asked for my judgement in the beauty contest. It made me feel important, and I want more of that.' She gazed wistfully at the plate she was drying. 'I want people to look up to me and value my opinion.'

Her mother carried the dishwater out of the back door and emptied it down the drain before coming back in. 'Sounds very much like the role of a mother to me.'

Cadi loved her mam and was keen not to upset her. 'Being a mother is a very important role, but not the one for me. I want to do something different – break away from the norm, pave my own way in life, be responsible for myself. Is that really so bad?'

Wiping her hands dry on her apron, Jill placed the cutlery in the drawer. 'Not at all, if you're a man ...' She wagged a chiding finger as her daughter made to protest. 'You may not like it, Cadi, but that's the long and short of it: we live in a man's world, and it's men what call the shots, not women.' She smiled kindly. 'Do you have any idea how hard it would be for a woman to take on the role of a man?'

'I only want a small piece of it,' said Cadi. 'There must be something a woman can do without a man's say-so?'

'If there is, then I've yet to hear about it – apart from being an actual queen, of course.' She gave her daughter a calculating stare. 'Tell you what, though, if there is summat out there, I reckon you'll be the one to find it; be damned good at it too, I shouldn't wonder.'

'Thanks, Mam. It's nice to know someone has a bit of faith in me.'

Jill removed her pinny and hung it up by the stove. 'Your father loves you with all his heart, but he's very old-fashioned when it comes to marriage and a woman's role in the world. As far as he's concerned, a woman's place is by the sink whilst the man goes out to earn a wage.'

A line creased Cadi's brow. 'Then why doesn't he object to you working as a seamstress?'

Jill laughed. 'Because he's no choice! In case you hadn't noticed, miners don't make a lot of money. We barely scrape by as it is, which is why he's so keen for you to marry Aled. He knows you wouldn't have to struggle like the rest of us.'

'Only I don't need to marry in order to have a comfortable life,' said Cadi firmly. 'And I'm going to prove that to him if it's the last thing I do, just you wait and see.'

Her mother lifted a chiding eyebrow. 'And how do you intend to do that whilst living in Rhos?'

A picture of Rhos formed in Cadi's mind. The damp and dismal house she lived in, the slag heap that she could see from her bedroom window, and the rows of identical stone houses that she passed on her way to work in the bakery. Her mother was right: there was nothing for her in Rhos. She turned to face her mother, half a smile forming on her lips. 'I don't, which is why I'm going to leave.'

18

Chapter One

July 1939

A year had passed since Cadi's reign and, despite her intentions, she still worked down the bakery alongside Poppy. Much to her annoyance, it seemed that her father had been correct when it came to the life choices of a girl from a small village, and leaving for pastures new had proved easier said than done, when you had nothing to go to. Although this hadn't dampened Cadi's desire to break free from the norm and, with rumours of war spreading fast, she thought she could see a way out of her humdrum existence.

She flourished a flier that she had picked up from the post office. 'Serve in the WAAF with the men who can fly! That's what it says here, and look, Poppy, look at her uniform, isn't that the smartest thing you've ever seen? She represents the sort of woman I aspire to be,' said Cadi as she waited for Poppy to fasten her coat. 'This is the perfect opportunity for us to get out of Rhos and see a bit of the world.'

'I'm sure you're right, and I'm all for it, but you wanted to be your own boss and you'd be far from that in the ATS or the WAAF, or whichever service it is you want to join. They'd be telling you when to get up, when to eat, when to go to sleep: more rules and regulations than you can poke a stick at,' reasoned Poppy.

'True,' mused Cadi, 'but we'd also be living away from home with a whole gaggle of other girls, doing a variety of different jobs, not like the bakery, where it's the same old thing, day in, day out.' She paused for thought. 'My auntie drove lorries in the last lot, I don't see why we couldn't do summat like that. Just think of it, Poppy, we'd get to drive all over the country. Imagine that? My dad's nigh on sixty and he's never so much as driven a car.'

Poppy belted her mackintosh and the girls bade their workmates goodbye before heading for home. 'It certainly would be something, but we can't guarantee we'd get a job as drivers. Knowing our luck, we'd end up peeling spuds in the NAAFI and, quite frankly, I'd rather be here baking buns than doing that.'

Feeling the drizzle begin to fall, Cadi opened up her brolly and put it over her and Poppy. 'The armed forces are huge. We could end up doing any manner of jobs – maybe chauffeuring pilots or even the prime minister. There's plenty of roles we can do that you don't need an education for.' An image of girls in the smart blue uniform of the Women's Auxiliary Air Force entered her mind. 'The most important thing is that we'd have our freedom,' she said. 'We'd be able to go to dances, with no …' She pulled a grumpy face and began to wag her finger in a disapproving fashion, as she imitated her father, 'Where do you think you're going? And you can get that muck off your face!'

A giggle escaped Poppy's lips as she recalled the time she and Cadi had decided to do their own hair and make-up for the flannel dance. 'We did rather plaster it on, so I could sort of see his point, but I don't think we did too badly, considering it was our first attempt.'

'Exactly. We weren't used to it,' said Cadi, 'and our mams didn't think we looked that bad, although mine did say we might have been a bit heavy-handed with the rouge.'

Poppy laughed. 'We looked like we'd done a marathon.'

'It's all part of growing up,' concluded Cadi, 'we all have to learn by our mistakes, but my dad would rather I never went anywhere or did anything.' She gazed dreamily at the hedgerows thick with an array of cow parsley, violets, harebells and foxgloves. 'If we join up, we'll be able to go to the cinema, cafés, dances, shopping – anything and everything – because we'll have no parents to stand in our way.'

Poppy's brow rose. 'And what about the corporal or sergeant, or whoever it is that would be in charge of us? Don't you think they'd have a say in what we did and when we did it? I can't see them letting us wander off, willy-nilly.'

'Granted, but we would get some free time and it would be ours to spend as we pleased, not like at home.'

'You make it sound idyllic,' said Poppy, adding, 'just like they do in that flier you've got, *especially* the ones for the WAAF: beautiful women in smart uniforms smiling away, all happy like they haven't got a care in the world, but I can't see life in the services being that easy. From what I've heard, they're really strict, with all sorts of rules and regulations, so we could be jumping out of the frying pan and into the fire.'

'I know it wouldn't be all fun and games, but we'd be free, independent from our parents and learning lots whilst we're about it,' insisted Cadi.

Poppy, ever the voice of reason, levelled with her friend. 'Even if what you're saying is right, we're both sixteen and I'm pretty sure that's too young to join up.'

Cadi tapped the tip of her forefinger against the side of her nose. 'I've been doing a bit of digging and, from what I can gather, the ones doing the recruiting don't take too close a look at your credentials, if you follow my meaning ...' Seeing the blank look on Poppy's face, she elaborated, 'They turn a blind eye to folk that've altered the date on their birth certificates and—' She got no further.

Poppy was wagging a reproving finger. 'You can stop right there. I'm not forging my birth certificate for no one.' She rolled her eyes. 'My mam'd go bonkers if she found out!'

Cadi looked horrified. 'We wouldn't *tell* our parents what we'd done, or of our intentions, come to that.'

'Don't you think they'd want to know why we wanted our birth certificates? Cos I don't keep mine tucked under me pillow, and I very much doubt you do, either.' She shook her head dismissively. 'Rhos is a small village and if we were to turn up at the recruiting office, I'd bet a pound to a penny we'd know the feller taking folk on, and they wouldn't need to see our certificates to know we was lying about our age.'

Cadi hadn't thought this far ahead, but ever one to think on her feet, she quickly rallied. 'My auntie – the one who drove lorries in the last war – lives in Liverpool. If we went to stay with her, we could sign up whilst we were there. As for our certificates, I know where mine's kept, and I'm sure you do too, and I very much doubt anyone would notice they'd gone missing.'

'And if they accept us? What do we say to our parents?'

Cadi grinned. 'Does it matter? Because by then it'll be too late for them to do anything about it.'

Poppy looked doubtful. 'Do you really think we could get away with it?'

Cadi shrugged. 'We'll never know unless we try, but if we don't, we'll end up baking bread until we wed, and I'd rather take my chances trying to sign up. That's even if we go to war, because there's still a chance we might not.'

'True,' conceded Poppy. 'I'm just not happy with the thought of lying about our intentions.'

As they approached the row of terraced houses, Cadi pulled Poppy to a halt. 'You can keep on living in a cramped two up, two down with the rest of your brothers and sisters, or you can join the services and have your own bed. I know I've had enough of sharing a room with my brothers, but at least I don't have to share a bed with them.'

Poppy instantly made up her mind. 'When you put it that way, I guess you can count me in. Only *not* the ATS, as their uniforms are awful *and* they're more like the fellers in the Army, and I'm not walkin' round in heavy boots and trousers for anyone.'

Cadi smiled. 'I don't think it's quite like that, Poppy.'

'Oh? And how do you know?'

'You know as well as I do that a woman isn't allowed to hold a gun or do any actual fighting. We have the nicer roles, like ferrying officers around and ...' She hesitated, because in truth she only knew what she'd heard on the grapevine or read about in magazines. 'And stuff like that,' she finished rather lamely.

'As long as you're not getting your hopes up too much,' warned Poppy.

With the drizzle turning heavy, Cadi pulled Poppy further under the umbrella. 'As long as I get away from Rhos, I don't much care what I end up doing,' she admitted, 'because anything's going to be better than the bakery.'

'It'll certainly be an adventure,' agreed Poppy.

Cadi smiled. She had won Poppy over. All she had to do now was hope that their parents would allow them to visit her auntie.

'So let's see if I've got this right,' said Dewi, his tone heavy with sarcasm. 'The same day Chamberlain announces we're at war with Germany, you decide you want to go and visit your mam's sister – a woman you've not seen for years – just "because"?' He cast his wife a withering glance. 'Your daughter must think I came down in the last shower! We all know why she's going, and your sister won't waste any time before filling Cadi's head with all kinds of fanciful rubbish.' Seeing the stern look cross his wife's face, he hesitated. 'Did you know about this?'

Jill held up her hands in a placatory manner. 'No, I did not. This is as much news to me as it is to you, and

24

I'd appreciate it if you didn't speak ill of our Flo because of this. It's hardly her fault the girls want to visit.'

Cadi's heart dropped, as she hadn't wanted to cause friction between her parents. 'Please don't argue. I just thought it would be nice to see her, and I could show Poppy where Mam grew up,' adding as a further incentive, 'she's never been to a city before.'

Dewi glared at his wife. 'Maybe not, but surely you wouldn't want them staying with *her*?'

Jill looked from Cadi to Dewi, her jaw twitching in a defensive manner. 'I'd rather she stayed with Flo than someone we don't know.'

Dewi's brow shot towards his hairline. 'Have you taken leave of your senses? We all know your Flo's got no sense of responsibility. I dread to think of the trouble our Cadi could get into, if she stayed with Flo.' He tutted grumpily. 'I wouldn't trust your sister to look after a dog, never mind a child.'

'Dad!' cried Cadi.

Jill bristled. 'There's no need to get nasty when it comes to Flo; she's never done you any harm.'

Dewi gave a loud 'harrumph' before falling silent. He glared accusingly at his daughter through narrowing eyes. His wife might not see past their daughter's façade, but Dewi could, and he was determined to winkle the truth out of Cadi. 'Let's hear it then, lady, and it'd better be good, if you think I'm going to agree to let you go gallivanting halfway across the country.'

Cadi crossed her fingers behind her back. 'They've all been talking about the Great War in work, and I remembered Auntie Flo saying she'd been in the first lot. I was telling them how she'd been a driver, and I thought it might be nice to go for a visit.'

He rolled his eyes. 'I *knew* it. You want to follow in your auntie's footsteps.'

Cadi feigned innocence. 'What makes you say that?'

'Because I'm not stupid. A blind man could see your intentions, even if your mam can't.'

'Mam's got nothing to do with this,' snapped Cadi. 'This was my idea, and I don't see why you're being so ill-tempered. How you can say Auntie Flo is irresponsible, when she works for the government, is beyond me.'

'Cos they don't know her like I do,' growled Dewi. He rubbed his face between his hands before regarding his daughter from over the top of steepled fingers. 'To decide that you want to go and visit a relative you barely know, when there's a war on, is idiotic. You've made it clear that you think you're too good to stay in Rhos, and this is the perfect opportunity for you to break free – or it would be if you were eighteen, only you're not, and I don't want you going off on some wild goose chase, with Jerry dropping bombs left, right and centre. If you really want to visit your auntie, you can wait until the war's over.' Leaning back in his chair, he picked up his paper and continued reading.

Cadi's mother gave her daughter an encouraging nod.

Cadi cleared her throat, regaining her father's attention. 'We've no idea how long the war will last. I know I'm not eighteen, but I do earn my own wages, and I have my own money. If I want to go and visit Auntie Flo, then I shall. Everyone knows Hitler will focus on

London, so I'm sure we'll be perfectly safe.' Her heart raced in her chest as the paper remained in front of her father's face. She waited for a second or two, but her father wasn't responding. 'Dad?'

Dewi folded down the top half of his paper and stared at Cadi, stony-faced. 'What?'

Cadi's words caught in her throat, but she was determined not to back down, not now. 'Did you hear what I said?'

His jaw flinched. 'How could I not hear you, when you're stood not more than two feet away from me?' He threw his wife a backward glance. 'I must say I'm surprised your mother has nothing to say on the matter, especially when you've just proved your naivety by saying that Hitler won't bomb Liverpool, because he will – it's a port, and a busy one to boot.'

Jill laid a reassuring hand on her husband's shoulder. 'Our Cadi's a sensible lass and despite what you've said, you know our Flo wouldn't let them come to any harm.'

'Beats me how you can say that with a straight face,' said Dewi. He gave a discontented snort before disappearing back behind the pages of his newspaper.

After another long pause Cadi tried again. 'Is that it?'

Sighing heavily, Dewi folded his paper and placed it on his knee. 'What do you want me to say? You've made your feelings perfectly clear, and it's obvious you don't give a damn what I think. So why should I waste my breath trying to talk sense into you, when you've clearly made your mind up?'

'I *do* care,' said Cadi quietly. 'I don't want to hurt or disappoint you, but this is *my* life and ...'

'And hang the rest of us,' muttered Dewi. He began to unfold the paper on his lap. 'If you've nothing else to add?'

Cadi got up from the chair and made her way to the door. Pausing momentarily, she spoke thickly through tears that threatened to get the better of her. 'I didn't want it to be this way. I wanted your approval – your support even.'

Dewi could hardly believe his ears. 'You wanted me to condone my daughter running off to Liverpool during a war in order join up? I'd never approve of you doing something like that, especially not at your age; you're still wet behind the ears, for God's sake.' He raised his voice, drowning out Cadi as she started to protest that she would soon be turning seventeen. 'You're *my* daughter, and no matter how old you are, you'll *always* be my child, and I'll do whatever it takes to protect you. Which is why I won't be giving you my blessing. Should anyone ask, I shall tell them the truth: that you're only sixteen. If I can't talk sense into you, then maybe they can. I'd hope to God your Auntie Flo will have summat to say, but she's as bad as the rest of you.' He heaved a sigh. 'I can't stop you going, but I'll be damned if I'll do anything to help you,' adding bitterly, 'unlike your mother.'

'At least Mam supports me, which is more than I can say for you,' said Cadi. She hesitated, her hand on the door handle. 'It's your fault I lied in the first place. I knew you'd try and stop me from leaving. You expect me to sit in a corner, baking buns, like a good little housewife. Any other father would be proud to think their daughter wanted to do her bit.'

Dewi jumped to his feet. 'Any father worth his salt wouldn't want to see his daughter going like a lamb to the slaughter!' He waved an angry finger under her nose. 'You really try my patience at times, young lady, which is why I have to keep reminding myself that you're barely out of nappies. When you come back—'

Cadi interrupted. 'Come back?'

He gave a short, patronising laugh. 'When you're a woman, you'll—'

Cadi cut him short once more. 'Just because I don't want to kowtow to a man, whilst chained to the kitchen sink, doesn't mean to say I'm not a woman.'

Dewi shot her a withering glance before sitting back down in his chair and disappearing behind his paper. 'Yes, dear.'

Cadi left the room before she said something she couldn't take back. There was no talking to her father once he had made up his mind. She would go to Liverpool and prove to him that she was more than capable of looking after herself. Maybe then he would admit that she wasn't the child he still thought her to be.

She pulled her knitted green shawl around her shoulders and had opened the front door when her mother called out from behind.

'Try not to take any notice of your father,' said Jill as she neatened Cadi's shawl, 'it's only natural he should worry. I'll have a word, see if I can't make him see sense.'

Cadi embraced her mother. 'Thanks, Mam. I thought I'd make myself scarce and see how Poppy got on with her folks, give him a chance to cool down.'

Jill nodded. 'Give me half an hour.'

Leaving her mother to talk to her father, Cadi walked the couple of paces to Poppy's house. Keeping her fingers crossed, she knocked a brief tattoo against the door. If Poppy's parents had denied their daughter passage to Liverpool, Cadi would be on her own, but after the conversation she had just had with her father, she was determined to go, with or without her pal.

The door opened and Poppy's youngest brother, Eifion, greeted her with a jammy smile. ''Ello, Cadi, you come to see our Poppy?'

Nodding, Cadi crouched down to Eifion's height and examined his face. 'Let me guess ... jam butties for your tea?'

His cheeks split into an astonished smile. 'How did you know that?'

She fluttered her fingers back and forth. 'Magic!'

Standing back to allow her in, he closed the door behind them. 'Our Poppy's in with me mam and dad. She says you and her's off to the city. Can I come?'

Cadi faltered mid-step, as she hardly wanted to walk in on her friend if things weren't going well. She held out her hand to Eifion and led him halfway up the stairs. 'What's your mam and dad said?'

He looked at her innocently. 'About what?'

'About her going to the city?'

'Oh, that.' He wiped his jammy mouth on his sleeve and looked at the residue. He gave her a shrewd grin. 'Magic, me bum. That's how you knew ...'

Nodding hastily, Cadi placed a finger to her lips. 'You're a clever boy, but this is really important: what did your parents say about the city?'

He shrugged. 'Dunno, cos I come to let you in.'

'Oh,' said Cadi, disappointed that he hadn't heard his parents' reaction.

Eifion looked down the stairs. 'Why are we sittin' 'ere?'

Cadi got to her feet. 'I didn't want to disturb your parents. Maybe it's better if I come back later—' She broke off as they heard the parlour door open.

Poppy's mother called through to her son. 'Who was at the door, Eifion?'

'Cadi,' he said before Cadi could stop him.

Smiling awkwardly, Cadi walked down the stairs and followed Eifion into the parlour. 'Sorry, Mrs H, I didn't want to intrude.'

The older woman raised an accusing eyebrow. 'Mmm, I bet you didn't.'

Cadi glanced anxiously at Poppy, who was sitting between her parents. Poppy winked at her friend. 'Come in, Cadi, Mam's only teasing.'

Cadi entered the parlour, turning to greet each of the Hardings as she did so. She wondered whether Poppy had continued with the ruse of wanting to go and visit Auntie Flo or whether she'd ended up spilling the beans, as Cadi had done.

Mr Harding was stuffing tobacco into the bowl of his pipe. 'I hear you want to whisk our Poppy off to Liverpool?'

Cadi nodded mutely.

'To see if we can join the services,' said Poppy. She glanced apologetically at Cadi.

Giving her friend a reassuring smile, Cadi waited with bated breath to hear the Hardings' thoughts.

Poppy's father lit the pipe and clenched it between his teeth whilst speaking out of the corner of his mouth. 'The village can't offer our Poppy the same opportunities the services can, and God only knows, we could do with the extra space.' He smiled fleetingly. 'What did your folks think of the idea?'

'Mam was all for it, but Dad's digging his heels in. He thinks we're too young, and that it's going to blow up in our faces.'

Mr Harding shrugged nonchalantly. 'We all know your father had his heart set on you and Aled Davies getting wed.'

Cadi rolled her eyes. 'I know he did, but even if I stayed, that would never happen.'

Mrs Harding smiled sympathetically at Cadi. 'I'm sure your father'll come round in time.'

'I hope so, because I'm going and that's all there is to it.'

'You have to lead your life as you see fit,' agreed Mrs Harding

'That's exactly what I told him, not that he liked hearing it,' said Cadi. 'Dad insists I'm still a child, but if that's true, it's only because he treats me like one. If I did as he wished and stayed at home, I'd never grow up.' She nodded tersely. 'If he wants me to act like an adult, then he needs to let me go!'

October 1939

A month had passed since Chamberlain's announcement and the girls had just finished their final shift in the bakery.

'I can't believe you're actually leaving,' said Matilda, one of their co-workers. 'I must say I rather envy you, but I don't think I'd be brave enough to leave home. You must promise to write and let me know how you're getting on, where you're living, who you've met …' She waved her hands in an excited fashion. 'Everything!'

Cadi fastened the wooden toggles on her coat as they made their way down the road. 'Will do, and you must fill us in on all the gossip whilst we're away.'

'Soon as I'm eighteen I'm out of here,' said Sophie, a shorthand typist who worked in the office. 'I fancy working for the War Office or something exciting like that.'

'Right in the thick of things,' said Poppy. 'You'd get to hear all the secret plans – you might even meet Chamberlain!'

'I could end up being his personal secretary,' mused Sophie. 'Imagine that.'

'I can't see me getting anything that grand,' said Cadi, 'but as long as I get away from here, I don't care what I end up doing.'

Matilda looked both ways as they reached the fork in the road; from here, she and Sophie would go one way, and Cadi and Poppy the other. 'Time to say cheerio.'

It was a tearful goodbye, with promises to stay in touch and to meet up in the future. The girls had just waved Matilda and Sophie off when they heard a familiar voice hail them from behind.

Cadi's heart sank. 'Why *him*?'

Poppy tucked her arm through Cadi's. 'I'd have thought you'd have enjoyed telling him of your new venture.'

'When you put it like that …' Cadi beamed smugly as Aled approached.

'What's going on?' said Aled. He nodded his head in the direction of Matilda and Sophie. 'I saw everyone hugging and kissing. If I didn't know any better, I'd have thought it an emotional goodbye—'

Eager to be the one boasting, for a change, Cadi cut him short. 'Then you'd have thought right.'

He looked after the other girls. 'Oh? Where are they going?'

Cadi frowned. Why did he automatically assume it was Matilda and Sophie leaving and not Poppy and herself? 'Not them! Us.'

His face fell. '*You?*'

Cadi could feel her temper rising. 'Yes, us! Why is that so hard to believe?'

Ignoring the question, Aled continued speaking. 'Where are you going?' adding, 'Wrexham?' with a scornful laugh.

'Liverpool,' said Poppy complacently.

Aled visibly baulked at the idea. 'Don't be silly.'

Cadi stamped her foot angrily. 'We're not being silly.'

'Why'd you want to go there?' He shot Cadi a sharp, patronising look. 'You do know there's a war on?'

Thoroughly fed up, and quite frankly insulted by Aled's response, Cadi spoke her mind. 'Of course we know there's a war on – that's why we're going, so that we can join up and do our bit.'

Aled stared at her in disbelief, before a smile cracked his lips. The girls were obviously having him on. 'Pull the other one, it's got bells on.'

'We are too,' said Poppy defiantly, 'and I think you're being jolly rude.'

He gaped at the girls. 'You're actually serious?'

'Why wouldn't we be?' snapped Cadi. She had always suspected Aled had a bad opinion of her but hearing it first-hand was proving infuriating.

'Because you're only a couple of kids. What are you? Fifteen? Sixteen? Certainly no more than that. The services are looking for women, not girls. What can you two possibly offer that would be of any use to the war effort?'

'I've just turned seventeen, and Cadi's not far off,' said Poppy. 'Besides, it's no skin off your nose where we go.'

But Cadi had already come up with the answer. She pointed an accusing finger at Aled. 'He's jealous because he has to stay on the farm, up to his knees in pig poo, whilst we get to live it up in the city, going to balls, swanky dances and posh shops.'

Aled spluttered a protest. 'I am *not* jealous. I just find it incredible that you're actually going ahead with this barmy plan.'

Cadi bridled. 'Barmy? *Barmy?* I'd have to be that, to stay here talking to you.' She thrust her arm through Poppy's. 'Come on, Poppy, I've had enough of listening to this rubbish.'

Raising his voice, Aled spoke his mind. 'You'll be back with your tails between your legs, you mark my words. The city's no place for a couple of kids.'

Furious beyond words, Cadi and Poppy marched off.

Poppy shook her head angrily. 'The nerve of that boy! All this time I've been standing up for him, saying he wasn't as bad as you thought him to be.'

Cadi spoke through thin lips. 'I always knew he was a wrong 'un, and he's proved it. Talk about showing your true colours.'

'That he has.' Poppy pulled an apologetic grimace. 'I'm sorry I ever doubted you.'

Cadi put her arm around her friend's shoulders. 'You tried to see the good in him. I can't hang you for that.'

Aled watched as they walked away. How could the girls' parents allow them to trot off to join the war, whilst his own father had point-blank refused even to consider letting him go?

He turned his thoughts to the day of Chamberlain's broadcast. They had been in the kitchen, listening to the wireless with bated breath. As soon as they heard the unthinkable, Aled had announced his intention to join the RAF. He had expected his mother to object, but not his father.

'I can't manage this place on my own, Aled, you know that,' his father had said reasonably. 'I understand that, to a young chap like yourself, war looks very glamorous and exciting, but the truth is far from that. Some would say you're damned lucky to be in a reserved occupation – and I'd be one of them. Far better that you stay on the farm with me and help feed the nation. You'd still be doing your bit, if that's what concerns you.'

Desperate to talk his father round, Aled had quickly come up with a solution. 'Couldn't one of the lads from the village take my place on the farm?'

His father had scoffed at such a suggestion. 'They're not farmers, they wouldn't know where to start.'

Aled raised an eyebrow. 'They'd soon pick it up, and I think I could do really well in the RAF – maybe even air crew.'

But his father had been resolute, and with his mother in tears at the thought of her boy going off to war, Aled had dropped the subject.

Now he turned on his heel. There was no way he was going to watch Cadi and Poppy chase their dreams and not do the same himself. He would talk to his father and make him see sense.

It was the following morning, and Cadi had woken to glorious sunshine flowing through her window. Shading her eyes from the bright light, she wondered what the time was, before remembering that today was the day she and Poppy were leaving for Liverpool. A slow smile spread across her cheeks as she slipped out of bed and went to pick up the ewer, ready to take downstairs; only, to her surprise, someone had half filled it with warm water. Passing the flannel over her skin, she mused that the next time she did this, it would be in Liverpool. Having washed and dressed, she headed down the steep staircase into the kitchen, where her family were already seated round the table eating their breakfast.

Her father was the first to look up from his porridge. 'I'd have thought you'd have been up at the crack of dawn, eager to get away,' he said sulkily.

'It took me a while to get to sleep,' Cadi admitted. 'Arwel was snoring like a pig most of the night.'

Arwel grinned. 'Rubbish! I don't snore.'

'You bloomin' well do,' yawned Alun, 'you were rumblin' away like one of the mine-carts.'

Arwel looked thoughtful. 'Now you mention it, I had a dream I was in one of them carts.'

Jill interrupted her sons' conversation. 'Are you all packed and ready for the off, dear?'

Cadi nodded as she took the empty seat next to her father. 'Not that it took me long, it's not as if I have an awful lot.'

Dylan picked up his empty bowl and took it over to the sink. 'Fancy our little sister leaving for the city. You're a proper grown-up now, Cadi.'

This comment was met with a quiet 'Hmph' from Cadi's father.

'Come on, Dad,' said Dylan. 'Our Cadi's got a sensible head on her shoulders, for her age.'

Dewi folded his arms on the table. 'I used to think so, but I don't call what she's doing sensible, even if you do.'

Dylan rolled his eyes. 'She'll be grand; and if she's not, then she can come home, can't you, Cadi?'

Cadi nodded, but in her heart she knew things would have to go very wrong indeed before she'd even consider returning home.

She looked to Dylan. 'Are you coming to see me off?'

He indicated his brothers. 'Us three have got to go to work, so we'll have to say our goodbyes here.'

As if taking this as their cue to leave, Alun and Arwel got up from the table and placed their dishes in the sink, as they waited their turn to hug their little sister goodbye and wish her well.

Speaking thickly through their embrace, Cadi hugged each of them tightly, promising that she would keep in touch.

'Don't forget to mention you've three handsome brothers, if you bump into any pretty Waafs,' said Alun as he placed his cap on his head.

'I have?' teased Cadi.

Alun winked at her. 'All right, just me then.'

The boys left amid a chorus of goodbyes and Cadi looked round the deserted kitchen. 'It's so quiet when they're not here. I'm really going to miss them.'

'You don't have to go,' said Dewi quickly, adding, 'it's not compulsory ...'

'I know it's not, but if I don't go now, I never will.'

'Would that really be so bad?' said Dewi. 'I've lived my whole life in the village and it's never done me any harm.'

'I know, Dad, but I'm not like you. I want to spread my wings, see what's out there.' Getting up from her seat, Cadi kissed the top of his head. 'We've been through all this.'

'I know, but I don't want you to feel you have to go through with it, to save face.'

'Don't worry. I'm doing this because I want to, not because I have to.'

'And what about Aled?'

She shrugged. 'What about him?'

'He'd have made a grand husband: plenty of money – and a home to call your own ...'

She shook her head. 'That's always been *your* dream for me, Dad, but it's not what *I* want.'

They were interrupted by someone knocking a familiar tattoo on the front door.

Cadi grinned. 'Come in, Poppy.'

39

Poppy was beaming as she entered the room. 'Are you still eating? Blimey, Cadi, I had my breakfast hours ago. I've been sitting in the parlour twiddling my thumbs for the past half-hour. Mam said I was getting on her and Dad's nerves, and that I was to come over and annoy you for a bit.'

Cadi giggled. 'Our Arwel kept me up with his snoring, so I overslept.' She finished the last spoonful of porridge. 'Done!'

Poppy drummed her heels on the floor in excitement. 'Let's go.'

Cadi nipped back upstairs and picked up her rucksack. Glancing round, she pulled back the curtain that separated her part of the room from the boys' part. Even with the curtain drawn back, the room was still too small. Hearing Poppy calling up from the bottom of the stairs, Cadi left the bedroom for what she hoped would be the final time.

Clattering down the stairs, she closed the door behind her and turned to bid Mr and Mrs Harding good morning.

'Are you sure you've got everything?' said Cadi's mother as they headed for the bus stop.

Cadi patted the rucksack that she had slung over her shoulder. 'Ration book, savings, identification, clothes, toothbrush and smalls.'

Poppy's mother looked expectantly at her daughter, who confirmed, for what she assured everyone else was the umpteenth time, that she too had everything she needed.

As they neared the stop, Cadi pointed ahead of them. 'Is that ours?'

'Hard to tell from here,' said Dewi, 'but I'm sure he'll wait ...' His words were lost on the girls, who were running towards the idling bus.

Seeing the girls hurrying towards him, the driver hastily stubbed out the cigarette he had been smoking with the toe of his boot.

'Is this the bus for Wrexham train station?' panted Cadi.

'It certainly is.' He glanced at the watch on his wrist. 'You're bang on time, hop aboard.'

Both girls hastily kissed their parents goodbye whilst the driver took his seat. Heading for the back of the bus, Cadi knelt on the seat and slid the top of the window open.

Tearing up, Jill called out to her daughter, 'Don't forget to give our love to your Auntie Flo.'

'I will!' was all Cadi managed to say before the bus pulled away from the kerb.

Sliding his arm around his wife's shoulders, Dewi waved the girls goodbye. 'She'll be back.'

Fishing in her coat pocket for a handkerchief, Jill dabbed her eyes. 'I wish I had your confidence.'

He gave her a comforting squeeze. 'Cadi might think she's going to have no problems joining up, but we both know she won't get into the services, and she'll soon run out of money, so she's not going to have much choice, is she? Your sister can't afford to keep two extra and, even if she could, you know she won't be able to stand looking after two kids – she more or less said so in her letter.'

Jill thought back to the day she had received the letter from her sister. The girls had been cock-a-hoop when they heard that Flo was willing to have them to stay whilst she was in Liverpool, but Flo had warned that her job took her all over the country and she could only put them up for a week before leaving Liverpool herself. It had meant that the girls' stay would only be short, but as they hadn't intended to stay there long-term it really made no difference to their plans.

'We should have our answer the same day we apply, and with a bit of luck our papers will arrive before Auntie has to shoot off,' Cadi had reasoned. 'We can ask them how long it will take, whilst we're at the recruiting office.'

Now, as Dewi slipped his hand into his wife's, he gave it a reassuring jiggle. 'I reckon Flo made that bit up about being relocated, so she'd have a good excuse to get rid of the girls before she got bored of them.'

'I don't know why you're so hard on Flo.'

Dewi frowned. 'What does she know about bringing up kids? She has no responsibilities, never has done, and …'

Jill stopped walking abruptly, staring deep into her husband's eyes. 'That's hardly her fault!'

A guilty look shadowed Dewi's face as he vindicated his opinion. 'She'll want to impress them, and they're very impressionable at that age.'

Jill shrugged. 'You've really got it in for our Flo.' She shook her head as Dewi went to speak. 'If the girls are successful, they'll be leaving Flo's before the week's out; and if they're not, they'll still be leaving, so I don't see the point in arguing.'

Dewi nodded. Jill was right. In a week's time Cadi would be safely home in the bosom of her family. All notions of leaving the village would be out of her system, and she would most likely accept Aled's proposal gratefully. He mulled over this thought. Aled's father, John, had been less than happy when he had heard that the girl he considered his future daughter-in-law was leaving Rhos in search of a new life, and had even questioned why Dewi had allowed his daughter to go in the first place. Rather than admit he'd had no say in the matter, Dewi had said it was only a phase – something Cadi had to get out of her system – and he was certain his daughter would soon be back. After all, better that than to admit he couldn't control his own daughter.

With their parents out of sight, both girls sank back into their seats.

Cadi gave an excited squeak. 'I can't believe we've actually done it! I always thought something would come along at the last minute and put a spanner in the works.'

'I know what you mean; it's almost too good to be true. I must have gone to sleep every night with my fingers crossed, praying that Liverpool wouldn't get bombed, because I knew if it did, my parents might change their minds.'

Cadi twisted in her seat to face Poppy. 'Me too. I was convinced there'd be a raid, or Auntie Flo would have to leave. I know I told Dad that it was my life and I was capable of living it on my own, but I might've thought twice if Auntie Flo wasn't living in Liverpool. I think the same thought had crossed his mind, and that's why he was so mean about her.'

'Your Auntie Flo's been a godsend all right. I can't wait to meet her – she sounds very different from any of the women we know.'

'She certainly is. Auntie Flo tends to live life for the moment. I'm not sure what she does exactly, but I do know it's something to do with the government.'

'Gosh,' exclaimed Poppy, clearly impressed, 'sounds intriguing. Do you think she works for the secret service?'

Cadi arched a singular eyebrow. 'I suppose she might, although I don't think she'd have welcomed us into her home if she were an undercover agent.'

'We could work for her,' suggested Poppy excitedly. 'After all, who's going to suspect two Welsh girls?'

Cadi grinned. 'Don't go getting your hopes up. I'm fairly sure she's a secretary or something equally dull.'

'Still more exciting than working down the bakery,' said Poppy.

Cadi stared wistfully out of the window. 'I can't wait to show you the city – you're going to love it.' A thought occurred to her. 'Can you swim?'

Poppy shook her head. 'Why on earth would I need to learn to swim, living in Rhos?'

Cadi shrugged. 'I suppose you're right. I guess Mam only taught me because there's a public baths by my grandparents' old house.' She hesitated. 'Thinking back, I'm pretty sure there's a public baths close to Auntie Flo's.'

Poppy was agog. 'How many public baths are there in Liverpool?'

Cadi beamed proudly; she might not be a Liverpudlian, but her mother was. 'Lots, possibly one in every district.'

44

Eager to hear more, Poppy continued, 'What else have I been missing out on?'

'Lots! Liverpool's like an Aladdin's cave, when it comes to all the different restaurants and cinemas ...' Cadi sighed wistfully. 'As for the shops, I guarantee you've never seen anything as grand as the ones in Liverpool.'

'Why? What's so different, surely a shop's a shop?'

'You don't get shops like these in Rhos *or* Wrexham,' said Cadi knowledgeably. 'I like Blacklers the best, they sell everything from ballgowns to buckets. I s'pose you could say there's something for everyone.'

'Sounds a bit like the market to me.'

Cadi smiled reminiscently. 'Believe you me, Poppy Harding, it is *nothing* like the market.' Adding as an afterthought, 'And since when have you seen a stall down the market selling ballgowns?'

'They do sell buckets, though, and clothes,' said Poppy a shade defensively.

Cadi folded her arms on the top of her satchel. 'Granted, but in Blacklers the gowns are made of silk and taffeta, because they only sell the very best.'

'Sounds posh – expensive too,' said Poppy. 'Not what I'd call something for everyone.'

Cadi drummed her fingers against the hessian of her satchel. 'I suppose it is expensive, especially compared to the Irish stalls – the locals call them Paddy's market – where you can get the same sort of stuff but a lot cheaper. The main attraction in Blacklers, or at least it was the main attraction for me, was their wonderful rocking horse. I believe it was called Blackie.' She sighed wistfully. 'I used to love going for a ride on him.'

Poppy's jaw dropped. 'They let you ride it?'

Cadi nodded. 'It might be a posh shop, but every-one's allowed to ride Blackie.' She gazed out of the window, a distant smile crossing her face. 'He was the most beautiful rocking horse, with a long silky mane and, from what I can remember, he was huge.'

'I always used to give the pit ponies a fuss whenever Mam took me to see Dad at the mine. I'd have done anything to take one of them home with me, but Dad said they were working ponies and not for fun.' Poppy pulled a downward smile. 'I knew we couldn't afford a real pony, but a rocking horse would've done.' She brightened. 'Can we go there tomorrow?'

'Of course we can, but only if you promise not to try and ride him. I think you're a bit big for that kind of thing now, don't you?'

'I s'pose so, but I'd still like to see him, unless your auntie has other plans of course?'

'I doubt it,' said Cadi. 'She'll probably be at work, and even if not, she's not the sort of woman who'd want to hang around with a couple of kids.'

'Oh? I thought your auntie was looking forward to us coming?'

'She is, but she's not got any kids of her own; she's what you'd call more of a career woman,' explained Cadi.

Poppy looked intrigued. 'Nothing like your mam then?'

'Gosh, no! You couldn't get two more different women if you tried. Mam's a housewife through and through, but not Auntie Flo – she's always on the go.'

Poppy watched as a couple of children waved to the bus driver. 'You told me that your father thinks your auntie to be irresponsible, despite the fact that she has an important job. Maybe he thinks she's irresponsible because, in his book, a woman's role is to be a wife and mother.'

'I reckon you're right. She did marry once, but that was a long time ago.'

'She's obviously not married any more; do you know what happened?'

Cadi grimaced. 'Not really, but I did hear Dad saying to Mam it was Flo's fault the marriage didn't last.'

'Sounds like you've got more in common with your aunt than your mam,' said Poppy.

'I know Dad thinks she's a bad influence, and that she'll fill my head with all sorts of nonsense.' Cadi tutted beneath her breath. 'No doubt by "nonsense" he meant an independent lifestyle. He's worried I'm going to take a leaf out of her book, but I don't see what's so bad about that; if she's happy, then surely that's all that matters?'

'Hardly the life he had carved out for you, though.'

'Only it's *my* life, and if I choose to be like Auntie Flo he should be happy for me,' Cadi said reasonably.

'You're his little girl, and he wants to keep you that way.'

'That's the trouble,' said Cadi. 'Dad still sees me as a child, and treats me like one. He probably thought I'd have no option other than to marry and settle down, which is why he's being so petulant about me going to Liverpool.'

The girls stopped speaking as the bus turned down the road into the train station. It had started to rain, and the driver turned the wipers on.

Poppy's stomach was full of butterflies. 'This is it! The start of a new life.'

'Good,' said Cadi with determination. 'The sooner I get on that train, the better. I've had enough of Rhos and the miserable weather we get here in north Wales – give me sunny old Liverpool any day of the week.'

Chapter Two

The journey to Liverpool proved confusing, with far more changes than the girls were expecting, although one thing had become apparent from their journey.

'Every serviceman or woman who boarded the train was a *lot* older than us,' said Poppy, who was feeling less confident at the prospect of a new life.

'I noticed that,' agreed Cadi, 'but it's still early days. There's probably lots of girls around our age, we just haven't seen them yet.'

Poppy, however, remained doubtful. 'I'm beginning to see why your dad didn't put up much of a fight.'

'Oh, I know, he made no secret of the fact he thought we were doomed because of our age. He thinks I'll fall at the first hurdle and come home without even trying, which is a bit of an insult,' said Cadi, 'because I thought he knew me better than that.'

'I don't think he's casting judgement on you,' said Poppy thoughtfully. 'Most people would come home straight away and, if you're honest with yourself, what *are* your plans if we don't get accepted?'

'To keep trying,' said Cadi. 'I've not come all this way only to roll over, should things go awry.'

'How long for, though?'

'As long as it takes,' said Cadi. 'Please don't let the folk on the train put you off, Poppy.'

'I'm not – I'm simply being realistic. Our savings, such as they are, won't last for ever, so we need a Plan B.'

Cadi puffed out her pigeon chest. 'We don't need a Plan B until Plan A falls through, otherwise we're admitting and accepting defeat before we've even tried.'

Poppy smiled slowly. 'Your father obviously thinks we're underprepared, and maybe we are, but with your grit and determination I'm certain summat'll come our way.'

The train pulled into Lime Street Station and Cadi scanned the platform for her auntie. 'I hope I recognise her, it's been—' She stopped short as a woman with neatly styled fair hair, wearing a smart two-piece suit, waved to her from the platform.

'Is that her?' asked Poppy. 'She's beautiful.'

'It certainly is,' grinned Cadi. 'You don't see many like her in Rhos.'

'You don't see *any* like her in Rhos,' confirmed Poppy. 'I didn't realise she was so posh.'

'She's not, she's just very smart, probably has something to do with her job.' As she spoke, Cadi stepped down from the train and approached her auntie, who welcomed her with open arms.

'Welcome to Liverpool. Did you have a good journey?'

Cadi nodded. 'Bit hectic, and we nearly boarded the wrong train at one point, but we're here now.' She gestured to Poppy. 'This is Poppy.'

Flo smiled brightly at Poppy. 'Hello, Poppy, I'm Flo.'

Poppy shook hands with the other woman. 'Hello, Mrs, er, Miss … What would you like me to call you?'

'Certainly not Mrs, or Miss – that's far too formal – so how about plain old Flo?' She glanced at Cadi. 'Same goes for you too. I've never liked the title "Auntie", it makes me feel as though I'm ready for the knacker's yard.'

Poppy giggled. 'You're far from that, M—' She quickly corrected herself, 'Flo.'

Flo smoothed a hand over her forehead. 'Very kind of you to say so, my dear, but the lines beg to differ!'

Poppy might not have known Flo for more than a few minutes, but she was already very impressed with the older woman, who was clean-cut and very forward thinking. Poppy was used to calling all adults by some title, whether it was Mr or Mrs, Auntie or Uncle. A slight crease furrowed her brow; she called some of her mother's friends "Auntie", even though they weren't blood relatives. The idea of calling an adult by her Christian name was very modern thinking indeed. It was no wonder Cadi's father was against Cadi staying with her aunt – someone who epitomised everything Cadi wanted to be.

Remembering Flo's busy lifestyle, Poppy asked the question now uppermost in her thoughts. 'Are you sure we're not putting you out?'

Flo waved a dismissive hand. 'I'd not have agreed to you coming, otherwise.'

'Poppy's convinced you're working undercover for the government,' explained Cadi pragmatically.

Poppy eyed Flo with anticipatory expectation. 'You don't look like the secretaries we get in the bakery …'

Flo smiled kindly. 'When you're working for the government they expect a certain standard.' Glancing around, she lowered her voice. 'I work for the War Office. Not terribly exciting, but in today's world one has to be careful what one says, as you never know who might be listening, but that's as secret as it gets, sorry to disappoint.'

Poppy appeared unperturbed. 'Still better than the bakery, and I bet you get to hear all the gossip.'

Flo winked. 'Well, there is that.'

Poppy gave Cadi a smug smile. 'I was sort of right; it is a little bit like being undercover.'

Flo tapped the side of her nose. 'I'm afraid I can't possibly comment: loose lips and all that.'

Poppy was in awe. 'I hope we end up doing summat like that.'

Flo continued to talk as she led the way out of the station. 'I heard from my sister that you've got your hearts set on joining up?'

Both girls nodded mutely.

'Admirable, but I'm afraid it isn't going to be a walk in the park. There's the age thing for a start, and even if you do get in, you'll have to start at the bottom like everyone else. That's six weeks of peeling spuds and square-bashing whilst you do your initial training.'

'We don't care,' said Cadi firmly. 'It's the independence that we really want.'

'And the uniforms,' added Poppy. 'I liked the ones the women were wearing on the train, they looked ever so smart.'

Flo arched an eyebrow. 'If you saw women in uniform, then they were very lucky, because most of the women joining up are still in civvies.'

Poppy beamed. 'Civvies! That's proper forces talk, that is.'

Flo chuckled. 'If you do get in, I reckon you'll take to service life like ducks to water.'

As they approached a line of taxis, Flo approached the driver who was parked at the front. After a brief conversation she signalled for the girls to come over.

Taking their places in the back of the cab, Flo sat between the girls. 'What are your plans for tomorrow?'

Cadi stared out of the window as the driver pulled away from the kerb. 'We thought we might have a look around the city, do a bit of sightseeing, that kind of thing, unless you've made other plans?'

'I'm ever so busy with work, so it suits me better if you girls can entertain yourselves.'

'Cadi's taking me to Blacklers,' Poppy gabbled happily, 'it sounds wonderful.'

'It is, but there are lots of lovely shops in the city, as well as the markets—'

Poppy interjected. 'Sorry, but did you say markets, as in more than one?'

'Heavens, yes!' laughed Flo. 'There's fruit-and-veg markets, clothes markets ...'

Poppy sank back into her seat. 'I reckon it's going to take more than a day to look round Liverpool.'

'Good God, yes, you'll need at least a week, and you still won't have seen everything even then,' said Flo.

The taxi drew to a halt at a set of traffic lights, and Poppy looked in awe at her surroundings. 'The buildings are *enormous*. I've never seen anything like them. I can barely see the top of that one ...' She gasped in awe. 'Is it me, or are there statues on the top of the building next to us?'

The taxi driver chuckled. 'There sure are, them's the Liver birds and they're on top of the Liver Building.'

'How on earth did they get statues up there?' marvelled Poppy, stopping only as she heard another chuckle escape the lips of their driver. She turned to Flo. 'I must sound very sheltered.'

Flo laid a reassuring hand on Poppy's. 'I wouldn't know where to start if someone dropped me in the heart of the countryside, so you could say we're all sheltered in our own way.'

'I hadn't thought of it like that,' considered Poppy as she looked across Flo to Cadi. 'I know you said Liverpool was grand, but I had no idea it was this grand. I don't think I'm going to get a wink of sleep tonight.'

'I'm glad you like it,' said Cadi. 'But there's lots more to see, so you'll need a good night's sleep.' She turned to Flo. 'Thanks ever so much for putting us up. I promise we won't get under your feet, and we'll be gone before you know it.'

Flo waved a dismissive hand. 'Don't worry about me. I only hope you get your papers in time – if you get in at all, of course – because I really do have to be gone by Friday, and I'm afraid my landlord won't allow anyone under the age of eighteen to stay in the flat on their own.'

Poppy, who was still staring open-mouthed at her surroundings, gave out a yelp. 'There's a boat floating up the pavement!'

Once again the driver let his amusement be known. 'That's not floating up the pavement, it's in the canal.'

'You should've brought me here years ago,' Poppy told Cadi, her voice wrapped in awe.

'Now you know why I was so keen to leave Rhos,' said Cadi.

Poppy nodded. 'I certainly do, and I don't blame you neither.' She beamed at her friend. 'Thanks for persuading me to come, Cadi, you really are the best friend a girl could have.'

Cadi grinned. 'Just keep everything crossed that we make it into the services.'

Crossing the fingers on both hands, Poppy held them up for Cadi to see. 'Let's hope this works, because I do *not* want to go home!'

When Cadi awoke the next morning she immediately sat up on one elbow because the noises coming from outside the bedroom window were a world away from the ones she had experienced at home.

Looking round, she found the alarm clock and stared bleary-eyed at the face. 'Seven o'clock.' She swung her legs out of bed and trotted over to Poppy, who was still slumbering. 'Wake up.'

Poppy stirred sleepily. 'What's up?'

'It's seven o'clock.'

'Then stop shouting and go back to sleep …' Poppy closed her eyes momentarily before opening them wide. 'Cadi?'

'Yes?'

'We're in Liverpool.'

Smiling, Cadi nodded slowly. 'Still want to go back to sleep?'

Poppy was already out of bed and pulling off her nightgown. 'Of course not. I want to get out there and see the sights.' She tiptoed across to the ewer and poured the water which the girls had fetched up the night before. 'It's jolly noisy outside, what's going on?'

Cadi went to the window and looked down to the street below. 'Lots of carts, a few cars, buses and lots and lots of people.' She turned to Poppy. 'It's much the same during the night: apart from the buses and cars, it seems Liverpool is a city that doesn't sleep.'

'We'd be lucky if we saw more than one car in Rhos,' said Poppy, who was enthusiastically towelling her face dry.

'I wonder if Flo's up?' Cadi mused. As the words left her lips she frowned. 'It may sound silly, but I don't like calling her Flo, it seems disrespectful somehow.'

'My mam would say it's modern, and Flo is a very fashionable woman.'

'I know, but it's almost as if she doesn't like the thought of being my aunt and doesn't want anyone else to know, or am I being silly? What do you think?'

'I think she was telling the truth when she said she thought it made her sound old,' Poppy said simply.

'I knew she'd be too busy with work, but I rather hoped she might want to show us around the city,' continued Cadi. 'I know I said I wasn't bothered, but I am a little bit.'

Poppy shrugged. 'Your father did imply your aunt was self-centred, so I don't know why you're surprised.'

'She hasn't seen me for a few years. I'd have thought she'd have wanted to spend a bit of time with her niece.'

'Oh, do stop bellyaching,' moaned Poppy. 'I don't wish to appear insensitive, but we came to Liverpool with one goal in mind, and your auntie – I mean Flo – is spending time with you when she can, but like she said …'

Cadi finished the sentence for her, ' … she's very busy with work, I know, I know.' Still staring out of the window, she indicated those of the building opposite. 'Have you noticed the tape on all the windows?'

Coming over to stand beside her friend, Poppy pulled a face. 'They were like that in Wrexham. Dad says it's to stop them shattering in case a bomb goes off nearby.'

Cadi glanced at the windows of the surrounding buildings. 'Looks like they're expecting a lot of bombs.'

Poppy shrugged. 'I dare say it's only a precaution; better to be safe than sorry, as it were.'

Flo's voice called out to them from across the hall-way, 'Morning, girls.'

They called back a greeting, and Cadi nipped across the linoleum floor and opened the door. 'I hope we didn't wake you?'

Flo, who was already dressed, shook her head. 'I'm off to work, but I've left a saucepan of porridge in the warming oven, and a pot of tea on the stove. You'll find the necessary utensils in the dresser. Did you sleep well?'

Cadi couldn't help but feel disappointed that her aunt wasn't going to have breakfast with them, but she did her best to hide it. 'Will we see you later?'

'Yes, I shall be back around teatime. If you'd like to make yourselves a sandwich, there's cheese or corned beef in the pantry, and I'll pick us up fish and chips for our tea, if that suits?'

Cadi nodded. 'What time would you like us back?'

'Six o'clock?'

'We'll see you later …' She hesitated. 'What about a key?'

Flo smiled. 'I've left one on a piece of string hanging from the letterbox. Anything else?'

'I don't think so,' said Cadi. 'Have a good day in work.'

'You too,' called Flo as she headed down the stairs that led to the flat.

Cadi turned back to Poppy. 'She didn't even stop for breakfast.'

'Well, you can't blame her for that,' said Poppy reasonably. 'If we'd been up earlier, we could've had breakfast with her.'

Cadi looked doubtful. 'If that was Mam, she would've woken us up so that we *could* have breakfast together.'

'Only she's not your mam, is she?' Poppy pointed out. 'And she's not used to kids, or living with other people, which is hardly her fault.'

Taking her place at the bowl, Cadi gasped as she felt the cold water against her skin. 'Tell you one thing, though.'

Poppy pulled her stocking over her toes. 'What's that?'

'She's not much of an undercover agent if she leaves a key hanging on a piece of string.'

Poppy giggled. 'That's true. On the other hand, she must be doing something exciting because she obviously loves her job.'

'More than she loves her family,' said Cadi.

Poppy tutted irritably. 'Don't be silly. Just because she's busy doesn't mean to say she doesn't love you. To be honest, Cadi, I don't see why you're getting so upset. You've not seen her for years, surely that told you summat?'

Cadi fastened the buttons on her cardigan. 'Ignore me, I'm being over-sensitive.' As she spoke she ran a brush through her hair before clipping it back out of her face. 'That's me done. C'mon, let's get us some breakfast.'

The girls soon found out where everything was kept and as they sat down to eat, Cadi gestured towards the newspaper Poppy was reading. 'Anything good?'

'Nope, same old, same old,' said Poppy. 'They're still calling it a "phoney war", and the more time goes on, the more I'm hoping they're right. That's why I'm not bothered about them taping up the windows.'

Cadi wasn't so certain. 'Dad says war is a bit like a game of chess: each side waiting to see what the other does before making a move.'

Poppy blew onto the spoonful of porridge poised before her lips. 'Do you think that's why Chamberlain's still building an army, so that we're ready for whatever comes?'

Cadi swilled the tea in the pot before topping up both her own and Poppy's cups. 'He'd be a fool not to.'

'Then why set an age limit?' said Poppy. 'I bet Hitler's allowing anyone and everyone to join up.' She hesitated as something that she had heard came back to her. 'He's got an army of children. I remember Mam saying they were a bit like Boy Scouts, but they were shouting for Hitler and marching like a proper army.'

'Well, *I* think that's ridiculous,' said Cadi, 'children can't fight wars!'

'Maybe that's why Chamberlain has an age restriction ...' said Poppy quietly.

Cadi scowled at her friend. 'Seventeen? I hardly call that children.'

Poppy decided to be diplomatic and not point out that whilst she was seventeen, Cadi herself was still sixteen for a few days yet. 'Either way, we'll soon find out at the recruiting office. When do you think we should go?'

'Tomorrow,' said Cadi decidedly. 'I don't know about you, but I need to practise changing my date of birth first.'

Poppy grimaced. 'Changing a two to a one isn't going to be easy; in fact I should imagine it's going to be impossible.' She looked worried. 'Don't you think both of us changing from a two to a one is going to look a tad fishy?'

'We're going to be hard pushed passing for eighteen as it is, so I don't think we should try and change it to a zero, even though that might be easier—'

With the porridge bowls empty, Cadi poured some of the water from the kettle into the sink and began to wash their pots. 'It's all about confidence, if we look and act the part, then we're halfway there.'

Unhooking a tea towel from its peg, Poppy began drying the dishes. 'Only I've never been good under pressure, which is why I told Mam and Dad the truth about Liverpool. If that lot down the recruiting office look at me funny, I'll go to pieces and spill the beans, I know I will.'

'Well, you needn't worry about that today.'

Poppy placed the bowls back into the cupboard. 'I needn't?'

'Nope. Today we do the shops and markets, and we'll tackle the recruiting office tomorrow.'

Poppy breathed a sigh of relief. 'Thank goodness for that – my palms are going sweaty at the mere thought of telling porkie pies.'

Cadi had taken their coats down from the pegs behind the door to the flat. She handed Poppy hers. 'Come on, Poppy Harding, let's take a gander around Liverpool. If that doesn't cheer you up, I don't know what will.'

It took the girls some time to figure out which bus would take them to the shops, but once they'd worked it out, they soon found themselves in the heart of the city.

'It's been a while since I was in Liverpool,' said Cadi, hooking her arm through Poppy's, 'but nothing's changed.' She pointed to a large building that stood on the corner of two streets. 'Blacklers!'

Poppy stared open-mouthed at the grand shop, which spanned several floors. 'You could fit every shop in Wrexham *and* Rhos in there, and probably the ones in between an' all.'

Cadi looked smug. 'Told you.'

Poppy continued to stare wide-eyed as Cadi led her inside. 'If we don't get into the services, I think we should try and get jobs in the city.'

'Do you mean to tell me you wouldn't want to go back to Rhos?' teased Cadi.

'No chance. I'm *never* going back; in fact I'm surprised your mam ever left. She must need her bumps read, who on earth would want to leave *this* for Rhos?'

'She met my dad when she was on her hols in Talacre,' said Cadi plainly. 'What with him working in Wales, and the mining company supplying cheaper rent than anything they could hope to get in Liverpool, it made good sense for them to live in Rhos after they got wed.'

Poppy peered at a pearl necklace beneath a glass shelf. 'She must've really loved him.'

Cadi chuckled softly. 'She most certainly does. Believe it or not, Mam also loves Rhos, *because* it's a lot quieter than the city, and less crowded too.'

'But that's what I love about the city,' said Poppy. 'Peace and quiet might be all right if you're old, like our parents, but not when you're our age.'

'Mam did come back to Liverpool for a while, when she was pregnant with me,' said Cadi, 'but it wasn't enough to make her want to stay.'

Poppy was trying on a pair of woollen gloves. 'What made her come back to Liverpool?'

'I was transverse.' Seeing the blank expression on her friend's face, Cadi went on to explain, 'It means I was lying sideways, and the doctors worried that they might lose me and Mam during the birth if we didn't have the right medical attention, so she came to stay with my grandparents.'

'Gosh, I didn't know that. Your poor mam must've been really scared.'

'Probably,' said Cadi. She picked up a cloche hat and placed it down delicately on her unruly curls. 'Obviously I wasn't there at the time, and my brothers were a lot younger, so they don't remember much, save that Dad couldn't cook to save his life.'

Poppy picked up a different pair of gloves and tried them on for size. 'If we hadn't been living in Gresford, Mam would've done the cooking for your dad.'

Cadi tweaked the brim of the cloche as she viewed her image in the mirror. 'Do you ever miss living there?'

'Not really. I was only five when we left, so I don't remember much about it.'

Cadi removed the hat and hooked her arm through Poppy's. 'Well, I'm glad you came to Rhos, else we'd never have met.'

Poppy pulled the glove off and placed it back on the counter. 'Destiny!'

'You're right. Had Mam not met Dad, I wouldn't be here; and had I not met you, I doubt I would've been brave enough to come to Liverpool on my own.'

The girls perused the shop until they had seen everything Blacklers had to offer. As they were heading out of the store, Poppy went over to the rocking horse, which stood near the entrance. She laid her hand on his mane. 'If only I were a few years younger.'

'Imagine if your Eifion was here,' said Cadi, 'I bet he'd love a ride on Blackie.'

'He certainly would.' A thought occurred to her. 'Do you think they'd let me go on with Eifion, just to make sure he didn't fall off?'

Cadi gave the horse a little push and watched it rock gently, as the memories of herself sitting on the horse whilst her mother placed an arm around her waist flooded back to her. 'If you're very lucky.'

'No harm in asking,' said Poppy as the two girls stepped out into the bright sunshine.

'I'll take you to Lewis's next,' said Cadi, 'it's not far from here.'

By the time they had finished admiring everything that Lewis's had on show, the girls decided it was time for lunch.

'We forgot to make sandwiches,' cried Poppy. 'That'll teach us to rush.'

'Not to worry, we'll grab something to eat in Lyons. I wanted to go there anyway to show you what it's like.'

The two girls entered the café and took a seat near the window.

'Mam always used to bring me here,' said Cadi. 'She reckoned it was good for people-watching.'

Poppy giggled. 'I've heard of bird-watching, but people?'

'Oh yes, you have to people-watch when you're having a bite to eat.'

The waitress approached the table and the girls ordered their sandwiches.

'I've never been anywhere this fancy,' whispered Poppy as the waitress went off to get their order.

'Believe me, Lyons isn't posh, not compared to some places,' said Cadi as she glanced out of the window. 'How do you feel about tomorrow?'

'Not good,' admitted Poppy. 'Coming to see the shops was a lovely idea, but it's left me feeling very much out of my depth.' She glanced at the passers-by, who were going about their business. 'Everyone else knows where they're going and what they're doing, none of this is new or special to them. To say I feel wet behind the ears is an understatement.'

'I've been thinking the same,' agreed Cadi. 'I know I said we could solve all our problems by changing the date on our certificates, but I can't see how we're going to do that without it looking a right mess.'

'I must admit I've been trying to imagine it in my mind's eye, and quite frankly all I see is a big ink blot.' Seeing the waitress arrive with their sandwiches, Poppy brightened. 'So if we're not going to change the date, what are we going to do?'

'The only thing I can think of is to say we've lost our certificates. It might sound far-fetched, but we could say we left them on the train or at home – anything really. The point being that they won't be able to tell us to nip back and fetch them, because Rhos is too far away.'

'So you're hoping they'll take us at face value?'

Cadi cast her friend a hopeful glance. 'Unless you can think of a better plan?'

Poppy shook her head without hesitation. 'Sorry, but no. I can't say as I was ever keen on the idea of messing with the dates in the first place, but I didn't see any other option. I'm guessing people lose their documents all the time, and it's more plausible than trying to make a two look like a one.'

'If we've a reasonable, plausible excuse and we appear confident, it just might work,' said Cadi, optimistically.

'Perhaps I should have a stiff whisky before I go in,' said Poppy glumly.

'Oh yes, what a terrific idea. Go in stinking of booze and green around the gills – that shouldn't raise too many eyebrows,' laughed Cadi, adding, 'You don't even like whisky. Not that I blame you, it's rotten stuff.'

Poppy crossed her fingers. 'Then we're going to have to hope the person doing the recruiting is half blind.'

'Tell you what: we'll go for a gander, see where the office is, what kind of people are going in, whether they're mainly men or women, young like us, or older, then go from there. If there's lots of girls our age going in, then we should be fine. After all, beggars can't be choosers, and there is a war on,' said Cadi decidedly.

Once they had finished their lunch the girls agreed to forget all thoughts of the following day and enjoy the rest of their time wandering around the city. As six o'clock loomed they hastened back to the flat, and were pleased to see that Flo was already there with fish and chips still wrapped in newspaper.

'That does smell good,' sniffed Poppy as she removed her shoes. 'My feet are killing me. I reckon I must've walked a hundred miles today.'

Flo addressed Poppy as she unwrapped their supper and placed it on three plates. 'Did you like the city?'

'Very much so,' said Poppy, liberally shaking salt over her chips.

'I wish we felt as buoyant about tomorrow's visit,' sighed Cadi ruefully.

'Why, what's happening tomorrow?' asked Flo, a forkful of fish poised before her lips.

Cadi felt rather annoyed that her aunt had seemingly forgotten what was so incredibly important to them, when it was, after all, their main reason for visiting. 'The recruiting office?'

'Oh, that,' said Flo airily. 'Why are you worried? There's nothing you can do about the outcome, so what's the sense in fretting?'

Cadi frowned. 'Because we want to join up – it's the whole reason why we're here,' she said, adding peevishly, 'I'd have thought you'd have understood that, what with your job and all.'

'Sorry, chuck, but I've got rather a lot on my mind at the moment.'

Not wishing any ill feeling, Poppy spoke out. 'A lot of people change their birth date on their certificates, but we're not going to do that because it's too complicated and it will be obvious that we've tampered with them, which means Plan A is a no-go.'

Flo nodded. 'Glad to hear it. The authorities aren't stupid – they'd have smelt a rat straight off the bat. Bearing that in mind, what's Plan B?'

Cadi finished her mouthful. 'We have an age-old plan in mind,' and she crossed her index and middle fingers.

Flo laughed. 'Fingers crossed?'

Poppy nodded. 'Who knows? It might actually work.'

'And if that fails, we're going to try out our winning smiles and good old Welsh charm,' said Cadi.

'And if *that* doesn't work we're going to lie through our teeth, saying we've lost our certificates,' said Poppy casually.

Flo started to cough as she laughed. 'Now *that* sounds like a plan, or one that could work at any rate.'

Cadi looked hopefully at her aunt. 'Does that mean you think we're in with a shot?'

'You've as good a chance as any, and certainly much better if you don't mess with an official document.' She eyed Cadi and Poppy curiously. 'I must say I'm a little surprised your parents are all right with this, especially your father, Cadi.'

Cadi pulled a face. 'To say Dad wasn't keen would be an understatement.' She looked over at Poppy. 'Poppy's parents were wonderful; they see this as a real opportunity.'

Flo gazed at Cadi. 'What about your mam?'

'She's behind me all the way. She knows I've had itchy feet for a long time, but there's not many choices for a girl with ambition, not in Rhos at any rate, but here ...'

'The land of opportunity,' agreed Flo.

'I wish my father was a bit more like my mam,' sighed Cadi, 'he's so old-fashioned.'

Flo shrugged. 'He's a man, what do you expect?'

Cadi might be annoyed at her father, but she was alarmed at hearing her aunt's forthright opinion. 'Not all men are like that.'

'I've yet to meet one who doesn't think the world starts and ends with him,' said Flo simply.

Poppy nodded. 'That sounds like Aled, the feller Cadi's dad wanted her to marry.'

Flo paused, a forkful of fish halfway to her mouth. 'Why on earth would he want you to marry someone like *that*?'

'Because Aled's a farmer's son, and Dad thinks I'll be sorted for life if I marry him, so he tried his best to keep me at home,' said Cadi.

'Didn't work, though, did it,' said Flo with an air of satisfaction.

Cadi stared at her aunt. 'How come you and Mam are so different?'

'Just are,' said Flo. 'I bet you're different from your brothers?'

Cadi laughed. 'I should jolly well hope I am!'

'There you are then, it's the same with me and your mam. She's quieter, more laid-back. I sometimes wish I was more like her, but we are who we are.'

Cadi knew her father had described his sister-in-law as selfish and she had begun to agree with him, but the more she talked to her aunt, the more she realised that Flo wasn't so much selfish as fiercely independent, and Cadi could hardly chastise her for that when she too craved her freedom.

'I wish you could have a word with my father.' She rolled her eyes. 'Talk about stuck in his ways—'

A chiding glance from Flo cut Cadi off mid-sentence. 'Your father might be a little misguided, but only because he cares about you, and you can't hold that against him. He's done everything he can to keep a roof over your family's head, and I think your mam's very lucky to have him.'

Cadi eyed her aunt inquisitively. 'I hope I'm not over-stepping the mark, but weren't you married at one stage?'

Flo averted her gaze from Cadi to her food. 'I was, but it didn't work out.'

Cadi stared at her aunt, but with no further explanation forthcoming, she indicated the fish with her fork. 'We don't get fish this fresh, do we, Poppy?'

Poppy shook her head. 'It's lovely.'

Cadi looked around the flat. 'You said in your letter that you have to leave at the end of the week. Do you move around a lot?'

Flo placed her knife and fork on her plate. 'I can be in Scotland one day and Devon the next, but I always come back to Liverpool, which is nice. It's good to have somewhere to call home.'

'I'm keeping everything crossed for tomorrow,' said Poppy. A frown creased her brow. 'I've just realised you didn't go to work in a uniform this morning, yet you said you worked for the War Office?'

Auntie Flo gave her a conspiratorial wink. 'Not everyone who works in the War Office wears a uniform.'

Poppy inhaled so sharply she began to cough, much to Cadi's amusement. 'You're not saying anything to convince our Poppy that you're not an undercover operative.'

Getting up from her seat, Auntie Flo took her plate over to the sink and rinsed it under the tap. 'My lips are sealed.'

'I wish Poppy's were, because she'll be bending my ear all night with tales of espionage.'

'I'd love to be a spy,' said Poppy as she took the dishes from Flo and placed them back into the cupboard.

Cadi gave a surprised cough. 'You wanted a stiff whisky before going into the recruiting office tomorrow, so how on earth would you cope under interrogation?'

Poppy grinned sheepishly. 'I never said I'd be good at it.'

With the dishes done, Flo got out the card table and the three women spent the evening playing rummy and discussing the war.

'What do you think about everyone calling this a "phoney war"?' said Poppy, as she fastidiously examined the cards she had been dealt.

Flo drummed her fingers against the table. 'Ever heard the expression "the quiet before the storm"?'

Poppy nodded. 'Is that what you think this is?'

'You can't expect to declare war on a man like Hitler and not get a response.'

Cadi looked surprised. 'Why'd you say "Hitler"? It's Germany we're at war with.'

Flo placed a card down before taking one from the top of the pack. 'Because if it weren't for Hitler, none of us would be in this pickle – he's the reason why Germany invaded Poland.'

Cadi glanced at the card her aunt had placed on the table and took it, before placing one of her own down. 'How can one man cause all this trouble?'

Flo shrugged indifferently. 'Most wars are because of one man stirring things up.'

Poppy took a card from the pack. 'We'll just have to hope he's bitten off more than he can chew. His armies must be pretty overstretched already.'

'But he's been planning this for a long time,' reasoned Flo, 'building up his army, his navy and his air force. He's more than prepared, which is more than I can say for us.'

'If that's the case, we should have quite a good chance of being accepted,' said Cadi, 'cos if what you're saying is right, they're going to need as many hands as they can get.'

Poppy looked beseechingly at Flo. 'Couldn't you put in a good word for us?'

Flo looked alarmed. 'Recommend two girls who I know to be underage? They'd fire me on the spot!'

Poppy deflated. 'Oh well, it was worth a try.'

'I admire your spirit – you'll need plenty of that if you get in.'

'*If* we get in,' repeated Poppy longingly. 'I really hope we do.'

As it got closer to midnight they decided to turn in, but they had no sooner climbed between the sheets than the air-raid siren sounded. Poppy and Cadi both leapt out of bed and were halfway across the room before they realised they had no idea where they were going.

Flo stepped onto the landing. She was lashing the cord on her dressing gown. 'I'm sure it'll be another false alarm – we've had lots of them – but we'd best go to the shelter to be on the safe side.'

Poppy let out a breath of relief. 'I'm glad you think it's a false alarm, but even so, it doesn't half bring it home, don't you think?'

'It certainly sharpens the mind,' agreed Cadi as they followed Flo down the stairs and into the yard. 'You say you've had a lot of these?'

Flo nodded. 'Golly, yes, nearly every night in the first few weeks of the war. It's eased off a little since then, but the lack of sleep doesn't do anyone any favours.'

'How long will we have to stay in the shelter?' said Poppy as they followed Flo down the steps into the underground shelter.

'Depends on what's going on up there,' said Flo. She settled herself onto a bench and indicated for the girls to join her on the adjoining benches. 'It can take a few hours, even all night, so you're best off trying to get some kip.'

Poppy looked up anxiously. 'You don't really think they're coming, do you?'

Flo smiled kindly. 'No, chuck, but it's best to be on the safe side.'

The girls stared round at the people who were entering the shelter. They ranged from old ladies who needed assistance to get down the steps, to young children who found the whole thing very exciting, to mothers who looked worn and tired.

Folding her coat, Flo rested her head against it.

'It's a little exciting, don't you think?' said Poppy as she too fashioned her coat into a pillow.

'It might be for us, but that old dear doesn't seem to think it's exciting,' said Cadi, indicating an elderly lady who appeared to be having difficulty getting comfortable. Cadi took her coat, which she was going to use as a pillow, and handed it to the old lady. 'Here, you can use this.'

Smiling gratefully, the old woman took the coat. 'Thank you, dear.' She plumped it up and laid her head against it, before looking up. 'That accent hails from Wales, if I'm any judge.'

Cadi nodded. 'Correct.'

The old lady cocked her head to one side, 'I don't know what's made you come this far afield, but if I were you, I'd've stayed put.'

'We're here to do our bit,' said Poppy proudly.

The woman squinted as she tried to focus on the two girls, and she was eyeing them incredulously. 'And your parents *let* you? Why, you can't be more than sixteen, mebbe seventeen at a push, but certainly not eighteen.'

'We look younger than we are,' said Poppy quietly.

The woman placed her head on the makeshift pillow. 'Oh well, I'm sure you know best. I only hope you know what you're getting yourselves into, as war isn't a place for women, lerralone youngsters.'

Poppy whispered to Cadi, 'We haven't a cat in hell's chance ...'

'She's guessing, and she's old,' Cadi assured her. Keeping her voice low, she continued, 'She had to squint to see us, I wouldn't pay much attention to her opinion.' Lying back down, she leaned her head against her hands. 'You heard what Flo said; we'd best get some sleep, we've a busy day ahead of us.'

She hadn't expected to go to sleep, but was surprised when she woke up a few hours later to hear the all-clear sounding. She retrieved her coat from the elderly lady, who thanked her for her kindness, adding, 'Go home, luv, the city's no place for young girls like yourself, especially in wartime.'

Cadi, Flo and Poppy trooped back to the flat, but with only half an hour left before the alarm clock was due to go off, they decided they might as well put the porridge on and have a leisurely breakfast.

Poppy rubbed her elbow. 'How anyone's meant to get any kip on one of those benches is anybody's guess.'

'You get used to them after a while,' said Flo. She added the oats to the simmering milk. 'What time are you heading down the recruiting office?'

Poppy rolled her eyes. 'I don't know whether we should bother, after that old woman guessing our age.'

Cadi sighed wearily. 'The worst they can do is turn us away, we've got to at least try.'

'That's the spirit,' said Flo briskly, 'and remember, even if it's a "no" today, it doesn't mean to say it's the end of your journey. There's plenty of jobs where you can still do your bit.'

Cadi looked up hopefully. 'Like what?'

'Messenger girls, if you've got access to a bicycle; or bringing tea and sandwiches to the wardens and fire-watchers who've been up all night ...'

'But they're voluntary posts,' said Poppy, 'and we can't live off thin air.'

'What about your job in the bakery?'

Cadi looked dismally into the cup of tea that Poppy had passed her. 'We don't want to go back. I thought you meant we could get work here.'

Flo was perplexed. 'I hadn't realised. I thought ...' She shook her head. 'I'm sorry, Cadi, I've obviously got my wires crossed. You see, even if you worked in a bakery in Liverpool, you'd not make enough to cover your rent, never mind feed yourselves.'

'Which is why we were pinning our hopes on the services taking us on.' She looked imploringly at her aunt. 'Is there no way we could stay with …'

Flo was shaking her head. 'I already told you, my job takes me all over the country. I did explain this in my letter.'

'I know, but couldn't you have a word with your boss, maybe explain …' Cadi began, but she could tell by the look on her aunt's face that her pleas were falling on deaf ears.

'I have to go where I'm told, there's no room for negotiation. I'm sorry, Cadi.'

Cadi nodded glumly. 'I understand, I shouldn't have asked.'

Flo stirred the porridge. 'I wish I could help, but my hands are tied.'

With nothing more to say on the matter, the three ate their breakfast in relative silence.

It was looking very much to Cadi as if their dreams were over before they'd even begun. She said as much later on that morning as she and Poppy headed to the town hall where they would attempt to sign up.

'I really don't want to go back to Rhos, but if this doesn't work we're not going to have much choice,' admitted Poppy.

'We have to remain positive,' said Cadi.

The girls reached the hall and watched the people going in and out. 'They're not eighteen,' said Poppy dejectedly, 'they're much older. We're going to look like a couple of sprogs compared to that lot. What do you think we should do?'

'Go in,' said Cadi, 'because I'll be damned if we've come all this way to not even try!'

Poppy drew a deep breath. 'Best foot forward and all that.'

The girls entered the building and followed the signs for the recruiting office. 'There's a queue,' said Cadi. 'I never thought people would be queuing.'

Poppy eyed the people ahead of them, then whispered to Cadi, 'On the bright side, this lot look a bit long in the tooth to be doing lots of physical work, and everyone knows you've got to be as fit as a flea to join the forces.'

Cadi brightened. 'If you put it that way, I reckon we could run rings around most of this lot. Maybe our luck's in after all.'

The queue went down faster than Poppy had hoped and before they knew it, it was their turn. The young man who sat behind the desk grinned as they approached.

'And what can I do for you, ladies?'

'We've come to join the services,' said Cadi, and Poppy nodded mutely.

He banished the grin and smiled kindly. 'Come on, girls, I wasn't born yesterday, and neither were you, and you weren't born eighteen years ago neither, so let's leave it at that, shall we?'

Cadi wanted to argue, to pretend she didn't know what he was implying, but he was being kind, so she took Poppy by the hand and together the two girls walked out of the building.

'My heart,' Poppy gasped, 'is trying to escape from my chest.' She jerked her head in the direction of the building behind them. 'I'm not cut out for this lying malarkey.'

Shading her eyes from the autumn sun, Cadi looked around them. 'So what now?'

Poppy shrugged. 'Get our stuff from your auntie's and go home, whilst we've still money to do so.'

'Is that what you want?'

'No!' cried Poppy. 'But what choice do we have?'

'I, for one, would rather stay here and work in a bakery than go home and do the same thing, and we do have until the end of the week.'

Poppy made a sweeping gesture with her arm. 'But where will we live? We can't rely on your aunt. She's already said that type of work won't cover the rent and, even if it did, we've no idea whether we can even get a room at our age.'

'Well, I'm not going home without trying,' said Cadi simply. 'Are you with me?'

Poppy opened her mouth to argue, then thought better of it. One of the reasons why she and Cadi were such great friends was because Cadi gave Poppy the guts to do things she wouldn't normally contemplate, and in turn Poppy gave Cadi support. In short, one couldn't function without the other. She nodded. 'Aren't I always?'

Cadi beamed. 'Then let's go get some lunch from Lyons and we can see if they've got any jobs going whilst we're there.'

By the end of the day both girls were exhausted. They had tried looking for work in every shop, café, restaurant, bakery and even the Chinese laundries, but there was little interest in employing two underage girls from Wales.

'You can see it in their faces as soon as we open our mouths,' moaned Poppy. 'I'm sure they think we're a couple of runaways.'

Cadi had to agree, albeit reluctantly. 'I'm afraid you're right, but I still think if we try hard enough ...'

Poppy yawned loudly, cutting her friend off. 'Well, I've had enough for one day. I say we go back to your aunt's and have us some tea.'

Cadi knew when she was beaten, so she nodded. 'Agreed! Tomorrow's another day, and who knows what it will bring.'

Back at the flat, they told Flo all about their day.

'I really hoped you might prove us all wrong and get accepted,' said Flo sympathetically, 'but it was always going to be a bit of a long shot.'

Cadi walked over to the window and looked out onto the street below. 'There's always tomorrow.'

'Even if you do get work—' Flo began, only to be cut short by her niece.

'We'll find summat,' said Cadi, 'a shared room, or a job where you live in. There has to be something.'

'I *know* you're disappointed, but don't you think it's best to admit defeat? You can always come back and try again when you're old enough,' suggested Flo.

Cadi turned her attention away from the window. 'Would you roll over, if someone told you to?'

'Well, no, but it's different for me,' said Flo.

'How? Just because you're older? That makes you as patronising as Dad.' As soon as the words left her mouth Cadi regretted them; she was being rude and she had no right, but far from being angry, her aunt spoke softly.

'Sometimes we all need to know when to admit defeat.' She patted the chair next to her and Cadi obediently sat down. 'Why do you think I got divorced, Cadi?'

Cadi could feel her face begin to colour. 'Because you wanted a career?'

'No! I got divorced because my husband wanted children, and I couldn't give him any.'

Cadi's mouth fell open. 'I'm so sorry, I didn't mean ...'

Flo placed her hands over Cadi's. 'No need for apologies. I know your father doesn't approve of me, and he probably filled your head with that rubbish because he thinks I should've tried harder to hold on to my marriage, but the truth is I didn't want my marriage to end; it was Frank who'd had enough.' She shrugged helplessly. 'I tried everything to make him stay, but I soon realised that if he really loved me – and I mean *really* loved me – I wouldn't have to persuade him, so I let him go. As soon as Frank left, I vowed to forget about men and throw myself into my career. It's not worth the pain, when you have to tell someone you can't give them children.'

Cadi hung her head in shame. 'Why would my father blame you for summat you had no control over?'

'I think he felt guilty that he and your mam had lots of children and I had none, so it was easier for him if he said I was at fault.'

'But that's ridiculous!'

Releasing Cadi's hands, Flo walked over to the oven and removed the corned-beef stew. 'Of course it is, but he's a man who doesn't know how to deal with his feelings. Far easier to blame me than face up to the truth.'

Poppy brought the plates out from the warming oven and placed them on the table. 'I'm not surprised you've thrown yourself into your career.'

Cadi stared at the plate of food her aunt had put in front of her. 'I know Dad can be stubborn, but I didn't think he could be so cold-hearted.'

Flo sat down opposite her. 'What your father thinks is irrelevant to me – something else that probably gets on his nerves. Now eat that up and get yourself an early night. Tomorrow's a new day, and hopefully it'll be filled with new opportunities. There's no sense in dwelling on the past.'

Cadi smiled sympathetically at her aunt. 'Will do.'

After clearing everything away, the girls headed for bed, but Cadi didn't sleep. She couldn't help but dwell on her father's words. She loved him dearly, but there was no getting away from the fact that he was a real bigot at times.

It was the last morning of their stay in Liverpool and the mood was sombre as they ate their breakfast. The girls had spent their time in the city desperately trying to seek employment, but it seemed their search was in vain.

Flo, having been up earlier than the girls, pointed at some sandwiches wrapped in greaseproof paper. 'I've made you some cheese-and-pickle sarnies.' She walked round the table and kissed Cadi on the top of her head. 'Promise me one thing.'

Cadi nodded.

81

'That you'll not give up on your dreams? I'd hate to see you go back to Rhos and not try again in a year's time.'

'I promise,' said Cadi, but Poppy noticed her friend hadn't looked her aunt in the eye when she made the statement.

'Good girl.' She turned to Poppy. 'Good luck. I hope I'll see you again in the not-too-distant future.'

'Of course, and thanks for everything you've done for us.'

Flo waved a nonchalant hand. 'My pleasure.' She glanced at the satchels by the front door. 'Ready for the off, I see.'

Cadi nodded. 'Didn't see the point in hanging around. We might as well catch the first train.'

Flo gave the girls a grim but reassuring smile. 'All good things come to those who wait, just you see.'

With that being said, they waved her off from the flat before returning to their breakfasts.

'I noticed you didn't make eye contact with your aunt when you promised not to give up on your dreams. Why was that?'

Cadi spoke through pursed lips. 'If Flo thinks I'd go back to my father now – *especially* after what she told us the other night – then she's another think coming.'

'I *knew* you were up to summat,' said Poppy excitedly, 'but what are we meant to do if we don't get jobs? We can't come back here – we'd get in dreadful trouble if someone reported us to the landlord.'

'We'll cross the bridge when we come to it,' said Cadi in between mouthfuls. 'Come on, Poppy, eat up, we've a lot of ground to cover.'

The girls ate their breakfast and cleared everything away, before gathering their belongings and heading out.

'So what's it to be?' said Poppy as they stood on the pavement.

Cadi locked the door and pushed the key back through the letterbox. 'I reckon we start with the chippie.'

'We've only just had breakfast!'

'I meant for jobs,' sighed Cadi.

'Oh, right, do you think it's worth a shot?'

'No harm in trying,' said Cadi, 'especially if they say yes. Come to that, there's plenty of places we didn't try yesterday. I know we steered clear of offices because we didn't see the point, but they still need to be cleaned, same as the public toilets, pubs, warehouses ...' A flicker of excitement entered her eye. 'We've not been thinking widely enough, Poppy, and it's time we started, because the closer we get to boarding that train, the lower my heart sinks.' She heaved a sigh. 'I know I say I won't be going back, but even I know that we'll not have any choice if we can't find anything, so it's up to us to roll our sleeves up.' She tucked her arm into Poppy's. 'I know we'll find something, I can feel it in my bones.'

Chapter Three

The girls had set off with much enthusiasm, agreeing that if they hadn't found work by the end of the day they would catch the train back to Wrexham. Full of eagerness and optimism, they felt sure their sheer will and determination would find them employment, but it seemed that every warehouse, factory and pub already had enough staff.

With the light beginning to fade and only an hour left before the last train for Wales was due to leave, Poppy was growing anxious.

'I know we said we wouldn't give up, but like Flo said, sometimes it's wiser to admit defeat, and I've no idea how far we are from the train station.' She glanced around her. The area they had wandered into looked bleak and dreary, with a lot of the houses having tatty hole-riddled curtains, whilst others had none at all. Poppy looked at one house in particular. Some of the panes of glass in the downstairs window were badly cracked, so much so that she had supposed it to be derelict, but looking through, she could see people moving around inside.

Poppy drew closer to Cadi as they passed one of the many courts. 'I don't like it round here, Cadi. There's hardly anyone on the streets and,' she pulled a disapproving face, 'it smells awful.'

Cadi didn't like the area any more than Poppy but she was determined to find something, if only to avoid going back home where she would be expected to marry Aled, who would undoubtedly take delight in crowing over her failure. She pointed out a public house a little further down the road. 'Last one, I promise. If they say no, we'll head back to the station.'

Poppy looked around her dubiously. 'Do you even know how to get to the station from here?'

They had been walking in what they believed to be a straight line for some time, and Cadi had been taking a keen interest in the buildings they passed, so she felt certain she could find her way back. However, as she looked at yet another court, she realised it appeared identical to one they had passed some time ago. Could she really find her way back? She no longer felt at all certain that she could, but she had come too far to admit that to Poppy, so she nodded. 'Yes, but it's probably better that we hurry, to be on the safe side.'

'I know we said we were willing to do anything to stay in Liverpool,' said Poppy, 'but do you really want to work in a pub round here? It's not like Mozart Street where your auntie lives, this is very different. I'm not even sure they *have* cleaners here.'

'If it means getting our foot through the door, then yes, I would work here, because it would only be until we find something better.'

They reached the pub, which the sign informed them was called the Bear's Paw, and Cadi gripped hold of Poppy's hand as she pushed the door open and slid quickly behind the blackout curtain. Inside, the air was thick with cigarette and pipe smoke, and the girls could barely hear themselves think for the shouts and yells of the clientele.

Poppy stared as a woman steadied herself against the wall, before tottering unsteadily towards the bar, whilst trying to pull the shoulder of her dress back into place. Hissing loudly into Cadi's ear, Poppy pointed at the woman. 'She's drunk!'

Cadi looked over to the barkeep who was in a heated argument with one of his customers. She had turned to tell Poppy she thought they should leave, when a sharp-faced woman flung an arm around Poppy's shoulders.

Poppy tried to duck out from under the woman's arm, but she held Poppy's shoulder in a vice-like grip. 'Now, now, don't struggle, I don't mean you no 'arm.'

A burly man with a hungry expression walked over. 'All right, Molly. These two new, are they?'

The woman who was known to the man as Molly nodded. 'I thought you didn't like women, Eric.'

The man licked his lips as he adjusted the waistband on his trousers. 'They have their uses.' He reached over to Poppy, his hand cupping her chin, whilst he addressed Molly from the corner of his mouth. 'How much?'

It was as these words left his lips that Cadi and Poppy both realised his intent. Kicking him hard in the shins, Cadi shoved Molly roughly as she yanked Poppy from the woman's grip. Seizing Poppy by the hand, she shouted over her shoulder, 'We're going to the

86

police.' The girls ran out of the pub and didn't stop until they were several streets away.

Leaning over to catch their breath, they had come to a halt at a crossroads. 'Sorry, Poppy,' panted Cadi, 'I had no idea.'

'I know,' breathed Poppy. 'Are we really going to the police?'

Cadi stood up. 'No, I only said that to scare him off.' She glanced around. 'Oh, Poppy ...'

Poppy shot up, expecting to see Eric or Molly in hot pursuit, but seeing that the coast was clear, she furrowed her brow. 'You scared me half to death. I thought they was following us.'

Cadi grimaced. 'Sorry, but I've just realised I haven't a clue where we are.'

Poppy too glanced around her, but was equally stumped. 'What are we going to do now?'

'I don't know,' wailed Cadi, 'I don't recognise any of this.'

'We've got to get to the station, Cadi. We'll have to find someone to ask for directions.'

Cadi had opened her mouth to agree when she was interrupted by the air-raid siren.

'Oh, bugger ...'

Poppy glanced round, looking for any sign of an air-raid shelter, but she could see nothing and it was only when a family left their home that the girls found someone to ask.

'Shelter?' The woman gave a short mirthless laugh as she hefted the smallest of her children into her arms. 'There's nowt as fancy as a shelter round these parts – best we've got is the arches.'

'Arches?' said Cadi.

The woman nodded. 'The railway arches.'

With no choice other than to follow behind, Poppy hissed to Cadi, 'I think they're all a bit strange round here. No one in their right minds would shelter under the railway! My dad said if we heard a siren we were to get as far away from the docks and railways as we could, because they're prime bombing targets …'

Cadi nodded. 'I don't understand it, either, but I'm sure they wouldn't tell people to go there if it wasn't safe. Besides, it's probably another false alarm.'

They reached the arches, joining many others, who were already crammed in.

Poppy looked hopefully around at the sea of faces. 'I bet one of these will know how to get to Lime Street Station.'

An elderly lady who'd overheard Poppy's comment blew her cheeks out. 'Lime Street? You're miles away.'

'But do you know how to get there from here?'

The woman scratched her head. 'Head south and away from the docks?'

'Which way's south?' said Cadi.

The woman grimaced apologetically. 'I'm no good at directions, luvvy, you'd be better off askin' someone else.'

Cadi turned to Poppy. 'I reckon we put our money together and see how much we've got and then, when they sound the all-clear, we can see if there's any taxis running – they'll know how to get to the station.'

Poppy took out her purse and Cadi did the same, and together they thought they had enough for their train fare home with a couple of shillings to spare. 'I've no idea how much a taxi will cost, so we'll have to hope for the best,' said Cadi as she dropped her money into Poppy's purse. 'We should probably keep all our money together for ease.'

Their experience under the arches was very different from the shelter in Mozart Street. There were no benches, just empty crates, or boxes that people had brought with them; and rather than being in an enclosed space that felt quite snug, they were exposed to the elements. 'Are you certain there's nowhere better to shelter? My pal's aunt lives in Mozart Street and they've a lovely—'

The young woman cut her off with a scornful laugh. 'Mozart Street? Why, I'd wager they've got champagne and bathrooms down their shelters!'

Poppy looked taken aback. 'No. But they do have a proper underground shelter, which is nowhere near the docks *or* railways.'

The woman shrugged dismissively. 'Lucky them. But that's not an option for the folks around here.' She turned to an older woman who was listening keenly, nodding her agreement. 'They wouldn't waste money building the folks round here a shelter.'

Cadi shook her head. 'That's awful; it shouldn't matter where you live.'

The older woman who had been openly eavesdropping pulled a face. 'Them in power look after their own, and that ain't us.' She eyed the girls studiously. 'Your pal says your aunt lives in Mozart Street, but you ain't from round these parts.'

'Rhos in Wales,' admitted Cadi. 'We came here looking for work, but it seems we're too young.' Feeling that introductions were needed, she continued, 'I'm Cadi, and this is my pal, Poppy.'

The woman smiled kindly. 'I'm Ethel, and if you ask me, one of the main troubles with war is the romance it portrays.'

Cadi and Poppy exchanged uncomprehending glances. 'Sorry, I think you've lost us,' said Cadi.

'Young 'uns like yourself see the glamorous posters, the fancy uniforms and them old war movies through rose-coloured specs, but what you don't see is the blood, the death and the sheer misery that war brings.'

Poppy swallowed. 'We know it'll be dangerous – we weren't going into this lightly.'

She gave them an old-fashioned look. '*Everyone* goes into it lightly; they'd not join up otherwise.'

'How do you mean?' said Cadi.

Ethel shifted position. 'No one joins up thinking they're going to get shot at or die.'

Cadi appeared to weigh this up in her mind. 'It *is* a bit different for women, though, cos we don't go into battle.'

Ethel's brow shot towards her hairline. 'Do you not think the Luftwaffe, when it comes – and come it will – won't target RAF bases over here? Or the ack-acks, not to mention the Navy. Good God, girl, women might not get a gun, but they're certainly put into the line of fire.' Seeing Cadi swallow, Ethel took pity on her. 'Sorry, luvvy, but speaking as one who lived through the last lot, I hate watching young 'uns like yourself walk into this, blinded by romance.'

'If you're so certain they'll come, then why on earth are you sheltering under a railway arch?' said Poppy, her voice hollow.

Ethel indicated the thick ceiling of bricks, whilst looking at the house opposite. 'Because this is better than a slate roof, and whilst we know they'll be aiming for the transport lines, they might miss and hit a house.' She shrugged, 'It's pot luck.'

Her words had had a sobering effect on the girls, who were both glancing anxiously at the cloud-studded sky.

Sensing their anxiety, Ethel followed their gaze. 'I wouldn't worry too much; these skies aren't good for bombing.'

Visibly relieved, Poppy eyed the woman with intrigue. 'Why, what's wrong with the sky?'

She smiled. 'Bombers like a clear sky, with a bright moon so they can see better – they call it a bomber's moon.'

As she finished speaking the all-clear sounded, much to Cadi and Poppy's relief. 'Do you know where we might find a taxi?' asked Cadi as they headed into the street.

'Now that I can help you with.' She pointed at the street ahead of them. 'Go up there and take the right fork, then take your next left and keep going until you see a sign for Plevin's Taxis. You'll have to hurry, mind, as he doesn't work after seven.'

Thanking Ethel for her help, the girls hurried off. 'I hope we can afford the fare,' said Cadi.

'I'm sure, if we explain our situation, the driver will take pity on us,' replied Poppy hopefully.

As the girls neared the fork in the road they heard a male voice call out from behind them. 'Oi, you two! Get back 'ere.'

Turning, Cadi instantly recognised the man from the Bear's Paw pub. Grabbing Poppy by the arm, she pulled her round the corner, then ducked into a doorway, holding a finger to her lips. Cadi and Poppy held their breath as their pursuer half jogged, half strutted past their hiding place. They waited until he was out of sight before venturing back out.

'I thought we'd seen the last of him,' said Poppy. 'How did he know where we were?'

'Sheer bad luck,' Cadi assured her. 'We were in the wrong place at the wrong time.'

Poppy rolled her eyes. 'We seem to be doing that a lot lately.'

Cadi ticked her fingers as she spoke. 'We got into a bit of a scrape in the Bear's Paw, then the air raid, and now running into that man again – if bad luck runs in threes, we've had our quota.'

'We'd best get a move on before that feller stops running his taxi for the evening,' said Poppy.

Trotting along the road, the two girls rounded the left-hand corner that Ethel had advised them to take, and Poppy pointed to a sign that she could just see at the top of the road. 'Thank goodness for that—'

Her words were cut off as a large, beefy hand slapped her hard on the shoulder, clipping her ear in the process. Before Poppy could get her breath back, her assailant spun her round to face him. It was the man from the Bear's Paw.

'Where the bloody hell d'you fink you're goin', Izzy ...' He squinted down at her as he tried to focus. He had clearly used the air raid as an opportunity to quaff as much ale as possible, judging by the stench of alcohol coming from his breath.

Realising that he didn't recognise them as the two girls in the Bear's Paw earlier, Poppy hastily explained that there had been a mistake and that she wasn't Izzy. Hoping that would be an end to the matter, she tried to pull away, but instead of releasing her the man doubled his grip, and Poppy's knees gave way as his thumb squeezed a nerve in her shoulder.

Seeing her friend collapse, Cadi yelled at him to let her go, but he wasn't even acknowledging her existence. His eyes were locked on Poppy's, and he was clearly enjoying watching her writhe in pain. Cadi tried pulling his arm off her friend, but it was no use; he was too strong.

'I *knew* you was up to no good when I went out …' He began pulling Poppy towards one of the houses. Seeing him fumbling for what Cadi assumed was a key, she knew that she had to act fast. Taking a running jump, she landed heavily on his back. She had hoped that this alone would make him let go of Poppy and start on her instead, but the man appeared unperturbed. Pulling a key out of his pocket, he tried to slot it into the lock.

Grabbing his hair with one hand, Cadi scratched and prodded his eyes, screaming from the top of her lungs for him to let Poppy go.

Bellowing angrily for her to get off, he momentarily released his grip on Poppy so that he could throw Cadi over his head. The wind was knocked out of her lungs as she landed heavily on the cobbles. Barely able to breathe, let alone move, she felt a tear trickling down the side of her cheek as she watched the beast of a man grab hold of Poppy's hair.

With pain engulfing every part of her body, Cadi tried to move, but it was no use. She had just begun to think that her friend's fate was sealed when a young man came running towards them. At first Cadi feared he might be a friend of Molly's or the drunken man, so she was relieved when he pulled Poppy free, then punched the older man, who buckled at the waist before falling onto the floor.

He held out a hand to Cadi. 'Come on, he won't stay down for long.'

Taking his hand, she winced in pain as she got to her feet. Still barely able to breathe, she croaked, 'I can't walk, let alone run.'

Before she could stop him, he had bent down and put her over his shoulder in the style of a fireman's lift. Cadi wanted to object, but as the young man carried her, she could see Eric beginning to get to his feet, yelling that he would ruddy well kill the lot of them.

Only when the three of them were a few streets away did the young man place Cadi back down. His eyes were full of concern as he spoke. 'Are you all right?'

Cadi gave a shy nod as she tried to hide her tear-stained face. 'Yes,' she replied, adding, 'thank you.'

Smiling at them both, he pushed his hair from his face. 'I'm Jeremy Thomas – my friends call me Jez.'

'Hello, Jez. I'm Poppy and this is my best pal, Cadi. We were on our way to Plevin's Taxis when that … that man …' Poppy shook her head, unable to go on.

Jez's jaw tightened. 'He's not a man, not a real one at any rate.' He furrowed his brow. 'Where are you from?'

Poppy went on to give Jez chapter and verse on everything from leaving Rhos to the moment he had come to their rescue.

'Dear me, you two know how to live dangerously! I don't know whether it's a good idea for you to go to Plevin's Taxis – not when it's on the same street that Eric lives on.'

'So that explains why we bumped into him again,' said Poppy. 'I don't suppose you know the way to Lime Street Station from here, or at least a different taxi service?'

Jez was staring fixedly at Cadi. 'Are you sure you're all right?'

Cadi was staring in horror at the palm of her hand. She turned it to face Poppy, who gasped. 'You're covered in blood!'

'It must've been from when he threw me over his shoulders,' said Cadi. She'd been trying very hard to control her emotions, but fear was getting the better of her, and she could feel the tears pricking her eyes. She turned round so that Poppy could see the back of her head. 'Is it bad?'

'I can't see, Cadi, but I think we should get you to a hospital ...' She fell silent as Cadi tried to shake her head, but the pain was too great.

'No, we'll miss our train.'

Poppy gaped at her friend. 'I think your head's a little more important than a train!'

'I'll be fine,' sniffed Cadi. 'I'm not having you miss the train, not on top of everything else.' Her bottom lip trembled miserably. 'You said you didn't like the look of the that pub, but I wouldn't listen. If I had, we'd be in the station waiting to get on the train.'

Poppy placed her arm around her friend's shoulders. 'It's not your fault that beast of a man picked on us.'

'Tell you what, why don't you let me take you to my friend,' suggested Jez. 'We'll be passing by hers on the way to the station, so it won't harm to pop in for ten minutes. She can take a look at your bonce and clean you up. You can hardly travel all the way back to Wales like that.'

'Thanks for the offer, and I really appreciate everything you've done for us, but we can manage—' Cadi began, only to be cut short by Poppy.

'No, we can't, we've proved that already, and whilst I'm all for independence, Jez is right, you can't go home looking like that – can you imagine what your father would say?' Without waiting for a reply, she turned to their new friend. 'Thank you, Jez, we'd love to accept your kind offer.'

Cadi, however, remained hesitant, as the last thing she wanted was to jump out of the frying pan into the fire, so she pulled Poppy to one side, hissing desperately into her ear, 'We don't know this Jez from Adam. He could be taking us anywhere.'

Poppy glanced at Jez, who was standing with his hands in his pockets, pushing around a piece of gravel with the toe of his boot. 'He just saved me – *us* – from that awful man, so do you really think he's not to be trusted?'

Cadi grimaced. 'I don't know, but I've made a real mess of things so far, and I don't want to add insult to injury.'

'Then go back home and see what your father has to say when he sees his daughter covered in blood,' said Poppy simply.

Cadi buried her face in her hands. 'I'm so sorry, Poppy.'

Poppy placed her arm around her friend. 'I've already told you, this isn't your fault. But we need to make a decision, and as I don't relish the idea of going home until we've had a chance to clean you up, I think we should take Jez up on his offer.'

Cadi fished a tissue from her coat pocket and blew her nose. As they approached Jez, he eyed them expectantly.

'Where does your friend live?' asked Cadi cautiously. 'I hope it's not near the Bear's Paw.'

His brow rose quickly. 'Good God, how do a couple of nice girls like you know about the Bear's Paw? It has to be the roughest pub in Liverpool. I'm not surprised you've got reservations if you think I'd take you somewhere like that.' He gave a snort of laughter. 'Maria wouldn't stand for the sort of nonsense they allow down the Paw.'

'Who's Maria?' asked Poppy.

'She's an old friend of the family, as well as being the landlady of my local, the Greyhound.'

'Landlady?' said Cadi. 'I didn't know a woman could run a pub?'

'Don't let Maria hear you say that – she's a big believer in equality for women.'

Cadi placed her hand to the back of her head, which was beginning to throb. 'Is it far from here?'

Jez pointed to the other end of the road, which stretched into the distance. 'Burlington Street, it won't take more than five minutes.'

Bringing her hand back for examination, Cadi was relieved to see there wasn't as much blood now. She told the others, adding, 'I've got a dreadful headache, though.'

'I'm not surprised,' said Poppy, 'as you landed on cobbles.'

As they approached the red-brick pub, the girls assumed they would be entering through the main door, but Jez led them round the back. 'Tradesmen's entrance,' he said, before knocking three times.

After a moment or two they heard the sound of approaching footsteps from the other side of the door and a woman's voice called out, 'Entrance is round the front.'

'It's me, Jez.'

They heard the sound of a key turning in the lock and the door swung open.

Peering over his shoulder, Cadi found herself looking at a tall, slender woman with dark, wavy hair and kind eyes.

Jez took a step back to introduce Poppy and Cadi to Maria, adding, 'I'm afraid Cadi took a bang to the head, when that pervy git Eric tried to take advantage of Poppy.'

Maria's eyes widened with horror. 'You girls are damned lucky you got away from him. What were you thinking?' she continued, without waiting for either girl to have a chance to answer. 'Still, you're safe now. The important thing now is making sure that head of yours doesn't get infected.'

She ushered them into a sizeable kitchen. Taking the kettle off the stove, she poured some of the water into a bowl. 'Luckily for you, I'd put the kettle on for a brew, so the water should be nice and hot.' She added a spoonful of salt and some cold water from the tap, then stirred the mixture. She turned to Jez. 'I need you to look after the bar whilst I take care of Cadi.' She indicated the kitchen dresser behind Poppy. 'Top drawer, you'll find some lengths of cloth – can you pass me one, please?'

Poppy did as she was asked, and watched as Maria tore the strip in two. Dunking one half into the water, she set about the task of cleaning Cadi's wound.

'It's only a small cut, but head-wounds can bleed something awful,' Maria explained as she rinsed the cloth in the water. She took a step back to examine her work, then nodded. Folding the other strip into a pad, she dabbed it in iodine before gently placing it against the wound, causing Cadi to yelp. 'Sorry, luv, but we can't risk infection.' Holding the pad in place, she asked Poppy to fetch another strip of cloth, which she wound around Cadi's injured head.

'Thanks, Maria,' said Cadi. 'I really didn't fancy going home with my head all bloodied.'

Wiping her hands on a towel, Maria leaned against the sink. 'Why are two young girls who aren't local to Liverpool wandering around these parts so late in the day?'

Cadi explained their quest to leave home for pastures new, and how their plans so far had been scuppered for one reason or another.

Maria placed the towel on a hook. 'You must've been desperate to go the Bear's Paw, and whilst I know you didn't want your folks to see you all bloodied, I think they'll want to know why you've a bandage wrapped round your head.'

'I've been giving that some thought,' said Poppy, 'and I think we should find us a bed and breakfast for the night, and catch the first train home.' She opened her duffel bag and rooted around for her purse. 'I know we had a few shillings extra ...'

She began to pull things out, then tipped the bag upside down. With tears forming in her eyes, she quickly put the contents back into her bag, checking each item thoroughly as she avoided Cadi's gaze. She placed her hands over her face and spoke thickly through her fingers. 'I've lost all our money. It was in my bag, but it must've come out when that—' She shook her head, unable to continue.

Cadi held Poppy's hand. 'Don't worry, we'll sort summat out.'

Folding her arms across her chest, Maria tipped her head to one side. 'How about if you stay here for the night. Come the morning, you can help me clean down and barrel up.' She wagged a warning finger at Cadi, 'Only if your head's better, that is, otherwise it'll just be me and Poppy. Your payment will be the train fare home.'

'Oh, Maria, that's ever so kind, and we really appreciate the offer, but we can't take the money – it's too much,' said Cadi.

Maria shrugged. 'Call it a loan then. You can send me a postal order if you really want to.' She eyed them curiously. 'What's so bad about where you live? I've always thought Wales was beautiful.'

'It is, but it's also boring and humdrum, not exciting like Liverpool,' said Cadi.

Maria indicated Cadi's bandages with a jerk of her head. 'That exciting enough for you?'

Cadi coloured. 'I was referring more to the liveliness of the city.'

'I know, queen, but where there's lots of people you'll often find trouble – certainly if you wander into the wrong area, like you did.'

'Are you in the right area then?' asked Poppy.

Maria laughed. 'Same area, but I believe in running a tight ship. I don't stand for any nonsense. First sign of trouble and they're out on their ears!'

Cadi eyed Maria's petite frame. 'I hope you don't mind my asking, but how do you do that exactly?'

'I remind them that this is my pub, and if they wish to carry on drinking here they'll respect my rules.'

Poppy was looking doubtful. 'But what if someone gets lairy? Or starts throwing their weight about? What do you do then?'

'I don't get that kind of trouble, because I nip it in the bud before it begins,' explained Maria. 'But for the more stubborn customer, there's always Bertie.'

Cadi frowned. 'Who's Bertie?'

Maria disappeared behind the bar, only to reappear a few seconds later holding a cricket bat. 'Bertie Bat.'

Poppy's eyes widened. 'I think the landlord down the Bear's Paw could do with meeting Bertie!'

Maria winked at the girls. 'I've never had to use Bertie once, but I'm a woman living on my own, serving alcohol to a room full of men.' She shrugged nonchalantly. 'I have Bertie just in case.'

Cadi looked at her host, full of admiration. 'Have you always been on your own?'

The smile vanished from Maria's lips. 'No, my husband – Bill – has gone over as part of the British Expeditionary Force.'

'Oh,' said Cadi quietly. She looked apologetically at Maria, who was looking grim. 'Sorry, I didn't think. Is that why you're the landlady?'

Nodding, Maria looked at the tiled floor beneath her feet. 'Bill said it would be better to put the pub in my name, just in case ...' She shook her head before looking back up. 'I can empathise with your parents. I didn't want Bill going to France any more than your parents wanted you to come to Liverpool, but Bill is fiercely patriotic and for him to sit by whilst others went to fight wasn't an option. I respected his decision because I love him, but it doesn't mean to say I'm happy about it.'

'A bit like my dad with me,' said Cadi.

'Very much so. It must have been hard for your father to watch his little girl go off into the wide blue yonder.' Maria glanced at Cadi's bandaged head. 'And you can understand why.'

Jez appeared from behind the bar. 'Everything all right?'

Maria nodded. 'I'll come through now.' She indicated a door in the corner of the room. 'That's the pantry – feel free to make yourselves a cheese butty. I've not got much in as I wasn't expecting company.' She winked at Jez as she passed him by. 'You too, Lancelot.'

Jez grinned. 'Don't mind if I do.'

Poppy disappeared into the pantry, before coming back out with a loaf of bread and a chunk of cheese. 'I'm starving! We've not had owt since lunch.'

Cadi rooted around in the dresser cupboards and drawers for the cutlery and plates. 'Me too. I know they say you shouldn't eat cheese before bed, but I can't see it disturbing my sleep.'

Jez leaned against the draining board. 'What do you think of Maria?'

Cadi handed the plates to Poppy. 'I think she's marvellous. In fact I'd say she's everything I aspire to be. I'd be happy if I turned out to be half the woman she is.'

Jez thanked Poppy for the sandwich and peered between the slices of bread. 'No onion?'

Laughing at his cheek, Poppy checked the pantry and returned with half an onion. She held it up. 'You too, Cadi?'

Cadi nodded. 'You can't beat cheese and onion.'

'Or pickle,' agreed Jez. He thanked Poppy for adding the onion and took a large bite, before nodding his approval slowly. He stowed his bite into the side of his cheek and held up a thumb. 'Champion!'

'Glad you approve,' said Poppy.

As he took a seat opposite Cadi, the air-raid siren sounded. 'Bugger and blast,' said Jez. He turned to the girls. 'Come on, we'd best get down the cellar.'

'Cellar?' said Poppy. 'Do you not have an air-raid shelter, either?'

He shook his head. 'Nope, and this is safer than going under the railway arches,' adding, 'probably safer than most shelters.'

As the girls entered the bar, they saw the backs of the men as they descended the stairs into the cellar. Maria ushered the trio forward. 'Take your sarnies with you, cos we could be down there the best part of the night.'

As they descended the steps, someone lit an oil lamp. The soft glow made the cellar look warm and welcoming. Maria indicated the crates, barrels and kegs that were lined up around the walls. 'Take a pew. It's not the

103

comfiest way to spend the night, but certainly the safest.'

'It must be a mistake,' said Poppy. 'This is the second siren we've had tonight.'

'Maybe,' said Maria, 'but I'd rather be safe than sorry … Oh, bugger, I've left the bloomin' till tray *again*.'

'I'll go,' said Jez, who was already halfway to his feet.

'No, you won't,' said Maria sharply. 'I might be prepared to take the risk, but I won't have someone else do it for me.' Before Jez could stop her, she had disappeared through the cellar door, reappearing a few seconds later with the tray to the till between her hands. 'I don't know why I keep forgetting the damned thing.'

'Probably because there's more important things to worry about than money,' Jez chastised her.

'Not when you've got none, there isn't,' said Maria.

'This is a lot better than the arches,' said Poppy. 'I can't believe they tell people to go and hide under railway lines.'

'Those with money've got shelters,' grumbled one of the Greyhound's patrons. 'You go down the likes of Ullet Road and you'll find more shelters than you can shake a stick at. The government don't care about folks like us.'

Poppy grimaced. 'It's a damned disgrace, if you ask me.'

The man who had spoken looked curiously at Poppy. 'You're not a local girl – where're you from?'

'Rhos,' said Poppy, 'it's a village in Wales.'

Keen to know more, the men listened to the girls' story and, when they finished, Maria brought out a pack of cards, a set of draughts and some dominoes.

The games helped to pass the time, and when the siren sounded the all-clear the girls were surprised to learn that they had been in the cellar for a couple of hours.

As the customers left the pub, Maria locked the doors and leaned her back against them. 'I'd normally collect the glasses ready for the morning, but it's getting late, so I think we'll worry about that tomorrow, especially as they might sound the sirens again at any moment.' She opened the door for Jez. 'There's always one straggler.'

Jez grinned. 'If you like, I'll pop by on my way to work in the morning.' He winked at Cadi. 'Make sure you get to the station in one piece?'

'That's really kind of you, Jez,' said Cadi.

'Right you are then.' He placed his fingers against the peak of his cap. 'Goodnight, girls, Maria.'

With Jez gone, Maria bolted the doors. 'Come on, girls, time for bed. I'll show you where you're sleeping whilst the kettle warms. That way, you can have a wash before turning in.' She led them through to the back of the bar and up some steep wooden steps, at the top of which were two rooms. She indicated the one to her left, 'That's my room, and this,' she opened the door latch and stepped through, 'is where you'll be sleeping.' Adding, 'Oh, bugger' as a voice from below called for her to 'Put that light out!' She hastened across the room and pulled the curtains shut, then opened an ottoman that stood between the single beds and pulled out a blanket, which she hung over the curtain rail. 'We never bothered putting blackout blinds in this room, cos there's only me and Bill here.' She placed the lamp on the ottoman. 'If you need the lavvy during the night, feel free to use the chamber pot under the bed, it's a damned sight warmer than a trip downstairs.'

She left the girls to look around the small but adequate room. 'We've landed on our feet here,' said Cadi approvingly.

'Haven't we just?' agreed Poppy. 'I wish we had our own pub – that would solve all our problems.'

'It's the only time I'd agree with my dad,' said Cadi thoughtfully, 'because whilst Maria has a firm hand on the helm, I don't think I'd be able to do what she does. I bet she'd have no qualms about sending that dreadful man off, with his tail between his legs.'

'True, I guess that comes with experience.'

Cadi sighed ruefully. 'I hate to say it, but I think Dad was right.'

Maria reappeared, two hand-towels draped over her left arm, and a tray containing a bowl of warm water and a bar of soap between her hands. 'Did I hear you say your father was right?'

Cadi nodded. 'We're too inexperienced to handle some situations. If Jez hadn't turned up this evening ...'

Maria placed the tray on the chest of drawers. 'What happened to you was horrible, but you're wiser for it. You've learned a lesson. We all have to learn by our mistakes, that's how we become older and wiser.'

'I think we've a way to go yet,' sighed Poppy.

Maria went over to the fireplace, where she quickly and expertly lit a fire. 'You'll get there.' She leaned back from the fire as it flamed into life. 'There we are! Soon be nice and toasty. Get yourselves cleaned up, and I'll see you in the morning, unless that pesky siren goes off again of course,' adding as she left the room, 'Holler if you need owt.'

As soon as Maria had gone, Cadi began to undress. 'I'm whacked. I reckon I'll be asleep before my head hits the pillow.' She took the flannel that was floating in the water and gently rubbed it against the bar of soap before passing it over her arms and neck. Closing her eyes, she felt the soothing effect of the warm water against her skin. Patting herself dry, she changed into her nightie, whilst Poppy took her turn at the sink.

'I wish we could start over,' sighed Poppy.

'Me too,' said Cadi, 'but out of curiosity, what would you have done differently?'

Poppy thought about this as she ran the flannel over her arms. 'Truthfully? I don't know; tried to prepare better, saved more money. You?'

Cadi prodded the fire with the poker. 'I don't think I'd have wasted the first day sightseeing, but would have knuckled down from the start.'

Poppy joined her friend by the fire. 'Quite frankly, right now I'm grateful that I'm here with you instead of …' She fell silent.

Cadi closed her eyes. 'Me too.' She stared idly at the flames. 'Bill can't be the only man who's given up his job to go to war. I reckon there'll be a shortage of workers before long.'

'Only we'll be long gone by then,' said Poppy.

'We can always come back,' reasoned Cadi.

Yawning, Poppy climbed into bed. 'If we do, there's no way I'm setting foot around these parts.'

Cadi slid between the cold sheets. 'Liverpool's a big place, and I bet Maria and Jez know plenty of people who need workers. As Dad's always said: it's not what you know, but *who* you know.'

Poppy leaned up on one elbow. 'What are you suggesting?'

Cadi's cheeks coloured. 'I know what you went through today was dreadful, but would it stop you wanting to leave Rhos?'

Poppy thought this through. Whilst it was true the ordeal had been terrifying, it was due to one person that they'd had the misfortune to encounter twice. Maria had lived in the same area as that man for years, yet she'd never had any problems with him. Poppy could return to Rhos and lead a quiet life, but would that really make her happy? Until this evening she had been desperate to stay in Liverpool. Making up her mind, she spoke slowly. 'If I could guarantee I'd never have to see that dreadful man again, I'd want to stay in Liverpool.'

Cadi smiled in the darkness. 'We've been extremely unlucky, and you've probably got more chance of finding a hen's tooth than you have of bumping into Eric again.'

Knowing how much it meant for Cadi to stay in Liverpool, Poppy nodded. 'We'll ask Maria and Jez, but if they don't know of anyone, we go home: agreed?'

Cadi's smile broadened. 'Agreed.' And with that sliver of hope, she slowly drifted to sleep.

When Cadi woke the next morning she saw that the fire was still lit, but only just, so she padded over and poked it back to life. With the fire blazing, she left their bedroom and stood on the landing for a moment, to see if she could hear any signs of life, but it seemed she was the only one awake. Taking the washing bowl they had used the previous evening, she tiptoed down the stairs and put the kettle on the hotplate. As she waited for the kettle to warm, she nipped into the bar and began to collect the empty glasses from the tables.

It was a neat little place, nicely laid out with seating areas, some of which were in stalls. Not being a patron of pubs, Cadi couldn't really judge whether this one was any better than the ones her father and brothers frequented; but according to her mother, public houses were rowdy, smelly places, full of tobacco smoke and alcohol. She wiped her forefinger along one of the tables and held it up for examination, and was pleased yet unsurprised to see that it was relatively clean. Maria had said she ran a tight ship and she meant it.

Cadi gathered the rest of the glasses and took them through to the kitchen. She then picked up the ashtrays and placed them all on one table, ready for cleaning. Heading back into the kitchen, she checked the kettle was warm, before pouring some of the water into a bowl and heading back upstairs.

As she entered the room, she started as Poppy wished her good morning.

'You were dead to the world when I left you,' said Cadi, placing the bowl on the chest of drawers. 'I thought you still were – which is why you damn near gave me a heart attack!' Remembering the previous evening's events, she hastily added, 'How are you? Did you sleep all right?'

Poppy grimaced. 'I didn't get to sleep for ages, because I kept thinking about that dreadful man, but when I did drop off, I slept like a log. What time is it?'

'If the clock in the kitchen is correct, it's five minutes to five. Talking of that beast, how are you feeling?'

Poppy yawned. 'All right, still a bit shaken up, but I suppose that's to be expected.' She glanced around. 'Is Maria up?'

'I've not heard her,' said Cadi. 'I thought I'd make a start on the pub whilst I waited for the water to warm up. If we make haste, I think we can have the glasses washed and the tables wiped down before Maria gets up.'

'Sounds good to me. How's your bonce?'

Cadi winced as she tentatively touched her injured head. 'Still smarts a bit – would you mind having a look?'

Poppy helped her friend remove the bandages and passed them over for Cadi to hold. 'There's not much blood on the pad,' said Poppy. Gently pulling Cadi's hair to one side, she peered at the cut. 'It doesn't look pink or gooey, so I don't think it's infected. Do you want me to have a go at re-bandaging it?'

'Thanks, Poppy, but it's probably best if we let the air get to it for a while,' said Cadi, folding the bandages neatly. 'That's what Mam always says is best for wounds.'

Poppy walked over to the window and looked out onto the street below whilst Cadi had a wash. 'It's still quite quiet out there, but there's a few people heading off to work. They're very different from the folk we saw on Mozart Street.'

Cadi carefully pulled her dress over her head, then joined Poppy by the window. 'Not surprising really, as the people living on Mozart Street are relatively well off, but this lot remind me of the folk back home.'

Poppy took her turn at the bowl. 'You mean, poor.'

Cadi pulled a brush through her hair, taking care not to go anywhere near her injury. 'Yes, same kind of people, just a different location.'

Poppy frowned. 'So if Burlington Street is considered rough, does that mean Rhos is too?'

Cadi gave Poppy a wan smile. 'Not to us, because we live there, but I dare say it is to outsiders.'

Poppy began to dress as she spoke. 'Has your aunt ever been to Rhos?'

Cadi thought about this for a moment. 'No, or at least not that I can remember. Why?'

'I was just wondering what Flo would make of somewhere like Rhos? Would she think it as rough as it is here, or would she see it differently because her sister lives there?'

'Interesting,' said Cadi, buckling her shoes. 'I wonder what people would make of Flo being my mother's sister. They probably wouldn't believe it because, let's face it, they're like chalk and cheese.'

When both girls had dressed, they dropped their voices as they headed down the stairs.

'I could say the same about you and your mam,' Poppy said. 'Perhaps it runs in your family? Where did your grandparents live?'

111

'Not far from Mozart Street. In a flat, like Flo. They were on the top floor.' She smiled wistfully. 'They had a cracking view of the park from their bedroom window.'

Poppy filled the kitchen sink with water and began washing the glasses. 'I wonder what they made of your mam marrying your dad?'

'Because he was a miner, you mean?' Cadi pulled a face. 'I don't remember them being unpleasant towards him when they came to visit – far from it – so I suppose it didn't bother them much.'

'What do you think about Flo, now you know she's only a career woman through circumstance?'

'I think I admire her now more than ever. It must've taken real gumption to start all over again. I only wish my father could see her for the woman she truly is, instead of worrying that I'll end up like her.'

'I can kind of see his point,' said Poppy as she handed Cadi another glass to dry. 'Flo is a very impressive woman who's taken control of her life. Your father may fear you will do the same, then regret it when you're older.'

'Only you can't live your life worrying about what might happen in the future, because life's too short. You've only got to look at what happened to Flo and her husband to see that.'

'Do you think she misses having children?'

Cadi nodded. 'That's why she's thrown herself into her job, so that she doesn't have time to think about it.'

Poppy rubbed her forehead with the back of her hand. 'I like your dad, I really do, but he's blaming Flo for not being able to have kids, which is really unfair, because it's not her fault she's different from everyone else.'

'That's Dad all over. He likes everything to be black and white: the women stay at home and have kids whilst the men go out to work, but life's not always like that,' said Cadi.

Poppy placed another glass on the drainer. 'I know you've said you want to be your own boss, or at least have a career of your own, but you haven't ruled out marriage and kids altogether, so your father's really worrying about what *might* happen.'

'Exactly!' said Cadi.

Poppy turned her thoughts back to Flo. 'Do you think Flo ever gets lonely? No husband or kids to come home to – I bet that flat is as quiet as the grave, with only her in it.'

Cadi pulled a face. 'She works hard, so she's probably happy to come home to some peace and quiet.'

'What about when she's old, though? I wouldn't like to think of her sitting in that flat on her own all day.'

'That's a long way off, anything could happen between now and then. I know she says she's sworn off men, but things change.'

'Morning!' Maria trilled as she stepped into the kitchen. She gestured for Cadi to turn round so that she could examine the back of her head. 'How does it feel?'

Cadi gave her a thumbs up. 'Loads better.'

'That's what I like to hear.' She placed an arm around Poppy's shoulders. 'How are you after your ordeal?'

Poppy shrugged. 'A bit jumpy, but I'm trying to put it behind me, so that I can move on.'

'It'll take time,' said Maria knowledgeably. Stepping back, she cast an approving glance over the gleaming glasses. 'This is a nice surprise, I must say.'

Poppy beamed. 'We wanted to get it all done before you came down, as a thank-you for all you've done for us.'

Maria called over her shoulder as she stepped through into the pantry. 'Well, you've certainly done that. Who's for toast, or would you prefer porridge?'

'Toast, please,' said Poppy and Cadi together.

'Right you are. If you pop the glasses onto the shelves below the bar, I'll fix us some tea and toast.'

'What do we do about the ashtrays?' asked Cadi.

Maria passed her a steel bucket. 'Put the contents in here and,' she fished out a grubby-looking cloth from under the sink and handed it to Poppy, 'you can give them a quick wipe over with this.'

Poppy did her best not to grimace as she took the cloth.

Maria called over her shoulder as she made her way into the kitchen. 'Back in a bit.'

Cadi emptied the ashtrays whilst Poppy wiped them clean. 'If I had a pub I wouldn't let anyone smoke,' said Poppy, a look of disgust on her face as she wiped the ash from one of the ashtrays.

Cadi turned her face to avoid a small cloud of ash as it rose up from the bucket. 'I don't think you'd have many customers. I couldn't see dad and the boys going to a pub if they weren't allowed to smoke.' A line furrowed her brow. 'Your dad smokes?'

'He smokes a pipe, which is very different from these nasty things – pipe smoke has a sweet sort of smell.'

'Can't say as I've noticed,' said Cadi. 'Mam won't let dad and the boys smoke in the house. She says it's hard enough to contend with coal dust, without adding fag ash into the mix.'

They finished the ashtrays as Maria called them through for breakfast. She pointed at the different jars as the girls washed their hands. 'There's jam, Marmite or butter – the choice is yours.'

Helping themselves to the different spreads, the girls settled down to eat.

Maria spoke as she spread a thin layer of Marmite on her toast. 'So what's the order for today?'

Cadi heaved a sigh. 'I know the sensible thing to say is "go home", but I can't help wondering if we haven't missed something.' She glanced at Maria. 'I don't suppose you have any friends in need of a couple of hard workers?' she asked, adding hastily, 'We'll do anything: clean, cook, carry – whatever's needed.'

Maria appeared to be deep in thought whilst eating her toast. 'When Bill first left, I never thought I'd be able to cope on my own, but through the help of friends and customers I've managed to scrape by, but scraping by and making a decent living aren't the same thing. I know I can't keep relying on friends and customers, but neither can I afford to pay a barmaid's wage—'

Fearing that Maria had got hold of the wrong end of the stick, Cadi interrupted. 'I wasn't implying you should give us a job.'

Maria waved a dismissive hand. 'As I was saying, I can't pay a proper wage, but if you wanted to live here rent-free and work for your keep, I could pay you a small wage each. But it would be small, sort of like pocket money.'

Cadi's heart rose in her chest. 'Do you really think it would work?'

Smiling, Maria nodded. 'I don't see why not. You see, when Bill went, he made sure everything was set up for me, but he hadn't thought about the heavy work. Changing barrels is one thing, but moving them?' She rolled her eyes. 'If you're a big, beefy man, then that's fine, but I can't do it on my own, so I've had to rely on others to help out.'

'Do you think Poppy and I could do it?'

Maria laughed. 'No, they're extremely heavy, but the three of us could.'

'Are you sure?' said Cadi.

Maria smiled. 'I wouldn't suggest it otherwise. Of course you don't have to, if you don't want to.'

'We'd love to,' cried Cadi, before glancing hastily at Poppy, who appeared cautious.

'That man,' she said to Maria, 'the one who attacked me, does he ever come in here?'

Maria's face was stern. 'No, he does not! Nor will he. I won't have men like him in my bar. The landlord down the Bear's Paw turns a blind eye to a lot of what goes on in his pub because he takes backhanders off everybody, but I'm not like that.'

'But what if he tries to come in?' said Poppy, still fretful.

'He won't,' said Maria simply, 'there's nothing for him here.' She lowered her voice, even though there was no fear of them being overheard. 'Men like Eric only want women for one thing, and he won't get that here, if you catch my meaning?'

Cadi nodded. 'He made it perfectly clear last night that he thought we were …' her jaw twitched, 'for sale.'

Maria's eyelids fluttered. 'Disgusting! Like I say, you're lucky you got away, but you needn't fear Eric, not whilst you're living here.'

Relieved to hear Maria's reassurance, Poppy's face dropped as another problem presented itself. 'Only aren't we too young to work in a pub?'

Maria replenished their teacups. 'You're too young to serve alcohol, but there's a lot more to running a pub than that. In fact with three of us, we might even be able to expand the business, and if we could do that, I might be able to afford to pay you a proper wage.'

'Expand how exactly? I've always thought a pub's a pub,' said Poppy.

Cadi was shaking her head wisely. 'Some pubs offer meals.' She glanced towards the stairs to their bedroom. 'And if Maria would agree to the three of us sharing her bedroom, we could even offer the spare room as a B&B.'

Maria nodded, a slow smile twitching her lips. 'I like your thinking! Being so close to the docks has its advantages. People coming into port need a place to stay, and we're perfectly located for that.'

'What about beds for me and Cadi?' asked Poppy thoughtfully.

Maria screwed her lips to one side, and for a moment she was lost deep in thought. 'I'm sure we've got a couple of camp beds in the loft. They may not be the comfiest, but they'd do for now.'

Cadi scanned the ceiling. 'I haven't noticed a loft hatch.'

'You wouldn't have; it's a separate staircase – it runs above the lavvies,' explained Maria.

Poppy too cast her eyes to the ceiling above them. 'Can we have a look after breakfast?'

'You certainly can,' smiled Maria. 'For a start, you're going to need to find those beds. But first,' she took her mug and rinsed it in the sink, 'we need to wipe the tables down and sweep the floor, ready for opening later today.' She had started to go through to the bar when she stopped abruptly. 'And I call myself a responsible woman! You've not contacted your parents to let them know you're all right.' She jerked her head towards a telephone that stood on a shelf behind the bar. 'I dare say your folks aren't on the telephone, but do they know someone who is?'

Both girls looked doubtful until Cadi cried, 'The bakery. They've got a telephone. We can ask Sophie to take a message to our folks.'

'Come on, I'll show you what to do.' She picked up the receiver and handed it to Cadi. 'When the operator speaks, ask her to connect you to … ?'

'Seth's Bakery,' confirmed Cadi. She did as Maria instructed and was pleased when she recognised the voice on the other end of the telephone. 'Hello, Sophie. It's me, Cadi.'

'Cadi,' cried Sophie. 'How are you?' She paused momentarily, before asking in an anxious voice, 'Is everything all right?'

Cadi was beaming as she replied, 'We're both fine. In fact that's why we're telephoning, to ask you to pass a message on to our parents.'

'Fire away. I've got a pen and paper.'

'Can you tell them we've secured jobs at the Greyhound pub, Burlington Street, Liverpool.'

'A pub! What happened to the services?'

'Too young,' Cadi admitted. 'So we started looking for work elsewhere, and that's when we came across the pub.'

'Is there anything else you'd like to add?'

'Nope, we'll write to explain everything. We just wanted them to know we're safe, in case they were worried.'

'Will do! Gosh, I can't believe you've left home. How's Liverpool?'

Aware that she was talking on someone else's time, Cadi cut the conversation short. 'Fabulous, but I've really got to go, so I'll drop you a line – tell you all about it.'

'Well, make sure you do. Give my love to Poppy.'

'I will. Ta-ra, Sophie.'

Cadi waited for her friend to say goodbye before replacing the receiver. 'Well, that's that done, and it won't just be our parents who know we're working in a pub, but the whole of Rhos.'

Poppy laughed. 'Good old Sophie, you can always rely on her to spread the word.'

Maria handed Poppy a broom. 'If you sweep, I'll get the mop and bucket.'

Cadi picked up the chairs and placed them on the tables whilst Poppy swept underneath. 'Do you believe in serendipity?'

'I never used to,' Poppy confessed, 'but it does rather seem as though events – or fate – have led us to Maria.'

'Exactly,' said Cadi. 'If we hadn't encountered that brute of a man, we'd never have met Jez or Maria.'

'Did I hear someone mention my name?' said Maria as she wrung out the mop.

'We were discussing our thoughts on fate, and whether we believe in it or not,' said Cadi.

'I'm a firm believer,' said Maria as she wiped the mop across the floor. 'I think that everything happens for a reason, be it good or bad.'

Someone knocked on the pub door, and a familiar voice called through, 'Anyone home?'

Maria called out to Jez as she slid the bolts back, 'Give it a push, it sticks summat wicked after it's been raining.'

Jez pushed the door open and beamed at the girls. 'Morning, all. Am I too early?'

Poppy rested her hands on top of the broom handle. 'Nope, because we're staying put.'

He raised a curious brow. 'Sorry?'

'Maria's asked us to stay on and help with the pub,' said Cadi simply, 'so we won't be needing your services as an escort after all.'

His eyes glittered as an approving smile tweaked his lips. 'I guess that means I'll be seeing a lot more of you?'

Maria rinsed the mop out. 'You certainly will. Tell you what, why don't you pop by after work and the girls can explain everything properly.'

Clearly delighted to hear the news, Jez was beaming like the cat that had got the cream. 'I shall look forward to it.' He winked at the girls. 'Ta-ra, ladies.'

'No prizes for guessing what's on his mind,' said Maria.

Cadi nodded. She knew what men wanted more than anything whilst out drinking. 'A free pint?'

Maria tutted. 'Free pint indeed! There's only one thing that's put a smile on that boy's face, and it's you.'

Cadi paused mid-wipe. '*Me?* It was Poppy he rescued.'

'That's as may be, but Jez was giving you the eye, not Poppy.'

Poppy giggled. 'First Aled, now Jez.'

Maria poured the water down the drain outside the door. 'Who's Aled?'

'No one!' snapped Cadi.

'He was considered the local catch back home,' supplied Poppy.

'A bit like measles,' muttered Cadi.

'Not your flavour then?' laughed Maria.

'Nope,' said Cadi firmly. 'Now can we stop discussing my non-existent love life and fetch these beds down from the attic?'

Maria winked at Poppy. 'Who's in charge here?'

Cadi began to apologise, but Maria waved her into silence. 'I'm only teasing. Come on.' She led them up a steep wooden staircase to the attic, only instead of leading to a loft hatch as the girls had expected, there was a door at the top of the stairs.

'It's a proper room,' breathed Cadi as they walked in.

Poppy walked over to the porthole-style window at the gable end of the roof. 'I can see for miles.'

'Why don't we all sleep up here and rent the two bedrooms out,' suggested Cadi.

Maria pulled a face as she looked around the dusty room. 'Because it's the attic?'

Cadi stepped over some boxes. 'I know, but it's lovely up here, and you've great views over the city. It's more than big enough for the three of us, and if we moved up here we wouldn't have to muck about with beds. Not only that, but we'd have two rooms to rent out.'

Maria stood with her head on one side, looking around the room. 'It would certainly make more sense financially ...' She fell silent as a voice called up from down below.

'Maria? I've got your delivery.'

'It's Stan,' said Maria. 'I'll deal with the delivery, if you girls set about finding those beds and clearing this room up, because I'm not sleeping in here until it's had a good mopping.'

As Maria disappeared down the steps, Poppy held a hand to her stomach. 'Every time I hear a man's voice, I'm like a cat on a hot tin roof.'

Cadi gave her friend a grim smile. 'It'll pass; like Maria said, that feller never comes here, so you've nowt to fear on that score.'

'I know, and I'm sure I'll be fine, given time.'

With that said, the girls began clearing the boxes and stacking them on top of each other. 'In less than a week we've got a new home, new jobs and you've even got yourself a new beau,' said Poppy.

Cadi took a sheet off an old chair and gave it a shake, causing clouds of dust to fill the air. 'Honestly!' she coughed. 'I don't know what Maria saw, but I didn't notice Jez looking at me any differently from the way he was looking at you.'

'Well, I did – he looks at you the same way I look at chocolate.' Poppy trotted over to the window and pushed it open, allowing the dust out. 'I don't see why you're objecting. I think he's lovely. I wouldn't mind him looking at me like that.'

'Like what?'

Poppy folded an old eiderdown and hugged it to her. 'Gooey-eyed.'

Cadi pulled a disapproving face. 'You make it sound like he's got conjunctivitis.'

Poppy emitted a shriek of laughter, which she hastily muffled with her hand. 'Honestly, Cadi. You know full well what I meant, but perhaps I should've said starry-eyed.'

'It certainly sounds better,' agreed Cadi. She fell silent as she clapped eyes on what appeared to be an old army camp bed. As she began to unroll it, she turned her thoughts to Jez. Had he looked at her any differently? She hadn't thought so, but she wasn't really paying attention. She conjured up an image of the boy in her mind. Dark-haired, brown-eyed, dimples when he smiled and a cleft in his chin. In her mind, she looked into his eyes. They twinkled at her. 'Oh, heck,' she said softly.

'What's wrong? Is it broken?'

Cadi shook her head. 'Nope.' She liked Jez, she really did, but she wasn't in the market for a boyfriend.

Dewi shook his head. 'A *barmaid*?'

Jill tutted loudly. 'Don't you listen? They *can't* be barmaids, they're too young – they'll be doing other things.'

'Like what?' said Dewi guardedly. 'I can only think of one other working woman's profession, if you're not a barmaid …'

Jill cried out in exasperation as she held up the letter from Cadi. 'For goodness' sake, Dewi! How could you possibly think that of our Cadi, *or* Poppy come to that? You know as well as I that they're going to provide evening meals as well as running a bed-and-breakfast.'

'Well, I don't like it,' grumbled Dewi. 'They're too young to be working in a pub, you should've told them to come home.'

'Don't be ridiculous. They're not children, despite what you might think.'

He looked up from his place at the table. 'I'm *not* being ridiculous. Do you even know the name of this pub?'

'The Greyhound – why?'

'Just wondered whereabouts it is. There's some pretty rough areas in Liverpool, as well you know.'

She pulled a face. 'Burlington Street, which I believe is in Vauxhall Ward.' She held up a hand as her husband spluttered a protest. 'It can't be a dive, if our Cadi's working there. Come on, Dewi, she's got more sense than that.'

'More sense!' growled Dewi. 'If she had any sense at all she'd not have gone running off in the first place. And exactly where is this pub? Is it close to the docks, because if so …'

Jill coloured. 'I know what you're going to say, but nowhere's safe during times of war, and it's not as if they're right on the docks.'

His brow shot up. 'So that's a yes, then.'

124

Jill sighed breathily. 'She's my daughter too.'

'Well, bloody well act like it!' snapped Dewi. 'Get out there and bring her back.'

Jill stared at her husband, aghast. 'She's not a child, Dewi. I can't drag her back and, what's more, you know it, otherwise you'd have tried yourself.'

Realising he'd hit a stalemate, Dewi tried another tack. 'Pubs are no place for a young girl. I want it known I don't approve.'

Jill fixed him with a wooden stare. 'Honestly, Dewi, who do you think you are?'

'Her father! Not that it seems to count for much.'

Jill let out a long-suffering sigh. 'Can we please drop the matter?'

As her husband returned to his newspaper, Jill continued peeling the vegetables for their tea. She had known Dewi would object to the girls' new occupation, and could even understand why. After all, she hadn't exactly been thrilled by the news, but she was proud of her daughter for finding herself a job and she was sure Dewi would be too, given time.

Chapter Four

November 1939

It had been a month since the girls had arrived in Liverpool, and what had started off as a nightmare had turned into a dream come true. Through their hard work and dedication they had turned the Greyhound from a run-of-the-mill pub into a successful B&B serving lunchtime and evening food. Maria looked after the bar whilst the girls attended to the B&B, as well as preparing the fare, which seemed to be going down a treat with the regulars.

'Simple but affordable, that's what your working man wants,' Maria had informed them when Poppy had questioned the need to serve food. 'Times are always hard for the folk living around these parts, and the coming of war just made everything worse, so why not give them a bit of a boost? I don't know a man alive who'd turn up his nose at a bit of home-cooked grub. Round these parts that's scouse, cottage pie, and a nice fruit crumble and custard for afters – you give them that and you'll not go far wrong.'

'As long as we're turning a profit,' said Cadi as she priced up her shopping list.

'You've got a proper little business head on you,' said Maria, glancing at the figures on Cadi's sheet.

Cadi, who had always been awful at maths, smiled as she looked up from her sums. 'I think running a business might be my forte, as it were, which is odd, because I couldn't do sums in school to save me life. But it's different when you're dealing with actual money. I probably got that from me mam – feeding our lot takes some careful budgeting.'

This conversation had taken place in their first trial week, but Poppy needn't have feared that their plan would fall flat. The men enjoyed coming into the pub for an evening meal, along with a pint or two, and the travellers residing at the B&B also preferred the home-cooked meals the girls prepared, compared to the pricier eating establishments to be found in the city.

Now, as Cadi finished smoothing down the sheet on the bed in readiness for their next guest, she stood back to admire her efforts. 'I'm not ashamed to admit I'm proud of what we've accomplished since first arriving. I reckon we must run the finest B&B this side of Liverpool. I know we're not exactly as grand as the Adelphi, but we're just as clean and comfortable.'

Poppy pushed a pillow into a clean case. 'And a heck of a lot cheaper too.'

'Glad you stayed and gave it a go?'

'Too right I am,' replied Poppy as she placed the pillow on the bed. 'What's more, I'm glad I never let that beast of a man scare me off.'

'Me too,' said Cadi, 'and I've noticed you don't jump as much whenever someone enters the pub.'

Poppy nodded. 'At first I was certain he was going to walk through the doors at any moment, but what Maria said was right: the Greyhound isn't for men like him.'

Even though Cadi knew Poppy's words were true, she was also very aware that the experience had dinted her friend's confidence, and she said as much to Poppy, who agreed.

'I'll get it back eventually. And working here is much better than working in the bakery, although probably not as exciting as whatever it is Flo does.' She hesitated as she fluffed the pillow up. 'I wonder where she is?'

'Goodness knows. Last time I spoke to her she was heading down south.'

'Probably off on some secret operation,' said Poppy. She placed a finger to her lips and winked at Cadi. 'All very hush-hush.'

'Honestly, Poppy, you and your theories.' Standing with her hands on her hips, Cadi admired her work. 'If anyone would've told me I'd enjoy making beds, I'd have thought them bonkers, but it really is satisfying when it's part of a business that you've helped to create.'

Poppy took the chrysanthemums that she had bought from the market and placed them in the vase on the windowsill. 'Taking pride in our work leads to satisfied customers, which in turn means more money in the till.'

'And whilst the Germans keep their bombs over that side of the water, we've nowt to worry about,' concluded Cadi.

Poppy pulled a guilty face. 'This is going to sound terrible, but do you ever worry about Bill coming back?'

Cadi gently closed the door to, before answering, 'Because you think we'd have to leave?'

'Don't you?'

'Yes, I do, but this war's going to go on for a long time yet, and whilst I'm hoping the Krauts never come over here, I'm afraid our boys will be overseas for a long time yet.'

A blush invaded Poppy's neckline. 'What's bad news for Maria is good for us.'

'Only it won't stay that way for ever, so we need to keep an ear to the ground just in case we need to move on.'

'I bet a certain someone would move heaven and earth to find us jobs, if it meant keeping you close by,' chuckled Poppy.

'Not this again!'

'But Jez is so sweet, and it's obvious he's keen on you. Why don't you give him a chance?' She gave Cadi a friendly nudge. 'I feel so sorry for him, standing at the bar hoping to catch a glimpse of you.'

Cadi picked up one of the pillowcases bound for the laundry. 'Oh, don't! I feel awful enough as it is, because I like him, but only as a friend, and it would be wrong for me to encourage him when I know it won't go beyond friendship.'

Poppy wagged a reproving finger. 'You wanted to prove that you're an independent woman, and you've done that, so why not give him a chance, see where it goes?'

Cadi frowned irritably. 'I'm too young to get tied down. You know what it's like: once you start courting, you end up spending all your time together, before getting married and having kids.' She held up a hand to quell Poppy's as-yet-unspoken objections. 'That's what happened with my parents and yours – it's inevitable.'

Poppy pulled a face. 'Not everyone lives happily ever after. Some people find out they're not suited.'

'Then what's the point?' reasoned Cadi. 'The whole idea is to find a mate to settle down with, and I'm not ready for that yet.'

Poppy collected the rest of the dirty sheets and bundled them into the wash bag before heading for the door. 'Well, I'd jump at the chance if I were you, especially with a corker like Jez.'

Cadi could feel herself getting annoyed. 'Have him, if that's what you want. Goodness only knows, I won't stand in your way.'

Poppy tutted. 'Don't be so coarse, Cadi. Besides, I wouldn't dream of being with a man who was in love with someone else.'

Cadi broke into startled laughter. 'Love! I'll admit he's keen, but *love*?'

'Don't you believe in love at first sight?' said Poppy, before remembering who she was talking to and answering her own question. 'Daft question – of course you don't. Well, I do, and I think Jez might too.'

'Well, in that case it's a definite "no",' said Cadi. She walked out of the room ahead of Poppy and descended the stairs. Calling out to Maria to let her know that they were going to do the laundry, the two girls left the pub.

'You're more like your auntie than I thought,' sighed Poppy. 'A shame really, because I always envisaged us being much like our parents, living on the same street with kiddies of a similar age.'

'Well, I'm sorry if I'm blowing your dream out of the water, but I can't court a feller just because you want me to.'

Entering the laundry they paused their conversation momentarily, as Cadi paid for the use of one of the cauldrons.

'I suppose there's plenty of time to change your mind,' continued Poppy as she dunked the sheets into the water.

'My point exactly,' agreed Cadi. 'Only, let's face it, if Jez really is the love of my life, don't you think wild horses wouldn't be able to stop me from being his belle?'

Poppy wiped the steam away from her brow with her forearm. 'I suppose so. Pity, though, cos I think you'd make a lovely couple.'

Taking a large pair of wooden tongs, Cadi stirred the sheets in the water. Every time Poppy quizzed her over her feelings for Jez, she always feared that her friend might accidentally uncover the truth, which was why she got so irritable. Cadi might not be ready for marriage, but she couldn't deny that she found Jez not only attractive but extremely good company. She hadn't realised how much she liked him until she found herself idly daydreaming about their first kiss, whilst preparing him a corned beef and tomato sandwich one Saturday lunchtime. The vision had taken her completely by surprise, so much so that she had made a promise to herself that she would keep him at arm's length, for fear her vision might come true.

Some time later, when the bedding had been washed and rinsed, the girls carried everything over to the mangles, where they stood waiting for one to become free.

'When we've finished with the wringer we'll have to hang them in the drying room,' said Poppy conversationally as they watched as a young woman a few years older than themselves thread her washing through the mangle. 'It's far too cold to hang them on the line.'

'I love carrying them home after they've been in the drying room,' said Cadi, 'because they're toasty warm.'

Poppy turned her back to the young woman whose mangle they were waiting to use. 'Is it me or is she taking her time?'

Cadi looked at the woman over Poppy's shoulder. 'She's not in a hurry, that's for sure,' she said, and as she continued to watch she added, 'Every time she turns the handle she winces as if she's in pain – maybe that's why she's taking so long.'

Poppy turned back to look. 'She does, doesn't she.'

Nodding, Cadi walked over to the woman. 'Would you like some help?'

Looking slightly guarded, the woman glanced around before giving a small nod. 'Are you sure you don't mind?'

In answer Cadi took over the turning of the handle. 'You thread them in and I'll do the turning.'

With Cadi doing most of the work, they soon got through the remaining items. Thanking Cadi for her help, the young woman gave a small gasp of pain as she bent to gather her laundry. Cadi and Poppy instinctively rushed to help, but the woman held up a hand.

'It's me back, it gives me gyp every now and then. I'll be right as rain in minute.'

Cadi frowned. How could someone so young be suffering from a bad back? 'Are you sure you're all right?' she asked, her concern growing as she noticed a scar that ran under the woman's eye on her left cheek.

The woman hefted the bagful of laundry over her shoulder. 'Yes, thank you.' She smiled fleetingly at them. 'I'd best be off, but thanks for your help.'

Cadi waited until she was out of earshot before mentioning the scar to Poppy. 'Did you see it?'

Poppy nodded. 'I did indeed! Poor bugger, I wonder how she got that?'

Cadi pulled a grim face. 'I dunno, but I bet it's got summat to do with her bad back.' She picked up a sheet and began to fold it with Poppy. 'It's strange ...'

Poppy looked around her. 'What is?'

'That poor woman must have been on the mangle for a while, judging by the amount of laundry she had, yet no one else came to help her, which seems odd because we've always found everyone to be helpful.'

Poppy watched as the young woman neared a group of older women gossiping idly. As she drew level the women fell quiet, dropping their heads until she had passed by. 'Did you see that?' hissed Poppy.

Cadi nodded slowly. 'They obviously know summat we don't. I wonder what?' She stopped speaking as one of the women, known to the girls as Lethia, broke free from the group and hastened towards them.

'Morning, girls, how's tricks?'

Cadi cast Lethia a shrewd look. 'Cut to the chase.'

Grinning, Lethia jerked her head in the direction the other woman had taken. 'I see you've met Isobel.'

Cadi continued turning the handle as she spoke. 'Was that her name? She didn't say.'

Lethia glanced back at the group of women who were watching with interest. 'Isobel normally keeps herself to herself. Quite frankly, we were surprised she let you help her.'

Poppy's forehead formed a crease. 'She told us she had a bad back.'

Lethia rolled her eyes. 'Bad back, my eye! More like her old feller's give her a good hiding – again.'

Cadi and Poppy stared at Lethia in stunned silence, before Cadi finally found her voice. 'Do you mean her husband?'

Lethia shook her head. 'Her dad – he's renowned for it. Poor little wretch can't do right for doing wrong, not in his eyes. That's how she ended up with that scar. My pal reckons he did it with his belt – pig of a man.'

'Why doesn't she leave him? It's not like she's not old enough,' asked Poppy incredulously.

'God knows! If it were me, I'd have left years ago.'

'What about her mam?' suggested Cadi, wringing out the last sheet. 'Doesn't she do anything to stop him?'

'Her mam's long gone; got herself a fancy man and trotted off into the wide blue yonder years back,' said Lethia informatively.

Cadi looked at her, aghast. 'Why on earth didn't she take her daughter with her? *Especially* if she knew what a brute of a man her husband was?'

'Goodness only knows,' said Lethia.

'How could she?' cried Poppy, adding, 'That poor woman, she must've been devastated when her mam left.'

The trio were heading towards the drying room. 'She was only young when her mam left,' said Lethia. 'I doubt she can even remember her.'

'What a dreadful thing to do to your own child,' said Poppy sadly.

Lethia nodded. 'On top of which, her father hasn't stopped punishing her since.'

Cadi stared at Lethia in disbelief. 'Why? It's not her fault her mam left.'

'As far as he's concerned, it's not a man's job to bring up a kid. And if his wife wanted to leave that much, she should've taken Isobel with her.'

'Oh my God. So he's making out like he's been lumbered with her?'

Lethia nodded glumly. 'Poor kid, it must be tough knowing neither of your parents wanted you.'

'Only if he doesn't want her, why doesn't he kick her out instead of using her as a punchbag all the time?' said Cadi thoughtfully.

'Because she keeps house for him,' said Lethia simply. 'From what we can gather, he sees it as her payment for staying behind.'

'Why can't he do his own bloomin' washing and shopping?' snapped Poppy. 'Lazy git.'

Lethia laughed. 'Because after a long day on the docks he prefers to go down the pub and get legless.'

'Oh, joy!' said Cadi sarcastically. 'So not only does Isobel have to put up with a miserable old so-'n'-so, but a drunk one to boot.'

Hearing one of the women hail her from behind, Lethia turned, giving a wave of acknowledgement.

'Look's like Viv's ready for the off.' She turned back to the girls. 'Gotta dash.'

With the last of the sheets pegged, the girls headed out of the laundry, telling the man in charge they would be back later to pick them up.

'That poor woman,' sighed Cadi. 'I can't stop thinking about how unhappy she must be.'

'I take it we're still talking about Isobel?'

Cadi nodded. 'I thought my dad was bad, but he's nothing compared to hers.'

'I still don't understand why she doesn't get up and walk out,' said Poppy. 'You did.'

'Yeah, but there was two of us,' Cadi pointed out, 'and she's on her own.'

'That wouldn't stop me,' said Poppy firmly. 'She'd be better off on the streets than living with him, and if she has half the luck we had, then who knows what opportunities await her.'

'I reckon it's fear of the unknown,' said Cadi. 'We always knew we could go home if it all went pear-shaped, but she hasn't got that option. In fact I should imagine things would be ten times worse for her if she had to go back.'

'We really are very lucky,' agreed Poppy, 'and I hate to sound ungrateful, but I do wish we could get out a bit more – and I don't mean to the laundry or the market.'

'It would be good to let our legs loose for an evening,' said Poppy.

Cadi held the door open for her as they entered the kitchen. 'It certainly would. I mean what's the point in living away from your parents if you can't let your hair down every now and then?'

'Only how?' reasoned Poppy. 'We're always changing the sheets, making breakfast or serving food. By the time we've finished the dishes it's too late to be thinking about going out.'

'I know, and I don't want to ask Maria for an evening off – not when she's done so much for us.'

'There's always the tea dances ...' Poppy began, much to Cadi's horror.

'I am not going to a tea dance. Blimey, Poppy, I want summat a bit glitzier than the village hall.'

Poppy retrieved a loaf of bread from the pantry and began cutting it into thin slices. 'Sunday's the only day off we get, so it's either a tea dance or nothing.'

Cadi began slicing some onions into a bowl. 'There's got to be another way round this. We're too young to be stuck indoors. Hellfire, I had more freedom in Rhos!'

Poppy waved the bread knife in a reproving fashion. 'Sometimes freedom comes at a price.'

Maria entered the kitchen from the bar. 'What's all this about freedom?'

Blushing to the roots of her hair, Cadi glanced at Poppy before replying. 'We were saying how well the business is doing.'

'Aha,' said Maria, giving each girl a wry smile. 'So successful that you've not got time to go out and do what young people do, am I right?'

Cadi nodded mutely, before voicing her thoughts. 'We're really grateful for everything you've done for us, and we're thrilled to bits the business is doing so well, but ...'

'You'd like a bit of time off to enjoy yourselves?'

Poppy nodded wretchedly. 'Only we understand that it isn't an option. There's no way you can run the pub and serve the meals at the same time, and we wouldn't ask you to.'

Maria held up a hand to silence Poppy. 'You don't have to ask, nor should you feel you must. You're two young girls who've just moved to the city, and it's only right you should want to have a bit of fun and experience your first dance without your parents watching your every move. So why not go tonight?'

Cadi gaped at her. 'What about the pub? You'll not cope on your own – you can't be serving behind the bar as well as dishing up food.'

Maria gave her a wan smile. 'I'll admit I haven't time to see to the B&B as well as prepare the menu for tonight's customers, but the rooms are ready and the guests have checked in, so if you girls can make a shepherd's pie or a fish pie – summat easy that I can simply dole out – I don't see there being a problem.' She grinned. 'We can leave the washing up till the morning.'

Cadi and Poppy thanked Maria profusely.

'We're really grateful, aren't we, Poppy?' enthused Cadi, but something was bothering Poppy.

'What'll we wear? I know I've not got owt suitable, and I'm pretty sure you haven't, either.'

Maria waved her hand dismissively. 'Don't worry, I'm sure I've got a couple of spare frocks in my wardrobe.'

'You really are a star,' sighed Cadi. 'You've come to our rescue on more than one occasion. I'm sure I don't know what we've done to deserve you.'

Maria laughed. 'You're not the only one who's been saved. If it weren't for you two, I could've ended up losing the pub.' She wagged an admonitory finger as the girls began to protest that this simply wasn't true. 'With the tax on beer going up, the punters aren't as willing to part with their hard-earned cash as they once were. We make more on meals and the B&B than we do on ale, and I couldn't do that on a regular basis, not on my own.'

A proud smile spread across Cadi's cheeks. 'Do you really think so?'

Maria nodded. 'I certainly do, which is why I don't want you getting bored and high-tailing it out of here, cos I wouldn't blame you if you did.'

Giggling, Cadi stopped slicing and dabbed at the tears that the onions had caused. 'You can tell you've never been to Rhos.'

'It must be pretty boring if you prefer being stuck in a pub, day in, day out.'

'Too right it is,' said Cadi.

'The Rose Queen Fete was good, though,' said Poppy.

Maria sighed, a far-away look in her eyes. 'I used to love going to the village fete.'

Poppy looked up from the sandwiches. 'I don't know why, but I assumed you'd always lived in the city.'

'I used to live in a small village just outside Liverpool,' said Maria. 'They used to hold a fete every year, and I got to be the Cornflower Queen.' She beamed at the memory. 'It was a wonderful event, with stalls, games, competitions and dances – those were the days!'

'In our village it was the Rose Queen,' said Cadi. 'It sounds very much like your fete, and I admit I loved every minute, but once is not enough for any girl. In fact it's part of the reason why we wanted to move away, so that we could go to all the wonderful halls and ballrooms and feel like queens all over again.'

'Then you're going to love the Grafton and the Locarno,' said Maria, 'but even though they're very fancy, you'll never feel as special as you did the day you were crowned Rose Queen.'

Cadi couldn't see how this could possibly be true. 'Why not?'

'Because on that day you were the only one in a special dress, but in the dance halls they'll all be dressed to the nines. You'll be one of many.'

'So it doesn't matter where we go or what we do, we'll never feel that special again?' said Poppy, a tad disappointed.

Maria laughed. 'Afraid so. Or at least not until you get wed.'

'That's what Mam said,' muttered Cadi dejectedly.

'There'll be plenty of things in your life that'll make you feel special,' said Maria, 'they just won't come with a crown and a fanfare.'

'Like what?' said Cadi sullenly.

Maria winked at her. 'Like when a certain young man looks at you like you're the only girl in the world.'

Poppy tried to swallow her smile. She knew exactly who Maria was referring to and guessed Cadi would too.

Seeing the expression on her friend's face, Cadi aimed a playful swipe in her direction. 'Don't start!'

Maria pretended to be deep in thought whilst tapping her chin with her forefinger. 'Hmm, now let me see: are there any men in these parts who are holding a torch for our Cadi?'

Poppy emitted a stifled giggle. 'Apart from Jez, you mean?'

'Oh, ha-ha.'

Maria gave Cadi a reproving glance. 'Don't knock it! When a man truly loves a woman he can make her feel like a queen whenever she walks into a room.'

'I am *not* rushing to court Jez just so I can feel special,' Cadi assured her friends. 'Now let's get a move on with these butties – we've fish to cook, potatoes to mash and laundry to fetch.'

'And if that isn't a change of subject, I don't know what is,' said Maria. 'If you need me, I'll be in the bar.'

By the time the girls had finished their chores, it was a mad rush to get ready in time for their first evening out. Maria had laid out several dresses that she thought suitable for the girls and, after some careful consideration, Poppy chose a dark-blue tea dress with a belted waist, and Cadi a lilac dress with a sweetheart neckline.

Maria pinned Poppy's long hair into rolls, but with Cadi having much shorter hair, there was not much she could do, other than pin it up on one side, as she normally did.

'You've the perfect hairstyle for a headband,' she informed Cadi as she thumbed down the eyebrow which she had just been plucking.

'Probably the closest I'll get to a crown,' said Cadi. She winced as Maria continued shaping her eyebrow. 'Why does beauty have to be so painful?'

'Growing up is painful,' said Poppy as she admired her own plucked eyebrows. 'Worth it, though, because my eyes look much bigger now.' She turned to face Maria. 'Do you think we should wear some make-up?'

Maria shrugged. 'It's up to you. Do you *want* to wear make-up?'

Poppy nodded enthusiastically. 'I need all the help I can get!'

Maria wagged her finger in rebuke at Poppy. 'There's nowt wrong with the way you look, Poppy Harding. Besides, this evening is all about having a bit of fun, *not* snaring a man.' Taking her make-up bag, Maria delved around until she found the lipstick and mascara. Instructing Poppy to sit still, she gently teased her lashes with the brush. 'Make-up isn't intended to change the way you look, but rather enhance the features you have.' She dabbed her finger against the lipstick, then gently wiped it across Poppy's lips. 'Perfect.'

Poppy stared at her image in the hand-held mirror. Turning her head from side to side so that she might see herself from all angles, she nodded approvingly. 'I never knew my eyelashes were so long.'

Cadi shuffled forward on her chair. 'Me next.'

Laughing, Maria started to apply Cadi's make-up. 'You'll be the belles of the ball.'

When she had finished, Poppy passed Cadi the mirror. 'I can't wait to see what everyone else thinks,' said Cadi as she admired her reflection.

'Who's "everybody"? Or do you mean Jez?'

Cadi blushed. She hadn't realised it when she said it, but that was exactly who she meant. Not that she was about to admit that to Poppy. 'No, I do not. I mean people in general.'

Poppy gave her friend a disbelieving grin. 'If you say so.'

'I do,' said Cadi firmly.

Maria pulled out a camera from her bedside cabinet. 'Come on, girls, let's take a photograph to mark the occasion. You can even send a copy home for your parents.'

'What a fantastic idea,' said Cadi. She placed her arm around Poppy's waist and the girls smiled for the camera when Maria instructed them to.

'There,' said Maria, putting the camera back into its case, 'now all you have to do is get out there and have the time of your lives.'

Cadi looked down at her kitten-heeled shoes, which Maria had loaned her. 'Only how do we get to the Locarno – can we walk or is it too far?'

'Too far,' said Maria, 'you'll have to catch the bus ... Oh, hello.' Her last comment was aimed at Jez, who was making his way towards them.

He cast an approving eye over the girls. 'My word. Where are you two off to?'

'The Locarno,' beamed Poppy.

'You're going to be fighting them off with sticks.' He cast a lingering look over Cadi's form. 'Has our Maria got a bargepole she can lend you?'

Cadi cursed the blush that was beginning to sweep over her neckline. 'Don't be daft.'

'I mean it,' said Jez, pushing his hands into his pockets. 'You look beautiful.'

Not knowing how to respond, Cadi found herself praying that someone would say something to divert the attention away from herself and was grateful when Poppy piped up.

'Well, we can't stand here all day,' she said, 'we've a bus to catch, only I'll be blowed if I know which one.'

'You'll need the number twenty-three, it comes every twenty minutes,' said Jez. He glanced at Poppy. 'I can walk you both to the bus stop, if you like?'

Poppy nodded. 'Yes, please, there seem to be a lot of nasty men living around these parts.'

Jez's brow furrowed. 'What makes you say that?'

Poppy told him about their encounter with Isobel.

His expression clouded over. 'This Isobel, was she a thin woman, a little older than me, with a small scar on her left cheek?'

Cadi eyed him with interest. 'You know her?'

He glanced at his feet before looking directly at Poppy. 'She's Eric's daughter,' adding for clarification, 'the man who attacked you.'

Poppy sank into one of the kitchen seats. 'Dear God, no wonder she's scared of him.'

Maria glanced at the clock above the mantel. 'Sorry to interrupt, but these girls had better get a move on if they're to catch the next bus.'

Cadi looked at Jez. 'Come on, we can talk as we walk.'

Bidding Maria goodbye, the trio left the pub.

'We helped Isobel do her laundry,' explained Cadi. 'We didn't know her name until Lethia told us.'

'I used to share the same school bus as Izzy,' said Jez. 'The poor kid was allus on her own, cos the other kids were scared of her dad, and so were their parents, especially after what happened when I tried to befriend her.'

'Why,' asked Cadi, 'what did he do?'

Jez blew his cheeks out. 'He went potty. Gripped hold of Izzy and dragged her off, before turning on me, and saying I'd better not go near her again or suffer the consequences. I was only eight at the time, and I don't mind admitting he frightened the life out of me. I told me nan, and whilst she was upset Eric had gone for me, she thought it best if I steered clear of Izzy, and after that little performance I wasn't the only one to stay away.'

Cadi asked the question that she and Poppy had both been wondering. 'That was a long time ago. She's a lot older now, so why doesn't she get up and leave?'

'I guess not everyone's as brave as you,' said Jez plainly.

She eyed him suspiciously. 'Are you poking fun at me?'

He shook his head fervently. 'No, I am not! It must have taken a deal of courage for you to go against your father's wishes.'

'It did, but I wouldn't pretend that my father's anything like hers, because he's not.'

'Still took guts, though,' said Jez. He indicated the bus stop ahead with a nod of his head. 'This is it.'

Poppy glanced over her shoulder to the pub at the bottom of the road. 'I know it's not far, but I'm still glad you came with us. Thanks, Jez.'

He touched the peak of his cap with his fingers. 'Glad I could be of assistance.' He rocked on his toes as he thought of something to say. 'What time do you suppose you'll be back?'

Poppy craned her neck to see if she could spy the bus. 'Not sure. When they kick us out probably ... Coo, that was good timing.'

145

Sensing the awkwardness between them, Cadi spoke first. 'Shall we see you tomorrow?'

Poppy began coughing into her hand in an effort to hide her amusement. Not a day had gone by since they arrived at the Greyhound that they hadn't seen Jez.

Cadi gave her friend a withering glance, but Jez appeared not to notice. 'It's Saturday tomorrer, so I'll pop round after work, see how you got on.' He screwed his lips to one side. 'Although I suppose I might see you later, depending on what time you get back.'

Poppy was waving at the bus driver to stop. 'See you later, Jez.' She took Cadi by the hand and the two of them stepped onto the bus before it had come to a complete halt. Selecting a window seat, they waved to Jez, who was looking rather forlorn.

'Poor bugger,' giggled Poppy, 'he must've been racking his brains for an excuse to come with us, but he could hardly go dancing dressed in his work clothes.'

'Stop trying to make me feel guilty,' said Cadi, as she watched Jez turn on his heel and walk back down the hill.

'I'm not,' protested Poppy, 'I'm just stating the obvious: that boy's smitten, and if he isn't at that stop awaiting your return, then I'm a monkey's uncle!'

Cadi blushed. 'What am I supposed to do? I've made sure I've done nothing to lead him on or give him the wrong impression.'

'Perhaps if you meet a feller tonight,' Poppy began, only to be shot down by Cadi.

'No, I've already said: I'm not interested in courting, no matter who the suitor is.'

*

146

As Jez walked away from the bus stop he wondered what he could do to change Cadi's mind about courting. He knew she liked him, he could tell by the way she looked at him, but she was fiercely independent, something that Jez found to be very attractive.

He entered the Greyhound and headed for the bar, where Maria was serving one of her older customers. Seeing Jez approaching, she smiled. 'By gum, you look like you've found a penny and lost a pound.'

He leaned against the bar. 'I have, or at least that's how it feels.'

She held up a half-pint glass and indicated the Burton pump handle. 'I take it you're here for more than a chat?'

'Aye, I need one of them to help drown me sorrows, although that's an expensive business nowadays, what with the government raising taxes and all.'

Maria filled the glass and passed it over. 'Are things really that bad?'

Jez took a sip, wiped the froth from his top lip and shrugged. 'It's like I know where the treasure is, but I haven't the foggiest how to get there.'

'Ah! I take it we're talking about Cadi?'

He took another sip, only this time he licked the foam away. 'We are indeed.'

Maria rested her hand on top of the pump handle. 'She's a smashing girl – they both are – but as you know, Cadi is adamant about carving out a life for herself without the help of a man.' She smiled kindly at Jez, who was looking glum. 'She's young, Jez, *very* young, and she's led a sheltered life in a small village. To these girls, Liverpool is a whole new playground and one they are eager to explore. It's not that she doesn't like you – she does; in fact I've caught her gazing at you on more than one occasion ...'

Jez sat to attention. 'You have? I thought I was imagining it.'

'Nope, I've caught her too, but she's a goal in mind, and she's not going to let anyone stand in her way.'

'I wouldn't stop her,' said Jez wretchedly. 'I want to help her.'

'I know you do, chuck, but that's the whole point. She wants to do it, whatever *it* is, on her own.'

'I'd happily take a back seat.'

Maria lifted her head as a customer approached the bar and asked for a half of bitter. Taking his glass, she filled it whilst still speaking to Jez. 'You'd mean to, but you'd want to take her places, show her the sights, spoil her rotten.'

His brow furrowed in incomprehension. 'What's so bad about that?'

'She wants to do those things with Poppy.' Feeling that Jez needed a simpler explanation, she continued, 'Our Cadi's a free spirit who needs to spread her wings, and you'd be clippin' them, love, whether you meant to or not.'

Jez stared miserably into his beer. 'So that's it. I'm doomed to stay single for the rest of my life.'

Maria muffled her mirth behind her hand. 'Goodness me! Just because you can't have Cadi doesn't mean to say you have to remain a bachelor.'

'It does,' said Jez vehemently, 'because Cadi's the only girl I'll ever be interested in.'

'Oh dear, you have got it bad.' She took payment for the drink and dropped the money into the till. 'Just because Cadi's not ready for a relationship now doesn't mean to say she'll never be ready.'

'But how long will that take?'

'I don't know, chuck. But if you love her, and I mean *really* love her, you'll be happy to wait,' said Maria simply.

Jez drained his glass and placed it on the bar. 'Looks like I'm going to need to have plenty of patience.'

The girls thought their first time at a city dance hall would be special and they weren't disappointed. The Locarno was better than they had imagined and, when they first arrived, they simply stood and stared.

'I've never seen anything like this,' breathed Poppy. 'How about you?'

Cadi shook her head. 'I've heard me mam talking about places like this, but you don't realise what they're like till you see them first-hand.' She glanced up at the glitter ball that hung above the dance floor. As it rotated, soft specks of light fell onto the dancers below, most of whom were women. She turned her attention to the bar. 'Do you feel old enough to be in here?'

Poppy followed her gaze to two women who were drinking some form of alcoholic drink in a fancy glass. 'I know what you mean, but we've as much right to be in here as they have.'

Cadi nodded to a table next to the dance floor. 'Do you want to sit and watch for a bit?'

'You bagsie the table and I'll get us a couple of lemonades.'

The girls did as they had planned, and after having watched everyone else, they decided to put the dance moves they had learned from their parents to the test.

'Give Jez two minutes in this place and he'd soon change his mind about me,' Cadi told Poppy as they stepped onto the dance floor.

Poppy pulled a face as she glanced around at the other dancers. 'I doubt it. He's probably been to the Locarno loads of times already.'

Her words left Cadi feeling very special indeed. Some of the women on the floor were beautiful, with meticulously styled hair. She felt sure that if Jez were to approach any of them, they'd gratefully accept his invitation to dance. He was young, tall, dark and handsome, with the kindest, warmest eyes that twinkled delightfully. Not to mention his dimpled cheeks and smiling cheekbones, which gave you the impression he was always happy and … Cadi stopped herself from going any further. No wonder Poppy was always making fun; she'd probably seen the way Cadi gazed at Jez whenever he was near. In fact Cadi herself had often given herself a shake when she found herself staring at him. For the first time she wondered whether forming a relationship would really be so bad.

You'd be dreadfully upset if you thought he was interested in another woman, she told herself, *but what's Jez meant to do? Hold on whilst you get yourself a career and experience a bit of life?* More to the point, was she willing to take the risk that Jez wouldn't get fed up of waiting? She thought of Flo and her husband. Flo had said that if her husband had truly loved her, he would have stayed whether or not they could have children, but was that really fair? If he was desperate to have children, then he would be giving up an awful lot. She then turned her thoughts to Izzy's mother, who had chosen her fling over her own daughter. Maybe children weren't the right decision for her; maybe that's why she'd had an affair in the first place. She would have to have a long, hard think about it all.

When the band stopped playing a few hours later, the girls couldn't hide their disappointment.

'Now I know how Cinderella felt when the clock struck midnight,' pouted Cadi.

Having collected their coats, Poppy handed Cadi hers. 'They say time flies when you're having fun. I'm glad none of the men asked me to dance – I think I'd have been too embarrassed. It's one thing dancing with your dad or your pal, but dancing with a boy who's a bit older than you?' The very thought sent a shiver down her back. 'No, I'm not ready for that yet.' She gave Cadi a sidelong glance as they walked to the bus stop. 'I would say I was surprised none of them asked you to dance, but you had a face like thunder whenever any of them came near you.'

This surprised Cadi. 'Did I?'

Poppy signalled the bus to stop, and the girls took a seat near the back so they could talk without being overheard. 'Yes, you did. Last time I saw you scowl like that was when we saw Aled ...'

Cadi scowled. 'What did you go and mention him for? I was having a nice evening.'

Poppy nodded. 'That's it, just like that!'

Cadi relented slightly. 'I supposed I'm a little guarded because I've heard the way my brothers talk about girls

151

they fancy, and I don't want a feller talking about me like that.'

Poppy stared at Cadi with intrigue. 'Why? What do they say?'

Cadi narrowed her eyes. 'Never you mind, save to say the girls would not be happy if they knew what was going on in the boys' heads.'

This had been the wrong thing to say, as Poppy was now determined to hear what it was that went through a boy's head when he saw a girl he liked.

Cadi wagged a reproachful finger. 'I love my brothers dearly, so I shall not repeat their words. All I will say is that most men – even nice ones like my brothers – think with something other than their brains.'

Poppy looked perplexed, before hazarding a guess. 'Their hearts?'

Cadi smiled. 'Yes, Poppy, their hearts!'

'Well, that doesn't sound too bad.'

Cadi rolled her eyes. 'For goodness' sake, Poppy, I was being flippant. I didn't mean their hearts, I meant they think with what's in their trousers.'

'Oh, I see.' She blushed. 'I didn't think your brothers were like that.'

Cadi shook her head. 'It doesn't make them bad, it makes them young men.'

Poppy knitted her brows as she looked uncertainly at Cadi. 'I don't think Jez thinks like that.'

Cadi pondered this thought for a moment before answering. 'I must admit, Jez has never looked at me as though I were a slab of steak in the butcher's window.'

Poppy spluttered a giggle. 'Honestly, Cadi. You aren't half blunt at times.'

Cadi shrugged. 'That's what you get when you grow up in a house full of men. Mam says knights in shining armour are a thing of the past.'

Poppy nudged Cadi. 'Jez is a proper knight, though. Coming to our rescue and saving us from that git Eric.'

Cadi shrugged in what she hoped was a carefree manner. 'Not every girl wants a knight in shining armour.' She realised as soon as the words left her mouth how ridiculous they sounded.

Poppy wrinkled her forehead. 'They don't?'

Luckily for Cadi, they had reached their stop and she was able to change the subject. The girls alighted and Cadi turned to Poppy. 'Looks like you're a monkey's uncle!'

'Sorry?'

'You said that if Jez wasn't waiting here for me on our return ...'

Poppy nodded. 'Then I'd be a monkey's uncle.'

'Now can we please stop talking about men? I've said it a thousand times! I don't want a man – he'll only get in the way. And if tonight was anything to go by, there's plenty more fun to be had. We've not been to any of the cinemas yet, and I'd like to go to the Grafton next time.'

Poppy threaded her arm through Cadi's. 'Me too, but do you think Maria will let us go again?'

'I hope so, but I suppose it'll depend on how she managed without us this evening.'

The girls entered the pub through the kitchen door and headed into the bar, where they found Maria collecting the last of the glasses.

'You're back! How'd it go?'

'Fantastic and wonderful, and everything in between,' said Poppy.

'How did you manage here?' asked Cadi cautiously. 'Was it busy?'

'Not too bad. The fish pie went down well – there's a little left, if you fancy it.'

'So you coped without us?' said Cadi.

'Of course I did, you set everything up beautifully. All I had to do was fill a plate and take the money.' She grinned. 'Are you asking out of concern, or because you'd like to go again?'

'Both,' admitted Cadi. 'Only I don't like the thought of us swanning off whilst you do all the work.'

Maria stood up with the tray of glasses. 'Don't be daft. It's not like you'll be going out every night of the week.'

'You sure you don't mind?' said Poppy. 'We feel really bad about ...'

Maria stopped on her way through to the kitchen. 'About what? Being young?' She continued through to the sink without waiting for an answer. 'You should be making the most of your life before you are too old, or before the war stops you from doing so.' She placed the glasses next to the sink. 'We may as well do these now, seeing as you're back.'

'You've done enough for one night – leave the glasses to us,' said Cadi.

'A kind offer, but I'd like to hear all about your evening. I've not been dancing for ever such a long time and I'd like to know if anything's changed.'

Pouring some hot water from the kettle into the sink, the three women set about cleaning the glasses whilst Cadi and Poppy told Maria all about their evening.

'It's a shame we can't all go out together,' sighed Cadi. 'I suppose it would be too much to close the pub on a Saturday evening?'

Maria's brow shot up. 'I should say so. Besides, it wouldn't feel right, me going dancing without my Bill.'

'Talking of fellers, did you see Jez after we left?' Cadi went on in what she hoped was a carefree manner.

'He came in for a couple of halves,' said Maria. She had promised Jez that she wouldn't mention his thoughts on Cadi and she intended to honour that promise, but it didn't mean to say she couldn't do a little fishing. 'Why?'

'Just wondered.'

Poppy took a cloth and rinsed it in the sink. 'She wants to know if he's been pining after her.'

'No, I don't,' said Cadi, frowning. 'I don't like to think of him being miserable.'

Maria thought Poppy was right, but she knew if she told the truth – that Jez was pining after Cadi – it would be the quickest way of dampening any flame that might ignite. 'I don't think you need feel guilty about Jez,' said Maria coolly. 'We all know you want more out of life than marriage and kids.'

Cadi dried the glass she had picked up. 'Good.' She waited a moment before adding, 'So he's not upset then?'

Maria tried to hide the grin that was twitching her lips. 'You can't worry about other folk – you have to live your life as you see fit.' Being careful not to divulge Jez's feelings, she continued cautiously, 'Jez is an attractive, sweet young man, who has plenty to offer.

There'll be plenty of women lining up to court him, so I wouldn't worry too much about his feelings.'

'Oh,' said Cadi, feeling slightly dejected. It was one thing for her to have Jez waiting in the wings, but another matter entirely to think he might be whisked away by someone else. 'Does Jez ever go dancing?'

Maria ran her tongue over her top lip as she tried to keep the smile from forming. 'I wouldn't know, chuck, he's a good deal younger than me. He'd probably like to, though.' She finished washing the large casserole dish and turned to face Cadi. 'For someone who's not interested in the opposite sex, you aren't half inquisitive when it comes to Jez.'

'I just wouldn't want him to get the wrong idea,' said Cadi, adding, in a bid to appear nonchalant, 'Have we had any more bookings for the B&B?'

'Yes. We've a couple of fellers from the RAF staying Saturday week. I've written their names down in the book. They're stopping over en route to Scotland.'

'Scotland?' gasped Cadi. 'Wouldn't it be quicker for them to fly?'

'It would be costly, and I don't think the RAF allow their men to use their kites like taxis.'

'I wonder what it'd be like to fly?' mused Cadi. 'It must be wonderful up there in the clouds, free as a bird.'

'Unless summat goes wrong,' said Poppy, who'd disappeared into the bar to clean down the tables, 'in which case, you'd be plummeting to earth faster than a peregrine falcon.'

'Blimey, I wouldn't want to get into a plane with you,' said Cadi, 'I'd be a nervous wreck!'

'Only stating the facts,' said Poppy. 'Are we ready to go up or is there summat else needs doing first?'

Maria covered a yawn with the back of her hand. 'I'm ready.'

'Me too,' agreed Cadi, also stifling a yawn. 'It must be all that dancing.'

Maria went into the bar to double-check the doors were bolted, whilst the girls headed up the stairs.

'I bet poor Izzy's never been dancing,' said Poppy as they entered their shared bedroom.

'Goodness me, no,' agreed Cadi. 'What made you think of her?'

Poppy undid the buttons on the front of her borrowed dress and pulled it over her head. 'To be honest, I've not *stopped* thinking about her. You see I was lucky, I got away from Eric, but she's stuck there with him. It seems wrong somehow that poor old Izzy's not more than a stone's throw away, yet her life couldn't be more different, purely because she has no means of escape.'

Maria entered the room and poured some water into the washbasin. 'Are you talking about Eric's daughter?'

Nodding, Cadi rolled her stockings down. 'I wish there was something we could do to help her. It's rotten she has to stay with that miserable old beggar.'

Maria wagged a reproachful finger. 'I know you mean well, but if you interfere, it'll be Izzy what pays the price.'

'Not if she's not there, she won't,' said Poppy. 'Surely there must be somewhere she could go?'

Maria shook her head. 'I wish there was, but I'm afraid she's up the creek without a paddle in sight.'

Tilting her head to one side, Poppy eyed Cadi thoughtfully. 'What about your Auntie Flo? Do you think she'd let Izzy stay with her?'

'She's in Dartmoor, or she was the last I heard,' cried Cadi, 'We can hardly let Izzy into her flat without her presence or knowledge.'

'When war was declared, I rather hoped Izzy would run off and join the services,' said Maria. 'She's old enough, so she shouldn't have a problem getting accepted.'

Cadi had a wash in the basin, before getting changed into her nightie. 'If Izzy could get hold of her details, and we could find somewhere for her to hide out until her papers arrived ...'

Poppy smiled. 'She'd be free!'

Maria looked sceptical. 'You make it sound incredibly easy.'

'If she could get her papers, it would be,' Cadi reasoned. 'I can't see any of the services allowing her father to march in and drag her out, can you?'

Maria sank down onto her bed. 'Well, no, but ...'

Poppy took her turn at the basin. 'How long does it take for someone to get their papers?'

Maria shrugged. 'A week, maybe two, which is a long time to hide from someone who's determined to find you, and Eric will not sit idly by; in fact I should think he'd move heaven and earth to find her.' She pointed a warning finger at both girls. 'And he won't care who gets in his way.' She jerked her head at Poppy. 'You should know that better than anyone.'

'I do,' said Poppy, 'which is why I'm determined to help Izzy in any way I can.'

Cadi puffed out her chest. 'Eric doesn't frighten me. Besides, he'd have to prove we had summat to do with it, and I'd report him to the police if he got nasty.'

'Like we did the first time, you mean,' said Poppy grimly. 'I don't wish to appear cynical, but it didn't exactly work out very well for us, now did it?'

'Threatening a man like Eric with scuffers would only enrage him further,' said Maria.

'It did,' admitted Cadi, 'that's why he chased us out of the Bear's Paw.'

Maria got changed into her nightie. 'As you already know, men like Eric see women as objects that needn't be suffered. If he thinks you're making a fool out of him, he wouldn't hesitate to burn this place to the ground whilst we slept in us beds.'

Poppy's head popped through her nightie. 'He'd *what*?'

Maria slipped between the bed sheets. 'He'd happily see us burn if he thought it saved him face.'

'Save face?' cried Cadi. 'You don't murder people to save face!'

Maria grimaced. 'Eric would, especially from a woman – he hates women, including his own daughter.'

'Izzy did nothing wrong; it was her mother who ran off with another man, not Izzy ...' Cadi started.

Maria heaved a sigh. 'Ever heard of the expression "Don't shoot the pack just because one dog has fleas"?'

Cadi and Poppy both shook their heads.

'It means don't tar everyone with the same brush – and that's exactly what Eric's done, only more so with Izzy because she's her mother's daughter. As far as Eric's concerned, the apple hasn't fallen far from the tree. He may not be able to punish her mother, but he can sure as hell make Izzy pay for her mother's actions.'

'But that's lunacy,' said Poppy as she blew out the lamp. 'Izzy isn't responsible for her mother's behaviour. As far as we're aware, she's never even tried leaving her father.'

'Doesn't that tell you something?' said Maria.

'Yes,' spluttered Cadi. 'That she's too scared, for fear of repercussions.'

'Not only that, but where would she go? It's not always as easy as walking out the door – there's other things to take into account.' Maria yawned audibly in the darkness. 'I don't know about you two, but I'm shattered, certainly far too tired to be talking about the likes of Eric.'

'I guess it has been rather a long day,' yawned Cadi. 'Goodnight, all.'

She listened as Poppy and Maria mumbled their goodnight wishes as they settled down to sleep.

Lying in the darkness, Cadi continued to think of Izzy. *What she needs is a friend to show her that she deserves a better life than the one she's got.* She nodded to herself. *Should our paths cross again, I shall be sure to offer the hand of friendship, and if she accepts that, I shall make sure Izzy gets as far away from her father as humanly possible.*

160

Chapter Five

March 1940

Aled Davies folded his arms across the steering wheel of the tractor and stared glumly at the field ahead of him. It had been nearly six months since Cadi and Poppy had left for Liverpool. He had expected them back within a matter of weeks, spouting tales of woe and disappointment, so it had come as an unpleasant surprise when he had heard the girls were both living and working in a pub. It wasn't so much that he wanted them to have failed, but it rubbed salt into the wound when it came to his own desire to leave Rhos in pursuit of a new and more exciting life. He had brought the matter up so many times with his parents that they had forbidden him to raise the matter again. As he gazed into the distance he turned his thoughts to the day his mother had banned the subject.

They had just been settling down for lunch when the postman – Gwyn – had arrived, bringing the news that Cadi and Poppy were happily settled in Liverpool.

'Not what they wanted,' said Gwyn as he sorted through the post in his bag, 'but they're making a silk purse out of a sow's ear by all accounts, turning the pub from a regular drinking hole into a B&B – even serving pub meals.'

'Good for them,' enthused John, Aled's father. 'I must say I'm very impressed with Cadi, although I always knew there was summat special about the girl, which is why I wanted our Aled to marry her, but as always, he left it too late.'

Aled ignored his father's words. Cadi had always been extremely prickly towards him, and he'd had no intention of asking her out on a date, never mind marrying her – no matter how pretty she might be, or how favourably his father might think of her.

As Gwyn left, John continued to sing the girls' praises. 'It can't be easy making your way in a new country, not for two young girls like them. I bet Dewi's mighty proud ...'

This was more than Aled could stand. 'How you can stand there singing their praises, when you know I want to do exactly what they've done, I do not know.' He paused momentarily before adding, 'Only I'd not be running some stinking pub, because I'd be in the RAF, I *know* I would, if only you'd give me the chance.'

Aled's mother, Gwen, stowed the envelopes in the pocket of her apron. 'Not this again.'

'If I'm getting on your nerves, I'll leave, simple as—' Aled began, only to be silenced by his father, who had slammed his fist down onto the kitchen table.

'Enough!' roared John. 'Your mam doesn't prepare a good meal just for you to spoil it with your sour face and ungrateful comments.'

Aled looked stunned. 'I only want to do what Cadi and Poppy have already done. Yet when I want to up sticks and leave, I'm accused of being ungrateful.'

'Because you've got a farm! You're already doing your bit by helping to feed the nation. Besides that, how the hell am I meant to run this place on my own?'

Aled breathed a weary sigh. 'As I've said a hundred times before, you can get some of the old fellers back. Or failing that, you could get one of the young lads in the village that are too young to join up, but don't want to work down the pits. Goodness only knows, there's plenty of them to be had.'

'And as I've said a thousand times already, I'm not going to pay them a wage when I've got you.'

'You're tight,' snapped Aled, 'that's your problem. You expect me to work here for handouts, never earning any real money of my own, and when I object, I'm labelled ungrateful.' He laughed incredulously. 'Nowhere in this village would you find someone to work for nothing and say they're grateful.'

'Maybe not, but I know plenty who'd work on a farm they're going to inherit and not whinge about it.'

Gwen rubbed her forehead between her fingers and thumb before throwing her hands up in exasperation. 'Are we really going to go over this again? Because I honestly don't see the point, when it always leads to the same outcome.' She pointed a finger at her husband. 'You end up storming out, and you,' here she pointed at Aled, 'end up backing down because you know you're wrong.'

Aled shook his head. His mother was quite right – their arguments always did end in the same way. He glanced up at her. 'Sorry, Mam, I know you don't like to see us argue.'

'No, I don't,' said Gwen, 'so from now on, the subject of you leaving is no longer up for discussion.'

And that had been that. Aled had never mentioned it again, and neither had his father. But that didn't mean to say Aled had forgotten his hopes and dreams for a life in the RAF. He just kept his thoughts to himself.

Now, as he continued to gaze at the meadow they were using to grow their hay, his thoughts swung round to Cadi. Aled knew her father hadn't wanted Cadi to go to Liverpool, but she had done so anyway. He wondered what his own father would do if he applied for the RAF behind his back. He tutted to himself, because he already knew the answer: his father would be furious and his mother upset, but there'd be very little they could do about it, once he was accepted. He sighed guiltily. Only then he'd be leaving his father in the lurch, which would be unfair of him. Not only that, but his father was correct in that they were doing their bit by supplying food to the nation. Without Aled to help, his father wouldn't be able to cope. He hesitated. Would that really be his fault? John had had ample opportunity to listen to his son and get someone else in, yet he'd refused to even contemplate the matter, and all because he'd have to part with his money. Aled remembered the time that he suggested his father get a Land Girl from the Women's Land Army to help. The idea had been met with outrage.

'A *woman*? How on earth is a woman meant to control the beasts? They're simply not strong enough.'

To Aled's surprise, he hadn't had to argue with his father on this matter because his mother had shot her husband down in flames. 'I used to haul buckets of water from that well, carrying two at a time with Aled strapped to my back, before we got the pump – not to mention pushing that ruddy great hand-cart into the village to pick up feed – and you say a woman wouldn't be strong enough? Shame on you, John Davies.'

Aled had left his father to get the dressing-down he deserved, but even though Gwen had read her husband the Riot Act, she'd not managed to change his mind. He had remained resolute that women weren't fit for farm work.

Aled tried to imagine his father working with someone other than himself. He felt certain John would be harder on someone he was having to pay, but Aled imagined that would be still be preferable to a life down the pit. It might also make his father appreciate Aled, and the work he did for free. A niggling doubt came to the forefront of his mind. If he decided that the RAF wasn't all he thought it to be, what then? He could hardly say he'd changed his mind and come back to the farm.

As a farmer's son, Aled had always been singled out because his family were landowners, but in the RAF he would be the same as everyone else. A small smile twitched his lips. It might have sounded strange to others, but he had always wanted to be the same as everyone else. His father believed that standing out from the crowd made you special, but Aled knew from bitter experience that it made you a target. His peers had made up their minds, long before he'd been introduced, that he was a spoiled little rich boy who thought himself above them. It hadn't mattered how hard he'd tried to change their minds, they'd singled him out from the word go by dubbing him 'Little Lord Fauntleroy'.

Now, Aled slid down from the tractor and, with the crank handle in one hand, turned the engine, which coughed, then spluttered into life. Why should he stay somewhere that caused him to feel morose?

His grandfather had once told him that life was all about taking risks, and that it was better to take a chance than regret not even trying. He jumped back onto the tractor. His mind was made up. He would apply for the RAF, then tell his parents what he'd done as soon as he got his acceptance. That way, his father would have plenty of time to get someone in, and Aled would be able to make peace with his parents before heading off on what he hoped would be the adventure of a lifetime.

May 1940

It had been some time since the girls' encounter with Izzy and whilst they had been disappointed they hadn't seen her again, they weren't altogether surprised.

'When you think about it, we'd been at the Greyhound for a couple of months before we first met her, so I'm guessing she doesn't come here very often,' Cadi said to Lethia as the girls scrubbed the cotton sheets against the washboards.

Lethia gave a sarcastic laugh. 'Doesn't come here often? I'm surprised Eric *ever* allows her to come to the laundry cos it costs money.'

Poppy grimaced. 'So how does she normally clean the bed linen?'

'She doesn't,' said Lethia simply.

Cadi pulled a disgusted face. 'Typical man.'

Lethia tilted her head to one side. 'Why are you so interested in Izzy?'

Poppy wrung out a pillowcase. She and Cadi had already discussed what they would say if Lethia questioned their interest, and they had agreed that they would keep it simple, saying they merely wanted to be friends. 'We thought it might be nice for her to have a friend – one her father knew nothing about.'

Lethia looked fearful. 'Be careful. I know you mean well, but Eric's a slippery customer who has eyes and ears where you'd least expect.'

Poppy looked nervously around her at the women, who were busy with their washing. 'You really think someone here would grass us up?'

'Not here, no, but there's people out there who'd not want to keep a secret from Eric, for fear of repercussions.'

Cadi pulled the sheet she was scrubbing out of the water. 'We'll bear that in mind, but as Izzy's not here, I doubt we'll ever get the opportunity.'

Lethia smiled. 'It was a nice thought, and you're good girls, just be careful.'

When the girls had hung the washing in the drying room they headed off to the Great Charlotte Street market to buy the ingredients for the blind scouse they were making for the evening meal. It was here that Cadi spied Izzy across the other side of the market. She gained Poppy's attention by nudging her frantically with her elbow and staring pointedly in Izzy's direction.

'Well, I'll be … !' whispered Poppy from the corner of her mouth. 'This is the last place I expected to see her, although I don't know why, because I suppose even Eric has to eat.'

'What should we do?' hissed Cadi.

Poppy glanced around the busy market. 'We can't talk to her here – it's too crowded.'

'But if we don't, we might not get another opportunity.'

As they spoke, Izzy was turning away from the stall she had been buying from.

'Quick!' said Cadi. She paid for the vegetables and the two girls dashed after Izzy.

'We can't just grab her,' puffed Poppy as they navigated their way through the people.

'Not to worry,' said Cadi, 'I've an idea.'

As they caught up with Izzy, Cadi took a carrot from her wicker basket and threw it onto the ground behind Izzy. Speaking loudly, she stooped to pick up the vegetable. 'Excuse me, but I think you've dropped this.'

Turning, Izzy looked down at Cadi, who was holding up the carrot. Frowning, she took the carrot and opened her bag. 'Thanks.' Still holding the carrot, she looked at the girls. 'This can't be mine – I didn't buy carrots.'

Cadi pretended to look surprised. 'Isn't it?' She looked into her basket. 'Silly me, it must be mine.'

As Izzy handed the vegetable back, her brow furrowed. 'Do I know you?'

Cadi smiled fleetingly. 'Sort of, we met a while back in the Chinese laundry.'

Izzy looked suspiciously from Cadi to Poppy. 'And you happen to bump into me here, so that you can give me a carrot back that isn't even mine?'

Cadi swallowed. Her plan had been last-minute, and she had been eager to fool the other shoppers. It hadn't occurred to her that Izzy might smell a rat. With no excuses presenting themselves, she gabbled the truth. 'We thought it might be nice to have a chat, but we know about your dad, and we didn't want to get you into any trouble.'

Izzy's eyes widened. 'And you thought you'd avoid suspicion by accosting me in a busy market over a dropped vegetable?'

Poppy grimaced. 'We hadn't expected to see you here. This was kind of a last-minute type of thing.'

Izzy glanced around her. 'Well, it was a bad one! You've caused more attention than if you'd simply approached me.'

Cadi gently bit her bottom lip. 'Sorry.'

Turning her back on the girls, Izzy spoke over her shoulder as she walked away. 'If you really want, you can meet me in the Chinese laundry after lunch tomorrow.'

Poppy was about to say that they had already done their washing when Cadi spoke up. 'We'll be there.'

Rather than watch Izzy go, Cadi took Poppy by the elbow and guided her through a different exit. It was only when they were outside that the two girls discussed their brief encounter.

Poppy was the first to speak. 'For a minute there I thought she was going to tell us where to get off.'

'Me too,' said Cadi excitedly, 'It worked, though, didn't it?'

'Luckily,' agreed Poppy, 'although my heart was in my mouth when she sussed us out.'

'Do you think anyone else knew what we were up to?'

Poppy mulled this over. 'If they did, then I don't think it matters, because Izzy wasn't happy to see us – that was obvious for all to see.'

'That's all that really matters,' said Cadi. 'Although I don't know what we're going to take to the laundry tomorrow.' She swapped the basket to her free arm. 'What do you think Maria will say when we tell her who we're meeting?'

'Do we have to mention it?' whined Poppy. 'Only I can't imagine Maria will be pleased to hear how we met Izzy in the first place, never mind the fact that we've made arrangements to meet her tomorrow.'

'We can't fib,' said Cadi. 'What would happen if Eric found out about our little plan and decided to pay Maria a visit?'

Poppy's eyelids fluttered. 'Don't! The very thought sends chills down my spine.'

'That's why I want to run it past Maria first,' said Cadi. 'If she says she thinks it's too risky, then I'll make an excuse to pop to the laundry tomorrow, maybe say I think I've left a pillowcase behind, or summat similar, and tell Izzy we've ...'

Poppy laid her hand on Cadi's arm. 'We've what? Changed our minds and decided to abandon her, like her mam?'

Cadi sighed wretchedly. 'What alternative is there? I wouldn't want to let her down, but—'

Once again Poppy interrupted her friend. 'Don't tell Maria. Look, we genuinely bumped into Izzy today, and for all Maria knows, we could genuinely bump into her again tomorrow. The only people who know the truth are you, me and Izzy. I know Izzy won't tell anyone because she's not that daft, and neither are we, so how's anyone going to find out? Why don't we meet with her tomorrow and see where we go from there.'

Cadi looked doubtful. 'I know what you're saying, but we have to be fair to Maria, especially after everything she's done for us.'

Poppy tilted her head to one side. 'How do we know that someone didn't click when they saw us talking to Izzy today? Who's to say the damage hasn't already been done? For all we know, Eric could already be on his way round to the Greyhound?'

Cadi puffed her cheeks out. 'All right. We'll see what happens tomorrow, but after that we really have to be straight with Maria.'

Poppy beamed. 'Agreed! For all we know, we could meet Izzy tomorrow only for her to tell us she doesn't want to see us again.'

They were so busy discussing the ins and outs of their plan that they nearly forgot to pick up the laundry. It was then that the perfect ruse came to them.

'We'll pretend we forgot the laundry,' said Poppy, her eyes shining with the cleverness of her plan. 'We'll say we were so busy nattering it completely slipped our minds – cos that's sort of true – and that way we can go back for it tomorrow.'

*

On their return to the pub, the girls immediately began the task of peeling the vegetables for the blind scouse, feeling grateful that Maria was too busy with a delivery to notice the lack of laundry. The three women didn't have time to chat until much later.

Maria addressed the girls as she passed through the kitchen to fetch a bar towel. 'Everything all right back here?'

'Spiffing,' said Poppy in a mock-posh accent.

'Good-o! The scouse is going down a treat.'

Cadi beamed with pride. 'You wait till they taste our jam roly-poly.'

'We've finished cooking,' said Poppy, 'so I can come through and collect empty glasses whilst Cadi doles out.'

Maria spun the bar towel above her head like a football rattle as she disappeared into the bar. 'Ta, chuck.'

Cadi breathed out. 'As someone once said, I'm not cut out for this lying malarkey.'

Poppy frowned as she removed her apron. 'Who's lying?'

'Well, we're not being truthful, are we?' Cadi pointed out.

'You worry too much,' said Poppy as she disappeared into the bar.

Cadi began to pour hot water into the sink, ready to start the washing up. She could see where Poppy was coming from, but she knew that the truth had a bad habit of coming out, which is why she'd ended up spilling the beans to her father all those months ago. On the other hand, this time tomorrow it would all be over. Only what would they say to Maria, should she enquire about the ins and outs of their supposedly accidental meeting with Izzy? Cadi placed the dishes in the water and found the dishcloth at the bottom of the sink. *This is why you should never lie,* thought Cadi to herself. *You're no good at it – never have been, never will be.*

A voice from behind caused her to jump. It was Jez. Laughing, she threw some soap bubbles at him. 'Blimey, Jez, you nigh on give me a heart attack.'

'Sorry, I didn't realise you were so deep in thought,' said Jez. 'I thought I'd save you girls a job by coming through for a bowl of your delicious-smelling blind scouse.'

Her hands covered in soapsuds, Cadi jerked her head in a backward motion at the pot of scouse behind her. 'Help yourself.'

Jez breathed in the wonderful smell, before putting two ladles-worth into his bowl. 'What were you thinking about when I came in just now?'

'Nothing much. How was your day?'

He settled down at the table and dipped his spoon into the stew. 'Busy, first with work, then running a few errands for me mam. Good job I did, mind you.'

'Oh? Why's that then?' said Cadi, still addressing him over her shoulder.

'Because that's when I found you'd left your laundry in the drying room.'

Cadi spun round to face him. 'What?'

Jez grinned sheepishly. 'I went to collect me mam's laundry, and Mr Chang said you hadn't come for yours and it was taking up room. So I offered to bring it back for you, only I forgot. Not to worry, though, they don't finish till nine-ish, so I'll pop back after I've had me scran.'

'There's really no need,' said Cadi quickly. 'Me and Poppy can pick it up tomorrow when we do our messages.'

Jez stared at her, a spoonful of scouse poised before his lips. He had thought Cadi would be pleased with his offer, but instead she looked disappointed. 'I don't mind going, and I did tell Mr Chang that I'd take it.'

Cadi turned back to the sink, careful to keep her back to him. 'I know, and I do appreciate the offer, but it's our mistake, and it's just as easy for us to pick it up in the morning.'

'I know you like to be independent, but it's only laundry, and I really don't mind …'

She drew a deep breath before letting it out slowly. Why couldn't he accept her decision and leave the matter be? 'It's very kind of you, Jez, and I know you mean well, but I'd really rather fetch it myself.'

The silence that followed was deafening to the point that Jez knew something was wrong. Standing up from his seat, he joined Cadi by the sink.

'We've not known each other that long, and even though I know you like to do everything yourself, this is more than that. What's wrong?'

Shaking her head, Cadi continued to wash the pots. 'Nothing's wrong! I don't know why you're being so persistent.'

He leaned against the draining board. 'Why won't you look me in the eye when you say that?'

She placed the plate she had been washing on the drainer and looked him square in the eye. Her

174

intention had been to tell him not to be so silly, and that she wasn't hiding anything. But as she gazed into his eyes, which radiated nothing but concern, she found herself speaking the truth. 'Because I'm rotten at lying, that's why.'

A slow grin graced his cheeks. 'I *knew* there was more to this than you were letting on, but what could possibly make you so keen on collecting your laundry tomorrer? After all, if you hadn't forgotten it today …' Seeing the look on her face, Jez slapped the palm of his hand against the drainer. 'I am dense at times! You didn't forget, did you?' It was both a question and a statement.

Turning back to the sink, she continued washing the pots, whilst Jez got a tea towel and began wiping them dry. Cadi glanced at him from the corner of her eye. 'If I tell you summat, do you promise not to tell?'

He drew the sign of the cross across his left breast. 'Cross my heart.'

Cadi told him all about their accidental meeting and consequent arranged rendezvous with Izzy.

He nodded wisely. 'In other words, you forgot the laundry accidentally on purpose, so that you'd have an excuse to go back tomorrer.'

'That's about the size of it, but if you go and pick it up we'd be stuck for an excuse.'

'Just as well I forgot it an' all, then,' grinned Jez.

Cadi put the last dish onto the drainer and gestured to the bowl of scouse on the table. 'For goodness' sake, please eat that before it goes cold.'

Passing her the tea towel, Jez sat back down to eat. 'If it's any consolation, I think you're doing the right thing. There's no sense in worrying Maria if nothing comes to fruition.'

Cadi was resting her forehead against her fingertips. 'I just feel terrible lying to her, and what's worse, I'm asking you to lie too.'

He gave her a wry smile. 'You're not asking me to – I'm offering.'

'Thanks, Jez, you really are one in a million. My only worry now is Eric.'

'Why would you worry about him?' said Jez, a line creasing his brow. 'It's not as if he knows you've made arrangements to meet his daughter.'

'True, but what if he finds out?'

He wrinkled his nose. 'I doubt it. It would be highly unlikely for the people that were in the market to be in Chang's Laundry at exactly the same time as the three of you, especially when you consider all the other Chinese laundries there are in Liverpool.'

Cadi still looked doubtful. 'But what if …'

'Ooh, two of my nan's pet hates. Ifs and buts!' Jez winked at her. 'You're letting your guilt get the better of you. Eric's not going to find out, and even if he did, so what? Two chance encounters – it's not as if you're running away with Izzy.'

'I know, but Maria put the willies up us, when she said she reckoned Eric would rather see us all dead in our beds than risk his daughter making a fool of him.'

Jez held up his hands. 'Whoa there. I thought you said Maria didn't know?'

Cadi grimaced. 'She doesn't, but we have had conversations about Izzy and her father, including one where I suggested we might be able to get Izzy away from him.'

He nodded sagely. 'Ah! *That*'s why you're imagining the worst, because you've already spoken about rescuing her from her father.'

'And because I'm a dreadful liar. I reckon one look at my guilty face and everyone will know what we've been up to.'

Jez continued eating his scouse as he mulled things over. 'Although I doubt that would even matter, because I can't see Izzy turning up.'

Cadi stared at him, frowning. 'Then why on earth would she agree to meet us?'

Jez scraped out the last spoonful of scouse. 'To shut you up?'

'Oh.' Cadi's shoulders sagged. This was something she hadn't thought of. She wiped her hands on the tea towel and began drying the rest of the pots. 'So all this worry, and Izzy might not even show up?'

Jez brought his dish over to the sink and tipped it in. 'It wouldn't surprise me.' He glanced through to the bar. 'I was going to stop for a swift half, but I think I'll make tracks. Can you do me a favour?'

'Anything.'

He sank to one knee. 'Marry me?'

Cadi stared at him open-mouthed, not knowing what to say until she saw the mischievous glint in his eye. She swiped him with her tea towel. 'You bloomin' swine!'

Laughing, Jez wagged a reproving finger. 'Never agree to anything unless you know what you're agreeing to.'

'So what did you really want then?' said Cadi, still giggling.

'I wanted to ask if you wouldn't mind keeping me in the loop?'

'Of course,' she said. 'Crikey, I'd have thought that went without saying.'

He smiled. 'Is it all right if I pop round tomorrow to see how you got on?'

Cadi was mid-nod when a thought occurred to her. 'Do you know where you'll be working?'

'Canada Dock – Why?'

'I'd prefer to come to you; that way, we can talk things through without fear of being overheard.'

A line creased his brow. 'But if you're going to tell Maria anyway ...'

She pulled the string of her apron, releasing the bow. 'Only if we decide to carry on meeting Izzy. If not, then I'd rather Maria didn't know we'd ever been plotting behind her back.'

'Mum's the word!' Jez said, giving her a large wink before heading for the door. He had just stepped outside when he remembered he hadn't paid for his meal. 'I'll forget my head next,' he said, pulling out his wallet from his trouser pocket.

Cadi shook her hands in a dismissive manner. 'This one's on the house.'

Grinning, Jez did something Cadi wasn't expecting. He leaned forward and kissed her softly on the cheek. 'Thanks, queen, see you tomorrer. I'll be on the last crane at the far end of the dock.'

Cadi held a hand to the cheek he had kissed and stared after him. It had been a gesture of gratitude, nothing more, but it had sent her heart racing and her tummy fluttering. His lips had been soft, and so gentle she had barely felt him. All thoughts of Izzy were gone. She had been kissed by Jez, only on the cheek, but it had meant more than she ever thought it could. So deep was she in her thoughts that she never heard Maria come in behind her.

'Cadi?'

She started. 'Sorry, I'm coming now.' As she followed Maria through, she spied Poppy chatting happily to some of the older customers. Every part of Cadi wanted to rush over to her friend and tell her about Jez's kiss, but she couldn't, because Poppy would want to know why Jez had kissed her in the first place. And in turn she would want to know why Cadi had given him a free meal, and she couldn't risk telling Poppy all that, with Maria only a few feet away. She would have to wait until tomorrow, even though she feared she might burst between now and then. She wondered what Poppy's response to her news might be. No doubt the other girl would tease her and say that Cadi was keen on Jez, but would that really matter? The more she thought about it, the more Cadi chastised herself for making a big deal over such a small episode. It wasn't as if he'd kissed her on the lips, or anything like that. If he had ... Cadi grinned. If he had, there was no way she would be able to keep it to herself.

Izzy nervously nibbled her fingernails. She very much hoped her father wouldn't get wind of her chance encounter with the two girls from the laundry, but how could she be sure? Her father had friends – she corrected herself, acquaintances – up and down Liverpool, and if they thought she was going behind his back they wouldn't hesitate to tell him.

Or was her paranoia getting the better of her? Whether it was or not she couldn't be certain, so she had decided to carry on as normal by making him his tea, giving him one less reason to complain when he came home from the pub – not that he needed an excuse.

As she paced nervously up and down her bedroom floor, she mulled over her meeting with the two relative strangers who seemed keen on becoming friends. The girl with the blonde bob had said something about Izzy's father. How did they know who her father was? It was something she would have to ask when she met them. She smiled. The carrot! She had thought it silly at the time, but now she realised it went to show that the girls were taking Izzy's well-being seriously.

She walked over to the window and looked down to the street below. Her father would be furious if he thought she was sneaking out behind his back, which is why she never did. She instinctively placed a hand to her scarred cheek and ran her finger over the slight ridge. Her father was strict, *very* strict, and there were many things that would send him off at the deep end. She would have to hope that word never got back to him, but if it did, she would shrug it off as a chance encounter.

Seeing her father stumbling down the street, Izzy quickly left the window and trotted down the stairs. If he saw her at the window he would only accuse her of spying on him, and nothing she could say would convince him otherwise.

The front door burst open and Eric half walked, half fell into the kitchen. She had hoped that with the price of alcohol soaring and measures shrinking, her father might not be able to get so drunk, but it hadn't made the slightest bit of difference, although it had given him something else to complain about.

He tried to focus on Izzy as he attempted to stand up. 'What choo starin' at?' he slurred, before landing heavily on one of the kitchen chairs.

Knowing better than to respond, she nipped over to the stove and ladled the vegetable stew she had prepared into a bowl. Placing it down before him, she warned him to be careful as it was hot. Being drunk, he chose not to listen and subsequently blamed Izzy when he scalded his tongue.

'Schtoopid cow,' Eric roared. 'You done that on purpose.' He picked up the bowl and threw it at Izzy, showering her with hot stew.

'I – I did say ...' mumbled Izzy as she tried to wipe the hot stew from her face.

But Eric wasn't for listening. 'Liar!' he yelled, pointing an accusing finger. 'Just like your bloody mam. Don't know why I expect any different – you're both cut from the same cloth.'

Izzy silently drew a deep breath whilst keeping her head down. She knew of old that it would be pointless to try and reason with him, drunk or otherwise. The only time she had ever dared to point out that she was nothing like her mother, Eric had rallied, saying he should have dumped her in the orphanage and gone off to find himself a better life, as her mother had. Izzy very much wanted to say that she wished he had, but she knew it would be an ungrateful thing to say because, no matter how bad things were at home, they could never be as bad as they would be in an orphanage. But it did make her wonder why her father hadn't abandoned her, as he suggested.

The answer had been apparent a few weeks later, when Eric had come flying back to their house; taking the stairs two at a time, he had informed his daughter that in no way was she to open the door to anyone, especially not the scuffers. Izzy supposed at the time that her father had been in a fight with one of the men down the docks. But bad news travels fast, and it wasn't long before she overheard the women in the laundry gossiping that her father had been involved in a punch-up with the captain of a merchant ship who had refused to hire him, accusing Eric of being drunk.

Again she touched her scar. At the time she had been so upset she hadn't thought of the consequences when she accused him of being no better than her mother. Izzy's eyelids fluttered as she recalled the incident. Eric had begun to walk away, when suddenly he spun back to face her; sliding his belt through the loops, he had begun raining blows down on her before she had time to protect herself from the vicious onslaught. The first lash had been straight across the left side of her cheek. Seeing the blood well up in her eye, she had thought for one dreadful minute that he had blinded her. She had screamed at him to stop, but her father had been in a blind rage and hadn't stopped until the buckle flew off the belt. Izzy had lain, curled in a ball, not daring to move until he'd gone. She supposed their neighbours must have heard, yet no one came round to stop him or see if she was all right. She knew they were just as frightened of Eric as she was, but she had hoped someone would do or say something. But no. The incident had taught Izzy one thing: she was on her own, no matter what.

When war had first been declared she had hoped her father might be called up, but of course, being a docker was a reserved occupation. She had suggested that she might join one of the services, thinking that if her father really blamed her for everything bad in his life he would welcome the chance to get rid of her, but instead he had turned it around on her, saying that if she even thought about joining up he would make sure it was the last thing she ever did. It seemed Izzy couldn't do right for doing wrong.

Now, as she waited for him to calm down, she took a dishcloth from the sink and mopped up the spilt stew from the table, muttering her apologies as she did so – not because she was in the wrong, but because it was easier to accept blame than argue, and it would hopefully be considerably less painful too. She got another bowl and ladled more stew into it before placing it down before him. Eric picked up his spoon so quickly that he caused her to flinch, but rather than strike her with the cutlery, he began to eat the stew, albeit grudgingly.

Leaving her father, who preferred to eat in peace, she went to the sink and mopped down the rest of her clothing, before picking up the bowl and stew that her father had flung at her. As she tidied up, Izzy turned her thoughts to the meeting the next day. Clearly no one had mentioned anything to her father about her seeing the girls in the market, because if they had, he would have said something by now, so she felt reassured that she was safe enough to go ahead as planned.

She would feel happier about the matter if she knew the girls would still want to be her friend after they got to know her properly, because anyone who knew Izzy or her father quickly learned that they were bad news.

Cadi was up betimes the following morning to prepare breakfast for the airman who was staying at the B&B. Having come in late the night before, she hadn't had much of a chance to speak to him, but this was often the case with air crew.

With the porridge simmering, Cadi sat down with a cup of tea and turned her thoughts to the day ahead and the possibilities that lay before them. Having had the previous night to think things over, she had decided not to tell Poppy about the kiss on cheek she had received from Jez. To do so would be making something out of nothing, and it would only get Poppy's hopes up that something could come of Jez's display of gratitude. Admittedly Cadi had been quite taken by his actions, but after some consideration she had come to the conclusion that her reaction to the kiss was quite natural. It didn't mean to say she was in love with Jez. Any kiss off a boy for the first time was bound to be exciting, and with it being unexpected, this had only added to the excitement. But when push came to shove, Jez had been thanking her for free food, nothing more.

Sensing movement on the other side of the bar, she got to her feet and went through to welcome their guest.

'Morning! Are you ready for breakfast?'

Still adjusting his tie, the airman nodded. 'That porridge smells good.'

'Tea?'

He nodded. 'Yes, please.'

Cadi disappeared into the back, reappearing a few moments later carrying a tray with a hot bowl of porridge and a pot of tea. 'I'll be back through with some toast, once you've finished your porridge.'

'That sounds wonderful, but I won't have time for toast as well.'

She pulled a disappointed face. 'That's a shame. Have you got far to go or shouldn't I be asking – loose lips and all that?'

He pretended to cast a scrutinising eye over her form. 'You don't look like a spy, but you never know,' he chuckled. 'I'm off to Plymouth, so yes, I've a fair way to go.'

'It must be very exciting getting to travel all over the country.' Her eyes rested on his flying insignia. 'Do you actually fly the planes or ...'

He tapped the badge. 'I do indeed, that's why I've got two wings.'

Cadi stared at him. 'So that's why they call it "getting your wings".'

He sprinkled some sugar over the top of his porridge. 'It certainly is.'

'I bet you get to fly all over the world.' She sighed dreamily. 'How terribly exciting that must be.'

He scooped his spoon into the porridge. 'I certainly can, and do. And you're right: it is very exciting, especially when the Luftwaffe are trying to shoot you down.'

The smile vanished from Cadi's lips. 'Sorry, I didn't mean to make light ...'

He winked at her. 'Don't worry about it. I meant what I said: it *is* exciting when you're outwitting the enemy and turning the tables on them, so that it's them plummeting down to earth and not you.'

'Gosh, you are brave,' said Cadi, her voice dripping with awe. 'I'd be terrified.'

He took a swig of his tea. 'Have you ever considered joining the services?'

She nodded shyly. 'I did in the beginning. My aunt was a driver in the last lot, and I thought that might be fun, but when we tried to sign up we were turned away for not being old enough.' She glanced around the pub. 'That's how we ended up here, and even though it wouldn't have been my first choice, I love running the B&B. Having said that, who knows what the future might bring? I'm still young, and I may change my mind when I turn eighteen.'

He feigned shock. 'You really think it will go on for that long?'

Realising what she had implied, she quickly began to backtrack, but the airman was laughing. 'I'm only teasing, luv.' Tilting his head to one side, he weighed her up. 'What are you? Seventeen?'

Cadi smiled coyly. 'I'll be eighteen in October.'

He shrugged. 'I can't see this war being over any time soon, so if you change your mind, I could be looking at what? A future Waaf, or Wren … ?'

'Whoever would be the first to say yes,' replied Cadi. 'Although I expect you'd recommend the WAAF?'

He finished his porridge before replying. 'Of course. The RAF – or it would be WAAF in your case – is the best the services have to offer. Best uniform, best jobs,' he winked, 'best-looking!'

Cadi laughed. 'Oh well, in that case it looks like it'd have to be the WAAF.'

He drained his tea. 'Good girl.' Standing up, he pulled his wallet out of his trouser pocket and paid for his bed and board. 'Who knows, maybe our paths will cross again some day.'

Cadi put the money into the till. 'You never know.'

She walked him over to the door and unbolted it. 'Goodbye, and safe journeys.'

He fixed his hat onto his head, then ripped off a smart salute. 'Until we meet again.'

She stood in the doorway watching him walk away. There was something to be said for a man in uniform, especially one so brave.

Poppy called out to her, causing her to jump, 'Morning! Was that our guest?'

Cadi closed the door behind her. 'It certainly was – he didn't have time for toast.'

Pouting her disappointment, Poppy walked over to the table where the airman had been seated and began to pile the empty dishes onto the tray. 'Shame, I'd have liked to have a natter. I do love hearing their stories. They lead such exciting lives compared to ours, don't you think?'

Cadi nodded. 'We had a chat whilst he ate his breakfast, and I must say he's given me food for thought.'

'Oh?' said Poppy, intrigued.

'He seemed to think the war will go on for some time yet, and that when we're old enough we'll be able to do what we came here to do.'

Poppy raised a brow. 'Join up?'

Cadi began loading the tray. 'Yup.'

'Are you considering it?'

Cadi shrugged. 'I dunno, I'm happy here. Besides, what would happen to Maria and the Greyhound? She's already said she couldn't manage to run a B&B as well as the pub and the meals. How about you?'

'I do still fancy the idea of becoming a Waaf. On the other hand, I'd not want to join up on my own, so I s'pose if you don't apply, then neither will I.'

Cadi ladled some of the porridge into two bowls and the girls sat down to eat.

'I wouldn't like to think I was holding you back,' confessed Cadi as she blew on a spoonful of porridge.

'You're not,' insisted Poppy, 'and I'm all right where I am for now. I'm just saying I haven't ruled it out.' She dipped her spoon into the porridge. The incident with Eric had left her feeling vulnerable, and she couldn't help thinking that life in the forces would give her the strength, knowledge and confidence to get herself out of a similar situation, should the need arise. She wouldn't admit this to Cadi of course, because she knew her friend still blamed herself for the attack. With that in mind, Poppy changed the subject. 'Have you thought any more about today's meeting with Izzy?'

Remembering last night's encounter with Jez, Cadi filled her friend in on every detail, apart from the thank-you kiss.

Poppy wrinkled the side of her nose. 'So you think she might not even turn up?'

'That's only Jez's opinion, but he wasn't there when we were speaking to her, and I think Izzy was pretty genuine, don't you?'

Poppy mulled this over as she ate her breakfast. 'It was her suggestion. If she really wanted to shut us up, all she had to do was tell us where to get off and walk away. After all, that's what I thought she was going to do at first.'

'Exactly. I suppose we shall have to wait and see.'

'It was ever so good of Jez to play along,' remarked Poppy, 'especially when he and Maria are such good friends.'

'I know, and I do feel awful about it, but he said it was his idea to keep shtum and I wasn't bending his arm to do anything he didn't want to do.'

Poppy nudged Cadi playfully. 'That's because he holds a torch for you!'

As thoughts of his parting kiss sprang to mind, her cheeks bloomed, something that did not go unnoticed by Poppy. 'Cadi?'

Keeping her eyes averted, Cadi felt her cheeks grow warmer.

With no response coming from her friend, Poppy pressed on. 'What aren't you telling me?'

Looking up, Cadi decided to come clean. She didn't want to think that Jez was jeopardising his relationship with Maria just so he could win favour with her. Before she had a chance to change her mind, she filled her friend in on the thank-you kiss.

A slow grin spread across Poppy's cheeks. 'I knew summat had happened. You kept smiling to yourself all last night, but whenever I asked you why, you'd fob me off. So when were you going to tell me?'

Cadi shook her head. 'I wasn't, because I knew what you'd say.'

Poppy gave a shrewd cough. 'So you knew it was more than a thank-you?'

Having finished her porridge, Cadi got up from her seat and began cleaning the dishes. 'No, because it *was* only a thank-you.'

'Do you think he'd kiss Maria or me like that if we'd give him a free supper?'

Cadi started to nod, until she caught Poppy's eye. 'Maybe not.'

'Exactly! He used the meal as an excuse to sneak a kiss.' She took a tea towel and began to dry the dishes. 'What did you say? When he kissed you, I mean?'

'Nothing,' said Cadi. 'I was a little surprised because it was totally unexpected, and he left straight after.'

'How did it make you feel?'

Cadi stared into the soapsuds. She and Poppy had been best friends for years, and if she tried to pull the wool over her friend's eyes, Poppy would see through her lies immediately. 'Don't read anything into this, but I felt as giddy as a schoolgirl.'

Poppy gave a short squeal of excitement, flagged into silence by Cadi, who feared Maria might hear.

'Sorry. But I *knew* you two were meant for each other!'

'For goodness' sake, Poppy, stop getting ahead of yourself. I only felt that way because it was my first kiss off a boy, but it was barely a peck on the cheek – it meant nothing, I know that now.'

Poppy gave a lopsided smile. 'Mighty oaks from little acorns grow.'

Cadi gave a half-hearted laugh. 'I think we've more important things to discuss than a fleeting peck on the cheek, don't you?'

Poppy stopped dreaming of a wedding where she would be bridesmaid. 'Our meeting with Izzy?'

Cadi nodded. 'I say we get the evening meal ready for the oven, then start the sarnies. After that, we can tell Maria that we've left the sheets in the laundry.' She pulled a rueful face as the last words left her lips.

'Don't feel bad, we have left them there,' said Poppy. 'We're not lying to Maria, only protecting her from the truth.'

'By gum, you don't half know how to dress summat up,' chuckled Cadi.

'It's true, though. What she doesn't know won't harm her, and if we decide there's summat she should know, we'll make sure we tell her, but there's no sense in worrying her over something that could be nothing.'

Maria entered the kitchen. 'Sounds ominous. Is there something I should know?'

Without skipping a beat Poppy answered, 'We forgot to bring the laundry home yesterday, so we're going to pick it up after lunch.'

'Is that it?' said Maria, eyeing them suspiciously. 'I wouldn't call that something to worry over.'

Poppy continued, committed to the path she was treading, 'We're trying to be responsible, and forgetting the washing isn't professional.'

Maria waved a dismissive hand. 'I've done it myself in the past. It's easy to do, once it goes into the drying room – out of sight, out of mind.'

Desperate to get off the subject, Cadi held up the pan of porridge. 'Would you like some?'

'Aye, that'd be grand, chuck. I've got to go down to the licensing office this morning. Apparently there's a couple of discrepancies that've cropped up regarding me running the pub. I dare say it's nowt to worry over – they probably need my signature on summat. Having said that, I won't be back until much later on today, so we've got no choice but to stay closed until this evening, so no sarnies today, girls.'

As Maria ate her breakfast, Cadi nipped out to the fishmonger's whilst Poppy prepared the potatoes for the pie topping.

Grateful to get away, Cadi vowed she would never fib to Maria again. *It's true what Mam always said,* she thought as she hurried down the road. *Once you tell one lie, you have to cover it up with another and another, until you don't know what's true any more.*

By the time Cadi returned with the fish, Maria had left for the licensing office. 'Haddock and skate,' she said, showing Poppy the bag.

Poppy wrinkled her nose. 'Skate's so awkward.'

Cadi shrugged. 'Beggars can't be choosers, not in this day and age.'

After a busy morning preparing food, the girls finally left for the laundry.

'I shall be jolly grateful when all this is behind us,' sighed Cadi.

Poppy grimaced. 'Me too.'

They entered the laundry and headed for the drying room, keeping an eye out for Izzy as they went.

'I can't see her anywhere,' hissed Poppy as they took the long way round.

'We should've been more precise with our times,' whispered Cadi. 'After lunch is too vague. For all we know, she could eat at … Ooh.' Nudging Poppy, she pointed to Izzy, who was at the mangles. 'She's here!'

The girls changed their heading for the mangles, keeping a lookout for any prying eyes as they went. Izzy, who had just pulled the last of her washing through, smiled shyly at them. 'I nearly didn't come,' she said quietly. 'What's all this about?'

Cadi swiftly introduced herself and Poppy, then explained as briefly as she could about their first meeting with Eric and the subsequent outcome.

Lowering her head, Izzy tutted softly. 'I'm so sorry – he must have thought I was sneaking out. I never have, but it doesn't stop him thinking I will.' A slight frown creased her forehead. 'Although I don't quite understand what this has to do with me, apart from mistaken identity of course.' She hesitated. 'Hang on a mo. How did you know who I was?'

'Your father called me "Izzy",' Poppy began.

But Izzy was shaking her head. 'There must be hundreds of Izzies livin' in Liverpool, besides which I don't remember introducing myself.'

Cadi's cheeks flamed. She thought she could see where the conversation was going and she didn't like it much.

Izzy, who had been deep in thought, looked up sharply from the mangle and stared at the other women washing their clothes, before turning her attention to the girls. 'There's only one way you could've found out who I was – you've been gossiping with that lot, haven't you?' She continued to speak over Cadi, who was trying to explain things from their point of view. 'You got me here so you could all have a good laugh!' Izzy shook her head angrily, her brown curls swaying limply around her shoulders. 'I'm not here to be the butt of someone else's joke.' A tear ran down her cheek as her bottom lip wobbled. 'And to think I was foolish enough to believe you might be genuine.'

'We *are*!' cried Cadi and Poppy together.

Cadi was wringing her hands as she spoke. 'I swear we didn't bring you here to poke fun – we would *never* do anything like that.'

'Then why?'

Cadi took a deep breath. 'We had no idea who you were, and I'll admit one of the girls mentioned your name.' She knew full well who that woman was, but there was no way she was going to drop Lethia into the mix. 'But that meant nothing until later, when we started talking about how we came to be living at the Greyhound with the feller that saved us from your dad. That's when we remembered Eric, and *that*'s when we put two and two together.'

Izzy looked utterly embarrassed and ashamed. 'I'm so sorry, I should never have leapt to conclusions like that.'

Cadi shrugged. 'Don't worry about it, I reckon I'd be paranoid if I had father like Eric. Once we realised who you were, we were understandably concerned. We've had first-hand experience of your dad's temper and, from what we've heard, it's not the first time he's lost it. If I were you, I'd want a friend in my corner, and *that*'s why we approached you.'

Izzy gave the girls an apologetic grimace. 'I know you say you've experienced my father's temper, but believe me, you've only seen a small part of it. You've no idea what it's like when he *really* loses his rag. And what's more, I don't want you to find out, so I hope you don't take offence when I say thanks for the offer, but—'

Realising what Izzy was about to say, Poppy cut her off mid-sentence. 'What about if we keep things low-key?' she suggested. 'Maybe meet in places where your father's unlikely to know anyone?'

Izzy looked doubtful. 'Being a docker, my father knows all sorts of people from all walks of life.' She began ticking them off on her fingers. 'Carters, dockers, warehousemen, sailors, to name but a few. And whilst they might not be his friends, they're as scared of him as I am, and they'd probably grass me up just to save their own necks.'

Feeling the argument slipping away from them, Cadi cast an eye around the laundry. 'Your father doesn't like women, so I dare say he wouldn't know any of the women in here.'

Izzy scoffed. 'Yes, he does, and even though he wouldn't give them the time of day, loose lips sink ships. They wouldn't mean to cause trouble, but a lot of them have got nothing better to do with their lives than gossip.'

Cadi started to object, but Poppy stopped her. 'She's right, because even though we weren't gossiping, we'd never have found out Izzy's name had it not cropped up in conversation.'

'And who's this Jez who rescued you from my dad?' asked Izzy apprehensively. 'Does he know you're meeting me here?

'Jeremy Thomas – only it's Jez to his pals,' said Cadi. 'And yes, he does know we're meeting you, but believe you me, he won't breathe a word.'

Feeling further explanation was needed, Poppy spoke up. 'He said he used to go on the same school bus as you. He said your dad went ballistic when he tried to befriend you?'

Izzy's cheeks coloured. 'I remember him now, poor bugger, he was only trying to be nice.' She studied the girls' faces. 'You say you want to be my friends, but why? You've heard what my dad does to people who try and befriend me.'

Cadi smiled kindly. 'So that we can be there for you. You see, Poppy got away from your father, but you're still stuck with him, mainly because you've got no one to help you get away.'

Looking terrified, Izzy held her hands up. 'Are you suggesting I run away?'

Cadi nodded enthusiastically. 'That's exactly what we're suggesting.'

Relating to Izzy's fear, Poppy butted in, 'Only you won't be on your own. You'd have me and Cadi helping you – just like Cadi helped me get away from your dad, because if she hadn't been there …'

Izzy eyed the girls as though they'd lost their minds. 'I don't think you quite understand what my father would do if I tried to leave, but I do, and believe me, he wouldn't take it lying down.'

'We're not suggesting you pack your bags and leave today,' reasoned Poppy, 'but we could make a plan.'

Izzy smiled gratefully at the girls. 'From your point of view, it's simple. Only it's really not, and whilst I

196

appreciate you trying to help, I don't think there's anything you can do to *really* help me.'

'So is that it?' said Cadi. 'Don't you even want to see us again?'

Picking up the clothes, Izzy headed for the drying room, indicating with her head that the girls should follow her. This had been the first time she had ever been able to tell anyone how she truly felt, and it was good to be able to vent her frustrations and feelings without fear of it getting back to her father. 'My dad used to watch my every move, even preventing me from getting the mail – goodness only knows why, it's not as if anyone was ever going to write to me – but he's stopped doing that in recent years. I s'pose he thinks I've no chance of making any friends, not after all this time.' Her cheeks coloured. 'I really am sorry I had a go at the pair of you before, but living with my dad makes me cagey. But if you're still game, then I'd very much like to take you up on your offer of friendship. *Not* running away, though, I don't think my nerves could take that.'

Cadi beamed. 'We certainly are, and don't worry, we'll take things at your pace.'

As they began to help Izzy hang her clothes up, Poppy looked at a couple of the women, who were craning their necks in order to get a better look. 'What'll you tell your father, if word does get back?'

Izzy followed her gaze and the women immediately turned their attention to the clothes they were washing. 'My father hates women! They may like to gossip and stir up trouble, but even this lot know better than to stir things up with him, not when they could end up bearing the brunt of his wrath. The worse they'd do is tell their husbands, but I very much doubt it'd go any further. Men don't gossip the same way women do.'

'Agreed, although having said that, we'll still keep everything as hush-hush as possible. I suggest we only meet in places where your father isn't likely to go,' said Cadi, 'because gossip's one thing, but seeing things with your own eyes is another matter entirely. Does anywhere spring to mind?'

Izzy nodded. 'Keep to the better parts of town. Dad never goes anywhere decent.' Her tummy fluttered. For the first time in her life she actually felt happy. That didn't mean to say her father would never beat her again, but it did mean that she would have friends to turn to when he did, and *that* would make all the difference. And if they were really careful, her father might never find out.

'Like where Auntie Flo lives,' said Poppy excitedly.

Nodding her agreement, Cadi elaborated, for Izzy's sake. 'She lives on Mozart Street, not far from Sefton Park.'

'A bit of a walk from here,' said Izzy, 'but I'd be up for that. I love the parks. I go in them most days after I've done my chores. What with Dad working from dawn to dusk, I have quite a bit of free time.'

Cadi eyed their new friend quizzically. 'I know you're scared of what your father would do if you tried to leave, but haven't you ever thought of leaving?'

Izzy laughed. 'All the time! But I've got nowhere to go, and no money to go anywhere with. And even if I had, I know Dad would find me, and when he did …' She shook her head darkly.

'That's how he makes sure you'll never leave,' said Poppy, absent-mindedly plucking a loose thread from the hem of her dress.

A line creased Izzy's brow. 'Sorry?'

'He keeps control by making sure that even if you plucked up the courage to leave, you couldn't, because you've got no money or friends.'

'Cold and calculating,' said Cadi.

'He is,' sighed Izzy, 'but at the same time if it weren't for him, I don't know where I'd be.'

Cadi helped Izzy hang one of the sheets. 'What do you mean?'

'He could've dumped me in an orphanage, and even though life is hell at home, it would be a damned sight worse there.' She gave the girls a knowing look. 'I'd rather live with Dad for the rest of me natural life than end up in the workhouse.'

'He's your father,' cried Cadi, 'it was his job to clothe and feed you.'

Izzy looked up sharply. 'It was me mam's too, but that didn't stop her beggaring off into the wide blue yonder.'

Poppy frowned. 'Hardly your fault.'

'Not if you listen to Dad.'

'Then I suggest you don't,' snapped Cadi. 'Sorry, Izzy, but I wouldn't listen to a word that left your father's lips, especially when it comes to the truth behind your mother's reasons for leaving.

Izzy looked wretched. 'I hear what you're saying, but she could've taken me with her, and as she didn't, I only have my father's account.' She shrugged. 'He's all the family I've got.'

'That's not how you treat family,' muttered Cadi.

'I know,' replied Izzy softly, 'and you're right, of course you are, but I can't – daren't – walk out on him, because no matter what he's done, he's still my father. I'm all he's got.'

'Then he should treat you better, because if you were happy, you wouldn't want to leave,' said Cadi reasonably.

'Only I'm not sure I do want to leave,' said Izzy, 'not when push comes to shove.'

Cadi and Poppy both cast her a look of pure disbelief.

Izzy relented under their gaze. 'If he didn't beat me or lose his temper at the drop of a hat, things might be different.'

'You can't teach an old dog new tricks,' said Poppy reasonably.

Izzy opened her mouth to say that her father might change, given time, then closed it again. 'I know what you're saying is right, but like I've said, I'm not ready to leave yet.'

That Izzy had already gone from saying she was too scared to leave home to saying she wasn't ready *yet* was, as far as Cadi was concerned, a start – and a good one at that. She smiled at her friends. 'So when shall we three meet again?'

Poppy stifled a laugh. 'You make us sound like witches!'

Izzy raised a sceptical brow. 'If my father could see us now, that's exactly what he'd call us: three witches plotting behind his back.'

'We wouldn't have to plot if he was reasonable,' said Poppy defensively. 'We're only being sneaky because we've been forced to, not because we want to.'

200

Izzy conceded that what Poppy said was true. They were doing exactly what her father had been accusing her of for years, but only because he had forced her hand. 'How about tomorrow?'

'Sounds good to me!' said Cadi, looking to Poppy for her approval. 'How about two o'clock tomorrow afternoon outside the Palm House in Sefton Park?'

Izzy held a hand to her tummy, which was alive with butterflies. 'I'll be there, although I think I'll be like a cat on a hot tin roof tonight.'

With everyone agreed, the two girls took their bag of dry laundry, which someone had placed by the door of the drying room, and bade their new friend goodbye before leaving. Once outside, Poppy took one handle of the bag and Cadi the other, so that they were both carrying it.

'I thought Izzy was going to send us away with a flea in our ear at first.'

'Wasn't it dreadful?' agreed Cadi. 'I really hadn't thought how it might look, with the two of us approaching her the way we did. But as soon as the words left her mouth, I knew exactly what she was thinking.'

'All's well that ends well, though,' mused Poppy, 'and if you ask me, I reckon we've done a cracking job. In fact it wouldn't surprise me if she left that evil so-'n'-so of a father before the month's out.'

'I dunno so much. She's a heart of gold, she'd never have stayed otherwise. Even I can see that leaving Eric will be extremely hard for Izzy, because the old blighter's guilted her into staying all this time.' Cadi shook her head angrily. 'Fancy telling your own child that her mother left because of her.'

'I know,' agreed Poppy. 'That only goes to show how evil he is. But he's done it in such a manner that Izzy actually feels like she owes him.'

'Indeed. And making sure that she doesn't have friends, or money, means she's stuck where she is.'

'Or at least she was,' said Poppy. 'I thought it was quite encouraging when she said she wasn't ready to leave home *yet*. At least it shows progress, because I think that before she met us, she'd resigned herself to living with Eric for the rest of her life.'

'Life is much easier with friends,' said Cadi. 'And with us behind her, I think she'll leave sooner rather than later, and we can help by finding her somewhere to run to.'

Poppy arched her eyebrows, a look of uncertainty clouding her face. 'We can?'

'Yes! Although I must admit I'm not entirely sure where, but we've plenty of time to figure that out.'

Poppy blew out her cheeks. 'I thought you were going to suggest she come and stay with us at the pub.'

'Blimey, Poppy. Maria'd go spare if we turned up with Izzy.'

'My thoughts exactly,' agreed Poppy.

'No, we'd have to find her a place far away from Eric, somewhere he'd never look for her …'

'We'll have to get our thinking caps on,' said Poppy.

'Maybe Jez'll think of summat – he's usually good at that sort of stuff. C'mon, let's see what he has to say,' said Cadi. And with that, the two girls made their way to Canada Dock.

*

As Izzy waited for her clothes to dry, she mulled over her meeting with the two girls. Never in her wildest dreams did she ever think she would have a friend on her side, yet here she was with two. It was funny how life worked out. Two girls who'd escaped their humdrum lives in Wales were trying to do the same for her. She smiled. Even if someone got word to her father of her meeting today, it would be worth the row, just to know that she had friends to talk to. Having said that, she would deny arranging to meet them, saying that it was simply two girls who had forgotten their laundry. After all, who could prove otherwise?

She sighed happily. Eric had been torturing her for years, safe in the knowledge that she had nowhere to go, but all that had changed now. For the first time ever, Izzy had a chance to get away from her father and his controlling ways. Her tummy gave an unpleasant lurch. She might feel brave now, with the girls only just departed, but when push came to shove, she knew it wouldn't be so easy. Then again, if she were ever to get away from her father, she would have to take a leap of faith at some time, and it would be a lot easier with friends by her side.

Chapter Six

The girls had arrived at Canada Dock and Poppy was standing on her tiptoes scanning the sea of identically dressed men to see if she could catch a glimpse of Jez's dark hair peeking out from beneath a flat cap. 'They're like peas in a pod – we'll never find him.'

'Yes, we will,' said Cadi assuredly. 'Jez said he was working on the crane at the far end of the dock. Come on.' Still lugging the laundry between them, the girls made their way through the men, some of whom whooped and hollered at them.

Poppy smiled shyly at the men who greeted the girls as they passed by. Speaking from the corner of her mouth, she addressed Cadi. 'I don't think they see many women down here.'

'The way they're behaving, you'd swear they'd *never* seen a woman,' chuckled Cadi as she wagged a reproving finger at a man who was blowing her a kiss.

Having heard the cries of his fellow workers, Jez waved frantically from the seat of his crane to the girls. 'Cadi, Poppy!' Seeing that he'd got their attention, he jumped down from the crane and made his way towards them.

Cadi jerked her thumb, indicating the men behind her. 'They're a loud lot.'

Grinning, Jez cast an eye over the men, who were watching with a keen interest. 'They allus get excited when they see summat in a frock.'

'They'd have a ball down the Chinese laundry,' quipped Poppy.

Jez roared with laughter. 'You tell 'em, Poppy.' He winked at Cadi. 'I've been dying to know how you got on, so how about you put this feller out of his misery and tell me what happened.'

Cadi told him of their brief encounter, and how Izzy had thought them to be taking her for a fool at first. She smiled brightly at Jez. 'It all came good in the end, though, and she's up for seeing us again, so we're meeting her by the Palm House in Sefton Park at two o'clock tomorrow.'

He blew a low whistle. 'Blimey, you have done well. I never thought she'd turn up to the first meeting, lerralone agree to another.' Gazing deep into Cadi's eyes, he winked again. 'I reckon it must be you.'

Poppy acted hurt. 'Oh, thanks. How come I don't get any of the credit?'

He performed a deep bow. 'Forgive me, dear Poppy.'

'Only cos it's you,' she chuckled, adding, 'bloomin' charmer.'

He grinned. 'I try my best.' Turning his attention back to Cadi, he pulled a rueful face. 'But often fail.'

Cadi rolled her eyes. 'You're right, Poppy, he is a charmer.' She looked at the men who were now hard at work. 'They're a cheerful lot, they must enjoy working here.'

Jez's brow shot towards his hairline. 'I'll have to tell them that – they like a good laugh.'

'But they looked so happy when we were walked through, full of smiles and waves,' said Cadi.

'I reckon that had more to do with you two than it does with this place.' Jez looked around the busy dockyard. 'Don't get me wrong; it's all right for men like me, working cranes and the like, but the dockers themselves are very poorly paid, and before the war they never knew whether they'd be working from one day to the next.'

'Every cloud ...' said Poppy, who always preferred to look on the brighter side of life.

He shrugged. 'Mebbe, mebbe not. They may have work in abundance, but we all know that when the bombing starts, it'll be the docks they aim for.'

Cadi eyed him sharply. 'Why do you say *when* – surely you mean *if*?'

Jez grimaced. 'Have you not been keeping abreast of the news?'

Both girls nodded.

'Every day,' said Poppy, 'but it's cities like London they're interested in, not Liverpool – we're too far north.'

He pushed his cap to the back of his head. 'If bombing the life out of London doesn't work, Hitler'll turn his attention to the rest of the country. And with Liverpool being a major trade route, we'll be next on his list. It's what we'd do, if the boot were on the other foot.' Seeing the forlorn look on the girls' faces, Jez gave an apologetic grimace. 'Sorry to burst your bubble, but

Hitler's determined to win, and he won't let a silly thing like distance stand in his way.'

Beginning to wish she had chosen a different topic of conversation, Cadi turned it back to Izzy. 'Then we'll have to stop Hitler before he gets this far. We did think Izzy might join up—' She fell silent as Jez held a finger to his lips.

'Not here – don't forget who her father is *and* where he works.'

Cadi spoke in hushed tones as she glanced wildly around her. 'You mean Eric's *here*?'

Jez shook his head. 'Not that I've seen, but he's well known down the docks.'

Cadi clasped her hand to her forehead. 'Of course. I forgot he was a docker.'

Jez pushed his hands into his pockets. 'Perhaps it was a bit silly of me to agree to your coming here, but I honestly didn't think you'd have anything to tell. I'm glad you have, though, because everyone needs a friend. I take it things went well?'

'*Very* well,' said Poppy.

'Does this mean you're going to tell Maria?'

'Oh yes,' said Poppy. 'We did say that if things progressed we would, and we're true to our word, aren't we, Cadi?'

Cadi nodded, but the doubtful look that clouded Jez's face was causing her concern. 'What's up?'

'Nothing. I was just wondering what you'll do if Maria forbids you to continue with your friendship.'

Cadi shook her head. 'She wouldn't do that – she's a good egg, is Maria. She'll be pleased as punch we've established a friendship. She'll …'

Jez remained doubtful. 'In principle, yes, but Maria has her livelihood to think of, and she won't want Eric causing her or her customers any trouble.'

'We're going to be so super-careful,' said Poppy. She looked over her shoulder, then gestured the others to come closer. 'We're only meeting in places that we know Eric, or anyone he knows, won't frequent. That's why Izzy suggested the park.'

Jez jerked his head in the direction of his crane. 'Come over here. We've less danger of being over-heard, and I think we need to talk this through before you go diving in head first.'

Following Jez, Cadi couldn't understand why he would want them to keep lying to Maria, especially when they were going to make sure Eric never found out. She said as much to him.

'I don't doubt you'll be careful and I trust you not to make any mistakes, but no matter how careful you are, Maria will always be fearful of the consequences. From her point of view, it's safer all round if you nip the friendship in the bud.' He smiled kindly. 'I want you to be certain you're doing the right thing, because once you've told her the truth, there'll be no taking it back.'

Cadi and Poppy stared glumly at each other. 'I don't want to lie to her,' said Cadi, 'not after everything Maria's done for us, but we *can't* leave Izzy with that dreadful excuse for a father.'

'So what are you going to do?' asked Jez. 'Tell Maria and risk everything, or keep shtum until you've sorted things out with Izzy?'

Cadi was looking at Poppy, who, guessing her friend's thoughts, nodded abruptly. 'It's our only choice.'

Cadi looked at Jez, her face a mask of shame. 'We'll keep quiet,' adding hastily, 'only for now, mind you. I don't intend to keep Maria in the dark for ever – it wouldn't be fair.'

Jez ran his tongue over his lips. 'Granted, but the longer you leave it, the harder it will be.'

'I know, but I don't want to let Izzy down, so we'll have to cross that bridge when we come to it.' She glanced shyly up at him. 'I'm sorry to ask you this again, Jez, but …' She got no further because, guessing what Cadi was about to say, he was already answering.

'My lips are sealed.'

'Thanks, Jez, you're a diamond.'

Performing a mock bow, he straightened up. Spreading his arms wide, he indicated the docks. 'A diamond in the rough!'

Cadi felt her cheeks grow warm. 'We're serving rhubarb crumble for tonight's pudding. I'm sure there'll be a little left over, if you fancy it?'

He licked his lips. 'I could go for a bit of rhubarb crumble, especially if it comes smothered in your delicious custard.' His eyes glittered flirtatiously as they settled on Cadi.

Swallowing shallowly, in the hope the others might not see, she gave him a shy smile. 'Custard too? You've the cheek of the devil, Jeremy Thomas.'

His eyes locked with Cadi's as he continued to twinkle at her. 'I get my devilishly good looks from him too.'

Shaking her head, but smiling fit to burst, she turned away. 'See you later, Jez.'

'Ta-ra, girls.'

As the girls walked away, Cadi was desperately trying to banish the smile that was giving away her innermost thoughts.

Once free of the docks, Poppy turned to Cadi. 'I've heard the expression "the air was electric" many times in the past, but by God, I've never experienced it until now.'

Cadi tutted. Even though she knew Poppy was right, she was not about to admit it. 'Honestly, Poppy, you've such an imagination.'

'I don't need imagination when I've got eyes in my head.'

'You must be seeing things then, because I am not going soppy over Jez,' said Cadi coolly.

Poppy smirked. 'You should try telling that to your face.'

Cadi cursed inwardly. She had been worried that her face might give the game away and she was right. What was it about Jez that made her go weak at the knees? She envisaged him as he had been just now and gave a heartfelt sigh of pure contentment. Was this how her mother had felt when she first met Dewi? If she had, then marrying the man she loved had resulted in what Cadi saw as a humdrum existence, with no end in sight. She turned her thoughts to a typical day in her mother's life. Up with the lark, so that she could feed the family their breakfast, as well as make everyone's lunch. After that she would do the pots and begin the task of trying to rid the house of mould and coal dust, the latter seeming to follow the men of the house, no matter how much they bathed. When she had finished that, she would do whatever sewing she had managed to acquire from the other women, who, in Cadi's eyes, looked down on her mother as if she was some sort of skivvy, often complaining that the work they gave her came back smelling like a coal fire, and even refusing to pay her the agreed price, as compensation for the aroma. Cadi was determined not to end up like her mother. She tutted beneath her breath.

Taking the bag of laundry from Cadi, Poppy slung it over her shoulder. 'I heard that.' She grinned at her friend. 'Or are you going to try and tell me I'm hearing things now?'

Cadi folded her arms defensively and then, realising it was futile to keep denying her feelings, she softened. 'All right, I admit it: I like him – a lot – but that doesn't mean to say I intend to act on my feelings.'

'Then you're a fool.' Poppy waved her hand to quieten Cadi, who had started to protest. 'Fellers like Jez don't crop up too often and if you don't act on your feelings, you run the risk of losing him.'

'But I don't want a relationship – I'm too young,' said Cadi wretchedly. 'I've my whole life ahead of me and I intend to make the most of it. You and I both know that if I were to give in to my feelings, I'd spend every moment of my free time with Jez, and that's *not* why I came to Liverpool.'

Deep in thought, Poppy spoke slowly. 'I know, but when love comes along you shouldn't turn your back on it, *especially* in times like these.'

'Bloomin' 'eck, Poppy! I like Jez, but *love*?'

Poppy's brow rose. 'I saw the way you were looking at each other. It was like summat you see in the movies.' She clicked her fingers. 'You was smouldering.'

Cadi went to object but stopped. She knew how she'd felt as Jez gazed at her, but she couldn't say how she'd looked. She glanced shyly at Poppy from the corner of her eye. 'Do you really think that's how we looked?'

Poppy nodded. 'Very much so. Blimey, Cadi, a *blind* man could've seen the love between you.'

'But we hardly know each other—' Cadi began, only for Poppy to cut her short once again.

'Love at first sight—' said Poppy simply.

This time it was Cadi who cut Poppy short. 'We've already been through this, and whilst you might have been right about Jez, I can honestly say I didn't fall in love with Jez the moment I clapped eyes on him. I was grateful that he'd come to your rescue, but that's where it ended.'

'That's because your ego was getting in the way, and you were miffed that we'd needed a man's help in the first place,' said Poppy truthfully, adding, 'not to mention being so winded that you could hardly move; and your head was bleedin', and you were worrying over what your dad was going to say.'

Cadi turned her thoughts back to that night. Poppy was right. And on top of it all, she had been so scared about what might have happened, had Jez not come to their rescue, that she hadn't really paid much attention to the young man who had saved them. Even if she had, she felt sure it wasn't a case of love at first sight – or not for her at any rate. No, her feelings for

Jez had got stronger, the more she got to know him. But attraction-wise? She smiled to herself. She'd be a liar if she said she hadn't found him attractive from the word go.

She answered Poppy in the best way she could. 'I've never been in love with a man before, so I can't say whether I am or not.'

'How do you feel when you hear the name "Jez"?' asked Poppy. Cadi immediately tried to swallow her smile, but she was too late.

Poppy wagged an admonitory finger. 'Don't you go trying to pull the wool over my eyes, Cadi Williams.'

'Happy!' said Cadi. 'You wanted to know how I feel when I hear his name, and that's your answer: it makes me feel happy.'

'And what about the thought of seeing him?' probed Poppy.

'The same, only more so, because I look forward to seeing him.' She shrugged. 'I look forward to seeing the look on our customers' faces when they eat our grub, but that doesn't mean to say I love them.'

Poppy giggled. 'Fair enough, but how do you feel when it's time for Jez to leave?'

Cadi felt her heart sink at the mere thought. She looked at Poppy. 'Disappointed?'

Poppy clicked her fingers. 'You love your brothers, but did you feel disappointed at the thought of them leaving for work each morning?'

Cadi laughed. 'More like relieved.'

'And *that*,' said Poppy firmly, 'is the difference between loving someone and being in love with them.'

As they approached the Greyhound, Cadi pulled on Poppy's elbow. 'Hold up, shouldn't we get our stories straight before we go in?'

Poppy pulled a face. 'I'm not sure there's anything to get straight? We've been to pick up the laundry, like we said we would.'

'But we've been hours!' hissed Cadi, suddenly aware that they hadn't a good excuse to give Maria.

It suddenly dawned on Poppy that her friend was right: they had been far longer than they intended. 'Flippin' 'eck, I didn't realise how long we'd been. What shall we say?'

'That we called to see Jez,' said Cadi, who couldn't think of any reasonable explanation for their absence.

'All this time?' asked Poppy dubiously.

'Can you think of a better excuse?'

Shrugging, Poppy continued, 'We'll have to say we dawdled on the way back. Because I doubt Jez could stop work for hours.'

Agreeing that this was their only option, the girls went to open the door but found it still locked. Taking the key out from her skirt pocket, Cadi opened the door, calling out to Maria as she did so, but there was no response.

Placing the laundry on the kitchen table, Poppy picked up a piece of paper. She smiled with relief as she read it out loud: '*Had to go to a meeting with the brewery, back soon. Love, Maria.*'

'Thank goodness for that!'

Poppy, however, was frowning at the note. 'The licensing office this morning and the brewery this afternoon. You don't think anything's amiss, do you?'

214

Cadi shook her head. 'No, Maria said herself that she had to sign some paperwork, but it was nothing to worry about. And I expect the meeting with the brewery will be to discuss the prices.'

Poppy called over her shoulder as she took the laundry upstairs, 'I hope you're right, because it seems odd.'

Cadi mulled over her friend's fears, but quickly dismissed them. Maria wasn't worried, so why should they be? Feeling content that their worries were futile, she went through to the bar to make sure everything was shipshape.

It was much later that afternoon when Maria returned to the bar, and it was clear from the look on her face that she had not had a good day. Sitting heavily on one of the kitchen chairs, she fixed the girls with a wooden stare. For a moment Cadi's heart was in her mouth and she felt sure that Poppy's must be the same, for it was obvious by Maria's demeanour that she had heard about their rendezvous with Izzy.

Thinking it better that they owned up, Cadi was the first to speak. 'Sorry, Maria, we were going to tell you.'

Her brow creasing, Maria glared at her. 'You mean to tell me you know who's responsible for shooting their mouth off?'

'No!' said Cadi. She hesitated; perhaps Eric had complained to the pub because of them meeting Izzy. She continued cautiously, 'I'm not quite sure what's happened ...'

'The licensing office *and* the brewery want to close me down.'

Cadi's jaw dropped. 'Why?'

'Some busybody has decided to stir things up because they don't like the idea of a woman running her own bar.' She shook her head angrily. 'Only they're going to have to try a lot harder, because Maria Smyth doesn't run at the first sign of trouble. I stood my ground and told them they'd got it wrong, and until they could prove otherwise I wasn't going anywhere.'

Poppy passed Maria a cup of tea. 'I don't understand. I thought Bill put the licence in your name before he went away?'

'He did, but that's not the issue. Apparently, somebody's made an official complaint, saying I should have my licence revoked because I've got two underage girls serving behind the bar.' She rolled her eyes. 'Bill said not everyone would be happy with me taking over the licence, and he was right. The brewery called me in to say they wouldn't be selling me any more beer if I was employing underage barmaids, and the licensing office said they'd revoke my licence, should they find the rumour to be true. Of course I strongly denied their accusations, saying that you neither of you worked behind the bar, but they didn't believe me.' She heaved a sigh. 'Of course they had no proof, so they could only issue me with a warning, but I'll tell you summat for nothing: this is far from over. If I know that lot, they'll be keeping a close eye on us – probably even send someone round to test us out. So from now on, I don't want to see either of you girls on the other side of that door, not even to collect glasses. I wouldn't trust that lot as far as I can throw them.'

Cadi looked thoroughly dejected. 'I'm so sorry, Maria – all this because of us!'

Maria shook her head sharply. 'None of this is your fault. This is the result of some busybody who fancied a pub for themselves ...' Tilting her head to one side, she eyed Cadi quizzically. 'When I first came in, you started to apologise for something?'

Cadi stared at Maria, her mind racing with thoughts and excuses, and she was grateful when Poppy came to her rescue.

'Cadi thought you'd heard that we'd been dilly-dallying when we were out. We were a lot longer than we said we'd be, so we've had to rush a bit to get eve-rything ready.'

'Oh,' she waved a dismissive hand, 'there's nowt wrong with dilly-dallying. I thought you meant you'd served someone behind the bar and that's why I was in trouble, or that you knew who this Welsh feller was.'

'No,' said Cadi promptly. 'We know the rules, and we'd not do owt to break them.' She hesitated. 'What Welsh feller?'

'They said they'd had an anonymous tip-off by some feller with a Welsh accent.'

Cadi curled her fists into balls. 'I bet you, a pound to a penny, it was Aled.'

Maria wrinkled her brow. 'Aled? Where have I heard that name before?'

'Aled lives in Rhos. When he found out we were coming to Liverpool he was horrid, saying that we'd soon be back with our tails between our legs,' explained Cadi, 'When I last got a letter from Sophie – my friend at the bakery – she said she couldn't wait to see the look on Aled's face when he knew how well things were going for us.'

Maria tutted angrily. 'I remember now, you mentioned him when you first arrived at the pub. For goodness' sake, doesn't he realise that his childish act of vengeance could've caused me to lose my licence?'

'It wouldn't bother Aled even if it did. He would've been so angry about hearing that we'd proved him wrong, he'd do anything to spoil things for us, even if that meant you losing the pub.'

'Well, I can't take any chances, especially now they're looking for me to make a mistake.' She glanced at her watch. 'I'd better get a move on, in case they accuse me of opening up late.'

As she walked through to open the pub doors, Cadi stared at Poppy. 'I don't know what's worse: the thought that she'd found out about Izzy or the fact that Aled's snitched on us.'

'Be fair, Cadi, you don't *know* it was Aled, you're just assuming …'

Cadi flapped her arms about in an exasperated manner. 'Who else could it have been?'

'Aled doesn't even live around here, but there's plenty of Welsh fellers that visit the pub – it could've been any one of them.'

'Only they aren't holding a grudge, like Aled,' said Cadi.

'Innocent until proven guilty,' said Poppy reasonably.

'Whether it was him or not makes no odds. Like Maria said, we've got to be on our guard.' Taking a knife, Cadi poked it into the fish pie. 'I'll show that Aled he can't always get everything he wants. I'm going to make sure the Greyhound goes from strength to strength.'

'That's the spirit,' said Poppy. 'They say that success is the best form of revenge.'

Cadi looked through to make sure Maria was out of earshot before speaking. 'Bloomin' good job we decided not to tell her the truth about Izzy. I reckon she'd definitely have said no to us meeting her, what with everything else she has going on.'

'She's certainly got enough worries without us adding to them,' agreed Poppy. 'As my mam always says: least said, soonest mended.'

'Mum's the word,' said Cadi.

Having spent the last month on tenterhooks whilst waiting for his papers to arrive, Aled was overjoyed when the postman handed him an official-looking envelope.

'I'm guessing this is the reason you've been watching me like a hawk each time I come to the farm,' said Gwyn.

Aled nodded. 'Don't say owt to Mam and Dad, will you? I've not told them I've signed up yet.'

Gwyn tapped the side of his nose. 'As a member of His Majesty's Postal Service, I am sworn to secrecy when it comes to another person's mail.' He glanced eagerly at the envelope. 'I hope it's good news.'

'If you hang on a mo, I can tell you.' Aled slit the envelope open and scanned the contents. He looked up and a huge grin donned his cheeks. 'It's from the RAF. I'm to report to Padgate for basic training in a fortnight's time.'

Gwyn was clearly impressed. 'Well done, Aled. The RAF, eh? I'm sure your folks'll be cock-a-hoop when they hear the good news.'

Aled looked highly sceptical. 'I very much doubt it. Dad wants me to stay put, so does me mam, and they're going to be anything but pleased.' He tucked the envelope into his trouser pocket. 'Here goes nothing! See you tomorrow, Gwyn, if me mam hasn't killed me before then, of course.'

'Good luck, Aled, although I'm sure you won't need it.'

Aled glanced anxiously at the farmhouse where his parents were having their morning cup of tea. This was one conversation he was not looking forward to. He entered the kitchen to find his parents eyeing him with deep suspicion, his father stony-faced, his mother anxious.

John spoke through thin lips. 'So you're off then, despite our asking you not to.'

Aled stared at them in stunned silence before finally finding his voice. 'How could you possibly know, when I've only just found out myself?'

'Because we weren't born yesterday,' snapped John. 'You've been like a cat on a hot tin roof for the past few weeks. I knew there was summat up, but even I didn't think you could be this devious.' He tutted. 'Standing there all smiles, looking so chuffed with yourself; and Gwyn no better.'

Aled gaped at his father. 'You've been spying on me?'

A muscle twitched in John's jaw. 'No, I ruddy well have not. I happened to be in the barn when I seen Gwyn handing you the envelope – just as bloomin' well, if you ask me, cos I dare say you'd never have bothered telling us otherwise. More than likely would have upped and left without so much as a goodbye.'

'I didn't want to say owt in case I wasn't accepted. It seemed pointless upsetting the apple cart, but I was going to tell you.' Seeing the disappointment on his mother's face, Aled continued, 'I've been accepted into the RAF, and I leave for Padgate in two weeks.'

Scraping his chair as he stood up, John muttered, 'You're a selfish fool,' before walking out.

'You knew he'd be disappointed,' said Gwen, 'but he'll get used to the idea, given time.' She smiled timidly. 'He's worried – we both are, it's only natural.'

Sitting down in the chair that his father had just vacated, Aled handed his mother the letter. 'I'll be fine, Mam. It's what I want to do. Flying an aeroplane is far more exciting than driving a tractor.'

Gwen gave him an old-fashioned look. 'Far more dangerous too, but if it's what you really want ...'

A look of relief swept Aled's features. 'Thanks, Mam.'

Reaching across the table, she took his hand in hers. 'You're my son, and I love you. I may not always approve of your decisions and choices, but if they make you happy, then who am I to judge?'

'What's made you change your tune? Because you were dead set against it before?' Aled asked cautiously. He didn't wish to upset the only ally he had.

'You must've been desperate to go behind our backs, and I want you to be happy; safe, but happy.'

'Why can't Dad see that?'

His mother laughed. 'Because he's a man, which means he's naturally stubborn and pig-headed.' She wagged a finger as Aled tried to object, 'As are you, and it's pointless to pretend otherwise, especially when you've stuck to your guns and gone against your father's wishes.'

Aled conceded defeat. 'Aye, I suppose you're right.' He glanced out of the window towards the farmyard. 'I only wish he'd see things from my point of view.'

'Deep down he does, which is why he knew you'd join up sooner or later.'

Aled sounded surprised. 'He did? Then why did he go off at the deep end?'

She heaved an exasperated sigh. 'Because he's worried summat bad'll happen to you! Air crew is one of the most dangerous jobs a serviceman can do, but you're over eighteen and that means you don't need his permission. If the boot were on the other foot, he'd have done exactly the same thing, which is why he's put word out that he might be looking for help on the farm sometime in the near future.'

Aled's brow rose. 'I had no idea.'

Gwen folded the tea towel and laid it on the table. 'Of course you didn't, you've been too tied up in your own affairs to notice what's going on under your own nose.'

'Is that why Alun Williams has been coming over?'

'Dad wanted to be sure that Alun wasn't leaving the mines out of desperation, and that he really was interested in farming.'

'Blow me down! I thought ...' He hesitated. 'I don't really know what I thought.'

'I expect that's where your father's gone,' said Gwen calmly, 'to tell Alun he can start in a couple of weeks.'

Aled wrinkled his brow. 'Does Cadi know?'

Gwen pulled a face. 'I don't know – why do you ask?'

'No reason.' Aled gazed at the letter in his hands. It seemed the war was changing everybody's lives. Cadi was living in Liverpool, having the time of her life by all accounts; and he, Aled, was off to join the RAF, whilst Cadi's brother Alun took his place on the farm. Life was about to get very interesting!

It was the day of their first official meeting at the Palm House, and Jez had agreed to go with the girls to meet Izzy.

'Are you sure she won't mind me tagging along?' he asked Cadi.

'I wouldn't have thought so. After all, if it weren't for you, none of this would be happening.'

'All this sneaking about reminds me of your Aunt Flo,' said Izzy, the excitement in her voice rising as she continued, 'I bet she does this when she goes wherever it is she goes.'

Cadi gave her friend a shrewd smile. 'How on earth you get that from her last letter is beyond me. There was no suggestion of spying or sneaking around – far from it, she said she was bored to tears in the land of Haggis.'

Poppy tapped the side of her nose. 'Scotland.'

'Yes, Poppy, Scotland. She only said "the land of Haggis" because she works for the War Office and she doesn't want to risk her letter falling into enemy hands, but that's about as exciting as it gets.'

223

Poppy pouted. 'I *know* she said she was bored to tears, but she's hardly likely to tell you the truth, is she?' Once again she tapped the side of her nose. 'I've been talking to the fellers that come into the pub on a stopover, and they say women in the services get to lead really exciting lives, delivering top-secret messages across the country and making important phone calls, as well as letting those in charge know where our boys are in the world. And that's the ones they can talk about. Your aunt can't even tell us what she does, not properly, and to me that speaks volumes.'

'Well, you're the only one,' said Cadi before pointing to Izzy, who was standing outside the Palm House. Fighting the urge to call out, in case she drew unwanted attention, she hissed 'There she is' from the corner of her mouth.

Seeing them approach, Izzy smiled shyly, soft dimples appearing in her cheeks, as Cadi reacquainted her with Jez. 'I hear you're a regular knight in shining armour,' said Izzy.

Jez nudged Cadi playfully. 'Is that how you've been describing me?'

Cadi blushed, even though she knew Jez was only joshing. 'I don't think those were my exact words ...'

Poppy, however, was eager to learn whether Eric had any inkling of their rendezvous. 'What did your dad say last night? Anything? Or do you think he's clueless?'

'Clueless,' said Izzy happily. She looked at Jez. 'I feel I should apologise for my father's behaviour, not just for what he did outside school all those years ago, but for what he *tried* to do to Poppy.'

Jez furrowed his brow. 'Why? It's not your fault he can't keep his hands to himself.'

'I know, but …'

'No buts,' said Cadi, wagging a reproachful finger. 'You're not responsible for your father's actions.'

Izzy smiled weakly. 'I find it so embarrassing because he's my father. I suppose that's why I'm always apologising for him.'

'Well, it's about time you stopped,' said Poppy. 'I'm sure nobody thinks you approve of his actions.'

'Hard to say, when everyone avoids you like the plague,' said Izzy miserably.

'They probably don't want to get involved,' said Jez diplomatically.

Izzy smiled appreciatively at Cadi and Poppy. 'These two did, and they aren't even from these parts.'

'It's easier for us,' said Cadi, '*because* Eric doesn't know who we are.'

Jez grinned. 'Just rode him like a donkey …'

Izzy gave Cadi an enquiring glance. 'What's this?'

Cadi explained how she'd jumped on Eric's back, and Izzy laughed until her sides ached. 'Oh, Cadi, I'm sorry for laughing, but the image of you sitting on top of my dad, like you were riding some sort of wild bull.' She wiped the tears from her cheeks with the backs of her hands. 'I wish I'd been there.' She hesitated. 'You were ever so brave, though, weren't you in the least bit frightened?'

Cadi shook her head fervently. 'He was attacking my friend and I knew I had to stop him. I didn't even think of the consequences.'

'You're like that woman,' said Izzy. She was lost in thought for a moment before whipping her head up. 'Boadicea!'

Cadi burst into laughter. 'I don't think I'm *that* brave.'

'I think you are,' said Izzy, in a voice filled with admiration. 'I think you're wonderful.'

Blushing to her ears, Cadi shyly thanked Izzy for her praise. 'It's very kind of you to say so, but I don't think I could take on the might of the Roman Empire.'

'You did more than I did,' said Poppy. 'I was as much use as a chocolate teapot.'

Waving a dismissive hand, Cadi decided to change the subject in order to spare her blushes. 'Who's up for a walk by the lake?'

They all agreed this would be lovely and, with Poppy and Izzy falling into step, Jez pulled Cadi to one side.

'I think you've got an admirer.'

'I know, and I feel a bit of a fraud, because it's different for me—' Cadi began, only to be cut short by Jez.

'You're feisty by nature. If it were you living under Eric's roof, you'd have gone long since.' He winked at her. 'I think you're just the sort of friend Izzy needs, to give her the strength to get away from that beast of a man.'

'Do you really think so?' said Cadi.

'I certainly do. You're a special girl, Cadi Williams. You might not see it, but I'm telling you, you are.' He held out his arm and Cadi slipped her hand through the crook of his elbow.

'I hope you're right, Jez, because I'd like nothing better than to get Izzy away from him.'

'A feisty nature is both a blessing and a curse,' said Jez.

'How?'

He chucked her under her chin. 'It's a blessing because it makes you who you are, but it's a curse because those same qualities keep me at arm's length.'

Cadi's cheeks, which were only just beginning to fade from the praise of her friends, coloured anew. 'I do like you, Jez, really I do, but I don't feel as if I'm ready for a relationship yet.' She smiled apologetically up at him.

He pulled her close. Her choice of words had given him fresh hope. 'Yet? That's good enough for me! They say patience is a virtue and quite frankly, my dear, you're worth waiting for.'

Looking into his eyes, which twinkled down at her, Cadi wondered how long she could keep denying herself his love.

July 1940

It had been several weeks since that first meeting in Sefton Park and the four friends now met on a regular basis.

'I always thought I was going to be like one of those birds in the aviary,' said Izzy, indicating the large building that housed the feathered creatures.

'You still are, in a way,' said Poppy.

'Ye-es,' Izzy began slowly, 'only it's different now, because I have the two of you, and Jez, and believe me, that's given me more freedom than I've ever had.'

The sun beat down on the three girls as they made their way to the lake, and Cadi couldn't help but notice that Izzy was wearing a cardigan. 'Aren't you hot?' Seeing the hunted look shrouding Izzy's face, she sighed breathily. 'Oh, Izzy, please tell me he's not been at it again?'

Izzy gave a small nod. 'I can't remember a week going by without my dad giving me a clout for one reason or another.'

Cadi linked arms with Izzy. 'This is getting silly. You shouldn't have to live like this, not now you've got us. You've really got to get away from him, Izzy.'

Izzy heaved a sigh. 'I know, but I'm still not ready.'

'What on earth are you waiting for?' said Cadi, adding desperately, 'Another scar like that one?'

'No,' said Izzy. She covered the scar with her hand. 'That was a mistake – he didn't mean to go that far.'

'Tosh!' snapped Cadi. 'You don't give someone a scar like that by accident. I bet he never even apologised.'

Izzy eyed her friends imploringly. 'Can't we change the subject? I hate talking about my dad.'

Cadi tutted beneath her breath. 'I don't mean to upset you, Izzy, but we can't help worrying about you, and what Eric'll do next.'

'I know and I'm grateful for your concern, truly I am, but this is something I'm going to have to deal with in my own time, and I can't say when that will be.'

Cadi wanted to continue, and make her friend see sense, but she knew that to do so would only make Izzy retreat further into her shell.

Squinting into the distance, Poppy grinned. The perfect change of subject was heading their way. 'Here comes Jez.' She wagged a reproving finger at Cadi. 'You're always talking about your independence, yet you and Jez might as well be joined at the hip.'

'It's not the same as being in a proper relationship, though. If we were, I'd feel obliged to ask him places, and we'd get bogged down in relationship etiquette. As it is, I don't have to worry about Jez getting the wrong idea if I speak to another feller, and vice versa.' She smiled with smug confidence. 'It's *much* better this way.'

'Only neither of you do that anyway,' Poppy pointed out, 'but I suppose if it makes you feel better ...'

'It does,' said Cadi. 'Right now, I'm happy being friends.'

Jez called over to the girls as he approached. 'Afternoon, ladies. How's tricks?'

'Same old,' said Cadi. 'You?'

Beaming fit to burst, Jez ran his fingers through his hair. 'I've been promoted.'

Cadi clapped her hands together. 'That's wonderful news. What to?'

'Supervisor,' he said, tucking his thumbs into his braces. 'So from now on, I'll be the one in charge.'

'That's fabulous news, Jez,' said Cadi. 'I can see you're thrilled to bits, and quite rightly so.'

Still beaming, he placed a hand to his cheeks. 'I've not stopped smiling all morning. More responsibility means more money.' Unbuttoning his collar, he looked at Izzy. 'Aren't you hot in that cardie?'

In truth, Izzy was beginning to feel woozy from the heat, so rather than make a fool out of herself, she took off her cardigan and swiftly tied it around her waist.

Cadi, Poppy and Jez stared at the purple bruises that covered her forearms.

A muscle in Jez's jaw flinched. 'Bloody great bully. I'd like to see him try and do that to me.'

Izzy smiled wanly. 'Don't be daft. He'd never try and pick on someone his own size. Besides, it's me he's cross with.'

'Why?' said Poppy promptly. 'What could you possibly have done that would have warranted such a reaction?'

'Blind scouse,' replied Izzy. 'Dad got it in his head that I'd said we was having scouse for tea, but when he found out there was no meat in it, he accused me of lying.' She rolled her eyes. 'Just like me mam used to.'

Cadi stiffened. 'I don't reckon he got it wrong, I think he was using that as an excuse to take his temper out on you. But either way, you don't do that to someone.' Adding as an afterthought, 'Especially not someone you love.'

'If the fellers down the docks knew—' Jez began, but Izzy was quick to cut him short.

'Well, they don't,' she said, 'and what's more, I'd prefer it if we could keep it that way.'

'Why are you protecting him?' said Cadi, utterly perplexed at her friend's loyalty. 'He's a pig, and a brute to boot. He doesn't deserve your protection.'

'The men he works with hold him in high regard,' explained Izzy.

'Only because they don't know the truth,' spluttered Cadi.

'And if they find out the truth, who do you think he'll blame? Not only that, but if they stop giving him work, he'd be at home with me all day. Which is more than I could stand.'

'I wouldn't want to make things worse for you, so it looks as though I've got no choice other than to hold my tongue,' said Jez wretchedly, 'but only because I think you're right, and he'd take it out on you.'

'So can we agree to leave it?' said Izzy. 'This is the only time of day I truly get to be happy, and I don't want to spend it talking about *him*.'

'Of course,' said Poppy. 'Let's go see if we can spot any water boatmen. I love watching them skim across the surface of the water.'

As they walked, Cadi turned her thoughts to her own parents. She had spoken to her mother earlier in the day and caught up with all the gossip from back home, including the fact that her brother, Alun, had started working on Aled's father's farm.

'He's loving every second of it,' Jill had told Cadi. 'It's all he talks about when he comes home.'

'I'm surprised they let Aled join the RAF,' said Cadi as she fiddled with the telephone wire. 'What with farming being a reserved occupation.'

There was a lengthy pause before her mother answered. 'Land Girls are ten-a-penny, and it's a pity the same can't be said about air crew. Speaking of which, didn't you say you've had a few pilots staying at the B&B?'

Cadi smiled. 'We certainly have. And I'm pleased to say we send them on their way refreshed, with full bellies and a song in their heart.'

'Aw, I always said you'd do a good job, no matter what you turned your hand to, and it sounds like you've done just that,' said Jill, her voice oozing with pride.

'The B&B's booked up months in advance, and we get people coming from all over Liverpool to eat our food.'

'That'll please your father,' chuckled Jill.

Cadi rolled her eyes. 'Honestly, Mam, why can't he accept that he was wrong?'

Her mother laughed into the receiver. 'Because he's convinced the Greyhound's some kind of hellhole frequented by the dregs of society.'

Cadi had a sudden thought. 'Why don't you bring him over for a visit? You could come for a weekend break, stay with us in the pub?' Her voice got more excited as she thought it through. 'It would be wonderful to see you both, and I know you haven't had a proper break in years! Come on, Mam, say you'll at least consider it?'

She heard Jill blow out her cheeks lengthily before replying, 'It would be nice, and we do need a break. I suppose it can't hurt to ask.'

Cadi beamed. 'Thanks, Mam. I'll keep everything crossed that Dad listens to you.'

'I'll let you know how I get on,' said Jill. She hesitated. 'You never know, with Aled working for the RAF, he might pop in for a night or two.'

Cadi stiffened. She'd had no desire to see Aled previously, and certainly not after he'd tried to get Maria closed down. Only there was no point in saying any of this, because her mother would only say Cadi had no proof that it was Aled who'd telephoned the licensing office. More importantly, albeit annoyingly, Cadi knew her mother would be right. She tried to imagine Aled out of his wellies and in an RAF uniform. No doubt he would be a pilot and would thoroughly enjoy waving his achievement in her face, lording it over her as he ordered his meal, and complaining that the room wasn't up to his standards. This bit she did mention to her mother, but Jill didn't seem as certain.

'The services change people, love. I very much doubt Aled will be the same person he once was.'

'No,' agreed Cadi. 'He'll probably be even more pompous and conceited!'

Jill had laughed down the phone. 'That lad will never be able to do right for doing wrong, not in your eyes.'

Now, as the others settled down on the banks of the lake, Cadi sat beside them, dipping her fingers into the sparkling water. 'Guess who's gone into the RAF?'

Knowing that Cadi had been speaking to her mother earlier that day, Poppy sat up. 'One of your brothers?'

'Aled.'

'No!' said Poppy, her voice thick with disbelief. 'Are you sure you got it right?'

Cadi nodded. 'Alun's replaced him on the farm.'

Jez pricked up his ears. 'Is Aled one of your brothers?'

'Aled's the man Cadi's father wanted her to marry,' said Poppy promptly.

'Oh?' said Jez. He was hoping to appear nonchalant, but inside he was fighting the urge to ask a hundred questions.

Cadi gave Poppy a withering glance, before turning to Jez. 'He's also the feller that shopped Maria to the authorities.'

Jez furrowed his brow. 'I thought Maria didn't know who'd blown the whistle on her, save that it was some feller with a Welsh accent?'

'The brewery didn't give her a name, but Aled wasn't happy when he heard we were leaving to go to Liverpool and a sneaky underhand manoeuvre like this is right up his alley,' snapped Cadi bitterly. 'I knew what he was like from the start, but would my father listen?'

Poppy rolled her eyes. 'We've no proof that it was Aled. And even if it was, we're still here, so his plan didn't work.'

'Thank goodness,' remarked Jez. Eager to side with Cadi, he continued, 'But for the grace of God, Aled might have been successful.'

Izzy was wrinkling her brow. 'Why on earth was your father so keen for you to marry someone so horrid?'

Cadi pulled a face. 'Because Aled's father is a landowner running a successful farm, which in Dad's eyes makes him the perfect catch.'

'Rumour has it his family have plenty of money,' Poppy added absent-mindedly. 'There's a lot of women who would see him as ideal marriage material.'

Cadi shrugged. 'Bully for them! Even if I liked Aled – which I don't – I really couldn't give a monkey's how much of anything he has. He's not the man for me, nor will he ever be.'

Jez fell silent as the three women continued to talk. Up until now Jez had believed that he was the only man on Cadi's horizon, and whilst he should have been assured by her response that he had nothing to fear from Aled, he had heard that the more someone appeared to dislike another person, the more they were hiding their true feelings. Staring glumly into the water, he listened with half an ear as Cadi continued to tell the others that if Aled ever turned up at the B&B she would fill his mattress with itching powder. He nodded thoughtfully to himself. *The lady doth protest too much!* Not only that, but if she really hated this Aled, surely she wouldn't allow him to set foot in the pub?

Feeling certain that Cadi secretly held a torch for the farmer, Jez would simply have to hope that the other man never showed his face down the Greyhound.

With the time getting on, Izzy got to her feet. 'I'd better be off, so's I can get his tea on before he comes home.'

'You sound like Cinderella,' said Cadi. 'Rushing home before her carriage turns into a pumpkin.'

Izzy smiled faintly. 'I suppose I am a bit like Cinderella.'

'Only without the happy ending,' said Poppy. 'Unless you've changed your mind of course?'

'Like I said, I'll think about it,' reaffirmed Izzy.

'You always say that,' said Cadi with a wry smile.

'Softly, softly, catchee monkey,' said Jez.

'Jez is right,' said Izzy. 'I'll leave, but in my own time.'

'You'll be too long in the tooth to join up, at this rate,' observed Poppy casually.

Poppy might have been joking, but something in her words struck a chord with Izzy. Her first response had been to laugh, but no one knew how long the war would go on for. Her secret hope had been that the government would conscript women as it had the men, because that way she could have blamed the government for making her leave. But what if it never did? She voiced her thoughts to the others.

'You could be waiting for ever,' said Jez. 'I wish we'd known your thoughts before.'

'Why?' said Izzy quizzically. 'What difference would it have made?'

He nodded at her arm. 'You'd not have had those bruises, for a start.'

She wrinkled her brow, still unclear as to what he was getting at.

'Because you'd have left already,' explained Cadi. 'Or at least we'd have hoped you would.'

'Do you really think they won't conscript women?' asked Izzy anxiously. 'I know they've already taken on lots, so they definitely need us, whether it be delivering messages across the country, taking the sailors their post or working as a wireless operator.'

'Blimey! It's clear to see you've given this some serious thought,' said Cadi, 'but what if the war ends before the government conscripts women? Have you thought about that? You'd be stuck with your father for ever.'

Izzy pulled her cardigan from around her waist and pushed her arm into one of the sleeves. 'I'll wait until my bruises go, then see how I feel.'

'And you think he won't give you more bruises, once that lot have gone?' said Cadi, arching a brow in query.

Izzy gave her friends a grim smile. 'Probably, which is why I shall make certain I do everything I can to appease him.' She held up a hand as the others began to protest that it had never been Izzy who was at fault. 'Let me do things at my own pace.'

August 1940

The months that followed the licensing complaint had been trying all round. Not just because Maria was suspicious of every customer, believing them to be working undercover either for the brewery or for the licensing offices, but also because the girls kept forgetting that they weren't allowed to collect glasses any more, and every time they accidentally wandered through to the bar they were met with an exasperated cry of 'Back to the kitchen, please' from Maria.

As time went on, the girls got used to their new boundaries, and life became a little easier when Maria had a tip-off that one of their new regulars had in fact been working for the brewery.

'I know you suspected Aled, Cadi, but for all we know, the licensing offices might've made the whole thing up, just to shut me down and renew the licence to a man. So whilst we can relax a little, I still don't want you in the bar until you're old enough. And as you'll both be turning eighteen soon, we won't have to tread on eggshells for too much longer.'

'When I was little I was always wishing to be older than I was,' Cadi told Poppy and Maria. 'Mam always used to say I was wishing my life away. I didn't understand her objections then and I still don't, because the day that I turn eighteen I can kiss all my worries goodbye.'

Maria gave Cadi a shrewd look as she wiped her hands on a tea towel. 'Sorry to disappoint, luvvy, but as far as I'm concerned, eighteen is when all your worries start.'

Cadi and Poppy stared at her, aghast. 'How on earth do you work that out?' said Poppy. 'When you're eighteen you can drink, serve drinks, join the services and do anything you want without getting your parents' consent – in fact everything that you couldn't do when you were seventeen. What's so bad about that?'

'It's bad because you're considered responsible for your own actions, in the eyes of the law,' explained Maria. 'For example, when you were being accused of serving drinks underage, it wasn't you that was going to get into trouble, but me. I'm the adult, therefore I'm the one who's liable for your actions. Same as if you were caught drinking underage in a pub – it'd be the landlord that'd get into trouble; you'd just get a rollicking from the scuffers, and possibly your parents.' She wagged a warning finger. 'And if you're a feller, you can get called up for service whether you want to go or not, and maybe even sent to the front line, so think on.'

Cadi looked crestfallen. 'I thought being eighteen meant we'd be footloose and fancy free, but you make it sound the exact opposite.'

Maria smiled kindly. 'Being eighteen comes with its pros as well as its cons.'

'Now I see what my mam was on about,' muttered Cadi glumly.

Poppy nudged her arm. 'Come on, it's not all bad – we'll have our freedom.'

'At a price!' said Cadi. She looked at Maria. 'Is that why people say that your school years are the best in your life?'

Maria grinned. 'Possibly, although you don't think so at the time.'

'I couldn't wait to leave school,' said Poppy. 'I was never any good at it.'

'Me neither,' agreed Cadi.

Hearing someone enter the bar, Maria walked through to see to the customer.

'Have you thought any more about joining the services when you turn eighteen?' Poppy asked Cadi.

Cadi pulled a disgruntled face. 'Knowing my luck, I'd end up on the same base as Aled, and I couldn't stand the thought of having to call him sir and saluting him every time he walked past.'

'Ooh, you're right there. I hadn't thought of that,' admitted Poppy. 'He'd be lapping it up.'

'I wouldn't be able to keep it zipped,' admitted Cadi, 'I know I wouldn't, and then what? Court-martialled for telling Aled he's an interfering, pompous pig.'

Poppy quickly stifled a shriek of laughter behind her fingers. 'Cadi! You can't call a pilot a pig.'

'Exactly,' said Cadi. 'And that's why I'm not bothering with the services. First of all, I love working in the B&B – it's almost like it's my baby, if that makes sense?'

Poppy frowned. 'Not really. Work's work, if you ask me.'

'I thought you loved working here,' said Cadi, clearly disappointed.

'It's all right, but I don't enjoy it as much as you. I find changing the bedding a bind and I hate scrubbing sheets, but I'll grant you it's better than working in the bakery.'

Not realising that Poppy felt so strongly, Cadi continued, 'If the B&B's not for you, then what is?'

Poppy shrugged. 'Dunno. I suppose I've still to find my niche.'

Knowing that her friend had never ruled out the services, Cadi probed further. 'You still want to join up, don't you?'

Poppy pulled an awkward smile. 'I do, but not on my own, so I guess I'm stuck here for the time being – unless you have a change of heart of course,' she added hopefully.

'Sorry, Poppy, but I can't see that happening any time soon,' confessed Cadi. 'It's such a shame we don't know anyone else who's considering—' she began, before stopping abruptly. 'Only we do, or at least I think she would, if she thought she was going in with a friend.'

Poppy stared blankly at Cadi until the penny dropped. 'Izzy?'

'Exactly. I don't know why we didn't think of it before.'

'Because we're underage?' hazarded Poppy.

'True,' agreed Cadi, 'but you're going to be eighteen in less than a month – that should be more than enough time for Izzy's bruises to go. What do you think?'

Poppy couldn't hide her disappointment. 'I dunno. I'd love to join the services, but I wanted to do it with you.'

'I know, Poppy, but even if Aled wasn't in the RAF, we still couldn't both leave Maria – it really wouldn't be fair.' Cadi reached across the kitchen table and clasped Poppy's hands. 'You know how much I love running the B&B, and I honestly can't say I'd feel the same about the services, but that shouldn't stop you following your dreams, as long as they *are* still your dreams.'

Nodding miserably, Poppy felt the tears coming. 'I can't believe we're talking about going our separate ways. It doesn't seem right.'

Cadi laid her cards on the table. 'Be honest: if you saw Izzy going off to the join the WAAF, how would it make you feel?'

Poppy dropped her gaze. 'Jealous.' She looked back up. 'Why wouldn't it you?' she continued, before Cadi had a chance to reply. 'What happened to experiencing a bit of life? The services would be perfect for that.'

'I *am* experiencing life,' said Cadi with assurance. 'You always said you didn't think I'd cope with all the rules and regulations, and you were right. I love being my own boss.'

'You're not, though,' said Poppy sullenly, 'not really. It's Maria what holds the licence, not you.'

'Agreed, but it was us who created the B&B, Poppy. We started it from scratch and we run every part of it, from the bookings, to cooking the breakfasts, even providing meals for those that want them. And that's all down to us, *not* Maria.'

'I know,' said Poppy dejectedly, 'but why did you tell Jez you weren't ready for a relationship? I thought, by that, you meant you wanted to spread your wings a bit more, and I think Jez was under the same impression?'

'You're right, I do want to spread my wings. And I'm rather hoping to have my own business one of these days, so that I can truly be my own boss, just like Maria.'

Poppy's eyes widened. 'You want to run a pub?'

'Not a pub,' said Cadi, hastily. 'I've got my heart set on a café or tea room – something like that.'

'Gosh, you are a dark horse!' said Poppy.

'Not really. I'm still young, Poppy, and I might well change my mind again before the year's out, which is why I've not mentioned it until now.' She sighed heavily. 'I don't want to be like my mam, jumping into marriage before I've had a chance to live a little first.'

'So that's it, then?' said Poppy softly.

'I guess so,' said Cadi, adding hurriedly, 'but if we go our separate ways, it doesn't mean to say we can't be friends any more. We can write, telephone, visit – all sorts of things. And you haven't even applied yet, so it'll be ages before you go.'

Poppy stared at her oldest, dearest friend. 'It feels like you want me to go.'

Cadi's jaw dropped. 'I don't! I want what's best for you, what makes *you* happy. I'd keep you here in a heartbeat, but that would be selfish of me. In fact I'd be worse than my father, and that's how I know that even though we're closer than sisters, you'd end up resenting me, because that's the way I'd started to feel towards him.'

'I know,' said Poppy, the words leaving her lips in almost a whisper. 'I just wish things were different.'

'Me too, but maybe that's part and parcel of growing up: you have to make decisions that you might not like. Maria did say it wouldn't be easy.'

'I didn't think it would happen this soon,' said Poppy. She hated the idea of leaving Cadi, but at the same time she very much wanted to experience life as a Waaf. And Cadi was right: Poppy was already resenting her friend for wanting to stay in Liverpool. Pulling herself together, she tried to put on a brave face. 'We're seeing Izzy on Friday, perhaps we should put it to her: see what she says?'

'What if she says no?' said Cadi.

Poppy thought this through carefully before answering. 'I still want to join, so I guess I need to stop relying on other people and take responsibility for myself. So whatever the outcome, I shall be doing just that.'

Maria poked her head around the door. 'Two cottage pies, please – full veg on one, and all but carrots on the other. Ta.'

Poppy stood up. 'Right you are. I'll give you a shout when we've plated up.'

As they doled out the food onto the plates, she turned her thoughts to how things would be for Cadi, once she'd gone. 'Do you think you'll manage without me?'

'It won't be anywhere near as much fun,' said Cadi, 'and I'll have to work a lot harder, especially when it comes to washing the sheets, but I'll manage because I'll have to.'

'I won't miss doing the laundry,' admitted Poppy. 'I'm pretty sure it's one of the few jobs they don't ask you to do in the services.'

Cadi picked up the potato-peeling knife. 'Good job you're a dab hand with one of these, because from what I hear, they make you peel mountains of potatoes.'

The girls spent the rest of the evening discussing Poppy's future in the services and, as Maria called time, they had both come to accept the decision.

'I won't tell Maria yet, not until we know what's going on with Izzy,' said Poppy as the girls prepared themselves for bed.

'It'll be a surprise for Maria,' mused Cadi.

Poppy shrugged. 'She knows we tried joining up when we first came to Liverpool, so I dare say maybe not. And at least you're staying behind, so she won't have to worry about finding someone to take over the running of the B&B.' A smile hovered on Poppy's lips. 'Jez'll be relieved.'

'I expect he will, not that it'll make any difference—' Cadi began, only to be cut short by her friend.

'Oh, come on, Cadi,' said Poppy, her voice muffled as she pulled her nightgown over her head. 'If you're not planning on joining up, then what's stopping you? You already know you want your future to be in Liverpool, so why not complete the jigsaw with Jez?'

'I've told you why: I don't want to end up like my mam,' spluttered Cadi. 'Not only that, but I'd gone from wanting to join the services to running a B&B in a matter of months, so who's to say I won't change my mind again? And that's my point, Poppy. I'm still too young to know exactly what it is I want to do, and it would be unfair of me to include Jez in my life when even I don't know where I'm heading.'

'Fair enough,' conceded Poppy. Hearing Maria ascending the stairs, she placed a finger to her lips, signalling Cadi to be quiet.

Later that night, as Cadi lay in her bed, she thought about the conversation she and Poppy had had in the kitchen. It seemed that one minute they had been talking about Izzy, and the next they were planning to go their separate ways! *No more Poppy*, thought Cadi, as a solitary tear tracked its way down her cheek.

Poppy too was thinking about their conversation, and how she would be going off to enjoy pastures new, whilst her friend stayed behind. She heaved a sigh. Moving on was definitely the right decision, but that didn't mean to say it wouldn't come without a great deal of sadness. Wondering what her parents would say when they knew she was leaving the pub without Cadi, she wiped a tear from her eye. Growing up wasn't proving to be as much fun as she first thought.

The next day the girls decided to run the idea past Jez while they waited for Izzy and see what he thought of their proposal.

'Two birds, one stone,' said Jez. 'It's kind of like the best of both worlds.' As he spoke, he skimmed a stone across the lake and they each silently counted the number of bounces.

'Eight!' cried Cadi. 'I'm lucky if I get more than one. What's the secret?'

Picking up a stone, he inspected it for smoothness and beckoned Cadi over. 'Come here and I'll show you.' He handed her the stone, then placed his arms around her. Brushing his chin against her shoulder, he cupped his hand around hers and positioned her correctly. 'You need the right angle,' said Jez informatively, 'after that, it's all down to the flick of the wrist. Let your hand go limp and I'll guide it for you.'

Cadi did as she was told, but she was finding it hard to concentrate when the warmth of Jez's breath was sending a delightful sensation down her neck.

Oblivious of the effect he was having on her, Jez took control of her hand and together they sent the stone skimming across the surface of the lake. Cadi squealed with delight as they counted three bounces. 'Oh, Jez, I did it!' She turned to Poppy. 'Did you see?'

Poppy gave her friend a small round of applause. 'Well done, you.' She sat down on the bank. 'Everything's changing.'

'I wouldn't call skimming stones—' Cadi began, but Poppy was shaking her head.

'I mean there once was a time when you wouldn't dream of letting a feller show you how to do summat. I remember when Aled tried to show you how to knock coconuts off their shies.' She giggled softly. 'I think he had more chance of hell freezing over than of you taking his advice.'

'That was different, though,' said Cadi as she began searching through the pebbles beneath her feet. 'Aled was being patronising. Jez was trying to help.'

'Nope,' said Poppy casually, 'it's more than that: you've changed a lot.'

Cadi looked up. 'I have?'

Poppy nodded. 'You're far more relaxed. Nowhere near as guarded as you once were.'

Cadi mulled this over as she looked for the smoothest pebbles. 'I guess I don't feel I have to prove myself any more.'

'Who were you trying to prove yourself to?' asked Poppy.

Cadi gave a brief grimace. 'If you'd asked me that a while back, I'd have probably said Dad, but I still haven't proved myself to him, so I guess I was trying to prove it to myself.'

'Prove what, though?' said Jez, who felt like he was getting a little lost in the conversation.

'That I can survive without the help of a man,' said Cadi simply. She began ticking off her achievements on her fingers. 'I left home, found employment – one where I haven't got a man telling me what to do, I might add – and I've built on that, making it better than it was.' She smiled hastily at Poppy. 'Of course I'm including you in all of my achievements, because we did it together.'

Picking up another stone, Jez handed it to Cadi. 'Do you think your father will ever accept your accomplishments?'

Cadi pulled a rueful face. 'I doubt it. He'll probably insist until his last breath that I could have had a better life if I'd stayed in Rhos and married Aled.'

'I know this Aled's father owns some land,' said Jez, 'but what's *so* special about him that makes your father so keen for you and him to get together?'

Cadi rolled her eyes. 'Darned if I know.'

'Yes, you do,' cried Poppy indignantly. 'He's handsome.' She wagged a finger as Cadi began to protest. 'He is, Cadi, whether you like to admit it or not. Not just that, but Aled lives in the same village, so you'd always be close by, *and* you'd never have to worry about money.'

'He sounds perfect,' said Jez, quietly.

'Maybe to you,' said Cadi resolutely, 'but *not* to me.'

Jez couldn't help wondering: if Cadi was going to turn down someone as perfect as Aled, how on earth did a dockworker like himself stand a chance?

Cadi picked up a pebble and showed it to Jez. 'How about this one?'

Taking the stone, he nodded as he handed it back. 'Perfect! Now remember to slant the stone sufficiently to hit the water, but not go in.'

Nodding, Cadi did as Jez had shown her, only this time without his assistance, and when the stone left her hand, they all watched it bounce across the water. Beaming with delight, she bent down to find another stone. 'You're a brilliant teacher, Jez. One lesson and I'm getting five bounces.'

Poppy shaded her eyes with her hand as she scoured the park for a sign of Izzy. 'She's awfully late. Do you think she's all right?'

Cadi's tummy lurched unpleasantly. She could only think of two reasons why their friend was late. Either Izzy was caught up running messages, or Eric had found out about their secret meetings. She said as much to her friends.

Jez picked up another stone, weighted it in his hand, then skimmed it across the water, causing ripples. 'You can forget her being late because of chores. Meeting us is the highlight of Izzy's day. She always ensures she has plenty of time for unseen eventualities.'

Poppy stared at him, her eyes rounding. 'You think Eric's found out?'

'Maybe. I remember the time he gave her that scar across her eye. She didn't show up to school for at least a month.' He shook his head ruefully. 'When she came back it was obvious what had happened. Not that anyone asked her outright, of course. What's the point?

248

She'd only have lied, said it was summat she'd done by accident.'

Cadi shook her head, sending her blonde curls bouncing around her shoulders. 'Why didn't someone intervene? I understand you couldn't do anything, Jez, as you were only a kid yourself, but what about the teachers?'

Jez shrugged. 'Dunno. If they did say summat, we never got to hear of it; and even if they did, Eric obviously didn't listen, because it wasn't the last time Izzy was kept from school, only to return a short while later with fading bruises.'

Cadi and Poppy exchanged glances. 'So where do we go from here?' asked Poppy anxiously. 'We can't arrange to meet her again without seeing her first, but we can't go to her house, in case someone sees us and tells Eric.'

'It seems that we're stuck between a rock and a hard place,' said Jez. He sat down on the grass between Cadi and Poppy. 'This is going to take some careful consideration.'

The three discussed various options, all of which drew a blank for one reason or another, until Poppy had the bright idea of a letter. 'Eric leaves before the mail arrives,' she said slowly, 'so he won't know Izzy's received anything, and I very much doubt the postman will say owt. So if we write her a letter, saying Cadi and I will be at the Palm House at two o'clock every day, then she's bound to be able to come, sooner or later.'

'Only what if she doesn't?' said Cadi. 'What if Eric's threatened her so badly she never goes out again?'

This suggestion was quickly dismissed by Jez. 'There's no way Eric's going to do his own laundry. You mark my words, Izzy will be back out, once the bruising and swelling's gone down.'

They had written the letter later that evening whilst Maria was busy behind the bar. Deciding it to be beneficial, they had informed Izzy of Poppy's intention to join the services. 'That way,' said Poppy, as she licked the envelope, 'she'll have a heads-up and it might even persuade her to leave the house earlier.'

'I wish we could do more to help,' said Cadi.

Jez smiled encouragingly. 'You're offering Izzy a way out, and that's more than anyone else round here has done.'

Sealing the envelope, Poppy licked the stamp and fixed it into place. 'All we have to do now, is hope for the best.'

Having Cadi, Poppy and Jez as friends was the best thing that could ever have happened to Izzy. As a child she had never been able to comprehend why her father had forbidden her to have any pals of her own, but since meeting the girls she now understood perfectly. Part of growing up is about learning what's normal and what's not, and Eric had obviously feared that if Izzy went round to a pal's house for tea, she would quickly learn that her life was not normal. This had been confirmed when comparing notes with the girls. Their reactions to her tales had given her validation that it was her father to blame for his temper, and not Izzy herself.

The girls had often talked about Izzy escaping her father, a topic that unsettled her, because even though it was a rotten life, it was the only one she knew, and fear of the unknown made her jittery. A small smile tweaked the corners of her mouth. It might make her feel uneasy, but at least they were giving her hopes for a better future – something she'd never had until they came along. She mused on how the mere thought of knowing that she had people on her side, to pick her up when she was feeling low, was invaluable. Her friends had given her the strength to believe in herself and see her father for what he was: a man of low self-esteem, who chose to crush others in order to make himself feel better.

Before Cadi, Poppy and Jez had come into her life, Izzy used to dread waking up in the morning, fearing that she would inadvertently do something to annoy her father and provoke his wrath. Since their arrival all that had changed. Each morning she would wake up happy in the knowledge that she would be meeting her friends later in the day and they would spend many a happy hour chatting or playing games such as hide-and-seek or tag. She supposed ruefully now that she must have been naive to expect her new-found happiness to last.

Staring glumly out of the window to the street below, she recalled the day of the ... She hesitated. Before meeting the girls, she would have referred to it as an overreaction on her father's part, but now she could see it for what it was: an attack. She had been cleaning out the dresser when she had inadvertently uncovered a couple of old photographs. Taking a closer look at the people in the first picture had taken her breath away. She had no memories of her mother and, apart from her father's word, she couldn't be certain whether she resembled her or not. So to discover a photograph of her mother in a wedding dress had come as quite a shock. Keen to see more, Izzy had fished out the magnifying glass that her father used for the small print in the newspapers and examined the photo in close detail. She had the same eyes, mouth and nose as her mam – only her hair was different. Her mother had beautiful thick curls, whereas Izzy's curls were fine and limp. Staring at the photograph, Izzy imagined what she would say to her mother if she could hear her. She knew the answer before the question had left her mind. *Why did you leave me with him? You must've known what he was like, yet you walked out without so much as a backward glance.* She then wondered what her mother's response might be. Would she care? Would she cry? Would she mumble some ridiculous excuse or would she have something plausible to say? Had Eric beaten his wife into leaving and, if so, why hadn't she taken Izzy with her?

As she continued to gaze at the photograph, she willed herself to be angry at the woman who'd walked out on her, but how could she be, when she didn't know the answers to any of her questions? She turned her attention to the second photograph. It was Izzy's mother, and Eric, only they were both older, and Izzy's mother held a baby – which Izzy assumed to be herself – on her knee. Izzy stared into her mother's eyes. She looked distraught, anxious even. Izzy looked to Eric who was looking at the photographer with a hate and loathing which Izzy knew all too well. Feeling a sense of unease, she concentrated on her mother. She was a lot larger than she had been in the first photograph and her curls were no longer plump as they once were. Turning it over Izzy looked at the back where someone had written their names and dated it the 7th of July 1920. Izzy had been so engrossed with her finding, she hadn't heard her father enter the room. Wanting to know what had caught his daughter's attention, he had ripped the wedding photo from her hands. As his eyes settled on the picture, Izzy could see the anger swelling inside him.

'And you wonder why I don't trust you,' Eric had growled, 'when you're the spit of that bitch of a woman?' His hands trembling with rage, he maliciously tore the photograph up and threw it onto the floor. Not wanting to lose the only connection she had with her mother, Izzy had knelt down to gather up the pieces whilst secreting the remaining picture in her skirt pocket.

Now, as she gingerly touched her swollen eye, she realised that this had been a stupid thing to do. Her father had been angry enough on seeing the photograph, but the thought that his daughter was keen to keep it had tipped him over the edge. He removed his belt with one swift motion and rained down the lashes on Izzy, who cowered in the corner. Clutching the remains of the photograph in her fingers, she curled into a ball, in a bid to protect herself from the onslaught.

When Eric had delivered what Izzy believed to be his final stroke, she peeked out from behind her arm. Seeing his daughter looking up at him reignited his anger and he delivered one last blow, catching her across the side of her face and splitting her lip. Smothering her scream in the crook of her elbow, Izzy curled back into a ball.

Whether her father knew he had gone too far she couldn't be sure, but he had soon retreated, leaving the house in favour of the pub. As she uncurled, she noticed that her skirt and the floor beneath it were damp; at first she couldn't understand why she was wet until she realised it stemmed from her crotch. Izzy would have cried in self-pity, but Eric had beaten her too many times for her to start feeling sorry for herself. Getting to her feet, Izzy examined her face in the mirror, watching as her eye began to puff up and close. She turned her attention to the blood running from the cut on her lip. Fishing for a piece of tissue out of her skirt pocket, she tentatively dabbed it dry. How could she meet the girls tomorrow, looking like this? Even though they were fully aware of Eric's temper, Izzy would still feel embarrassed and ashamed that she had tried to defend his actions in the past.

Now, seeing the postman coming down the street, she was a little surprised that he appeared to push a white envelope through their letterbox, as all their post usually came in brown ones, being bills and the like. Descending the stairs, she went to the mat by the door and picked up the envelopes. Her eyes widened as she read her name on the outside of the white one, and she immediately ripped it open and read the contents. Happy tears formed in her eyes. She had always known that Cadi, Poppy and Jez were special friends, but this just went to prove it.

Dearest Izzy,

We do hope this letter finds you safe and well. We know things can be awkward, and you can't always come and see us for one reason or another, so we've come up with a plan. We shall go to the aviary outside the Palm House every day at two o'clock. We would love to see you, no matter the circumstances, so please do try and come to see us if you can.

Poppy is going into the services, but I'm staying put. We think it would be wonderful if you decided to go along with her – perhaps even sign up together – but if you feel you're unable to, then that's fine too. Please do let us know if you're well, as we worry so about you.

Fondest wishes, Cadi and Poppy

Tucking the letter into her skirt pocket, Izzy went to the parlour and inspected her reflection in the mirror that stood atop the sideboard. The swelling had gone down considerably over the past week or so, but the bruising was still visible. If she had been the sort of girl who used make-up, she thought she would have been able to conceal the bruises beneath a heavy layer of foundation. But her father wouldn't allow anything like that in his house, claiming it was the mask of a tart – she rolled her eyes – the same as her mother.

Sitting down at the kitchen table, she drew the letter out of her pocket and read it through to make sure she had got the details correct, before placing it in the fire-place and setting it alight. Eric wouldn't dream of checking Izzy for letters, because it wouldn't cross his mind that somebody might write to her, but even so, she wasn't prepared to take any chances.

As she watched the flames lick the corner of the letter, she turned her thoughts to the suggestion that she and Poppy join up together. Until recently she had been intent on standing by her father, reasoning that he couldn't treat her this way for ever, but now she questioned how many beatings it would take for Eric to finally concede that she wasn't such a bad daughter? She'd always done his bidding and had never gone against his wishes, yet that hadn't made the blindest bit of difference.

She tried to envisage what her life would have been like, had Cadi and Poppy not come into it, and grimaced. It would have been awful, and she had to admit that with or without them, she would still have received her latest beating – the only difference being that she now had someone to turn to. So why hadn't she grasped that opportunity with both hands and left already? *Because you've been so scared of what might happen that you daren't even try,* she thought to herself. *If you don't do it now, you never will, and the next time he raises his hand, he really might go too far.* With this thought clear in her mind, she came to a decision. Eric hadn't banned her from going out – he really didn't care who saw Izzy. As far as he was concerned, she had got what she deserved. It was she who chose to stay at home, rather than see people staring at her in horror whilst whispering behind their hands, knowing full well they were all probably saying what she was thinking: 'What's wrong with her? Why doesn't she leave?'

Izzy gave a short, hollow laugh. Leaving was easier said than done, especially when she had nowhere to go, and no one to go there with. She knew it would only be a matter of time before Eric hounded her down and thrashed her for doing exactly what her mother had done. The fact that her mother had left him for another man, and left Izzy for her freedom, wouldn't enter her father's mind, as he would still tar them with the same brush.

Only now she wouldn't have to go on her own, because Poppy would be going with her. And whilst her friends hadn't written down a specific timeline, Izzy assumed they would join up, then wait for their acceptance papers to come through.

In the meantime she would have to make sure she did nothing to annoy her father. She tutted beneath her breath. How could she do that, when anything could set him off? She would have to keep everything crossed that this last beating had been enough to satisfy him for some time to come. This brought her to another train of thought. How long did it take, from applying to join, to actually leaving for the services? She'd overheard conversations in the market where people had said it ranged from days to weeks.

Whatever the answer, she would just have to hope it was sooner rather than later, because she was leaving!

Eager to hear if there was any news on Izzy, Jez knocked on the back door of the Greyhound. 'It's me, Jez.'

Cadi opened the door and stepped outside. Taking him by the crook of the elbow, she walked him up the road until they were out of earshot.

He raised his brow hopefully. 'I take it you have news?'

Cadi shook her head. 'I guessed why you'd come calling, and Maria's in the kitchen, so ...'

He nodded wisely. 'So you thought it best to talk out here.'

She smiled meekly at him. 'I still feel awful about you having to lie to Maria on our behalf. I swear my cheeks turn scarlet every time she mentions your name.'

Jez placed his arm around her shoulders. 'That's because you're a good girl and you don't like lying to your friends. But you have to remember, you're only lying to protect her from the truth, as am I.'

Cadi wished fervently that she might lay her head on his shoulder and relax into his embrace, but she already felt as though she was taking advantage of Jez as it was, without leading him on. This thought made her pause. Would it be leading him on if she *wanted* him to do it? That was a good question, but she thought she already knew the answer. It would be leading him on, because she didn't wish to pursue a relationship with him – not yet at any rate. Why couldn't Jez have come into her life at a later date? She grimaced. If he had, goodness only knows what would have happened to Poppy; and not only that, but there's no way they'd ever have met Maria. Cadi chastised herself inwardly. Jez had come into their lives for a reason and, whether she liked it or not, she had a feeling his role in their lives was not yet over.

Realising she'd not said anything for a while, she spoke up. 'I'll feel a lot happier when we know what's happened to Izzy.'

Jez squeezed her shoulders, sending delightful sensations throughout her body. 'I'm afraid we probably know the answer as to what's happened to Izzy,' said Jez. 'You simply have to keep your fingers crossed that Eric hasn't hit her too badly this time.'

Cadi came to a halt. 'I wish she'd see through him and leave, because the sooner she does, the sooner we can stop lying to Maria.'

They turned back towards the pub. 'If anyone can persuade Izzy to leave her father, it's you.'

She hid the shy smile that donned her lips. 'I hope you're right.'

Jez absent-mindedly kissed the top of her head in a friendly fashion. 'I *know* I'm right!'

Chapter Seven

September 1940

It was several days after receiving the letter, and even though her blackened eye was still clearly visible, Izzy had finally summoned up the courage to go to Sefton Park and see if her friends had remained true to their word. As she approached the Palm House she could see Cadi and Poppy waving in order to get her attention. Beaming with relief, she waved back and headed over to the girls, who were already walking towards her.

'I worried you might have given up on me,' confided Izzy as they drew nearer.

'Never,' cried Cadi. 'I must say, it really is awfully good to see you again, although I'd prefer to see you without a black eye. Are you all right?'

Izzy nodded. 'I'll live.'

'We've been imagining all sorts,' admitted Poppy.

'Yeah, and none of it good,' confirmed Cadi, as she gestured to Izzy's black eye and thick lip with a jerk of her head. 'What was his excuse this time: stew too hot or too cold?'

Izzy filled the girls in on the photographs.

Cadi could hardly contain her anger. 'You mean he took the only photographs you had of your mother and destroyed them?'

Izzy twisted her lips to the side. 'Not entirely. I managed to keep the one of the three of us hidden, but it wasn't my favourite. Mum didn't look as pretty as she had in the wedding one.' She smiled softly. 'We're like peas in a pod, except that she's got thick curly hair.'

'Well I'm glad you managed to salvage something, but you can't keep excusing his behaviour,' cried Poppy. 'What Eric did was wrong, and you shouldn't just accept it.' Peeved that Izzy still appeared to be justifying her father's behaviour, she wagged a finger at her. 'That man's rotten to the core and nothing will ever change that.'

Nodding meekly, Izzy gave the girls a grim smile. 'I know. I suppose I always have, but I've never seen him as angry as he was this time, and it makes me wonder how far he would go, which is why I've made my mind up to join the services.'

Poppy inhaled sharply. '*Really?*'

Cadi was clapping her hands excitedly. 'Good for you, Izzy!'

Relieved that she was finally able to share the good news with her pals, Izzy explained how she had come to her decision. 'I realised that I could never please my father, because I'm not the one he's angry at.' She shrugged in a nonchalant manner. 'I could spend the rest of my life trying to make up for something someone else did, and he still wouldn't be satisfied.'

Cadi blew her cheeks out. It seemed Izzy really was intent on leaving her father. 'I don't care what made you change your mind,' she said. 'I'm only grateful you did.'

'So what happens next?' said Izzy. 'I don't suppose we can apply today – only I've brought my birth certificate, just in case?'

Cadi and Poppy exchanged looks, before breaking into delighted laughter.

Seeing the bewildered look on Izzy's face, Cadi explained the reason behind their mirth. 'For you to say you want to leave is one thing, but to hear you say you want to leave this very minute is even better.'

'So can we?' asked Izzy excitedly. 'Only I've been dreaming about this day ever since I received your letter and quite frankly, I can't wait to be off. In fact the sooner, the better.'

'Strike whilst the iron's hot,' agreed Poppy. 'Only I've not got my papers with me, so perhaps we'd be better leaving this until tomorrow?' Seeing the disappointment on Izzy's face, she continued, 'Cadi and I only have a few hours in the afternoon and we won't have time, not on top of everything else we have to do.'

Cadi cleared her throat. 'I've got to learn to cope without you sooner or later, so why not start today? After all, there's no real reason why you shouldn't, and I'd rather you do it now, in case summat happens to change Izzy's mind.' She eyed Izzy gravely. 'You do realise that once you've signed up there's no going back?'

Izzy nodded assuredly. 'Trust me, nothing is going to change my mind, so if you'd rather wait an extra day, it won't make the blindest bit of difference, not as far as I'm concerned.'

Poppy looked expectantly at her. 'You say you've got the necessary papers with you to join up?'

In answer, Izzy pulled her birth certificate from her skirt pocket. 'Like I said, I've not thought of anything else.'

Poppy smiled bravely at her oldest friend. 'Then that's settled it. I'll get my papers and tell Maria that I've decided to join up. I'll just not mention who with – not yet. That's fair enough, don't you think?'

'Best to keep shtum until you're on the train, I reckon,' said Cadi. 'I don't see the sense in poking the bear when there's no need.' She turned to Izzy. 'Are you all right to wait here whilst Poppy fetches her certificate?'

Izzy's tummy fluttered with excitement. 'I won't move an inch.'

The girls jogged down and out of the park. 'I can't believe it,' said Poppy excitedly. 'I'm actually going to join the WAAF or ATS or …' she clapped her hands enthusiastically, 'whoever'll have me!'

'I can't believe Izzy's going with you,' said Cadi. 'How do you think Maria will take the news when she hears you're joining up? She might be a little surprised you're doing it so quickly.'

'She won't bat an eyelid – you know what Maria's like, she takes everything in her stride. I'll tell her I've been thinking about it for a while and decided today was the day,' said Poppy, 'which is true, when you think about it.'

Poppy was quite correct that Maria took the news exactly as she predicted. Standing at the kitchen door, Cadi waved Poppy off. 'I'll keep everything crossed for you.'

Back inside the kitchen, Maria eyed Cadi thoughtfully. 'So how come you're not going with her? I thought you two were inseparable?'

Cadi shrugged. She had no qualms about telling Maria the truth. 'We did talk about it, but I think I've found my niche, as it were. Poppy's been happy here too, but she's been eager to try life as a servicewoman for some time now.'

'So your staying has nothing to do with a certain young gentleman?' asked Maria, arching an eyebrow.

Cadi laughed. 'You're as bad as Poppy! But in answer to your question: no, my decision has nothing to do with Jez.'

Racing to the park, Poppy was relieved and delighted to see that Izzy hadn't changed her mind. 'Ready?'

Izzy nodded. 'As I'll ever be.'

Before they set off, Poppy unzipped her handbag and produced a headscarf, which she handed to Izzy. 'We've never ventured into the city together before, so I think it's best if you put this on. What do you think?'

In answer, Izzy took the scarf and tied it around her head. She looked at Poppy. 'Better?'

Poppy tweaked the sides of the scarf so that they hid part of Izzy's face. 'Much!'

Linking arms, they began walking to the recruiting office.

'I don't think I've ever felt so nervous in all my life,' confessed Izzy as they approached the entrance to the office.

'You'll be fine,' Poppy reassured her, 'but if it's any consolation, I'm nervous too. This is a big step we're taking, and last time I came here it didn't exactly pan out as I'd planned.'

The girls had hoped they would be the only ones wanting to join up that day, and were therefore disappointed to find themselves standing at the back of a rather long queue – something that Izzy didn't relish.

'I'm scared someone's going to recognise me and go blabbing to my dad.'

Poppy looked up and down the line of hopefuls. 'If you keep your head down, I reckon you should be fine. They all seem too caught up in their own affairs to be nosing around seeing who's here.'

To the girls' relief, they soon reached the front of the queue. Having given their names and addresses, they held their breath as the young man inspected their birth certificates and handed them back.

'Go home and wait for your papers to arrive.'

Izzy glanced at Poppy. 'Is that it? Are we in?'

Nodding, the young man glanced impatiently at the lengthy queue behind the girls. 'You sure are. Now if you wouldn't mind moving along ...'

'How long will it be before we get our papers?' asked Izzy anxiously.

He turned his attention from the queue back to Izzy. 'Shouldn't be too long – maybe a couple of weeks at the most. Now if you don't mind?'

Almost giddy with relief, the girls headed out of the office.

Not stopping to celebrate, Poppy slipped her arm through Izzy's and gave it a squeeze. 'Not long now and we'll be bona fide members of His Majesty's armed forces.'

'I can't believe we've actually done it,' said Izzy. She removed the headscarf and handed it back to Poppy. 'All I have to do now is make sure I'm the first to reach the post.'

'You will be, because you *always* are,' Poppy assured her. 'Just make sure you hand the letter to me or Cadi, so that we can look after it for you – that way you won't have to worry about your father finding it by accident.'

Izzy smiled fondly at Poppy. 'I don't know what would have become of me if you two hadn't come into my life, but I'm certainly glad you did.'

'So are we,' affirmed Poppy. 'As soon as we heard who your father was, we knew there was no way we could sit idly by.'

'You're my angels!'

Poppy's cheeks coloured. 'I dunno about that.'

But Izzy was resolute. 'Take it from me. I've lived round this area my whole life and none of the others have so much as lifted a finger in my defence, cos they were too scared of what my dad would do to them if they did. But that didn't stop you and Cadi.'

'True, but until now we've been meeting in secret, so your dad doesn't know we exist, and I'd like to keep it that way,' said Poppy. 'Not only for our sake, but for Maria too, because I certainly wouldn't want her to get caught in the crossfire.'

'Trust me,' smiled Izzy, 'my father hasn't got a clue.'

The wait had been agonising. Poppy had received her papers within a week of applying, yet there was no sign of Izzy's.

'We applied together, so surely we should find out around the same time,' said Izzy, her tone rising anxiously. 'I don't understand it. We've not had any post at all, and we usually get something even if it's once a week.'

'Maybe a mix-up at the sorting office?' suggested Poppy.

'Ooh, there's a thought. They reckon the mail's taking for ever nowadays,' said Cadi. 'But how will you know if that's what's happened?'

'Perhaps go back to the recruiting office and ask them?' suggested Jez.

'Not if my life depended on it,' said Izzy firmly. 'It was bad enough taking the risk the first time around. I don't fancy pushing my luck a second time.'

'Ask your postie?' volunteered Poppy.

'What? And have him know I'm expecting something? No fear! He might mention summat to Dad.'

A frown creased Cadi's brow. 'I thought your dad never saw the postie?'

'He doesn't, but the fewer chances I take the better; and the fewer people who know, the less chance there is of Dad finding out.' Izzy nibbled the edge of her thumbnail. Whilst she was sure the lack of mail was nothing to worry about, it was unusual. Two weeks had passed since Poppy's acceptance and she was going to be heading for Sandhurst in a week and a half's time.

'The mail is getting in a bit of a muddle, what with the war and all,' said Jez informatively. 'I expect that's what's happened. The office staff have been whingeing about it at work, because it's affected the payroll.'

Cadi brightened. 'There you are! Even big compan-ies like the one Jez works for are having problems. I'm sure it's nothing to worry about.'

Izzy glanced at Poppy. 'Have you told your mam and dad yet?'

'I certainly have, and they were that proud, Mam started crying.'

There came a harrumph from Cadi, who aired her grievance. 'Aye, and they told my mam and dad. And Dad was straight on the blower, demanding to know why I wasn't going with Poppy. I told him I wanted to stay at the pub, and he muttered something I can't repeat before handing the phone back to Mam.'

Izzy grimaced. 'He wasn't too chuffed then?'

'I'd say furious about covers it,' sighed Cadi. 'Mam says he'd rather I was in the WAAF than in a pub.'

'He won't have it that the Greyhound's a lovely B&B as well as a pub,' said Poppy. 'He needs to come and see you – that'd soon change his mind.'

'I've told him to, but he says he's too busy doing a real job,' said Cadi, rolling her eyes. 'Dad won't be happy until I'm back in that bakery, but that's never going to happen.'

Jez smiled to himself. When he had first heard of Poppy's plans to join up, he had lived in fear that Cadi would change her mind and do the same, so to hear her confirm that she wanted to stay in Liverpool was music to his ears.

Believing that Jez had been correct about the missing papers, they laid the matter to rest, until he came and met the girls out of the blue a few days later in Sefton Park.

Seeing him approach, Cadi wiped her skirt free from grass as she leapt to her feet. 'Hello. Fancy seeing you here!'

Jez smiled back grimly. 'I'm afraid this isn't a social visit.' He glanced past Cadi to Izzy, who was still sitting on the grass beside Poppy. 'I think I know where your letter's gone.'

Izzy's heart dropped. She did not like the look on Jez's face. 'Where?' she asked in hollow tones.

Jez pulled his cap from his head and squeezed the brim between his fingers. 'I was up Huskisson Dock this morning when I saw your dad. He was talking to the postman, and I'd swear I saw the postie hand him some mail.'

Izzy shot to her feet, her features leaden. She stared Jez square in the eye. 'Why would he do that?'

Jez glanced at the other two girls. 'I dunno, but if I were to hazard a guess, I'd say someone's been blabbing and given Eric a heads-up. It would explain why you haven't received your instructions, yet Poppy received hers weeks ago. I think yours have been sent, but been intercepted en route, as it were.'

Everyone began talking at once, and Izzy hastily waved the girls into silence as she thought this through. 'If that was the case, then why hasn't Dad said something?' She looked at Cadi, Poppy, then Jez. 'We all know he's got a temper on him. Can you really see him keeping shtum when he finally has something to hold over me?'

'That's exactly what I would've thought,' said Jez. 'Only after giving it some consideration, I reckon Eric's looking at the bigger picture.'

Izzy looked blank. 'I don't understand.'

'If he confronts you now, you'll know you've been accepted and you'll still have time to leave. But if he confronts you *afterwards*, when your date has been and gone, it'll be too late for you to do anything about it.'

'Jesus wept!' cried Cadi. 'You mean he's biding his time?'

Jez nodded. 'I reckon so.'

'So he knows,' whispered Izzy. She looked up, tears forming in her eyes. 'He's going to ruddy well kill me.'

'No, he won't,' snapped Cadi, 'because you aren't going back.'

Poppy added her thoughts to the conversation. 'I think we need to box clever on this one, because whether we like it or not, Eric's holding all the cards.'

Cadi placed her arm around Izzy's shoulders. 'So what do you suggest?'

'That Izzy carries on as if she's clueless. That way, Eric won't get his dander up, and Izzy might have time to retrieve the papers. After all, I can't see him keeping them at work, can you?'

'How do we know he hasn't burned them?' said Cadi.

Izzy gave a grim smile. 'And deny himself the opportunity to gloat? To show his power over me? Not a chance! He'll want to wave those papers under my nose *before* he burns them ...' She fell silent as a thought entered her mind. 'Just like I did when I received the letter off you lot.' She clapped a hand to her head. 'I never got rid of the ashes. I didn't even check to make sure the whole letter burned. Oh my God, for all I know, he might've been able to read some of it. I was so excited at the thought of joining up, I didn't think to go back and check.'

Cadi's mouth had gone dry. 'We signed that letter.'

Izzy shook her head. 'He won't have a clue who you are – only that you're my friends. Maybe that's why he's been getting the postman to deliver the mail to him at work, so that he can see if you write to me again.'

'What if he asks around?' said Poppy nervously. 'There can't be many Cadis living in the ward, so it wouldn't take him long to find out who we are and where we're staying.'

Izzy was wringing her hands. 'I'm so sorry – I've been an idiot. I was so excited that I never stopped to think, and now everyone might have to pay for my mistake.'

'We're making a lot of assumptions here,' said Jez levelly. 'For all we know, Eric could've seen the burnt paper in the grate and got suspicious, but he might not actually *know* anything.'

'I hope you're right and that we're making mountains out of molehills,' said Poppy. 'I'd feel a lot better if I thought Eric didn't know who we are.'

'All we can do is hope,' said Izzy miserably. 'I'll go back and start searching for my acceptance papers. If I find them, I'll put them back in their place until the day before we're due to leave.'

'Then what, because he's bound to check?' said Poppy.

'As it'll only be for one night, I'll sleep rough if need be.'

'I'll be glad when we're sitting on that train bound for Sandhurst,' said Poppy fervently.

'What do we do in the meantime?' said Cadi. 'Are we still going to meet up every day, or do we think that's taking an unnecessary risk?'

'Given what we suspect, I think it's taking unnecessary risks,' said Izzy. 'I'll come and meet you on Friday, so that I can tell you whether I've found anything. It'll be hard to say what to do after that, because a lot will depend on my findings, if any.'

With that said, they had all gone their separate ways, with Izzy on her own, and Jez, Poppy and Cadi leaving together.

'What a stroke of luck it was, you seeing that postman,' said Cadi. 'Izzy's plans would've been well and truly scuppered otherwise.'

'Coming to the ladies' rescue once again,' agreed Poppy. 'Fingers crossed you're in time.'

'I only hope Izzy can hold her nerve,' said Jez, 'as it won't be easy sharing a house with someone who you know to be hiding a secret.'

'I'm amazed Eric's kept his cool all this time,' said Cadi.

'That's what worries me the most,' said Jez, fixing his cap onto his head once more. 'Eric's not exactly known for his patience, so I reckon he's going to do something bad – really bad.'

Cadi felt her stomach jolt. 'Like what? He's already split Izzy's lip and given her a black eye, so how much worse could it be?'

'I don't know,' admitted Jez, 'and that's what scares me.'

*

As soon as Izzy got home she made a beeline for her father's room, where she began her search. Even though she knew he would not be home for hours, the thought of him walking in to find her searching his room put the fear of God in her. So she swiftly checked behind the bed and under the mattress, but there was no sign of any paperwork, not even an empty envelope. Heading downstairs, she began searching beneath the chair cushions, but still nothing. She began to think the others had been wrong and that he'd destroyed her papers, when she stumbled across her father's money box whilst searching the parlour cupboard. As soon as she saw it, her heart sank into her boots. The key to the box was on a string around her father's neck and he only took if off at night before bed; worse still, he kept it under his pillow as he slept, so getting her hands on it was going to be nigh on impossible.

She carefully placed the box back in the cupboard, then went to sit on one of the kitchen chairs whilst she racked her brains to see if there was anything she could say or do that would give her father cause to hand her the key, but she could think of no real excuse that would persuade him to do so. She did contemplate breaking into the box, but quickly dismissed the idea as fruitless – especially if she was wrong and he hadn't hidden the papers inside. She placed her face in her hands as the enormity of the situation swept over her. She knew the answer to her predicament, but the mere thought of it chilled her to the core. There was only one way of getting that key: she would have to sneak into his room as he slept and keep her fingers crossed that he didn't wake as she tried to slip the key from beneath his pillow. Images of her father's eyes suddenly popping wide open as he gripped her wrist kept presenting themselves, and Izzy knew she would have to have nerves of steel to go ahead with her scheme.

She spent the rest of the day devising a plan that would ensure her father slept soundly. Even though he quite often slept deeply after having too much to drink, she feared that alcohol alone wouldn't be enough; she would have to give him something that would knock him out. So she ventured out to the chemist and asked for something that would help her get a good night's sleep. The tablets proved expensive, but they would be worth it if they did their job. Paying for them out of her housekeeping money, Izzy then had to use her best bargaining skills to bring down the price of their evening meal of meat-and-potato pie, a treat that she knew her father couldn't turn his nose up at.

When she got home she set about making the pie, carefully lacing it with crushed sleeping tablets. She knew her father would be going to the pub after his tea, because he always did, but this didn't bother Izzy too much; if her father appeared sleepy, the landlord would assume it was down to the alcohol, and he and one of the customers would carry Eric home, as they had done on many previous occasions.

That night when her father came in, she wordlessly cut him a large slice of the pie and covered it with gravy. Looking up from his food, he stared at her empty plate. 'Why aren't you having any?'

She placed a hand to her stomach. 'I've had a bit of a gippy tummy. I'll see how I go and mebbe have some later.'

With no reason to doubt her word, Eric tucked into the pie, whilst Izzy tidied up. Her outward appearance was calm and collected, but inside her heart was racing in her chest, and her tummy really was feeling gippy. Every time she heard his cutlery clatter against the plate, she half expected to hear him complain of a funny taste, but it seemed Eric was blissfully unaware of any additives. It was an enormous relief to Izzy when he cleared his plate, collected his cap from the hook by the door and left the house without a word of praise. Any other time it would have irked her that her father hadn't so much as said thank you, but tonight she couldn't have cared less. So far her plan was working a treat!

Wanting to remain busy to keep her mind off her father, Izzy cleared the table, completed the dishes and headed to her bed, where she awaited her father's return with bated breath.

It was several hours later when the front door was half pushed, half kicked open, and her father stumbled in, cursing loudly as he tripped over his own feet. Heading for the stairs, he fell up the first few. Swearing as his head hit the step above him, he crawled to the top, before stripping off and heaving himself into bed. Izzy tiptoed towards his door to see if there was any further movement coming from her father's room, but as she neared she heard snoring, softly at first, then louder. She gently pushed the door open with her fingertips and peeked through to check all was well, before crawling across the floor on her hands and knees. Kneeling beside his head, she gently slid her hand under his pillow until she felt the string; looping it around her forefinger, she slowly teased it out, taking great care not to disturb her father as she did so. With the key firmly in her hand, she quickly crawled backwards out of the room, keeping an eye on her father. She did not turn her back on him until she had closed the door to his bedroom.

Stealing down the stairs as silently as she could, she pulled the cupboard door open and removed the box. With sweat beading her brow, she held her breath as she pushed the key into the lock and opened the lid. Seeing a brown envelope on top, she turned it over. As she had suspected it was addressed to herself. Tears pricked her eyes – there was no more pretending or wishful thinking; her father knew of her plans, of that there was now no doubt. Placing the box down, she pulled the papers out of the open envelope and read the contents, before putting everything back exactly as she had found it. For two pins she would have taken the papers there and then and made a run for it, but of course her father would know what she had done, and he wouldn't rest until he had hunted her down. No, she would have to take the papers the night before she was due to leave, as she had planned. She felt slightly easier about this, knowing that all she had to do was the same as she had done tonight.

That Friday when Izzy met the girls she told them of her findings.

'And is it the same day as me?' asked Poppy anxiously.

'Same day, same train, same location,' confirmed Izzy.

'You took one hell of a risk, Izzy,' said Cadi, her voice filled with admiration. 'You've got guts, I'll give you that, but the thought that you've got to do it again is making me feel quite ill.'

'Me too,' said Poppy. 'You're jolly lucky he didn't wake the first time, but how can you be sure he won't wake next time?'

Izzy gave a hollow laugh. 'Because I've got the rest of the sleeping tablets and I shall use them all.'

Feeling more assured, Cadi settled onto the grass. 'I seem to remember you once referring to me as Boadicea, but from where I'm sitting, I think you fit that title far better than me.'

Looking quite proud of herself, Izzy knelt down beside Cadi. 'I'd never have had the courage before I met up with you and Poppy. I suppose you must be rubbing off on me.'

Poppy, however, was still thinking about what was to come. 'We aren't out of the woods yet. Supposing you manage to nick your own letter, then what?'

'I'll wait until morning and leave before Dad has a chance to wake,' said Izzy as if this was the simplest thing in the world. 'Our train leaves at nine a.m., so I won't have long to wait. I'll head for Sefton Park. He's never thought to look for me there before, so I reckon I should be safe enough.'

It was evening time before Cadi had a chance to fill Jez in on Izzy's findings.

Jez stared wide-eyed at Cadi. 'And there I was, thinking she wouldn't say boo to a goose, and there's our Izzy acting like a spy, lacing Eric with drugs and getting him drunk.'

Cadi giggled. 'She says we've rubbed off on her.'

'You must have, because that's not the Izzy we all know,' said Jez firmly. He glanced towards the back door of the pub. 'Do you think Maria's getting suspicious?'

Cadi looked perplexed. 'No, why would she?'

'You keep fielding me whenever you've got news to impart,' said Jez reasonably. 'I'd have thought that would've raised an eyebrow or two.'

'She's never mentioned anything. I think she's probably too busy to notice.'

He grinned wickedly at her. 'Perhaps she thinks we're carrying on.'

Blushing to the roots of her hair, Cadi slapped him playfully on the arm. 'Jeremy Thomas, I'm sure Maria knows I'm not that type of girl!'

'More's the pity,' chuckled Jez, quickly ducking out of Cadi's reach before she had a chance to connect. He placed a friendly arm around her shoulders. 'All joking aside, I think you're a cracking lass, and you've worked wonders on our Izzy.'

For the first time since she met Jez, Cadi placed her arm around his waist. As he naturally leaned into her embrace, Cadi fought the urge to give in to her feelings. It was an emotional time, and she knew her senses were heightened with all that was going on. If she were to turn to face him, she felt certain her body language would encourage him to lean down and kiss her and, quite frankly, she had neither the strength nor the urge to turn him away. For two pins she would give in to her desires, but that would be unfair to Jez, and Cadi thought way too much of him to do that to him.

*

It was the day before their intended departure, and Izzy was making her father another pie. The first time she had done this she had used four of the tablets, but this time she intended to use the remaining six. After all, she wanted to make certain that he didn't wake until she was long gone.

With the pie cooking in the oven, she nipped upstairs and packed a few possessions into a satchel that Cadi had loaned her, before going back down and starting on the dishes. She had been like a cat on a hot tin roof all day, and she worried that her nerves might give the game away. In order to avoid any suspicion, she had carefully marked out a slice of pie for herself, taking great care to make sure it didn't contain any of the crushed tablets. That way her father wouldn't bat an eyelid when she sat down to eat with him.

Back down in the kitchen, her heart leapt as she heard her father enter the house. Keen to keep every-thing as normal as possible, she prepared the plates whilst her father washed his hands in the sink. He shook the water from his fingers before wiping them dry. Turning from the sink, he stared at the generous slices of pie.

'What's the occasion?'

Izzy felt her heart skip a beat. Knowing that her father was aware of her intention to leave, she had taken great care to ensure he didn't realise she was on to him by keeping everything normal. The one thing she hadn't considered was that serving a meat-and-potato pie twice in as many weeks could arouse his suspicion, but she was quick to react. 'We have very little meat, with rationing – hardly enough to go round – but if you put it in a pie, it goes further.' She gave her father a furtive glance, but he seemed satisfied with her explanation. Or at least he didn't argue, instead asking for more gravy, which she dutifully fetched.

They ate their meal in silence and, as usual, her father headed for the pub. Izzy smiled as she heard the door slam behind him. This would be the last time she ever cooked that ungrateful man a meal, or did his pots. Tomorrow she would be a free woman!

Cadi and Poppy were in the kitchen of the Greyhound, busying themselves so that they didn't dwell on the knowledge that their friend was taking the biggest risk of her life in order to gain her freedom.

'I can't stop thinking about Izzy,' said Cadi as she wiped the table down for the second time. 'What if Eric catches her? What if he doesn't eat the pie? What if ...'

'You can't think that way,' said Poppy, although it was obvious from her face that she was equally concerned. 'There's no reason to suppose her father won't eat the pie, or not go for a drink afterwards. I very much doubt Izzy will oversleep, either, so you needn't worry yourself about that—' She stopped speaking as Jez knocked briefly before entering the kitchen.

'I can't stop worrying something's going to go wrong. I must've walked past their house at least half a dozen times. I'm surprised I haven't worn a path in the cobbles.'

Cadi ushered him inside. 'I'm the same, but Poppy's more optimistic.'

Jez sat down heavily on one of the kitchen chairs. 'If he kept that bloomin' key anywhere other than under his pillow, I wouldn't worry as much.'

'It worked the first time, so I can't see why it would go wrong tonight, especially when she's put even more tablets in his pie,' said Poppy reasonably.

'Well, I won't rest until you're both on that train,' said Jez firmly, 'which is why I've taken tomorrer off.'

Cadi placed a hand on his shoulder. 'How about a nice bit of corned-beef hash to take your mind off things?'

Jez shook his head. 'I'm too worried to eat.' His nostrils flared as Cadi placed a modest portion on a plate. 'On the other hand, there's no sense in worrying on an empty stomach!'

Laughing softly, she placed the plate before him and fetched some cutlery. 'I can't imagine anything putting you off your food, Jez.'

Izzy was sitting on the edge of her bed, waiting for her father to return. Her plan had been to stay up all night, leaving in the small hours. But as she waited she felt her lids begin to droop. Shaking herself awake, she chastised herself for being so silly. For one dreadful moment she questioned whether she had got the slices of pie mixed up, but she quickly dismissed this idea as paranoia. After all, she'd been very careful to mark her slice with an 'I'. On the other hand, there was no getting away from the fact that she was feeling unusually tired, so maybe the number of tablets had meant that some of them had seeped into her side of the pie. Fighting to keep awake, she wondered whether her father was already fast asleep on his bar stool.

She nibbled her bottom lip. If he'd not had much to drink, it would definitely raise an eyebrow or two if he was very sleepy, but on the other hand, would that really matter, as she would be long gone before questions could be raised. Yawning, she turned her mind back to the meal. She had worried that the extra tablets might be noticed by her father, but as with the first time, he had seemed completely oblivious, even asking for more gravy part-way through. Supposing that the anxiety and apprehension were causing her drowsiness, she allowed herself forty winks.

Eric sat on his bar stool, a glass of bitter shandy in his hands. When he'd first come across a burnt piece of paper in the fire grate, he knew his daughter had been up to something, which was why he'd decided to intercept the mail. And when he opened the papers confirming that she'd applied for the WAAF, he knew he was correct. Even so, he thought that with the evidence hidden, that would be an end to the matter, which just went to prove how wrong he was.

The landlord was watching him keenly from behind the bar as Eric nursed his drink. 'You sure you're all right, Eric? You're normally a bitter man – I didn't realise you knew what shandy was, never mind drank any of it.'

'Sometimes you need a clear head, and this is one of them times,' said Eric, gazing at the bubbles that ran up the inside of his glass.

Wiping a glass dry, the landlord held it up to the light. He didn't normally have any conversation with Eric other than to ask what drink he wanted and, on the odd occasion, explain why he was throwing him out of the pub. This was a whole new territory. 'Sounds serious?' he ventured.

'It is,' confirmed Eric, still staring at the bubbles rising up the glass. 'I've got a snake in the grass and I intend to deal with it.'

Knowing how nasty Eric's reputation was, the landlord decided not to continue the conversation, instead turning his attention to another customer in need of service.

Eric glanced up at the clock. He reckoned another hour should do it. He turned his mind to the last time he had eaten Izzy's meat-and-potato pie. He hadn't suspected a thing, until falling asleep within moments of entering the pub. He'd either caught his daughter's gippy tummy or something else was awry. It was only when he'd checked his box the following morning that he knew for certain that Izzy was on to him. Eric had placed the envelope address side down in the box, yet when he checked, it was the right way up. Of course he couldn't prove anything, and there was always the outside chance that he had been mistaken, but if he wanted to be sure, the answer was simple: don't get drunk; and see what, if anything, occurs. And to be on the safe side, swap the damned plates!

Izzy jolted awake as she heard the front door slam. Blinking, she glanced around her, but it was still dark, so she couldn't have been asleep for too long. Pricking up her ears, she listened for signs that her father was inebriated, and smiled as she heard him stumbling up the stairs. She waited for him to enter his bedroom, but everything had gone quiet. Creeping to her bedroom door, she tentatively cracked it open and peered through the gap. Her father had half collapsed on the top stair, so that he was facing her room in a slouched position.

Erring on the side of caution, she spoke hesitantly. 'Dad?' She waited but there was no response. Taking her satchel, she placed it over her shoulder, then bent down so that she was opposite him. Studiously studying his face for any sign that he was about to wake up, Izzy felt satisfied that Eric appeared to be dead to the world. Holding her breath, she leaned forward and unhooked the key from under his shirt. She was just about to pull it over his head when Eric's hand shot out at lightning speed, gripping her fingers so hard that she could feel the key cutting into the palm of her hand.

'I knew it!' he hissed through gritted teeth. 'Sneaky, conniving little bitch, I bloody well *knew* it.'

Horrified at her father's sobriety, Izzy stared at him open-mouthed as she tried to find an explanation for her current position, but it was clear Eric wasn't interested in listening to her excuses. He knew what she'd been up to and so he'd played along, hoping to catch her in the act, and he had been successful.

'Running off to join the WAAF! I can't say as I'm surprised – you're no better than your mam, never have been, never will be – but I'll tell you this for nothing, Izzy Taylor: you'll not leave this house unless it's over my dead body.'

Seeing her hopes of freedom vanishing before her eyes, Izzy shook her head. 'You can't make me stay. I'm twenty-two years old.'

Furious at his daughter's show of insubordination, he pushed her back towards her room. As Izzy stumbled, she was still holding the key, the string to which snapped free. Falling onto her back, she heard her father roar with rage. Looking between her feet, she could see that he was unbuckling his belt. Knowing what was about to come, she instinctively kicked out with both feet. She had only done it to push him away, but it seemed Eric was closer to the top of the stairs than she realised. Screaming fit to kill, he tumbled head over heels down the stairs to the tiled hallway below. Jumping up, Izzy stared at his recumbent form. Fearing the worst, she raced down the stairs. She might not like the way he treated her, but he was still her father, and Izzy was no murderer – intentional or otherwise.

Tears streaming down her face, she knelt down beside him. 'Please don't be dead. I didn't mean to hurt you – I just wanted what was rightfully mine.' Removing her satchel, she placed it beneath his head. 'I'm sorry, Dad. I promise I won't leave, if you'll only wake up …'

Eric opened a bleary eye and stared up at her. He blinked several times before his eyes fell to the key, which Izzy still clutched in her hand. 'You tried to kill me,' he roared accusingly.

Izzy looked at him in horror. 'No, I would *never*—' She stopped short. She could see the fury in her father's eyes and knew then that he was convinced she'd done it on purpose.

His face turning puce with anger, his face shook as he bellowed the words, 'I'm going to ruddy well kill you!'

Whipping her satchel from under his head, Izzy ran out of the house, with her father in hot pursuit. Running as fast as her feet could carry her, she realised to her horror that she had left her papers in the cupboard. Her only option was to double back, and she hoped she could get them before he realised her mistake.

She raced around the corner of their road and quickly ducked down beneath some bins. Panting hard, she struggled to hold her breath as her father ran past. Checking to make sure he was out of sight, she ran back to the house, whipped open the cupboard and was about to undo the box when she realised she was wasting precious time. Tucking the box beneath her arm, Izzy ran out into the night, hoping against hope that she didn't bump into her father.

Maria stood at the top of the stairs, fastening the belt on her dressing gown. 'Hold your horses – I'm comin' as fast as I can.'

Cadi and Poppy had appeared by her side, both giving the other fretful glances. Someone was hammering their fists in earnest against the pub door and, given the circumstances, they guessed it was either Izzy or her father.

'It's all right, Maria, I'll get it,' panted Cadi as she hastened to get to the door before Maria. Leaning against the door panel, she tried listening for a hint as to who was on the other side, but Maria, blissfully unaware of the evening's events, pulled Cadi out of the way and deftly unbolted the door before the girls could stop her.

'No!' cried Poppy and Cadi together, but they were too late. Maria was opening the door.

Izzy quickly stepped inside and leaned against the door, which she closed behind her. She was panting heavily and the look on her face said it all. 'Sorry, girls, I know I shouldn't have come, but as I'm sure you've already guessed, Dad knows *everything*.'

Maria subjected the girls to a steely glare. 'Does he now?' she said stiffly. 'Well, it appears he knows a darned sight more than I do.'

Ushering Izzy away from the door, Cadi swiftly slid the bolts across and jerked her head in the direction of the kitchen. 'This is going to take some explaining.'

Believing that a cup of tea always made everything better, Maria instinctively filled the kettle and lit the stove as the girls trooped into the kitchen. Folding her arms across her chest, she stared at each of them in turn, before finally settling on Cadi. 'This had better be good.'

Cadi started with the night the three of them had discussed Izzy's predicament, leading up to the moment she and Poppy had left her on Friday.

'We didn't want to keep it from you,' cried Poppy earnestly, 'but we thought you might forbid us from seeing Izzy again, and we couldn't turn our backs on her. And the more time went on, the harder it became to say something.' She looked at Maria through tear-brimmed eyes. 'We really do appreciate everything you've done for us, which is why we feel so bad about lying to you. But we couldn't give Izzy the elbow, especially when we found out how badly Eric was beating her.' She hung her head in shame. 'We really are dreadfully sorry.'

'Belting her,' corrected Cadi, her bottom lip trembling as she fought back the tears. 'Cos that's how Izzy got that scar across her cheek,' adding as further proof, '*and* the one on her lip.'

Maria calmly scooped tea into the pot as their actions sank in. 'I can't pretend I'm not angry at you for lying to me, because I am,' she said sternly. 'You should've given me the benefit of the doubt and at least *asked* my opinion, rather than assuming I'd be cross. Having said that, I don't blame you for not turning your back on Izzy, and I'd like to say I wouldn't have asked you to. But Eric's a dangerous man, and this is—' Maria had been about to say 'none of our business' when she stopped short. Seeing Izzy seated at the table, with the visible scars of her father's anger clear for all to see, Maria realised it was her duty to make it her business, so she continued on a different route. 'We should make it our business to see that men like Eric are stopped.'

'So did we do the right thing?' asked Poppy cautiously.

'You did what you thought was right at the time. And seeing as Izzy is free from that beast of a man, I'd say that yes, you did the right thing. But next time tell someone, because finding out this way doesn't give anyone time to prepare for what might happen.' She flicked her gaze towards Izzy. 'Should we be expecting a visit from your father?'

Izzy shook her head and then, holding the corner of her bottom lip gently between her teeth, she shrugged. 'I dunno, I don't think so, but I can't be sure.'

'I reckon he'll turn up tomorrow when you're at the train station—' Poppy began, only to be interrupted by Cadi.

'No, he won't, because he'd have to drag Izzy off the train in order to make her stay, and there'd be too many witnesses.' She glanced at Izzy. 'What with all the excitement, I haven't asked you what went wrong. Something obviously did, because we weren't meant to see you until tomorrow morning.'

Izzy told them everything, including the switched pie, and Eric's fall down the stairs.

Maria's gaze was fixed on the box, which none of them had noticed until Izzy put it on the table. 'What's in it?'

Izzy opened the box and pulled out her letter of acceptance. 'This, and some other stuff.'

Maria peered into the box, then cursed gently beneath her breath. 'You have to be kidding me!'

Intrigued, Cadi stepped forward for a better look, then wished she hadn't. 'Flippin' heck, Izzy, he's going to go spare.'

Izzy groaned as she too looked into the box. 'Dad's money! I forgot it was in there.' Pulling it out, she began to count. 'He's going to go more than spare – there's over twenty-two quid in here.'

'Where on earth did someone like Eric get that kind of money?' asked Poppy with anxious curiosity.

'Dunno, but I can't see it being from anything legal,' said Izzy plainly, 'cos dockers don't make that kind of money.'

As the words left her lips, somebody thumped furiously against the back door, causing them all to start. Maria picked up an empty bottle of ginger beer and placed a finger to her lips. Signalling the girls to remain quiet, she called through the door, 'We're not open!'

'It's me, Jez.'

Frowning, Maria placed the bottle down and opened the door. She ushered him in, then quickly bolted the door behind him. 'What on earth caused you to bang on the door like that? I thought ...'

Jez stared at the money on the table. 'What the—' He hesitated. 'So that's why Eric's on the warpath.'

Izzy's face dropped. 'Why? What's he doing?'

'He's shouting blue murder, that's what. Banging on people's doors and accusing them of stealing his money and hiding his daughter.' He stared at the box. 'I thought the bit about stealing his money was a crock of rubbish, but I can see that for once Eric was telling the truth.' He glanced incredulously at Izzy. 'Why on earth did you nick his dosh? You must've realised it would only make matters worse?'

Izzy ran through the evening's events for Jez's benefit, finishing with an explanation as to how she'd only intended to take her papers, but had ended up with the box. 'I didn't have time to think and, truth be known, I'd forgotten all about the money.'

A worried frown creased Jez's brow. 'Well, Eric hasn't forgotten about it and nor will he – not until he gets it back.'

'Gets it *back*?' said Poppy, her eyes widening at the thought of having to return the money.

Maria stared fixedly at the money. 'Izzy can't keep it – it's not hers to keep.'

Jez picked up the money and fanned it out. 'The quicker we get this back to Eric, the better.'

Cadi raised a quizzical eyebrow. 'So what do you suggest we do?'

'Well, give it back of course,' said Maria. Fetching another cup for Jez, she poured the tea into four cups. 'It sure as hell can't stay here.'

'And who do you suggest does that?' said Jez, placing the money back in the box, 'because whoever returns it will get the blame for nicking it in the first place.'

Pushing the lid down, Maria spoke plainly. 'Well, it can't stay here.'

Izzy stood up. 'This is my fault, so I'll put it back.'

Everyone in the room said 'no' in unison.

'Out of the question,' said Maria. 'I'm the oldest, I'll do it.'

Jez grabbed the box before they could stop him. 'If anyone's going to do it, it's me. I'm faster and bigger than any of you. Eric'll think twice before trying to lay one on me.'

The four women gaped as he swept out of the room. Grabbing her coat, Cadi followed behind, shunning the protests of her friends. 'He's not going on his own.'

Once outside, she looked around for Jez and could just make him out in the distance. He was right about one thing: he was a lot faster than the girls. Trotting along behind, she kept close to the buildings, praying that the air-raid siren wouldn't sound. She stole through the night, using only the moonlight to guide her way. She knew she should be scared, but there was something about sneaking around in the dead of night that Cadi found quite thrilling. Believing that Jez would be annoyed if he knew she was following him, she stopped short as she watched him approach the open door to Izzy's house.

Cadi felt a wave of admiration as she watched Jez returning the box as though it were the easiest thing in the world. She was about to go over and congratulate him on a job well done, when her attention turned to something moving across the road. Her heart sank. It was Eric – he must have seen Jez, because he was making his way stealthily towards the house. She watched as he bent down and picked something up. Seeing him weighing it in his hand, Cadi guessed it to be a rock or a brick. Realising that Jez knew nothing of Eric's presence and the weapon he held, she had only a few seconds to come to a decision. Running towards the house, she yelled a warning as she reached the threshold just behind Eric, who jumped nervously. Holding the brick up in a threatening manner, he threw his back against the wall. 'Who the hell are you?'

Cadi's eyes darted sideways to Jez, who was out of Eric's line of sight, holding his finger to his lips. Thinking on her feet, she tried to look complacent. 'Who am I? You're the one sneaking around, breaking into people's houses with a brick.'

Eric stared at the girl before him. There was something about the situation that didn't ring true. He spoke in suspicious tones. 'What's a young girl like you doing wandering round the streets so late at night?'

She swallowed hard. 'Fire-watching. I was just coming off my shift when I saw you.'

He stared at her through narrowing eyes. 'Where's your helmet?'

Cadi reached up and patted her head. 'I must've left it on the roof! Oh, bother, I'd best go and get it.'

As she spoke she was frantically trying to work out how she could persuade Eric to move away from the house, so that Jez might get out unseen.

Eric looked up at the rooftops. 'Fire-watching, eh?' he said, in disbelieving tones. 'Which roof were you on?'

Seeing this as an opportunity to lead Eric away from the house, Cadi walked a little way up the road whilst keeping her eyes turned up to the roofs, hoping against hope to see a fire-watcher in situ.

Eric's hand landed heavily on her shoulder. 'I knew there was summat wrong with what you were sayin',' he cried with an air of triumph, 'cos why would I be usin' a brick to break into a house what's got its front door wide open?'

Cadi froze, whilst she tried to think of an explanation. Luckily for her, she didn't need one.

'All right, Cadi, are you looking for me?' said Jez, jogging up from behind.

Smiling with relief, she turned to face him. 'Yes. Why aren't you at your post?' She glanced meaningfully at the rooftops of the houses nearby. 'You're not much use fire-watching on the ground, are you?' She threaded her arm through Jez's. 'I don't suppose you saw my helmet whilst you were up there?' As she spoke she walked with slow determination away from Eric.

She had expected him to call them out, but it seemed he had something more urgent on his mind.

Jez turned to Cadi. 'What on earth were you thinking?'

'That you shouldn't have gone off on your own like that. And I was right!' hissed Cadi.

'You shouldn't have put yourself in harm's way.' He glanced back at the house. 'Are you ready to run?'

A frown creased her brow. 'Is he still behind us?'

Jez shook his head.

'Then why would we need to run?' asked Cadi.

'Eric's no fool – he's gone to see if the money's been returned. Once he sees it's back, he'll know it was me who put it there. And it won't take him long to put two and two together and realise that we must know where Izzy is—' He broke off as Eric came flying out of his house, yelling fit to kill. Jez grabbed Cadi by the hand. 'See!'

'Where are we going?' gasped Cadi as Jez led her down a street that didn't head towards the pub.

'We can't go to the Greyhound, because we'll be leading him straight to Izzy,' panted Jez, 'so we'll go to my office down the docks. I've got the keys, so we can hide there till the coast is clear.'

Cadi allowed Jez to guide her through unknown alleys and streets until they reached the dock where he worked. In truth she had expected Eric to give up long back, but it seemed his determination to find his daughter meant that he was never too far behind. Still panting heavily, Jez opened the door to the office and ushered Cadi inside, before closing it quietly behind him and turning the key in the lock. Crouching down, he held a finger to his lips as he pointed to the dock outside.

Cadi listened to the silence, which was broken by the slap of heavy feet running towards the office. With her heart rising in her chest, she waited with bated breath to see whether Eric was going to try to come into the office, but thankfully he continued straight past.

Breathing hard, the two friends sat side-by-side on the floor. Reaching across, Jez took Cadi's hand in his and gave it a friendly shake. 'Don't ever say I don't take you anywhere!'

Cadi began to giggle, but she was still too out of breath. 'You certainly know how to show a girl an exciting time.'

He chuckled softly. 'If you ever allow me to take you on a proper date, I promise it won't be anywhere near as exciting, exhausting or downright dangerous.'

'What?' said Cadi, feigning disappointment. 'No running for my life?'

Jez stifled his laughter behind his hand. With his eyes growing wide, he looked pointedly at the door of the office.

Cadi's face dropped. She too had heard someone come to a halt outside the door. Holding their breath, they waited to see what would happen and were both relieved when they heard footsteps going away from them.

Jez sank his head back against the filing cabinet. 'We'll give it five minutes, then skedaddle.'

'Where do you think Eric's gone?'

Jez shrugged. 'Probably back home.' He gave a hollow laugh. 'In case somebody really does rob him.'

They waited for five minutes before getting up to leave. Opening the door, Jez nearly cried out when he saw someone standing in the doorway. He drew a deep breath. 'Arthur! What the hell are you trying to do? Scare me to death?'

The man known to Jez as Arthur stepped inside. 'We got wind that some people were hanging around. I thought some bugger was out to nick the stock.' He frowned. 'Why am I explaining myself to you, when you're the one locked in the office with ...' Looking past Jez, he raised an accusing eyebrow. With a knowing smile twitching his lips, he finished his sentence, '... a young lady?'

Jez clapped his hand on Arthur's shoulder. 'You know what it's like, mate – can't get a bit of privacy for love nor money back home.'

Laughing raucously, Arthur wiggled his eyebrows in a suggestive manner. 'I do, mate, I do.' Clearing his throat, he winked at Jez in a conspiratorial fashion. 'I'll leave you to it, but make sure you lock up when you've finished.'

Jez held up a hand. 'No need, we were just leaving.'

Hearing Arthur chuckling to himself as they walked past, Cadi waited until they were out of earshot before chastising Jez. 'Why did you say that? He thinks we were,' she hesitated, 'you *know* – and you didn't say a thing to change his mind. In fact you encouraged him to think that.'

'And what would you have me tell him? That we were hiding?'

She nodded. 'Better that than him think I'm some kind of tart.'

Much to her annoyance, Jez began to chuckle, stopping only when Cadi punched him in the arm. 'Don't laugh – it's not funny.'

He straightened his face. 'In all seriousness, if I'd told him we were hiding, he'd want to know who from. And then I'd either have to make up some cock-and-bull story or tell him the truth, which would be way too risky, especially as Arthur probably knows Eric. Word would soon get out and, with Eric being a docker, he'd be bound to get wind of it sooner or later. And I don't want to be looking over my shoulder for the rest of my life.'

She heaved a sigh. 'Let's hope Arthur doesn't recognise me, should he see me again.'

'What about me?' cried Jez. 'I'll have a rotten reputation now, and I didn't even get a kiss.

'Oh dear!' said Cadi, her voice heavy with sarcasm. 'How awful it will be to have your mates thinking you managed to bag a girl in your office. You can say what you like, but we both know they'd be slapping you on the back and congratulating you for your efforts. Whereas if word gets out that *I* was that girl, no one will be slapping me on the back, or congratulating me – quite the opposite.'

His cheeks colouring, Jez pushed his hands into his pockets. 'Sorry, Cadi, I guess that's me told.'

'Not so much you, but society,' said Cadi. 'It's always been the same: one rule for men, and a different one for women. My brothers talk about girls in a manner that would make you blush – well, maybe not you, but certainly Poppy – and yet no one bats an eyelid; but if a woman were to make the same comments about a man, she'd be branded a slut.'

'You're right,' said Jez hastily, 'and it's wrong. But I don't want you to think I'm like that, because I'm not.' He frowned. 'Crikey, my nan'd kill me.'

Cadi hooked her arm through his. 'Your nan sounds like a lovely lady.'

Glad for a change of subject, Jez continued, 'She is; you two would get on like a house on fire. You'll have to meet her one of these days.'

'I'd like that.' Cadi hesitated as she broached the question that had been on her mind for quite some time. 'You never talk about your mam and dad – is there a reason for that?'

He nodded. 'I'm a foundling, so I wouldn't know who my real parents were if I fell over them.'

Cadi's heart was melting. How could anyone abandon Jez? 'How did you end up with your nan?' She faltered mid-step. 'I'm guessing she's not your real nan?'

'You guessed correctly. As for how I ended up with my nan? It was her doorstep they left me on.'

Cadi squeezed his arm in hers. 'If you ask me, she's done a cracking job of bringing you up.'

Jez smiled shyly. 'She's a grand old lass – can't cook for toffee, but that doesn't matter. I'm just grateful she took me in and didn't hand me over to the orphanage, because she could've done.'

Cadi held his arm tight. The thought of her Jez in an orphanage was more than she could stand. Eager to get away from his upsetting past, she turned the conversation to the others, who would no doubt be awaiting their return.

'We've been gone a while, I hope they aren't worrying about us.'

He winked at her, the moonlight twinkling in his eyes. 'Maria knows I'd not let anything happen to you.'

Cadi took a firm hold of herself. Why did Jez have such an effect on her? She pushed on with the conversation. 'What do you think Eric will do now?'

'I dare say he's going to be like a bear like a sore head for a couple of days, after his tumble down the stairs, and I'm jolly glad I'm not going to be the one working with him. But other than that, what can he do? Izzy's gone, and he doesn't know where. The only thing he knows for certain is the time of her train tomorrow, but there's not a cat in hell's chance he'll try going down there to fetch her back.'

Cadi began to relax. 'You said earlier that you've got tomorrow off. Does that mean you're going to wave them goodbye?'

'Of course. I've grown quite attached to our Poppy, especially her apple crumble!'

She smiled. 'Funny how things turn out, isn't it?'

'Why, did she use to be a rotten cook?'

She nudged him playfully with her elbow. 'Not at all, you cheeky swine! I was on about how I've always been adamant that I don't need the help of any man, but I'm beginning to see that men do have their uses . . .' She slapped Jez on his bicep in a bid to quell his laughter.

'I'm so glad I can be useful,' he said, still chuckling softly.

Shooting him a withering glance, she continued, 'Stop teasing. You know full well what I mean. Women can't always cope without a man's assistance – much as it pains me to admit it.'

He ruffled the top of her hair affectionately. 'I'm only joshing.'

Cadi pouted. 'It's all right for you. Men can do anything, which is why they get the better money. Women are like second-class citizens, and all because they're not as physically strong as men.'

He arched an eyebrow. 'Why do I suddenly feel like the enemy?'

'You're not,' said Cadi reassuringly. 'I'm referring to men in general. My dad and brothers work down a mine, yet you never hear of females working down the pits.'

'You should be grateful,' said Jez. 'Mining is really dangerous, as well as dirty and arduous.'

'I know, and I don't mean to make light of their work, but it would be nice if women were at least given the option.'

'You're a regular suffragette, aren't you? Please don't go throwing yourself in front of anything …' He feigned pain as she punched his arm. 'You're wrong – women are as strong as men.' He gave her a cheesy grin. 'You sure make me go weak at the knees.'

'Good job I know you're only joking.'

Laughing, he placed his arm around Cadi's shoulders and pulled her close. 'Indeed I was – apart from the bit about the knees, of course.'

'You're a real charmer, Jeremy Thomas.'

Jez shot her a sidelong glance. 'Please don't call me by my full name – that normally only happens when I'm in trouble.'

'Carry on as you are and you *will* be in trouble,' said Cadi. They turned onto Burlington Street. 'Home at last,' she said. 'I shall be grateful for my bed tonight.'

'I should imagine you will,' conceded Jez, 'you've done a fair bit of running.'

Yawning, Cadi glanced around for any signs of life, but with the blackout it was impossible to tell. 'Are you coming in for a bit?'

'Nah, I'll say goodnight here, but I'll be back before brekker tomorrer.'

Standing on tiptoe, she kissed his cheek. 'Thanks for everything, Jez, you're a star.'

He winked at her. 'My pleasure, and if it means more thank-you kisses, I shall have to see what else I can pull out of the hat.'

Jez waited until she had gone in before heading off, whistling softly. Things were looking up. Cadi was beginning to change her opinions; she'd already decided not to join the services, and now she conceded that men weren't the enemy – or at least he wasn't. If he played his cards right, and did as his nan advised, Cadi would see him for what he was. A young man who had fallen hopelessly in love with a Welsh lass.

Cadi entered the kitchen and, apologising for the look of concern on her friends' faces, she spoke quickly. 'Long story short: Eric's got his money back, and he doesn't know where you are.'

'You've been gone ages,' said Poppy. 'Where've you been?'

Cadi grinned. 'Hiding in Jez's office down the docks.'

Maria nodded. 'I knew you'd be all right. That boy would put his life on the line for you. Where is he now?'

'He's gone home,' said Cadi, 'but he'll be back before breakfast, to see the girls off.'

'Good,' said Izzy. 'I wouldn't want to leave without thanking Jez – and that goes for you too.'

'Don't mention it,' said Cadi, 'Despite the imminent danger, I rather enjoyed myself.'

'You're getting more like your Auntie Flo with every day that passes,' remarked Poppy. 'It wouldn't surprise me if you ended up following in her footsteps.'

Cadi waved a dismissive hand. 'I don't think I could take much more excitement.'

'I'm just glad it's all over,' said Izzy, 'and that my dad didn't catch you or Jez in the act.'

Cadi grimaced. 'That's not quite true. You see, not only does he know what I look like, but I've spoken to him too.'

Maria's brow shot towards her hairline. 'How?'

Stifling a yawn, Cadi looked pointedly at the ceiling above them. 'I'll tell you as we're getting ready for bed.'

Maria ducked down behind the bar before coming back with Bertie Bat. 'I'll feel a deal safer with this by my side.'

Izzy's eyes widened. 'My dad's in for a nasty surprise, should he decide to turn up uninvited.'

Poppy gave a firm nod. 'We'll certainly give him a bad headache.'

Feeling reassured, they changed into their nighties as Cadi relayed the night's events.

'Flippin' heck, Cadi Williams, you don't half like to live life on the edge,' chuckled Poppy. 'I'll never forget you jumping on Eric's back the night he mistook me for Izzy – you were like one of them rodeo riders.'

'If I'd have been a bit stronger we wouldn't have needed Jez's assistance,' said Cadi thoughtfully.

'And we'd never have met Maria or stayed in Liverpool,' Poppy reminded them. 'So it's just as well he came along when he did.'

Having agreed to top and tail for the night, Izzy grinned as she climbed into the bottom of Poppy's bed. 'Just think, if you'd not met Jez, I'd never have met the two of you and I'd still be stuck at home.'

'I wonder what Eric's doing now?' mused Maria.

Cadi yawned. 'As he spent most of the night chasing me and Jez around like a headless chicken, I should imagine he's whacked.'

Izzy smiled. 'Serves the bugger right.'

Bidding each other goodnight, the girls all settled down to sleep. As the snores resonated around the room, Cadi turned her thoughts to Jez and how differently life would have turned out if it wasn't for him. She'd looked for a more exciting life and she'd found it. Maybe it was time she gave in to her emotions and accepted his affection.

Aled covered his mouth with the back of his hand and yawned. Life in the RAF hadn't turned out quite as he had imagined. Admittedly all his information had come from war movies and newsreels depicting handsome, courageous men dashing to their aircraft, returning home only a few hours later to be hailed as conquering heroes. What they hadn't shown was men jogging around the parade ground in the howling wind and pouring rain whilst their flight sergeant screamed commands at them.

Hearing the bugler sounding reveille, Aled jumped out of bed and glanced out of the window. The wind was blowing the rain sideways and he was certain he had heard the sound of thunder rumbling in the distance. Seeing the men around him stirring, he made his way to the ablutions before all the cubicles could be claimed.

When he had first arrived for training a few weeks prior, he had unwittingly assumed there would be a toilet for each man, so had been rather surprised to find himself in a lengthy queue leading almost all the way back to his hut. This had been the first lesson of many, and the biggest one of all: how to share. As an only child, Aled had always had his own possessions, but in the RAF you shared just about everything, from toothpaste to boot polish.

Then there was the food. On the farm everything was fresh – quite the opposite of the fare they served in the cookhouse, which Aled found dire, to say the least. In his opinion the RAF used the cheapest ingredients, cooked and served by people who had little to no training.

He would have thought about quitting, had it not been for the camaraderie and the sense of belonging. Here everyone was treated equally. It didn't matter where you came from or who you were: you all had to go through the square-bashing and eat the same God-awful food. None of the men in his hut had shown the slightest interest in the fact that he was the son of a farmer, which was fine by Aled, who, for the first time in his life, was just considered one of the lads.

Now, having left the ablutions, he got changed into his uniform and headed out to the parade ground to join his fellow trainees. The force of the rain stung his eyes, but Aled knew better than to complain.

Once the drill was over, they waited for the command to fall out before heading to the cookhouse, and even though he knew it would be a lousy breakfast of runny porridge and toast, Aled was looking forward to getting fed. As he jogged across the yard he was hailed by Daphne, a Waaf who had come to the station the same day as he had. The two had hit it off immediately when they discovered that they were both the only children of farmers.

'What weather!' said Daphne, shaking the rain off her jacket.

Aled rubbed his hands together in an effort to warm up. 'You'd think I'd be used to it, living in Wales.'

She gave him a shrewd smile. 'Regretting leaving your life as a farmer?'

'Never! The food may be awful, the drill incessant and the routine tedious, but I'm still away from my parents and one step closer to being a pilot.'

Daphne sneezed into her handkerchief. 'If you don't catch your death first. Honestly, you'd think they'd wait until it'd eased off.'

Aled put on a haughty voice. 'I say, Herr Hitler, would you mind awfully if we asked you not to fly today, only the weather's pretty foul this side of the Channel.'

Daphne giggled. 'I see your point – best to be prepared for anything, eh?'

'I reckon that's why they do it, or maybe they simply enjoy watching us suffer.' He grimaced as he looked down at the bowl of grey porridge that the cook had just placed on his tray. 'If they don't kill us through exercise, they'll do it through food.'

Daphne dug him in the ribs with her elbow. 'Shh. Cooks have ears – feelings too – and if you don't want them doing summat awful to your food ...'

Aled wrinkled his forehead as he looked into his porridge. 'By the looks of it, they've already done something awful to it.'

'There's nowt wrong wi' the food we serve,' said the cook defensively. 'There is a war on, you know.'

'Really?' said Aled, his voice heavy with sarcasm. 'I hadn't noticed! Had you noticed, Daph?'

Daphne slapped him playfully on his forearm. 'C'mon, you sarky blighter.'

'My mam makes a crackin' porridge, with or without milk,' mused Aled. 'I don't see why this lot can't do the same.'

She raised her brow. 'Maybe because they don't live on a farm?' She shook her head as Aled went to protest. 'No matter what your mam might have told you, porridge that's been made with water is horrid, so if hers is better, it's because she's adding summat – probably a dash of milk. That's the beauty of living on a farm.'

They both placed their trays on a table. 'I'm not going to argue, because I dare say you're right,' conceded Aled. 'The lads I used to go to school with often said I was a privileged child. I didn't think I was at the time, but I suppose I must have been.'

'You've never known anything different. To you, nipping down to get a couple of eggs is as easy as pulling an apple off the tree, but others have to pay for apples and eggs.'

Aled dipped his spoon into the porridge. 'You're making me sound spoilt.'

'You are,' said Daphne, adding hastily, 'as am I. Or at least we are compared to some. What we take for granted, others don't – simple as that.'

Aled turned his thoughts to Cadi and Poppy, who had been allowed to leave Rhos without much fuss, and said as much to Daphne. 'From my point of view, they're the ones who were spoilt, because they were allowed to do what they wanted, whereas my parents kicked up a right old dust when I said I wanted to join the RAF.'

'It's different for girls. We don't have the same opportunities as men, and I expect their parents realised that; mine certainly did.'

'Oh?'

She shrugged. 'When Mam and Dad retire, I can't run the farm on my own, so I need summat to fall back on. The WAAF is full of opportunities and, given the right training, the world is my oyster.'

Aled scraped the last of the porridge out from his bowl. 'Whose words were those, because they don't sound as though they came from you?'

'Dad!' She gave him a wry smile. 'I'm a farmer to my bones, but Dad reckons I need another string to my bow. It was his idea for me to join up.'

Aled furrowed his brow. 'Do you think you've got what it takes to run the farm?'

'I do, but as far as my father's concerned, it's not "the farmer needs a wife" so much as "the farm girl needs a husband".'

'We should swap parents,' said Aled, with a hint of bitterness.

Daphne played with the remainder of her porridge. 'What do you think you'll do when it's all over?'

'Dunno, depends on what I end up as. If I get my wings, I'll stay on: if not ...' He shrugged.

Daphne nodded, deep in thought. When she had learned that Aled was a farmer she had made it her business to get close to him. Not only was he handsome and witty, but he was also perfect marriage material for a girl who wanted a farmer as a husband. Only listening to him now, it seemed that Aled had no desire to go back to farming – certainly not if he passed muster. She would have to be patient and hope he never got his wings.

Watching Daphne as she continued to scoop her porridge from one side of the dish to the other, Aled mused that he had never been able to talk to any of the girls in the village the way he did to Daphne. With hindsight, he realised it wasn't because she was special, but more because she had a similar background. He tried to think if he'd ever acted like a brat in front of the village children. He grimaced as an image came to mind of him telling the others – boasting to the others, he corrected himself – about his mother's cooking, the meals they had every Sunday, the pond with ducks that sat behind the house and the horses he rode to market. He hadn't meant to boast, and thought if he told them what his life was like they would admire him and want to be his friend, but he could see now that this had merely driven a deeper wedge between them. He had always blamed them for not accepting him into the bosom of their group, but with hindsight it was he who had caused the divide. He looked at Daphne as she talked of her training. She was pretty, sweet and a jolly good friend, but would she make a suitable girlfriend? His thoughts turned to Cadi, as they had a lot lately. He wondered what she would make of him in uniform. Would she be impressed? He was surprised to find that it would bother him if she wasn't, mainly because he thought her worth impressing. An image of Cadi in her cotton dress, with her crown of roses nestled on her unruly hair, formed in his mind. He smiled to himself. Her hair was as unruly as her nature. Cadi was strong-willed, independent and feisty. His grin broadened. He would never have thought so back in Rhos, but now he felt certain that Cadi was exactly the kind of woman he was after. Only she lived in Liverpool and he was in London, or he was for now at any rate. Fingers entwined, he rested his lips against his knuckles as he tried to come up with an excuse to see Cadi.

It was the morning after the night before, and the girls were up betimes. Cadi was preparing the porridge whilst Izzy and Poppy peeled the potatoes for the mash that would be served with the sausage casserole later that evening.

Cadi pouted as she stirred the porridge. 'I can't believe you're going to be gone in a matter of hours.'

'Me neither,' said Poppy. 'Even though I'm thrilled at the thought of what lies ahead, I won't half miss you.'

'Me too,' said Izzy, who couldn't contain her excitement.

'I want regular letters,' said Cadi, 'at least three times a week.'

Jez knocked a brief tattoo against the back door before letting himself in. 'Morning, all!'

There followed a chorus of hellos.

'Would you like some porridge?' said Cadi, holding up the ladle.

In answer Jez fetched himself a bowl from the sideboard and placed it with the others. 'You know me, never one to turn down a free meal.'

'I dare say you need it, after all the running we did last night,' said Cadi. 'I'm aching in places I never knew existed.'

Jez wriggled his eyebrows suggestively. 'What you need is a massage …'

Cadi giggled. 'Not off you I don't, you cheeky blighter!'

'Have you heard anything?' Izzy asked timorously.

Sinking into a vacant chair, Jez picked up a potato. 'Nope, all's quiet on the Western Front, so I'm hoping we can rest easy.'

Poppy passed him a knife. 'Maria's going to stay behind whilst we go to the station. That way she can make a start on the lunchtime sarnies.'

Jez began to peel the potato. 'Talking of Maria, where is she?'

Cadi began ladling the porridge into bowls. 'Gone to Paddy's market. I got the impression she's not keen on goodbyes.' Leaving the porridge to cool, she helped the others finish the potatoes.

'Sounds about right. I've known Maria for years, and whilst she might come across as a no-nonsense businesswoman, she's as soft as putty with a heart of gold, and I know she thinks a lot of you girls,' said Jez. 'Maria and Bill were never blessed with kids, and I fancy she looked on the two of you as daughters.'

Poppy stared open-mouthed at Jez. 'I nearly called her Mam the other day, but stopped myself in the nick of time.'

Cadi dropped a peeled potato into the saucepan. 'Maria's nurturing nature makes her a good hostess because she enjoys looking after people.'

'I wish she was still here,' said Poppy, 'so that I could give her another hug.'

Jez popped the last potato into the pan. 'That's probably why she's gone – stiff upper lip and all that.'

Izzy glanced at the clock above the mantel as she submerged the potatoes in cold water. 'I hate to interrupt, but we really should get a shuffle on, if we're to get to the station on time.'

For the next few minutes the only noise in the kitchen was the sound of spoons scraping against bowls. With breakfast finished and the washing up done, they left the pub.

As they walked, Cadi threaded her arm through Poppy's. 'You must come back as soon as you get some leave.' She glanced across at Izzy. 'You too, Izzy, because I dare say things will have well and truly cooled down by then.'

Making their way to Lime street, the friends chattered excitedly about the girls' expectations of life in the WAAF, and it wasn't long before they found themselves standing at the foot of the steps that led to the glass-domed station.

Izzy glanced at the only train on the platform. 'That one *must* be ours.'

Jez trotted up the steps ahead of them. 'I'll check.'

Izzy clutched a hand to her tummy as they followed behind. 'I hope the station has a lavvy – my tummy's doing somersaults.'

Poppy pointed to the Ladies. 'It's over there – do you want me to come with you?'

Izzy waved a dismissive hand as she trotted off in the direction of the toilets. 'I'll be fine.'

Poppy and Cadi walked towards Jez, who was chatting to a porter. He smiled as the girls approached. 'This is it!' He looked round. 'Where's Izzy?'

Poppy jerked her head in the direction of the toilets. 'Call of nature.'

Cadi kept her arm firmly in Poppy's. 'I wonder when I'll see you again?'

'You can always change your mind?' suggested Poppy hopefully.

Jez placed his arm around Cadi's shoulders. 'Forget it! She's staying here. Quite frankly, I can't go back to eating my nan's version of cooking.'

Cadi shook her head. 'I bet you'd not dare say that to your nan.'

He baulked at the very suggestion. 'Damn right I wouldn't – she'd have my guts for garters.'

Standing on tiptoe, Poppy glanced around them. 'Can anyone see Izzy? She's not going to know where to find us, and the platform's getting quite crowded.'

Cadi sighed. 'I'll go and find her – you two stay here.' Looking at the train, she counted the carriages so that she could find her way back to the exact spot. 'Shan't be long, and keep your eyes peeled in the meantime.'

Cadi left Jez and Poppy scanning the crowd as she weaved her way through the people to the lavatories. Once inside, it took only a matter of seconds for her to establish that the toilets were empty. Going back out, she looked desperately around her. Where was Izzy? She thought they had ruled out Eric turning up at the station, but what if … ? Her attention was caught by Jez, who was waving furiously at her. Izzy was standing between him and Poppy.

Sighing with relief, Cadi began squeezing her way through the crowd, but the throng was so dense that she barely had room to move. So when she heard an objection from one of the passengers, she assumed she must have accidentally trodden on them. Turning to apologise, she found herself looking at Eric, who was staring at her with an air of defiance.

'I *knew* it was you,' snarled Eric. 'Where's my daughter?'

Careful not to glance in Izzy's direction, Cadi kept her eyes fixed on him. 'Hell would have to freeze over before I'd tell you. Why don't you leave her alone?'

'She nicked my money,' said Eric through gritted teeth.

'No, she didn't. Or at least not intentionally. Izzy only wanted her papers, and she's every right to them. If she wasn't so scared that you'd turn up and give her another belting, she'd never have taken the box.'

He eyed her incredulously. 'Don't try and make me out to be the one who's at fault here. I'm not the one nickin' other people's money.'

'We brought it back,' said Cadi evenly, 'so what's your problem?'

Eric gripped her elbow painfully. 'My *problem* is folk what poke their noses into other people's business.'

'No, it's not,' snapped Cadi, as she wrenched her arm from his grip. 'You're angry because your daughter's left you, just like your wife did. Is it any wonder, when you've spent the last God-knows-how-many years pushing her away? Always accusing her of being the spit of her mam, when in actual fact she'd done nothing wrong.'

He stared at her in amazement. 'Nothing wrong? She ran off with my money, after kicking me down the stairs, I might add. You mark my words, if I was dead, she'd never have returned the money.'

Cadi frowned. 'You really don't see it, do you? Izzy only ran off because you wouldn't let her leave, you hid her acceptance papers and, when she tried to get them back, you threatened to give her a good belting. What was she meant to do – lie there and take it?'

Eric gaped at her. He was not used to someone answering him back. 'What's any of this got to do with *you*?' he said in withering tones.

Cadi could feel her temper rising. Not only was Eric oblivious of his misdeeds, but he was also causing her to lose last precious minutes with Poppy. 'I'll tell you what it's got to do with me. Izzy is my friend, and I don't like seeing my friends being bullied. She's gone and she's *never* coming back, so why don't you sling your hook and crawl back under the rock you came from?'

'You should learn to respect your elders,' roared Eric. He brought his hand round in a sweeping motion, but

Cadi managed to duck down in the nick of time, leaving his fist to connect with a serviceman who was standing behind her.

Seeing the size of the soldier he had accidentally hit, Eric floundered. 'It wasn't meant for you.' He pointed a finger at Cadi. 'It was meant for that little bitch.'

The man, who was dressed in khaki green, raised his brow. 'You meant to hit *her*, with the force you just hit me?'

Eric's eyes darted around his skull as he tried to think of an appropriate response that would make the soldier see things from his point of view, but Cadi was already speaking.

'Apparently I don't respect my elders.'

The soldier took his hat off and passed it to one of his friends. 'Really? Then how's about I give your elder here a little lesson in how to respect women ...'

Eric turned, hoping to run for it, but the people around him were packed in like sardines.

Cadi raised her hand. 'You can't hit an old man, it wouldn't be fair. Not only that, but I wouldn't see anyone get into trouble because of him – he's not worth it.' She placed her hands on her hips and turned to Eric. 'You never taught Izzy to respect you, despite belting her to within an inch of her life. That's why she's left you, Eric. She could've taken your money, but she's no thief. Although I must say I'm rather intrigued to know where a docker lays his hands on that kind of money – a question that I dare say the scuffers would want answering.'

Eric was ashen-faced. 'Ain't none of your business where I get my money from.'

'Twenty-odd quid?' said Cadi in a voice loud enough to attract attention. 'How does a docker get that kind of money?'

He waved a trembling finger at her, but, catching the soldier's eye, dropped his hand. 'You'd best give me a wide berth, that's all I can say!'

Cadi smiled. 'Just like every other woman in your life.'

His jaw twitching angrily, Eric spat at Cadi's feet. 'I should've got rid of her whilst I had the chance.'

Cadi stared at his retreating back, before thanking the soldier for his intervention.

He placed his cap back on his head. 'I'm not sure I did anything. You seemed to have the matter under control.'

Making her apologies as she squeezed her way to her friends, Cadi waved her hands in a placatory manner as Poppy, Izzy and Jez asked her whether she knew what had been going on further down the platform.

'Eric,' said Cadi simply. 'But don't worry, he won't be bothering you again, Izzy.' She quickly explained what had taken place.

'Why didn't you let that soldier clock him one?' asked Jez.

'Because I don't want anyone getting into trouble over that man. He's nothing but a bully.'

Izzy smiled apologetically. 'I'm so sorry ...'

Cadi wagged a reproving finger. 'You've got to stop apologising for your father's actions. What he does is no more your fault than it is mine. He said he wished he'd got rid of you when he had the chance, and if I'd

316

thought about it at the time, I'd have said, "I bet she wishes the same".'

Izzy rolled her eyes. 'He's talking about the orphanage. He always used to say I should be grateful he hadn't dumped me on their doorstep the day me mam left.'

Poppy indicated the porter who was calling for everyone to board. 'Sorry, girls, but it's time we were off.'

Cadi embraced her oldest friend. 'Take care of yourself, and don't forget: you can phone as well as write.'

As tears trickled down Poppy's cheeks, Jez placed his arms around both girls.

'The Three Musketeers,' said Cadi, her lip trembling as she spoke.

'One for all and ...' began Jez.

'All for one!' chorused Poppy and Cadi together.

Cadi looked over to Izzy. 'Only I seem to remember that there were four musketeers.'

Izzy came over and joined in their embrace, until the train's shrill whistle signalled for them to break apart.

Taking their bags, the girls boarded the train.

Standing behind Cadi, Jez put his hands on her shoulders. 'Cheer up, queen, this isn't goodbye.'

'I know,' said Cadi as she leaned her head against him, 'but it is the end of an era.' She started as the train's wheels squealed loudly when they gained traction.

Pushing the window on the carriage door down, Poppy and Izzy stood side by side, waving frantically at their friends.

'Bye, Jez,' yelled Poppy. 'Ta-ra, Cadi, see you soon.'

'Make sure you take care of each other,' cried Cadi, 'and good luck with everything.'

Waving back, Cadi and Jez followed the train as it pulled away from the platform. Only when the girls were out of sight did they turn back.

'I feel hollow,' said Cadi, 'as though a part of me is missing.'

'Poppy's been a huge part of your life,' said Jez, 'and you've shared all kinds of adventures.'

'Only now she's on an adventure without me,' sniffed Cadi, 'and that doesn't seem natural.'

Not wishing Cadi to leave, but equally not wishing to see her unhappy, Jez spoke selflessly. 'You could always join her.'

To his relief, she shook her head. 'It's not for me – or not at the moment. For now my place is here, with you and Maria.'

Jez beamed down at her. 'You've really settled here, haven't you?'

'I certainly have. Liverpool's my home now and I love everything about it. I've never been this happy anywhere else. I'm not sure whether it's the lifestyle or the people, or both.'

'I think it's because of the people,' said Jez, 'or at least I'd like to think it is.'

Cadi eyed him from beneath her lashes. 'When I told my folks about wanting to join the services, they couldn't understand why, because I'd always said I wanted to be my own boss, and being in the services means taking orders and doing what I'm told.'

'That's true,' said Jez, 'so why *did* you want to join?'

She pulled a face. 'I was desperate to leave Rhos and a married life that I had no intention of leading. I thought it was my only way out. It's only by chance that I met you and Maria, and of course that led to the job in the Greyhound, where I *am* my own boss, or as good as.'

'So do you think all that business with Eric happened to guide you in the right direction? Like fate?'

She nodded then shrugged. 'Maybe.'

Jez held up a finger. 'You still take orders from Maria, though?'

She wrinkled her brow. 'Maria doesn't order us about.'

'She did at first – she had to, else you'd not have known what to do.'

'That's different,' said Cadi slowly.

'Is it? I know she wouldn't bark orders, but your working hours are very unsociable – not like if you were in the services.' Jez stopped speaking as he realised he could be unwittingly persuading his friend to leave.

'I know, but …' Cadi shook her head. 'It's different, because I'm responsible for the B&B, and in a way I answer to myself. I can have time off if I want it, but I won't earn a wage if I do. If I were in the services, I wouldn't be able to do that.'

'True, but it comes with its disadvantages,' said Jez. 'I've spent lunchtimes and evenings with you, but we're either with Izzy and Poppy or you're working. It would be nice if we could spend some real time together – maybe go dancing or to the movies, summat like that?'

Cadi nodded. 'I know, and whilst Poppy and I did get to go dancing on the odd occasion, it was not as often as we'd have liked. And I agree that the girls will have a much better social life in the WAAF, but it does come at a cost.'

Fearing that he'd never get to spend any time with Cadi, Jez voiced his thoughts. 'What'll happen now Poppy's gone? You rarely had time off before, but you'll never have any now,' he said simply. 'You're too young to be working all the time. In some respects Izzy had more freedom than you.'

This was a bitter pill to swallow, made worse by the fact that her friend was speaking the truth. 'Maybe now that Poppy's gone we can hire someone to take her place.' She glanced up at Jez. 'Just for the odd evening shift.'

'All you can do is ask Maria and see what she says,' suggested Jez.

Cadi walked on in silence as she contemplated Jez's suggestion. It would be wonderful if she could get at least one evening off a week, but who could they find who would be prepared to work such few hours? Most people wanted to work a five-day week. This was something she would have to give some careful consideration to.

Chapter Eight

March 1941

More than four months had passed since Poppy and Izzy's departure and a lot had happened during that time. The Luftwaffe had shattered Christmas with a three-night raid – something that none of them had been expecting. Whether or not the Luftwaffe had been testing the water to see what the reaction of the British would be, nobody knew, but all were thankful when the Germans ceased their attack.

Cadi had been serving behind the bar a few weeks after her eighteenth birthday when a man she didn't know had approached the bar asking for Maria. Cadi had just turned to fetch the other woman through when Maria appeared in the doorway that divided the bar from the kitchen. Before Cadi had a chance to speak, Maria ran round the other side of the bar and jumped into the stranger's arms.

'Bill!'

Cadi stared open-mouthed. She had seen pictures of Bill, but they looked nothing like the man who stood before her. His left eye and ear were both heavily bandaged, and his left leg was encased in plaster.

The bar had fallen silent as Bill explained his injuries. Trapped in occupied France, he and a couple of mates had faced a dangerous journey to the coast across ground still sown with bombs and tripwires. Had it not been for a feral cat setting off a hidden mine, they would never have survived.

'I'd been closest, so I took the worst of the shrapnel,' Bill explained. 'Somehow my mates persuaded a French fishing boat to take us on board, and that's how we got back to Blighty. They don't think I'll ever recover the sight in my left eye or the hearing in my ear, so you'll have to shout, as I'm a bit Mutt 'n' Jeff on the left side. There is some good news, though – they've said I can get an office job once my wounds have healed.' He heaved a heartfelt sigh. 'Left to me, I'd be out somewhere like a shot doing my bit, but not if I'm a liability.'

With his tale told, Maria had taken him through to the back and left Cadi to continue serving. When Jez had come in later on that evening, Cadi had told him of Bill's arrival.

'Poor sod,' said Jez, 'but it could've been worse.'

'If it hadn't been for that poor cat, Bill might not be here at all,' agreed Cadi.

At first she had worried that Bill's presence might change things, and in some respects it did, because they could no longer offer two rooms at the B&B. However, this had taken some of the pressure off Cadi's shoulders, and with Bill back behind the bar until his injuries healed, she was able to live the sociable life of a young woman.

Jez had been delighted to take Cadi all over Liverpool, and she had enjoyed every minute of their time together. Dancing with Poppy had always been fun, but dancing with Jez was a whole new experience. Much to Cadi's delight, he turned out to be a brilliant dancer, never putting a foot wrong, not only on the dance floor but in the way he behaved towards her. This only cemented her feelings towards him, and it had been at one of these dances that the inevitable – as far as Poppy was concerned – happened.

Jez had, as always, been the perfect gentleman, and as he held Cadi close during the last dance of the evening, she had found herself yearning for him to cast his gentlemanly behaviour aside. As the music faded she had looked up into his eyes and melted as they twinkled down at her. She couldn't say what exactly, but something changed between them, and the gaze of affection turned into something far more intense. Without having to say a word, they both knew what was going to happen, and as they flitted their attention between each other's mouth and eyes, their lips finally met. Having never been kissed before, Cadi had always worried she might get it wrong somehow. But Jez had been gentle and the kiss so natural that she felt as if she'd been kissing him her whole life. With not a sliver of space between their bodies, her heart raced as he continued to kiss her until the lights illuminated the room.

She might not have been able to tell Poppy in person, but she had rung the Sandhurst NAAFI the very next day to tell her friend the news.

Cadi had leaned back from the earpiece as Poppy squealed excitedly down the phone. 'Didn't I say?' she said, after she had calmed down. 'I *knew* you two would make a perfect couple and I was right.'

'You were indeed, although I always knew you were – it was simply my fear of being tied down that got in the way.'

Poppy giggled. 'Isn't that what the fellers are supposed to say?'

'Talking of fellers,' said Cadi, swiftly changing the subject, 'are you and Izzy fighting them off with sticks?'

There was a short pause before Poppy's voice came coyly down the receiver. 'I dunno about fighting them off, but there's more fellers here than you can poke a stick at. I feel like a kid in a sweet shop.'

This time it was Cadi's turn to giggle. 'Poppy! I don't think I've ever heard you talk that way about the opposite sex.' She hesitated, as that wasn't the only thing about Poppy that had altered. 'You seem to have changed quite a bit – you sound more ...' Cadi fell silent as she tried to think of the right word.

'Confident,' said Poppy simply. 'I know I wasn't exactly huge, but I've lost a fair bit of weight being here; the exercise is doing me the world of good, and driving gives you a real sense of freedom. I know you say you love being running the B&B, but I really think you'd be in your element here, because when you're driving it feels like you really are your own boss. And when something goes wrong, you can fix it yourself. I've already ruined one pair of stockings ...'

'Stockings! What on earth would you need your stockings for?'

'Fan belt,' said Poppy plainly.

'I don't even know what one of those is,' admitted Cadi. 'You really are learning new things.'

'And all that helps with my confidence. Women really do lead sheltered lives, when it comes down to it, but when you start learning all the things men already know, it makes you feel more like an equal.'

'Sounds idyllic,' said Cadi.

'It is,' cried Poppy. 'So why don't you come and join us?'

Cadi smiled and her silence spoke volumes.

'Jez!' said Poppy

'Amongst other things,' admitted Cadi. 'Is there anything you don't like about the WAAF?'

'The food's dire, and you have to look after your own cutlery – only they call them irons; they make you dunk them in a huge tub of boiling hot water, and quite often I'm sure they come out with more than they went in with. That's enough about me, though. I want to hear about you and Jez: are you joined at the hip?'

'Ye-es, although I'm glad we are. I love spending time with him, Poppy, and I wouldn't have it any other way. I miss him terribly when he's at work, and I find myself watching the door for his arrival.'

'I bet Maria's cock-a-hoop.'

'That's putting it mildly. She's already planning the wedding.'

'Wedding?' said Poppy, her tone lifting.

'Not yet,' giggled Cadi. 'So you can stop getting ahead of yourself.'

'You are serious, though?' hazarded Poppy.

'He took me to meet his nan, so I'd say so.'

'Well! That's practically an offer of marriage,' said Poppy knowledgeably. 'Meeting the folks is a serious thing – what's she like?'

'Adorable. She's kind, funny, and she dotes on Jez. We got on like a house on fire.'

'What about your folks? What did they say, although I can imagine your father wasn't best pleased?'

'That's an understatement. Dad tried to draw comparisons between Jez and Aled, saying that a docker's wage wasn't enough to support one person, never mind two people, unlike a farmer.'

'Didn't you explain that Jez is a supervisor, *not* a docker?'

'Of course, but according to Dad a supervisor is a "glorified docker". Honestly, Poppy, in some respects my father is as pig-headed as Eric when it comes to not seeing things from someone else's point of view.'

'Well, he'll have to come round sooner or later, because I can't see Jez going anywhere.'

Now, as Cadi placed the pint she had been pulling on the bar, she took Jez's money. 'Do you realise I've not been home for well over a year, and it's all because of my father?'

Taking a sip, Jez wiped the froth from his top lip. 'If you believe he's never going to come round to your way of thinking, then you might as well go back sooner rather than later.'

'Why? So he can point out everything that he believes to be wrong in my life? Because that's what he'll do, and he won't like it when I tell him he hasn't got a clue what he's talking about. He'll get in a mood and storm out, and I'll be left with Mum asking me to see things from his point of view. But why should I, when he won't do the same? I've asked them to come to the pub more times than I care to remember, but they refuse, on the grounds that Dad's a total and utter—'

Jez held up a hand. 'Whoa there! I can see you're not happy.'

'Not happy? Would you be happy if your father—' She ceased speaking immediately, 'Oh Jez, I'm so sorry, I didn't think.'

He gave a nonchalant shrug. 'Not to worry. But for the record, if my father were around and acting like yours, I would hope that one of us would take the higher ground, especially when there's a war on.'

Cadi rested her hands over the top of the pump handle. 'I couldn't agree more, and seeing as he's not only the eldest, but the one who's being the most objectionable, I think it should be him.'

Maria, who had been listening with half an ear, walked over. 'If you were saying "she", not "he", you do realise you'd not have this problem?'

'Yes! Because a woman would listen to reason.'

'Am I getting picked on again?' asked Jez cautiously.

Maria waved her tea towel at him. 'We never include you in these chats, on account of you not being like most men.'

He cocked a quizzical eyebrow. 'Should I be flattered?'

'Yes,' chorused both women.

'You can tell you've been brought up by a woman,' said Maria. 'None of that macho rubbish.'

'Of course,' said Cadi. 'I hadn't thought of it before, but that makes perfect sense.'

'Am I right in saying that this is still good?' ventured Jez, who wasn't sure whether the girls were making him out to be a sissy or not.

'Very good,' said Cadi. 'Don't change for anyone, Jez – you're perfect just as you are!'

He was beaming. 'I'll have to tell Nan,' he paused, before adding, 'or maybe not, as she'll only cook me something as a treat.'

'I don't believe your nan's cooking can be that bad,' chuckled Cadi.

Jez took a few gulps of his beer before answering. 'Depends on what she's making. As a general rule of thumb, if it needs heating in any way it's doomed before she starts.'

Cadi let out a shriek of laughter. 'I bet she makes wonderful food.'

'She makes the best butties, for which I'm grateful, otherwise I would've died of hunger – or food poisoning – a long time ago.'

'So is that the only reason why you're with me?' purred Cadi. 'For food?'

He gave her one of his cheesy grins. 'Don't be silly – the beer has a lot to do with it.' He dodged out of the way as Cadi leaned across the bar. 'I'm only joshing.'

Laughing, Maria shook her head. 'The sooner you two get married, the better.'

Cadi's face fell.

'Good God, surely the idea of marrying me isn't that bad?' said Jez in hurt tones.

She smiled fleetingly. 'Unless my father changes his attitude, what'll happen on my wedding day? Every girl dreams of her father giving them away, but mine's barely talking to me. If he doesn't approve of our relationship, I can hardly see him giving his blessing, never mind walking me down the aisle.'

'Which is why you should make the effort to go and see him,' said Jez patiently.

Cadi nodded. 'I will, because you're right, one of us has to relent; and if that's me, then so be it.'

Maria looked expectantly at the door to the pub. 'I'm fed up to the back teeth of people booking and then not bothering to turn up.'

'Not another one,' tutted Cadi disgustedly. 'Can't you complain to the RAF?'

'They aren't interested. As far as they're concerned, we should be more understanding.'

'Don't they understand that this is our bread and butter?'

Maria shrugged. 'Apparently those three little words can get you out of anything.'

Jez lifted his head. '"I love you?"'

'"We're at war",' said Maria. 'It seems to be a get-out clause for just about everything nowadays.'

As she spoke the door to the pub swung open and a young man in RAF uniform entered. Smiling broadly, he approached the bar. 'Hello, Cadi, long time no see.'

Cadi blinked as she stared at the stranger, only realising after a second or two exactly who she was looking at. 'Aled!'

He grinned. 'You do remember me then. I thought I'd pop by and see how you're getting on with your new venture.'

Hearing the strong lilt of his Welsh accent, Jez looked the other man up and down. '*The* Aled?'

Aled raised an eyebrow. 'Sounds like you've been talking about me, and there I was thinking you never cared.'

'You've got a nerve,' said Cadi, her tone leaden.

Aled looked perplexed. 'Apparently I was right. Although I'm not entirely sure what warrants such a reaction?'

'You know exactly what I'm talking about,' snapped Cadi. 'You told lies about Maria using underage staff to serve beer.' She tutted bitterly. 'As if you didn't know.'

Aled gaped at her. He hadn't the foggiest idea what she was on about, so he said as much. Adding, 'Why would I? What would be the point?'

'Because you were jealous of me leaving home whilst you were stuck on the smelly farm,' said Cadi.

Aled pointed at his jacket. 'Only I'm not stuck on the farm, and I haven't been for a long time. I don't know where you get your notions from, but they're ludicrous.'

Cadi placed her hands on her hips. 'Oh, please! How many other Welsh men are there who'd go out of their way to cause such trouble?'

He stared at her incredulously. How could she seriously think he would do such a thing, instead of seeing the most obvious answer? 'Well, I can think of one straight off the bat.'

'Oh aye, who?' said Cadi, her eyes narrowing.

'Your father, that's who,' snapped Aled.

She stared at him, her mouth dropping open. She wanted to deny his accusations, but how could she, when they'd just been discussing how much her father disapproved of her life. She glanced at Maria. 'Oh my God ...'

Aled cleared his throat, swinging Cadi's attention back to him.

'It really wasn't you?' she asked hoarsely.

'No,' repeated Aled, adding in kinder tones, 'Bloomin' 'eck, Cadi. I know I could be a bit of a swine when we were growing up, but I'd never set out to destroy someone else's dreams, particularly when they matched my own.'

Embarrassed at her outburst, Cadi lowered her gaze. 'I'm so sorry, Aled, I really am. I don't know why, but your name was the first that sprang to mind.'

He chuckled softly. 'I think we've had our wires crossed quite often, but that's a world away from something as vindictive as this. Not that I'm accusing your father of being vindictive,' he added hastily.

She waved a hand. 'Don't stick up for him, because that's exactly what he is. He couldn't persuade me to come home, so he obviously thought he'd force me to.' She held a hand to her forehead. 'I don't know why I didn't see it sooner.'

'Because he's your father,' said Jez, 'and you didn't want to think badly of him.'

She held her hand out to Aled. 'Can we start again?'

Accepting the offer of an apology, Aled shook her hand. 'Good idea. And whilst we're at it, why don't we clear up a few other things?'

Cadi nodded mutely. She was thoroughly embarrassed and ashamed that she had been so quick to judge Aled; not only that, but she felt certain he was going to recap the many other occasions when she had accused him of doing her wrong. Her eyes flickered over his uniform. He looked a lot smarter than he did in overalls and wellies.

'I didn't cover you in manure on purpose that day, and I did mean to apologise. But you did look rather absurd, and the crosser you got, the more ridiculous you looked – for which I am well and truly sorry.' He drew a deep breath before continuing. 'I also seem to remember pulling a chair out when you were about to sit down. Again I can only apologise, because I really didn't do it on purpose.'

An image of herself covered in manure formed in Cadi's mind, and a giggle escaped her lips. 'I suppose I did look rather comical – not that I thought so at the time.'

Aled arched an eyebrow. 'Am I forgiven?'

Cadi nodded, adding, 'I can only hope you look where you're going when you're flying your kite!'

Aled laughed. 'You don't have to look where you're going when you're sitting in the arse-end of a plane.'

Cadi's smile vanished in an instant. 'Tail-end Charlie?'

'That's me!' he said jovially. 'Point and shoot and try not to get shot. It couldn't be more simple, apart from the not-getting-shot bit of course.'

'Oh, I always assumed ...'

'What?' said Aled, a smirk playing on his lips. 'That the great Aled would become a pilot?' The smirk broadened into a grin. 'Not got the brains, apparently.' A slight frown creased his brow. 'Shame really, cos I always thought I was rather good at maths.'

For a moment Cadi wondered if he was poking fun at the time he had offered to tutor her, but could see by his face that the thought hadn't crossed his mind.

She felt her cheeks grow warm. All her life she had thought Aled to be the bad one, but she could see now that she had been the one assuming everything, and so far she'd been wrong on all counts. She looked at the beer pumps. 'Can I buy you a drink by way of an apology?'

'Don't be daft, and there's really no need to keep apologising ...' Aled began, but Cadi insisted.

She pointed to the Burton pump handle. 'This do you?'

'Yes, but it really isn't necessary.'

'It'll make me feel better,' said Cadi. 'I know you're in the RAF, and what you do, but how's everything otherwise?'

Thanking Cadi for the drink, Aled took a sip. 'Wonderful. In fact I couldn't be happier. I don't mind admitting it was a bit of a shock to the system at first, but once you get used to it, service life is grand.'

'What took you so long to join up?' asked Cadi.

'My father and yours have quite a bit in common, when it comes to keeping their kids at home.'

'They have?' said Cadi, her interest piqued.

'God, yes. My father was fighting tooth and nail to keep me on the farm.' Aled took another sip of his beer, then chuckled. 'You were right when you said I was jealous of you swanning off into the sunset whilst I was stuck on the farm, up to my knees in pig poop. When I heard how well you were doing in Liverpool, I figured if two young girls could do it, then so could I. So I snuck off and enlisted behind their backs. Dad was furious, Mum not so much.'

'He's got our Alun working for him now, though,' said Cadi casually.

'He certainly has, and for once in his life he's having to pay someone a proper wage, which is more than I ever got.'

Cadi's eyes widened. 'He didn't pay you?'

Aled grinned. 'Nope. He'd buy me everything I needed, and if I wanted something in particular he'd get it for me, but he never physically handed me my own money.'

'Well, I'll be ...! My father thinks you're rolling in it.' She started to laugh. 'Would you mind awfully if I told him?'

Aled shook his head. 'Go for it! I expect the news would raise a few eyebrows.'

'It would.' She glanced at Jez, who was sitting quietly. 'How rude of me. Aled, meet Jez, my boyfriend.'

The two men shook hands, but Jez noticed a slight dulling in Aled's eyes when Cadi referred to him as her boyfriend. When Aled had first come in, Jez had been hopeful that Cadi would send him packing with a flea in his ear – as she had always said she would – so it had come as a nasty surprise when Cadi not only forgave Aled his past misdemeanours, but offered the hand of friendship.

It seemed typical to Jez that just as he got the girl of his dreams, a handsome daredevil walked into her life. Cadi might think her father would change his mind about Aled once he heard that money was tight on the farm, but Jez didn't think so. It would be the land and the security of the farm that her father found appealing, and the money would come when Aled took over from his parents.

He then wondered what Cadi's father would say when she went home and told him how Aled had suggested that it was he who had reported Maria. No doubt Cadi's father would not thank Aled for telling tales. It might even cause him to change his tune and decide that Jez wasn't so bad after all.

'What's making you smile?' asked Cadi curiously.

Jez shrugged. 'Just thinking: we're always talking about how things turn out, and this evening's been a prime example.'

Cadi mulled his words over. He was right: had Aled not arrived, she would never have known how devious her father could be; and neither would she have known that she had got Aled all wrong. He wasn't the pompous, stuck-up, spotty little oik she had once accused him of being. Far from it; he was humble, unassuming and, she smiled, the spots were gone, a neat moustache in their place. She wondered what Poppy would think if she could see Aled now. She would have to tell her friend how much the man she had once referred to as her nemesis had changed.

Aled sat back on his bar stool. 'Where's Poppy?'

Cadi explained how Poppy had joined the WAAF with their friend Izzy.

Aled eyed Cadi inquisitively. 'Why didn't you sign up? I thought that's why you'd left home in the first place?'

'It was,' admitted Cadi, 'but life got in the way.'

He furrowed his brow. 'How d'you mean?'

She waved a hand around the bar. 'This place – not only is it my place of work, but it's my home and I love it here. I more or less run the B&B, and now that I'm old enough to serve behind the bar, I do that too. I'm not sure I could stand taking orders from some jumped-up sergeant.'

'What does Poppy think of the WAAF?'

'She loves it! She's a driver in the MT.' She grinned. 'I can't imagine our Poppy behind the wheel of a lorry.'

As she spoke someone else entered the bar. It was a woman in WAAF uniform. Cadi had opened her mouth to say that they had no more rooms for the night, when Aled turned to greet the newcomer.

'You found us then.'

Eyeing Cadi with extreme disapproval, the woman nodded curtly. 'I must admit I hoped I'd got the wrong address at first.' She cast a disapproving eye around the bar. 'Are you really staying here?'

'I certainly am.' Aled swivelled on his seat. 'Cadi, this is Daphne – we're stationed at the same base.'

Cadi stared at the woman in her smart uniform. She was around the same height as her, with dark hair and equally dark eyes. Cadi never compared herself to anyone, but she now found herself doing just that. Cadi was wearing her favourite dress, a beautiful blue frock with a sweetheart neckline and black court shoes; she loved her outfit, and not only because Jez had bought it for her as a Christmas present. It always made her feel smart and important, but it paled in comparison to the neat uniform that Daphne was wearing.

She cursed herself inwardly for comparing herself to such a rude individual. The woman might look smart, but she clearly had no manners. If it was left to Cadi, she would have shown Daphne the door, but as she was a friend of Aled's, she decided to give the woman the benefit of the doubt.

Smiling sweetly, she raised her hand to the glasses above her head. 'Hello, Daphne, can I get you something to drink?'

The woman glanced around the bar as though she thought having a drink here would make her ill. 'No thank you.'

Cadi shrugged her indifference. 'As you wish,' and she turned her attention back to Aled. 'We're doing corned-beef hash with mash and onion gravy, if you'd like some?'

Aled was about to nod when Daphne began to protest. 'Oh no, Aled, can't we go somewhere a little,' she wrinkled her nose as she eyed her surroundings, 'more suitable?'

Cadi stared icily at the other woman. She knew, from what Poppy had told her, that the cookhouse wasn't a patch on the meals they served in the Greyhound. She glanced at Aled. She'd never have described Poppy as a friend of Aled's, but she wanted to get under Daphne's skin. 'Our pal Poppy's in the WAAF and she reckons the food to be pretty grim, and the surroundings even worse, with some disgusting great bin full of boiling water that you have to dip your irons in.' She shot the woman a sarcastic smile, the words leaving her lips like knives. 'I'm afraid we can't stoop to the standards you're used to.'

Roaring with laughter, Aled clapped his hands together. 'She's spot on!' Still grinning, he turned to Daphne, who was scowling at Cadi. 'Come on, Daph, you're always complaining about the grub. And as for that water you have to dip your irons in, they probably come out dirtier than they went in.'

'Which is why I wanted to go somewhere with a little more class,' said Daphne stiffly. 'I know you wanted to drop your stuff off and say a quick hello, but surely we don't have to spend the whole evening here?'

Cadi had been watching Daphne as she spoke to Aled. The woman was looking at him as though she thought him the most wonderful man in the world. *So she's jealous!* thought Cadi. *Only why be jealous of me? Surely Aled must have told her that we never used to get along?* But whether Aled had or hadn't, it didn't make the slightest bit of difference to Daphne, who seemed hell-bent on getting him as far away from Cadi as she could. It was something that annoyed Cadi, who had done nothing to provoke such a reaction. Reaching across the bar, she replenished Aled's empty glass. 'It would be a shame for you to shoot off so soon, especially when we're just getting to know each other again.'

Jez shifted his weight. 'Unless Aled would like to show Daphne a bit of the city?'

Completely ignoring his suggestion, Aled looked at Daphne. 'Are we saying two plates of corned-beef hash or only the one?'

Daphne glanced at Jez, then turned her gaze back to Aled, who was staring fixedly at her. Realising that he wasn't going to take heed of Jez's proposal, she tutted before replying 'Two' rather sullenly.

'Wonderful!' said Cadi. 'If you'd like to take a seat, I'll fetch them through.'

Jez leaned over from the bar. 'Need a hand?'

Cadi shook her head. 'We're only plating up – shan't be a mo.'

Jez watched as Daphne began to walk towards the back of the pub, but Aled called her back. 'Don't go all the way over there, silly. Let's sit here.' He indicated a table closer to the bar.

Maria had followed Cadi into the kitchen. 'Well, well, well! It seems you've ruffled someone's feathers.'

'I know, but I don't see why. It's not as if Aled and I are best buddies,' said Cadi as she doled out the food onto the plates.

'That's not what she thinks,' said Maria as she watched the pair through the kitchen door. 'And a blind man could see the twinkle in his eye when he speaks to you.'

Cadi frowned. 'I don't think so.'

Maria popped a slice of carrot into her mouth. 'Why don't you ask Jez, cos I'm not the only one who's noticed.'

Cadi picked up the plates. 'What on earth makes you think that?'

'Because I've got eyes in my head, and so has Jez. Poor bugger's face dropped when Aled walked in, and I can't say as I blame him. It's only natural he should feel threatened by someone as smart and handsome as Aled, especially the way he looks at you.' Maria shook her head. 'Whether you realise it or not, Jez has competition – and he knows it.'

'I think I know who I'm interested in, and it's *not* Aled.'

Tilting her head to one side, Maria viewed Cadi inquisitively. 'Maybe not, but I'd wager the feeling isn't mutual.'

'Don't be daft; he's with his girlfriend,' insisted Cadi.

'So why did you buy him a drink and persuade him to stay here for the evening?'

'To annoy Daphne,' said Cadi tartly. 'You heard the way she spoke about the Greyhound.'

'I did, and if that's the way she feels, I'd rather she took her opinions elsewhere. The last thing I'd want to do is spend an evening with someone who doesn't want to be here. I'm surprised you do. I know you say you only did it to annoy Daphne, but aren't you in the least bit curious as to why he's really here?'

'All right, so I'm curious,' admitted Cadi, 'who wouldn't be? He's like a completely different feller to the one I left behind.'

'Well, you be careful, cos you're playing with fire. Daphne sees you as a threat, and who can blame her, when you look so glamorous.'

Cadi looked down at her dress. 'Me? Glamorous? Daphne looks like one of those women in the posters. Or the movies.'

Maria looked at Cadi. 'You're wearing a flattering dress, which emphasises your body in all the right places. Not only that, but you're your own woman. From where I'm standing, it's obvious why Daphne's acting the way she is.'

Cadi put the plates onto a tray along with the cutlery. 'If we stand here nattering, she really will have summat to complain about.'

'True.'

Cadi took the tray through and placed everything on the table. 'Any condiments?'

'Salt,' said Daphne.

Cadi fought the urge to point out that the woman hadn't even tasted the food. 'How about you, Aled, can I get you anything else?'

He winked at her. 'I'm sure it's perfect as it is.'

As she turned from the table, Cadi saw Daphne roll her eyes. So Maria was right. She took the salt back to the table and placed it down beside Daphne.

Back at the bar, Jez turned his attention from Aled and Daphne to Cadi. 'Fancy him coming to see you after all this time.'

Cadi stared at Daphne, who was looking at her food disdainfully as she pushed it around her plate. 'You see how Daphne is?'

Jez nodded.

'That's what Aled used to be like, which is why I couldn't stand him. It seems odd that he's changed so much, yet he still finds someone like Daphne attractive.'

'She's a bit of a whinger all right,' agreed Jez, 'but I'm guessing that's because she's jealous.'

Cadi whipped round to look at him. 'She is, isn't she? Maria said as much.'

'Not surprising really. It's obvious Aled didn't come here just to say hello,' said Jez.

'Of course not. He came over for a good nose, and to see where I ended up. He's just curious.' She wiped the bar with the cloth. 'Not half as curious as my dad's going to be, when I tell him I know the truth.'

'Have you decided what you're going to do about going home?'

She nodded. 'I'm going to go back and give my father a piece of my mind – a *large* piece. That should dampen his fire when it comes to me and Aled, *especially* when I tell him how Aled turned up at the pub with his girl-friend in tow.'

Jez looked at Daphne. 'His girlfriend? Are you sure? Only he didn't introduce her as such.'

Cadi gave a short, knowing laugh. 'If she isn't, then trust me, she soon will be. She's got her sights set on Aled and she'll not let anyone stand in her way until she gets what she wants.'

'Didn't win tonight, though, did she?' said Jez.

'Softly, softly, catchee monkey,' said Cadi wisely. 'He may have won this battle, but she'll win the war, because I can guarantee Aled won't be coming back here after tonight.'

Jez felt himself relax. He knew Cadi wouldn't do anything behind his back, but that didn't mean she couldn't break things off with him and start a fresh relationship with Aled. As far as Jez was concerned, the sooner the other man left, the better.

It was the morning after Aled's stay, and Cadi was up early seeing to his breakfast. When she went into the bar Aled had taken a seat by the window.

'Good morning! I trust you slept well?'

Aled stifled a yawn behind his hand. 'I did indeed! So well, I didn't want to get up.'

'What time do you have to leave at?'

He glanced at the watch on his wrist. 'I've got half an hour yet, so I've plenty of time.'

Placing the tray of porridge, toast and a pot of tea on the table, Cadi began unloading it. 'It's been lovely to see you, although I don't think Daphne likes it here much.'

He wrinkled an eyebrow. 'Yes, she was a tad vocal, wasn't she? Which is most unusual for her, as she's normally happy wherever she is.'

'Really? Because she came across as liking the finer things in life. Are her parents wealthy?'

Aled coughed on a chuckle. 'Good God no! They run a tenanted farm! As for being posh, I can understand why you'd think that, but you couldn't be further from the truth.'

'You do surprise me.'

'I think Daphne was having a bad day. She's always saying it's not easy being the only woman amongst so many men.'

Cadi sat down opposite him. 'I've been meaning to ask you about that. It's obviously no coincidence that the two of you are in the same city, so what gives?'

'She's the same as Poppy – a driver in the MT – and it's not just the two of us; the rest of the crew are staying in various lodgings throughout the city. It's hard getting us all under the same roof, so we invariably end up in different places.'

'So why did Daphne choose to come here?'

Aled gave her a shrewd smile. 'She says she finds the others hard to talk to, so I suggested she come and meet me here.'

'Ah.' Cadi nodded. 'I see! So maybe that's why she wasn't keen on sharing you.'

'Possibly.'

Having had enough of discussing Daphne, Cadi changed the topic. 'So what brings an entire crew to Liverpool for one night?'

'We're en route to pick up our new bomber,' explained Aled as he dug his spoon into the porridge, 'which is why we need Daphne to drive us up. Once she's dropped us off at our destination, she'll drive back, whilst we fly.'

Cadi found herself asking Aled something she never thought she would. 'Will I see you again?'

He flashed her a dazzling smile. 'Of course! I could come and see you or, if you'd prefer, you can come and see me.'

Standing up from her seat, she waited for him to finish his porridge before taking the bowl. 'That'd be nice. I've never been to Lincolnshire before.'

'It's very different to Rhos – and Liverpool, come to that. Very olde-worldy, chocolate-box houses and quaint streets. So I'm not sure it'd be your cup of tea ...'

'It sounds beautiful,' called Cadi over her shoulder as she took the bowl through to the kitchen.

'You'll have to come and see for yourself,' Aled called back, adding, 'I don't mind showing you around.'

Cadi came back through. 'Personal guide? I am honoured, but ...' Hearing someone knocking on the door, she stopped short. Sliding the bolts back, she opened the door and wasn't altogether surprised to see Daphne on the other side.

'You're early,' said Aled, as Cadi closed the door behind Daphne.

'The early bird and all that,' said Daphne as she stood halfway between the door and Aled's table. 'Are you ready?'

Aled frowned at his watch. 'No, I am not. I've still got my tea and toast.'

Seeing that Aled wasn't about to move any time soon, Daphne walked over and sat down opposite him.

Not wanting to start the day on an argument, Cadi decided to offer the hand of peace. 'Aled tells me you're in the MT? That's the same as my friend Poppy.'

'Have you never considered joining up?' asked Daphne, in tones that suggested she hoped the answer to be no.

'I have indeed,' said Cadi, her lips twitching with amusement as she saw the rueful look that crossed Daphne's face, 'but I decided I'd rather stay here.'

Daphne cast Cadi a superior glance. 'It's not for everybody. That's why they have the training process, so they can separate the wheat from the chaff.'

Cadi was livid. How dare the wretched woman throw her pleasantries back in her face by insinuating that Cadi was the chaff? 'If I can run a B&B as well as serving behind a bar, *and* provide meals, I'm pretty certain I could taxi folk from A to B in a little car.'

Seemingly unaware of the trouble that was brewing, Aled cut in, 'We couldn't all fit in the car – Daph's driving one of the wagons.'

Cadi wrinkled her nose in disgust. Daphne had started things, by putting down Cadi's career choice, and she was about to return the favour. 'How awful! You must have the devil's own job getting rid of the smell of oil and grease. However do you manage it?'

Daphne's eyes narrowed. 'With soap and water, same way as you get rid of the smell of stale ale and fags.'

Aled, now aware that things were getting heated, drained his cup. 'As you're here early, we might as well make a move.' Standing up, he approached Cadi. 'Thanks for everything, it's been great fun catching up. We'll have to do it again sometime.'

Leaning up, Cadi kissed him on the cheek. 'It's been good seeing you too, Maybe I'll take you up on the offer of a guided tour around Lincoln.' She knew she was being wicked. Under normal circumstances she'd never have dreamed of kissing Aled on the cheek, and had only done so to infuriate Daphne. The same was true of her mentioning the trip to Lincoln, so she was pleased to see that her actions had Daphne positively spitting feathers.

Aled beamed. 'I'll hold you to that.' He pecked her on the cheek before heading to the door. 'I'll give you a heads-up that it's me next time.'

Cadi walked them out of the pub, and watched as Aled and Daphne climbed into the cab of the lorry. Seeing the other girl start the engine and pull away from the kerb, Cadi noticed with delight the thunderous look Daphne shot her in her side-view mirror. No one slated the Greyhound and got away with it.

Peering around the door of the pub, Jez waved to gain Cadi's attention. 'Are you ready?'

Instead of going over, she beckoned him to join her by the bar. 'I'm waiting for a telephone call from Mam and Dad.'

'Are they calling for any reason in particular?'

'Yes, I told them I had some news to impart but wanted to do it over the 'phone. You see, I've thought it through and I think it's best if I tell them what I know, prior to visiting – see what their reaction is …' As if on cue, the telephone began to ring. Crossing her fingers, Cadi picked up the handset and spoke into the mouthpiece. 'Greyhound Public House, Cadi speaking, how may I help you?'

'Cadi!' cried Jill, her voice filled with glee.

'Mam! How are you?'

'So-so,' replied Jill. 'Missing you of course – especially your father, who's heard tell that you've seen Aled?'

'Yes, he came to stay over on his way to pick up a new bomber,' said Cadi. 'It's about Aled that I'm ringing.'

'Oh?'

Cadi heard her mother relay her words to her father, and Dewi came on the telephone.

'Mam says you've summat to tell us?'

'Yes, I have! For a start, where do you get off ringing the licensing office and telling them Maria's got two underage girls serving behind the bar? Just what did you think you'd accomplish? Because you failed, but in the process I ended up giving Aled a mouthful, because I thought he was to blame.'

There was a brief silence before her father spoke, rather coldly. 'It's not my fault that woman employs children to do her dirty work.'

'Dad!' cried Cadi. 'Maria didn't employ us to work behind the bar, we ran the B&B. And if you'd come to visit, like I asked you to, you could've seen that with your own eyes, but instead you choose to believe what you want to.'

There came a small 'hmmph' from the other end of the receiver.

'Have you nothing to say?'

'I hope you apologised to Aled for accusing him unfairly.'

Cadi was livid. 'Never mind Aled, although yes, I did apologise, because I do when I'm in the wrong,' adding bitterly, 'shame it doesn't run in the family.'

Ignoring her insinuation, Dewi continued. 'Did he accept your apology?'

'He was very gracious about the whole thing.'

She could hear her father smiling. 'Sounds like you got on well.'

Realising her father was getting his hopes up, Cadi decided to tell a small white lie. 'We did. I introduced him to Jez, and Aled introduced me to his girlfriend.' There came nothing but silence. 'Dad?'

'Cadi?'

Cadi heaved a sigh. 'Mam! Where's Dad? Did he hear what I said?'

'I think so, or that's to say he didn't look best pleased.'

'*He* didn't look best pleased! What about me? Maria too, come to that. Dad's stirring could've got her closed down, Mam—'

Jill cut her short. 'What *are* you on about, Cadi?'

Cadi repeated the conversation she had just had with her father.

'So *that's* why he's stormed off, the silly old fool.' She heaved an exasperated sigh. 'I'll have a word with him, love, although I can't promise anything. He's convinced you've done the wrong thing, and it doesn't matter what me or your brothers say. As far as your father's concerned, he knows best, and hearing that Aled's got a girlfriend won't have done anything to change his mind.'

'He's got to forget about me and Aled, because it's never going to happen. We live in separate worlds, and I'm with Jez now.' Seeing Jez smile, Cadi did too. 'The sooner Dad gets that through his thick skull, the better.'

'Now there's no need to be rude, Cadi. Your father loves you. That's why he wants the best – you're his only daughter …'

Cadi rolled her eyes. 'If he really loved me, he'd want me to be happy, and he clearly doesn't.'

'He does – but he goes about it the wrong way.' Jill sighed wearily. 'Why don't you come home for a weekend? He might listen if you're face-to-face.'

'You've already said he won't listen to you or the boys, so why to me?'

'Will you at least think about it?'

Cadi nodded. 'All right, but I can't promise anything.'

'That's all I ask. Take care of yourself, love.'

'You too. Give my love to the boys.'

'Will do. Ta-ra, Cadi.

'Bye, Mam.'

Replacing the handset, Cadi turned to Jez. 'Did you get the gist?'

'Just as you said it would be. But I think this might be the conversation you needed in order to break the ice.' He held up a hand as Cadi went to interject. 'I know your father stormed off, but that's because he didn't know what to say. You'd caught him red-handed and he couldn't deny it; not only that, but his plans to get you and Aled together have been well and truly foiled and he can hardly blame you for that. Give him time and I'm sure he'll come round. But it will take time, because he doesn't sound like the type of man who wants to admit he's wrong.'

'I hope you're right, Jez, because I hate fighting with him.'

'Give it a couple of weeks, and if he's not come to you by then, give him another call.'

'Why can't he be more like you?' muttered Cadi.

Jez grinned. 'I'm unique.'

'Modest too,' giggled Cadi.

He winked at Cadi. 'Another winning attribute.'

She picked up her handbag from behind the bar. 'Come on, you – we'd best get to the Grafton whilst you can still fit your head through the door.'

They boarded the tram that would take them to the dance hall and took a seat near the back. Jez placed an arm around Cadi's shoulders, sending a thrill of delight through her. They may have been courting for some time now, but she was still in the heady days of being with her first boyfriend.

'Have you heard from Poppy or Izzy?' Jez asked.

'Yes. Poppy's made arrangements to come home for the first week of May.'

'She has a week's leave already?'

'Yep, they were due a week's leave after training, but Poppy said she'd prefer to take it when the weather had improved. Izzy isn't coming back, though.'

'Not surprising. I wouldn't fancy bumping into her old man either, if I were her.'

'It's not that. She's loving life in the WAAF – so much so she doesn't want to leave.'

'She'll go places, with an attitude like that,' said Jez approvingly.

'Poppy reckons they've earmarked Izzy as sergeant material.'

Jez glanced out at the people waiting at the next stop. 'I'd never have put Izzy down as the sort of woman to give people orders – take them, yes.'

The tram came to a halt and the pair alighted along with a lot of other passengers. Cadi threaded her arm through Jez's as they stood in line. 'I sometimes wonder how I would've found life in the WAAF, had I gone with them, because they both seem to enjoy it.'

'I'm glad you didn't,' said Jez and, leaning forward, he kissed her tenderly. 'I know they say absence makes the heart grow fonder, but I'd far rather have you here with me.'

Blushing to the roots of her hair, Cadi glanced round to see if anyone was watching as they broke apart. However, it seemed the kiss, which meant everything to Cadi, meant nothing to those standing nearby.

The queue was quick to go down and it wasn't long before they were buying their drinks by the bar. Cadi looked out across the dance floor. 'Do you think people are right in thinking that Hitler's only interested in destroying London?'

Jez mulled it over as he sipped his drink. 'I'm afraid not. I reckon Christmas was a taste of what's to come – like a bit of a trial run to see how we'd react, before deciding what to do next.' Standing up, he held out a hand. 'C'mon, queen, let's have us some fun.'

Taking his hand, Cadi joined him on the dance floor. 'Whilst we still can, you mean?'

'Not necessarily. Don't forget the British Army is one of the best in the world. Our men are still out there, protecting the British Empire, and Churchill's determined to win – not like that bloomin' Chamberlain.'

Cadi relaxed into Jez's arms. She'd been keeping a keen eye on the news and, from what she could see, things were getting worse, not better. The British had underestimated the Germans, something that had been proved with the Christmas blitz. 'We will win, won't we?'

Squeezing her tight, Jez's lips brushed against her cheek. 'Of course we will.'

Satisfied that Jez was right, as always, Cadi rested her cheek against his chest.

1 May 1941

Cadi craned her neck as the train that Poppy was travelling on pulled into the station. Seeing her pal waving from one of the carriages, Cadi gave a small squeal of excitement. It had only been a couple of months since they had last seen each other, but to Cadi it felt like years.

'I want to know everything' were the first words out of Poppy's mouth. 'I know we've spoken over the phone, but you've not told me any of the nitty-gritty.'

'And neither would I, or at least certainly not over the phone. After all, a lady never tells,' smiled Cadi.

'Good job you're not a lady then,' Poppy laughed.

Cadi gave her friend a playful nudge. 'Cheeky!'

Swinging her kitbag up into her arms, Poppy walked towards the exit with Cadi. 'So come on then, don't leave me in suspenders.'

Cadi, who had been dying to renew the topic with her best friend, was happy to bring her up to date. 'We had our first kiss on the dance floor of the Grafton, as I told you. It wasn't planned, although I dare say a kiss never is, and his lips were as soft as a whisper.'

'And?' said Poppy, mugging furiously for more information.

'And what sort of girl do you take me for, Poppy Harding?'

'I don't mean *that*,' tutted Poppy. 'I meant, is that when he asked you to be his girlfriend?'

Cadi's brow furrowed. 'A very interesting question, because no, he didn't. In fact he never has; we've both sort of assumed that's the case. He introduced me to his nan as his girlfriend, and I introduced him to Aled as my boyfriend.'

'Aled!' mused Poppy. 'What was his face like when you introduced him to Jez?'

'I don't think he cared much, but Maria thinks Aled is holding a torch for me. And, judging by your question, I'm guessing you do too?'

'Last time the two of you met it was hardly a heart-felt goodbye. Yet out of all the places he could've stayed in Liverpool, he chose the Greyhound? That's no coincidence.'

'You're right,' agreed Cadi, 'he even said so himself.'

Poppy looked at her in surprise. 'He did?'

'Yes, he said he was curious to see how things had turned out for me because it had been such a long time.'

Poppy cast her friend a knowing glance. 'Let me put it this way. If Aled was staying in another B&B, would you have gone to see him?'

Cadi looked aghast. 'No, I would not. And not only because I believed him to be a snake in the grass; even before that, I'd not have been interested in any way, shape or ...' She fell silent as her brain caught up with her words. 'Oh.'

'Precisely,' said Poppy, with a smug smile.

Cadi hailed a tram and the two girls boarded. With no available seats, they held on to the ceiling straps. 'I think I might've made a mistake,' confessed Cadi quietly.

'Not to worry – no harm done.'

'Not that,' said Cadi. 'I mean the bit where I gave Aled a peck on the cheek and told him I might take him up on his offer of a guided tour round Lincoln.'

Poppy's eyes widened. 'You did *what*?'

Placing a finger to her lips, Cadi glanced around her. 'Perhaps this isn't the best place to air my dirty laundry.' She grimaced as she heard an elderly lady tut her disappointment.

The girls stood in silence as they waited for their stop. Descending from the tram, they resumed their conversation only once they were clear of prying ears.

'What on earth possessed you?' cried Poppy.

Sighing miserably, Cadi told her all about Daphne and her attitude towards Cadi and the Greyhound, as they began the walk home.

'So you thought you'd give her one in the eye whilst leading Aled on?'

'Yes,' said Cadi, quickly adding, 'I mean no!'

'Leading men on is playing with fire, Cadi Williams, and if word ever got back to Jez ...'

Cadi held a hand to her tummy. 'Oh, don't. I know I've been a fool, but it didn't mean anything.'

Poppy furrowed her brow. 'Why did you let this Daphne get under your skin?'

'Because she was making out like the Greyhound was a dive, and that I was no better, even implying that I was chaff,' confessed Cadi. 'I wanted to hurt her the way she had hurt me.'

'So you did it by making a beeline for her feller?' said Poppy.

'He's not Daphne's feller, but it's obvious she wants him to be – that's why she was being so vile towards me.'

'And you thought you'd make it better by pretending to be interested in Aled?'

Cadi sighed miserably. 'I wasn't thinking clearly.'

Poppy was shaking her head. 'There's more to this than meets the eye. It doesn't make sense that you would react in such a manner over some silly comments made by a woman you don't even know.'

'I swear that's all it was. Why else would I do it?'

'Let's think this through. If that had been anyone else – and I'm referring to Aled here – what would your response have been, if Daphne would've come in with exactly the same attitude? What would you have done or said?'

Cadi mulled this over. 'I'd still have been annoyed, but I wouldn't have tried to persuade the man to stay for a meal. In fact, I'd rather he left, so that we didn't have to listen to her nasty comments. We've always known you can't please all of the people all of the time, and we've had our fair share of disgruntled customers who've been disappointed, for one reason or another. Which is why Maria's told us we're not to react, but simply smile and nod.'

'The customer's always right,' agreed Poppy.

'I know,' said Cadi wretchedly, 'so why did I react so badly?'

'I think the answer's obvious,' concluded Poppy. 'You didn't want Aled thinking badly about you or your profession.'

'Of course I didn't, I'm proud of everything I've accomplished.' Cadi was blushing to the tips of her ears. 'But if I'm being honest, I was jealous of Daphne. She looked ever so smart in her uniform, and she made me feel quite inferior by comparison.'

Poppy eyed her sharply. 'Did you only feel that way because of the things she said or … ?'

Cadi shot her a sidelong glance. 'She made me feel inferior to her as soon as she walked in.'

'Uh-oh!'

'What?'

'When you phoned to tell me how much Aled had changed, I thought I could hear something in your voice, but this has confirmed it.' She smiled sympathetically. 'You liked him, didn't you?'

Cadi nodded mutely. 'As a person, yes, which is annoying because I wasn't expecting to.'

'Question is: how much?'

'He's a completely different feller to the one I thought he was – humble and unassuming.' Cadi shrugged.

'Aled was really nice, and if I weren't with Jez, I'd say he seemed like perfect boyfriend material?'

'Only you are,' Poppy reminded her friend.

'I know,' said Cadi irritably, 'so you needn't look at me like that, Poppy Harding, because I love Jez and I'm not interested in anyone else, no matter how much they may have changed. Never mind the fact that it's highly unlikely I'll ever see him again,' she added as an afterthought.

Ever the one to play devil's advocate, Poppy continued, 'Supposing Aled lived in Liverpool and you could see him on a daily basis, as you do Jez, how would you feel then?'

'Only he doesn't, does he, so I guess we'll never know,' Cadi said primly, adding, 'Why are you trying to cause me to doubt myself?'

'Because you're my best pal and I don't want to see you make a mistake. Not only that, but I think the world of Jez, and if you've got feelings for another man, then he deserves to know.'

'But you're suggesting scenarios that are never going to happen,' said Cadi briskly. 'And even if they did, none of us knows what the future holds. For all I know, Jez could fall in love with another woman.'

Poppy nodded. 'You're right. Ignore me. I'm making a mountain out of a molehill and poking my nose in where it's not wanted.'

'No, you're not,' said Cadi, 'you're trying to be a good pal to both of us. But honestly, Poppy, Jez is the man for me. And whilst I think you're right in suggesting that I wanted to impress Aled, maybe it's because I'm still on the defensive.'

Poppy nodded. 'You've spent years convinced that Aled was looking down his nose at you – it's probably become a bit of a habit.' She opened the door to the pub, where she was warmly greeted by Maria, who introduced her to Bill.

As Cadi stood in the background, watching them, she ran Poppy's theories through her mind. Was Poppy right? Had Cadi's feelings towards her old adversary changed? She had felt both impressed and humbled when she learned that Aled was a rear-gunner. She recalled how her tummy had sunk as she imagined him in the back of a bomber, with the Luftwaffe trying to gun him down. Seeing the look in his eyes, she instantly dismissed the image from her mind. She looked at Poppy, who was showing off her uniform. Of all the scenarios Poppy had put forward, not one had involved Aled's dangerous role. They all knew that tail-end Charlie was the most dangerous of the jobs for a member of the air crew. Had it not crossed Poppy's mind that Cadi felt sorry for him? It had Cadi's. Even before that night in the pub, had someone told her of Aled's new role, she would have felt the same. No one wanted to think of someone they had grown up with practically sacrificing themselves by sitting in such a vulnerable position.

Later that day, as the girls helped Maria to open up the pub, Cadi put her thoughts to Poppy, who agreed.

'We had what they call "the talk" within days of our initial training. In our case, it was Sergeant Mary Daniels who told us why war romances are frowned upon in the forces.'

358

'Because they don't want a population explosion?' ventured Cadi, much to Poppy's hilarity.

'No! Although you're quite right, because she did say she'd had to explain to more than one angry parent why their daughter was being discharged.' She gave Cadi a knowing look.

'Blimey. I was only joking.'

'I dare say you were, but joking aside, they say that most war romances only come about because people are in a hurry to get together, in case the worst happens.'

Cadi nodded. 'My dad's sister and her husband got together during the last lot, and they can't stand the sight of each other any more. But it's different for me and Jez, our relationship developed slowly. Goodness only knows, I made sure I was absolutely certain that I was doing the right thing before giving in to my emotions.'

'I know you did, and I feel silly for making such a fuss. I didn't mean to put the cat amongst the pigeons, but at the same time—'

She stopped short as Jez entered the bar. 'Poppy! Sorry I couldn't be there to greet you, but we're super-busy down the docks.'

With Jez present, all talk of Aled was on hold. Poppy regaled him with stories of her adventures, and Jez listened avidly. Being a popular member of the Greyhound staff, Poppy was welcomed back with open arms by the locals, who wished to hear all about her new life in the WAAF.

'I think I'm going hoarse,' she said as she placed another tray of empty glasses on the bar.

'You're certainly quite the heroine, as far as these fellers are concerned,' observed Jez.

Poppy leaned back against the bar. 'They're awfully sweet. You'd swear I was fighting the war single-handed, the way some of them speak—' She stopped short as the dreaded air-raid siren wailed its warning.

Maria lifted the hatch to the cellar and Cadi went outside to see if there were any stragglers in need of shelter, whilst Jez nipped out to fetch his nan.

Descending the steps into the cellar, Jez introduced Poppy to his nan, who grinned toothily as she settled down beside Poppy.

'Hello, Poppy. I'm Carrie, but they all call me "Auntie Carrie".'

Poppy smiled. This was the first time she had met Jez's nan, and she liked her already. 'Hello, Auntie Carrie. Would you like a cushion?'

Laughing, Carrie patted her ample bottom. 'I've plenty of padding of me own, thanks, chuck. Besides, I'm hopin' we won't be down here too long.' She shot Jez a chastising look. 'If it were up to me, I'd still be in me bed, but our Jez reckons the war's heating up.' She viewed Poppy through narrowing eyes. 'You're in the WAAF, so what do you think, is he right?'

With all eyes on Poppy, she began to wish that Auntie Carrie had chosen a different seat. 'Hitler doesn't give us advance warning, and it would be wrong for me to repeat rumours that have no—' She fell silent as Maria interrupted.

'Shhh!' The cellar fell silent as the occupants strained their ears. Nodding, Maria got to her feet. 'Someone's banging on the door.'

Bill put out a restraining hand. 'Sit back down – *I'll go.*'

'No, you won't,' said Maria firmly. 'You've only got one good eye, and everything's pitch-black up there.'

'Then it won't make any difference, will it?' said Bill, reasonably, but Maria wasn't listening.

'You can go next time.' Without another word she left, only to return, grim-faced, with the man who'd been knocking. She jerked her head towards the group, who were eyeing them with trepidation. 'Tell them.'

The man's voice quavered as he spoke. 'It's no false alarm – there's hundreds of 'em coming our way. The spotters said so; they reckon the sky went black cos they blocked out the stars.' He gulped as the last words left his lips.

Cadi, Poppy and Jez exchanged glances. 'That can't be true,' said Cadi. 'Surely we'd have heard something, if there was that many.'

Maria was leaning her head against Bill's chest, a solitary tear trickling down her cheek. 'It's true. I didn't see them for myself – I didn't have to, you can hear them clear as a bell. They sound like a swarm of bees, only louder.' Wiping the tear away, she glanced around the sea of worried faces. 'This is going to be nothing like it was at Christmas.'

'You mean you think it's going to be worse?' ventured Cadi. Crossing her fingers, she hoped that Maria was going to say no, and her heart sank as Maria nodded.

'Much worse.'

The people in the cellar fell silent once again, but this time the silence was broken by the distant thrum of the

Luftwaffe's engines, accompanied by the sound of bombs exploding as they rained down.

Clutching Jez's hand in hers, Cadi prayed for the Luftwaffe to go away.

'P'raps you was right about me not stopping in bed,' conceded Auntie Carrie as dust fell from the ceiling. Glancing over to Jez's nan, Caddie saw the older woman slip her hand into Jez's. 'We are safe down here, aren't we?'

Holding Maria in his arms, Bill nodded. 'Safe as houses, queen. This cellar is deeper than any shelter and a darned sight safer than your bed, so don't you worry.'

The bombing went on far longer than they'd have thought possible, and when the all-clear finally sounded and they emerged from the cellar, the sight that met their eyes was that of complete devastation. Whole streets lay in crumpled ruins, and those that still stood burned white from the phosphorus fires. Cadi heaved as the sharp smell of burning roofs and bodies invaded her nostrils.

She looked up to Jez, who was staring around them in horror. 'This is what they must mean by "hell on earth". You said the bombers were going to come back, and you were right,' she said, her voice barely above a whisper. Silent tears tracked a path down her cheek, now dirty with the soot that filled the air.

He nodded reluctantly. 'And for once I wish I'd been wrong.' He turned to Maria. 'Can Nan stay here whilst we go and help?'

Maria shot him a reproving glance. 'Of course she can. Dear God, Jez, you don't need to ask.' She turned to the old lady. 'Come on, Auntie Carrie, let's get you summat to drink and leave these young ones to help in any way they can.' Putting her arm around the old lady's shoulders, she addressed Cadi. 'As soon as I've got Auntie Carrie settled, I'll start making sarnies for the workers and survivors. Some folk will've lost everything, and a bit of human kindness will mean a lot.'

Cadi, Poppy and Jez headed towards the buildings that were still ablaze after being hit with incendiary bombs. 'I hope Aled and his crew give them Germans a taste of their own medicine, because we didn't do anything to deserve this,' snapped Cadi angrily.

Poppy's jaw twitched. 'Don't you worry, Cadi. Our boys won't have let this go by without some form of retaliation.'

Jez placed one arm around Cadi and the other around Poppy. 'Hitler's going to rue the day he messed with us, just you wait and see.'

As they neared the worst-hit areas, Cadi stared around her. 'I don't even know where we are – everything's gone,' she said quietly.

A man passing by looked at her solemnly. 'You're in hell, queen – or at least that's what it feels like.'

Cadi looked towards an old lady who appeared to be searching for something. Walking over, she laid a hand on the woman's elbow. 'Can I help you?'

The woman turned a tear-stained face to Cadi. 'I'm trying to find my home ...'

A warden hastened towards them. 'There you are, Mrs Wilkinson. You come with me – I've found you somewhere to stay.' He smiled kindly at Cadi over his shoulder. 'Thanks for looking after her.'

'I'm not sure I did much,' said Cadi, 'but we've come here to help. Can you point us in the right direction?'

He nodded to a van parked up by the kerb. 'Go to the WVS van, they'll tell you what needs doing.'

The three of them did as he had instructed, and the women in the van soon put them to work, clearing rubble from houses where they believed people to be trapped. They hadn't been at it for long before Cadi came across her first survivor. 'Over here!' she yelled to the warden who was in charge.

He climbed gingerly across the rubble to join Cadi. 'Have you found someone?'

She pointed to a woman who was sitting on a chair beneath the rubble. 'Down there. You wouldn't credit it, would you? The whole place comes down, but she's sitting there like nowt's happened.'

The warden called out to the young woman. 'Hello? Are you all right, luv?' With no response coming from the woman, he continued, 'Only I don't think this beam's going to protect you for much longer, so we need to get you out of here as quickly as we can.'

Seeing the beam he was referring to, Cadi turned to the others. 'There's one beam holding this whole thing up – talk about lucky.' A faint smile etching her cheeks, she turned back to the warden, but her face fell as she followed his gaze.

The woman was blinking up at them, her face stained with tears, dirt and blood. A small bundle lay in her arms. 'A baby!' cried Cadi and, kneeling down, she leaned as far over as she dared, holding her arms out, she looked into the woman's eyes. 'Pass your baby to me. Then we can concentrate on getting you out, but you need to hurry, cos this thing could come down at any moment.'

The woman shook her head, holding the baby tightly to her.

Cadi looked over her shoulder to where the warden stood looking down into the hole. 'Why's she being so silly? Do you think she's in shock?'

The warden wiped his nose on the back of his hand. 'Take a closer look.'

Cadi looked at the woman, then at the baby: clean-faced, eyes wide open, and silent as the … Hiding her tears behind her hands, Cadi spoke thickly through them. 'The baby … is it?'

The warden placed a hand on her shoulder. 'I'm afraid so, luv.'

Wiping the tears from her eyes, Cadi leaned back over, her bottom lip trembling as she tried to get her words out in a calming fashion. 'Pass me your baby – there's nothing else can be done, but if you stay down there …'

The woman, tears still streaming down her face, shook her head. 'I don't want to let her go.'

Cadi nodded abruptly, whilst fighting back the tears. 'I know you don't, but I *promise* I'll hand her straight back as soon as you're up here, is that all right with you?'

In answer, the woman got to her feet and passed the baby up. With the bundle in her arms, Cadi caught a glimpse of the small face: not a speck of dust or dirt, and large blue eyes that stared dully back. Cadi hastily looked away.

With the young mother now out of the hole, Cadi handed the baby over. 'She's beautiful.'

Nodding, the woman thanked Cadi, before being led away by a kind-looking middle-aged woman from the WVS van.

Choking on her tears, Cadi looked to the warden for answers. 'There wasn't a mark on that baby. How can she go through all that, only to die from the blast?'

He shrugged. 'It happens.'

The tears streamed down Cadi's cheeks. 'It shouldn't, though. None of this should be happening.' She turned to Poppy and Jez, who had come to join her from further down the rubble.

'Go home, Cadi,' urged Jez, as he placed his arm around her shoulders. 'You've done your bit.'

She shook her head. 'I can't, Jez, not whilst there's others still trapped.'

It was many hours later when the three of them returned to the pub.

'How's it going?' asked Maria anxiously.

Flopping into the nearest chair, Cadi held her face in her hands. 'We've barely scratched the surface, and I've seen things I wish I hadn't, although I dare say they'll visit me in my nightmares.' She cast Poppy a rueful glance. 'What a way to spend your leave.'

'They've certainly given us a good hammering,' admitted Poppy. Standing at the sink, she washed her hands free of soot, muck and other people's blood. 'We saved lives out there tonight. If you hadn't have found that woman, it might have been another life lost, and that's why we'll go back tomorrow.'

'What woman?' asked Maria, keen to hear the news.

Poppy explained, and Maria took Cadi in a tight embrace. 'You poor, poor thing – no one should have to go through summat like that.'

Cadi gave her a grim smile. 'I can walk away, but that poor woman can't. She'll have to deal with her loss for the rest of her life. I get off lightly in comparison.'

Jez, who had been resting his head on his arm, suddenly started. 'Where's me nan?'

Maria glanced towards the bar. 'In the pub, serving customers and having a good old chinwag.'

Cadi looked at Maria in amazement. 'You're open?'

Maria nodded. 'It's times like these folk need us the most – not only for a bit of normality, but as an escape from the reality. I explained that we wouldn't be serving evening meals and, even though they understood, you could tell they were a bit disappointed.'

Pushing herself up from her seat, Cadi headed for the pantry. 'Anything I can do to make folk feel better, I will. And if that's a bit of stew, then that's fine by me.'

Maria wagged an admonitory finger. 'You're like a dead dog, Cadi. Get yourself up them stairs and into a bath. You too, Poppy. And you needn't think you're getting away without a bath, neither, Jez – you can take your turn after the girls.'

Cadi ignored Maria's advice. 'Poppy can go first, and Jez can help me do the stew. We can sleep tonight.'

Despite her words, sleep would not come that night. The Luftwaffe, determined to continue their onslaught, came back in their hundreds and, just as they had the previous night, they all huddled in the safety of the cellar, waiting for the all-clear.

'They reckon the bombers buggered off early last night because of the unexpected change in the weather,' said Bill, as he tried to reassure the people who were watching small clouds of dust falling from the ceiling with frightened eyes. 'Let's hope the same happens tonight.'

As they listened to the dull thuds of bombs falling in the distance, Auntie Carrie got to her feet. 'I don't know about you lot, but I ain't goin' to let no Nazi dampen my spirits. How's about a singsong?'

The suggestion was a welcome one, and Auntie Carrie, as well as some of the older customers, burst into songs the likes of which Jez, Cadi and Poppy had never heard before. 'By all that's holy, your nan knows some crude songs,' chuckled Cadi as she and Poppy fell into fits of giggles.

Jez grinned. 'She's one in a million, that's for sure.'

Like the previous night, when the all-clear sounded, Cadi, Poppy and Jez headed for the city whilst Maria and Bill made refreshments, and Carrie dozed in one of the armchairs.

It was when Cadi and Jez popped back for more refreshments that Maria, who was talking on the telephone, called Cadi through. 'It's Aled.'

Wiping her dirty hands on a clean cloth, Cadi took the handset.

'Aled?'

'Cadi! How are you? I've been that worried.'

She smiled. 'That's really sweet of you, but there's no need to worry over me – we're fine. You?'

'Better for hearing you're all right. I don't suppose you've considered moving back to Rhos for a bit?'

'No, and nor would I,' said Cadi. 'I bet it hasn't made you want to return?'

'Golly, no. If anything, it's made us more determined than ever to stop the Luftwaffe in their tracks and we've a few tricks up our sleeves—'

The operator cut in, reminding them that they were being listened to. 'Careless talk costs lives!'

Cadi, who had practically jumped out of her skin on hearing the unexpected voice, giggled an apology. 'That's told us.'

'She's right, though. You can't talk on the phone the same as you can in person, which is why I thought I'd come over and see you on my next forty-eight-hour leave, if it's all right with you, of course?'

Cadi didn't know what to say. It would be rude to rebuff Aled's suggestion, especially after he'd rung to enquire about her welfare. On the other hand, how would Jez feel? She came to a hasty decision. If Jez truly loved her, he would trust her. 'That would be lovely – just let me know when.'

'Right you are. I shall be in touch,' came the gleeful response. 'And, Cadi?'

'Yes?'

'Look after yourself.'

She smiled. 'You too.'

She placed the handset back and trotted through to the kitchen. 'Sorry about that. Shall we go?'

Jez nodded. 'What did Aled want?'

Cadi took one of the baskets and the pair headed outside. 'He'd heard about the bombings – same as the rest of the world, I should imagine – and wanted to know if I was all right.'

'You were quite a while on the phone. Is that all he said?'

Cadi could feel her cheeks growing warmer. 'We got a telling-off from the operator for chatting about the war, and Aled said it would be easier to talk face-to-face, which is why he's coming over on his next forty-eight.'

'To stay at the Greyhound?' asked Jez.

'I expect so, he didn't really say.' She glanced at Jez, who was looking morose. 'Why?'

'Just think it's a bit odd that he wants to come back here, when he could use his leave to see his mam and dad.'

Cadi knew he was right, but she didn't want to admit it, so she thought of a feasible excuse. 'Not really. His father was no keener on him joining the RAF than mine was with me coming to Liverpool. Aled probably doesn't fancy going back for an earbashing.'

'S'pose.'

Cadi stopped in her tracks. 'Why the long face?'

'How would you feel if a female friend of mine came to stay with me for the weekend?' he asked sullenly.

Cadi's jaw clenched. 'I wouldn't give two hoots, because I trust you.' She began walking at a faster pace.

'I trust you too,' said Jez, jogging to keep up. 'It's Aled I'm not sure about. And who can blame me? Good-looking feller, impressive job, a hero by all accounts …'

Cadi stopped so sharply that Jez cannoned into the back of her. 'So you don't trust me!'

'I do—' Jez began, but Cadi, already annoyed that she had agreed to Aled coming over, was ready for an argument.

'If you really trusted me, you'd not be bothered what Aled looked like or what he did for a living, because you'd know it wouldn't matter to me.' She began walking again, the sandwiches bouncing precariously in the basket. 'Honestly, Jez, without trust, do we even have a relationship?'

Hurrying behind, Jez caught up with her. 'I do trust you, really I do, but when I look at Aled I can't help feeling like you've drawn the short straw.'

She spun round to face him. 'Why on earth would you think that?'

'When your father said I was a glorified docker, he hit the nail on the head, because that's exactly what I am. I don't wear a smart uniform or perform death-defying feats before breakfast – or at any other time of day for that matter.'

'Don't listen to my father. I certainly don't,' said Cadi. 'It doesn't matter what you do, or how you dress, or any of that stuff – it's what's in here that counts.' She laid the palm of her hand across his left breast. 'And Aled'll never have that, because he's not you!'

Putting his basket to the floor, Jez placed his arms around Cadi and kissed her tenderly. 'Sorry, queen, I guess the last couple of nights have got to me.'

She smiled ruefully at him. 'So you're not going to throw a tantrum if Aled comes over?'

He performed the three-fingered salute used by the Boy Scouts. 'Scouts' honour.'

Picking up her basket, Cadi tucked her arm into his. 'Good. Now let's get these butties to the workers before they start to curl.'

As they walked, Cadi cursed herself inwardly for making Jez feel badly about Aled. She had done it out of guilt, because she knew he had every right to feel

371

that way. And if he ever found out about their last goodbye – she drew a deep breath – then he really would have something to complain about.

It was Poppy's final day and they were all exhausted. Having spent most of the nights sheltering from the bombs and the days clearing the city, they'd hardly had any sleep. The bombing had left the city in ruins, and they had no idea whether the Luftwaffe was intending to strike again that night.

With Lime Street having suffered bomb damage, Poppy was catching a train from Central Station, and it was here that the girls said their goodbyes. Fighting hard to hold back the tears, Poppy leaned back from their embrace and, taking Cadi's hands in hers, she squeezed them tightly. '*Please* look after yourself, and try to get your head down for a few hours. You'll likely as not have an accident yourself if you don't get some proper kip soon.

Cadi smiled. 'Don't you worry about me, I'll be fine. Just you take care of yourself, and do give our love to Izzy.'

'Will do, and if Aled comes to visit, give him by best, won't you?'

Nodding, Cadi laughed. 'There once was a time you wouldn't give that boy the time of day, and yet here you are, wishing him well.'

Poppy gave a grim smile. 'I've greater sympathy and respect for him now that I've experienced the wrath of a bomber plane for myself. It can't be easy doing what they do, knowing that they're inflicting all kinds of misery on the German people.'

'And so they ruddy well should,' said Jez briskly. 'We didn't start this.'

'I know, but it's still not nice,' said Poppy calmly.

Bill took Poppy in a warm embrace. 'You're a grand lass, Poppy, with a heart of gold – don't ever lose that.'

She smiled round at them. 'Ta-ra, all, and say goodbye to Auntie Carrie for me, won't you, Jez?'

'Will do.' He grinned. 'Thanks for teaching her how to make pastry.'

Poppy laughed. 'My pleasure.'

She glanced at the huge clock that hung high above the platform. 'I'd best skedaddle, before the train leaves without me.'

They each gave her a final hug before seeing her aboard the train. Sliding the little carriage window across, Poppy pushed her hand out to wave as the train slowly made its way from the station.

With Poppy gone, they boarded the tram for home. Cadi yawned into the palm of her hand. 'I should think I could sleep for a month.'

'I don't know how much more we, or the city, can take,' said Maria, 'if they don't stop soon ...'

Half asleep, Cadi smiled as Jez kissed her cheek. Yawning, she rested her head against his shoulder. 'Poppy reckons the RAF have some of the best pilots in the world, so if anyone can stop the Luftwaffe, it's them.'

Jez kissed the top of her head. 'That's why I've been thinking about joining up.'

Cadi shot up, wide-eyed. 'Jez, no.'

'You said it yourself, Cadi. We need our boys in blue to stop them, and I want to be a part of that.'

'You're not doing this because of the conversation we had a few days ago, are you, because if you are—'

Jez shook his head. 'No! I'm doing this because I want to do my bit, same as Bill did.'

'And look what happened to him,' snapped Maria. 'Do you really want the same to happen to you?'

'Not everyone gets injured,' said Jez stiffly. 'If everyone thought that, where would we be?'

'Under Nazi rule, that's where,' said a man who was standing nearby.

'Precisely,' said Bill. 'That's why I joined, and it's why I want to go back, even if it is only a desk job.'

Cadi leaned against Jez's chest. She couldn't help thinking that Jez had been quite happy doing his job until Aled had come onto the scene. But she could hardly argue with him – it was his life after all.

Jez envisaged the shops such as Lewis's and Blacklers, which now stood as empty shells, with no windows or doors, and no sign of the finery that once stood inside. With half the walls missing, it was difficult to tell where one shop ended and another had begun. He then imagined himself in RAF uniform, shooting down those who dared to attack his country. The image looked good, especially with a pilot's brevet on his lapel.

Chapter Nine

Cadi had hoped that Jez's thoughts of joining the RAF would be short-lived, but he had signed up before the day was through. There had then followed an anxious wait whilst Cadi hoped fervently that Jez would be turned down.

Hearing his familiar tattoo against the back door, Cadi called for him to enter. Smiling a greeting, she soon stopped when she saw him proudly brandishing his papers.

'I'm in and they're sending me to Prestwich, two weeks from today.'

Cadi couldn't hide her disappointment. 'I've never even heard of Prestwich – how far away is it?'

'Manchester, so it's a fair way, probably two to three hours,' said Bill.

Relieved to hear that it wasn't as far as Lincoln, Cadi brightened, if only a little. 'I suppose that doesn't sound too bad. I worried they might send you to Scotland, or somewhere equally far afield.'

'And don't forget, that's only for my training. After that I might be sent somewhere closer to home,' said Jez hopefully.

'That would be wonderful, Jez. I do hope so.' Cadi raised an envelope that she had been holding in her hands. She didn't want to upset Jez, but knew it was better to be upfront about these matters. 'After all, if they can send Aled close by, then why not you?'

Noticing the envelope for the first time, Jez felt his heart sink. But knowing that Cadi didn't approve of jealousy, he tried his hardest to appear nonchalant. 'I didn't know Aled wrote to you.'

'He doesn't normally, and I must admit I was quite surprised to hear from him in this way.' As she spoke she pulled the letter from its envelope and unfolded it. 'It says he's not coming for a forty-eight any more, on account of being posted to RAF Speke.' She looked up from the letter. 'You won't believe this, but he's arriving the same day you leave.'

When she had said Aled wasn't coming for a forty-eight, Jez's heart had whooped for joy, but when she went on to say that he was being posted to RAF Speke, he felt as though he'd won a battle but lost the war. Aware that the room was silent, he tried to smile. 'That's nice.'

'Chin up! I've told you were my heart lies. Besides, I dare say I'll see very little of him, what with him being busy with his work, and me helping Maria in the pub as well as running the B&B, especially since Bill's been given a job in the town hall.'

Jez looked towards Bill, who was grinning like the cat who'd got the cream. 'I'm recruiting! So not in the thick of it, but it's summat, and it beats sitting round here all day feeling sorry for myself.'

This news pleased Jez for two reasons. First, he knew how difficult Bill had found it being at home when his pals were still fighting overseas; and second, because it meant Cadi would be too busy helping Maria to spend much time with her former acquaintance. 'I'm made up for you, pal, that's brilliant news,' said Jez, and he meant every word of it.

When Jez left the pub, he kicked a stone so that it bounced down the road in front of him. How typical was it that Aled was coming to Liverpool just as he was departing? If he didn't know any better, he'd say that Aled had concocted the whole affair – but even Jez knew that would be impossible. A small smile etched his lips. On the other hand, Bill's placement was most satisfactory, because there was no way Cadi would have time for dancing with only herself and Maria running the place. *Every cloud*, he thought to himself. He had envisaged being a pilot before this news, but knowing that he would be getting one up on Aled if he achieved this goal, he was now more determined than ever. He imagined Cadi's face as she admired the wings on his lapel – she looked impressed.

Aled climbed over the Elsan toilet and closed the blast doors behind him. He had received a letter that morning from Cadi saying that she looked forward to seeing him when he had the time. In her letter she had mentioned that her boyfriend had been accepted for basic training in Prestwich. This had been music to Aled's ears. After their last meeting he had gone home with a very different view of his one-time nemesis. He had always thought Cadi attractive, but back in Rhos she had come across as icy, aloof even – very different from the Cadi he had talked to in the Greyhound. Whilst she remained passionate and feisty, she was also warm and caring. Aled knew she had a boyfriend, but it wasn't like she had a ring on her finger or anything like that.

He frowned. What was it about Cadi that made him want to pursue her? After all, there were plenty of other women in the WAAF – and ones without boy-friends. A slow smile crossed his face as he placed the guns to 'fire' position. *You and Cadi are like peas in a pod*, Aled thought to himself. *You're both strong-willed and defiant, neither of you will let anyone stand in your way, and you find that irresistible. She's one of a kind and you want her for yourself!*

He wasn't the sort of man who chased another man's woman, but he and Cadi had history. And their fathers had always been hell-bent on the two of them getting together, so if he played his cards right, it looked as though the odds were very much stacked in his favour.

It was the day before Jez was due to leave and he had taken Cadi to Sefton Park, to enjoy the summer sun as it scat-tered its rays like diamonds across the surface of the lake.

'It doesn't seem more than five minutes since we sat here trying to persuade Izzy to leave.' Cadi smiled. 'Talking of whom, I got a letter from her this morning. She's loving the WAAF and intends to work her way up the ladder, just as Poppy said.' She giggled. 'She says she'd love to get Eric on the parade ground, so that she could teach him a thing or two.'

'Good old Izzy!' Jez gazed into the water. 'This is where I taught you to skim stones.'

'You did indeed,' said Cadi. 'So much has happened in such a short time. When I think back to the time when we discussed the war, and how I hoped it would never hit Liverpool as hard as it had London ...'

'Just before they started bombing,' said Jez. 'I'm going to miss our chats *and* our walks.'

Leaning over, Cadi kissed him softly on the cheek. 'Me too. I still can't believe you're going; in fact I don't think it'll sink in until I wave you goodbye tomorrow.' She looked at him from under thick lashes. 'Do you ever wish you'd not signed up?'

Jez hesitated before answering. If Aled wasn't coming to Liverpool, Jez would still be eager for the off. But as things stood? Not that he could admit that to Cadi, of course. He shook his head. 'I'll miss you like crazy, but after experiencing what it's like to be on the receiving end of them bombs, I think it's high time I doled some out.'

Cadi said nothing. She was hoping Jez wouldn't make it into air crew, preferring him to have both feet firmly on the ground. But if it was what Jez wanted ... She smiled as she looked into his deep-set eyes. 'You'll do us all proud, I know you will.'

Jez had promised himself that he wasn't going to mention Aled, but the man always seemed to be prevalent in his thoughts. He had racked his brains for a way to keep the two of them apart, but could think of nothing that would work, until he had spoken to his nan, who'd suggested that there was only one way a man could secure his woman until he returned.

'I know Cadi's allus been against marriage, but I think you might find she feels differently, now that you're going to be so far away from home.'

Jez had gaped at her. 'You're not suggesting we get married?'

'Good God, no! That's how you scare a woman like Cadi off, not keep her.' She smiled kindly at him. 'Although there is something you can give her that cements your relationship.'

Jez rubbed his chin thoughtfully. 'What's that?'

'A promise ring.'

Jez pulled face. 'Easier said than done, when I can't afford a ring.' He stopped as his nan pulled a ring from the fourth finger of her right hand and held it towards him. 'What's this?'

'It's my old promise ring. Willy—'

Jez held his hands up. 'I can't, Nan. Thanks for the offer, but it's too much.'

'Nonsense. I think a lot of Cadi, and I know she'll take good care of it.' She pushed the ring into the palm of his hand and closed his fingers over it. 'She's a good 'un, Jez, worth fighting for. And I reckon you're right about that Aled – a feller don't travel halfway across the country to see someone he's no interest in.'

Now, as Jez finished making a bracelet of daisies, he placed them around Cadi's wrist. His heart pounding in his chest, he summoned the courage to ask her the question uppermost in his mind. Kneeling up, he stared earnestly into her eyes. 'I've been having a long, hard think about life in general lately, and where it's going.'

'I should think you have,' said Cadi. 'Joining up is not for the faint-hearted.'

'I'm not talking about the RAF ...' He pushed his hand into his pocket and pulled out the ring, which he held up for her to see. 'I'm talking about you and me, and our lives.'

Cadi swallowed. She hadn't thought Jez had any intention of doing something like this, so she was completely unprepared.

Cradling her chin in his hand, he gazed into her eyes. 'I know you've always been independent and there's no reason why that should change. You're too precious for me to try and clip your wings, but there's no getting away from the fact that I'm moving to pastures new and we may be apart for a long time. Having said that, I know that no matter where I go, you'll always be the girl for me. And I love you with all my heart, which is why I'm asking if you'll accept my promise ring.'

Cadi beamed. 'Of course I will, Jez, it's beautiful.' She allowed him to slide the ring onto her right hand. Leaning forward, she kissed his cheek before whispering in his ear, 'I love you too, Jeremy Thomas.'

Jez couldn't be more pleased. As things had turned out, his nan's suggestion had been a good one. All morning he had had visions of Cadi refusing the ring, saying it was too much too soon, so when she accepted with such glee, he felt like the cock of the walk.

Cupping her face in his hands, he kissed her gently. 'You've just made me the happiest man alive.'

The two of them spent the morning lazing in the sunshine whilst discussing a code to stop the censors being too heavy-handed with their correspondence.

'I got a letter from Izzy and it looked as though someone had been making a paper doily,' said Cadi. 'I can't believe she would say something that would warrant such heavy censorship.'

'Maria said her letters from Bill were always full of holes,' agreed Jez. 'We're going to have to write our code down so that we don't forget it.'

They had gone to Lyons for their lunch, then spent the rest of the afternoon skimming stones and strolling around the park. With the sun setting, they walked back to the Greyhound, and Cadi invited Jez in so that they could spend the evening together, but he declined the offer.

'My nan's looked after me when others didn't want to, so I've said I'd spend my last evening with her, playing cards and reminiscing. If you'd like to join us, you're more than welcome ...'

Cadi shook her head. 'It's important that you and your nan spend this time together. I know she's said she'd rather say goodbye at home, as opposed to seeing you off at the station, so that will be *our* time.'

Jez kissed her goodbye before quickly heading off to tell his nan that Cadi had accepted his ring.

Inside the pub Cadi was instantly quizzed by Maria, who noticed the ring straight off the bat.

'I knew he'd do summat like this, cos he's a soppy sod at heart,' cooed Maria as she admired the posy ring. 'Did he say where he got it from?'

'It was his nan's,' said Cadi, her eyes shining as she too admired the ring. 'I thought he was going to propose, and I don't mind admitting my heart was in my mouth.'

Bill looked up from his paper. 'What would you have said, d'you reckon?'

As she stared at the ring, an image of Jez – his eyes twinkling into hers – appeared in her mind's eye. A half smile crossed her lips. Jez had always been happy-go-lucky; even when the Luftwaffe were doing their worst, he had been there, trying his utmost to cheer everyone up. There wasn't a bad bone in his body, and she doubted she'd ever find a man to match him. 'I reckon I'd have said yes.'

Maria clapped her hands together. 'Oh, Cadi.'

Cadi laughed. 'He's not asked me, Maria.'

'I know, but he will, and when he does,' she drummed her feet against the floor, 'marriage and babies!'

Bill rolled his eyes as he slid back beneath his paper. 'Good God, woman, he's not even proposed and you've got 'em married with a gaggle of babbies round their ankles.'

'I just wish he wasn't going,' said Cadi miserably.

'He'll be back,' said Maria with firm assurance.

'How can you be so confident?'

She shrugged. 'Cos he's not the sort to get shot.'

Bill choked as he removed his pipe from between his teeth. 'Did I hear that right?'

Maria nodded. 'Indeed you did. Why, is there summat wrong with what I said?'

Knitting his brows, Bill conceded that it was better not to say anything. 'No, dear, nothing at all.'

Cadi smiled at Maria. 'I hope you're right, because I rather like Jez the way he is.'

Maria winked. 'Call it a feeling in my waters, or women's intuition – call it what you will, but I'm telling you, that boy's coming home.'

When Jez walked into the parlour, his nan was ready and waiting, with the card table set up and a plate of sandwiches to hand.

'What did she say?'

Jez beamed. 'Yes!'

'That's the ticket.' She pushed a letter towards Jez. 'This come for you earlier. I don't recognise the writing, and whoever wrote it made it out to Jez – a bit odd, don't you think?'

Jez stared at the envelope. Who would be writing to him in such an unofficial capacity? Slitting it open, he scanned the contents, his heart dropping into his boots.

Carrie reached over to hold his hand, a worried frown etched on her heavily wrinkled brow. 'Is it bad news, luv?'

He nodded. 'Remember I told you about that girl Daphne, the one who came to the pub with Aled?'

'I do.'

He passed Carrie the letter and she began to read it aloud.

'Dear Jez. You may not remember me, but my name is Daphne and I came to the pub when Aled was staying there ...' Carrie fell silent as she continued to read.

'I thought you should know that Cadi seems intent on making a play for my Aled. Not that she'd admit it of

course, but seeing is believing, and she was all over him when we left the pub – she even kissed him goodbye! I could barely believe my ears when she suggested she might come and see him in Lincoln. I did very much hope that once they were parted this would bring an end to the matter, but it seems Aled is being relocated to RAF Speke.

I must admit I wasn't too concerned, believing you'd be around to keep an eye on them, but Aled tells me you've joined the RAF.

I do hope you don't think I'm interfering, because I'm really not. I just thought you should be aware of what's going on.'

Carrie made a hissing noise between her teeth. 'Poisonous little …' She glanced up at Jez. 'You don't believe any of this tosh, do you?'

He shook his head hesitantly. 'Only why would she say these things if they aren't true?'

'To try and manipulate you into warning Cadi off or …' a slow, knowing smile tweaked her lips, 'or to make you propose to Cadi.' She folded the letter and pushed it back into its envelope. 'If I were you, I'd take that round to Cadi.'

'Why on earth would I want to do that?'

'So that Cadi knows what you're having to deal with. Fancy sending you a letter like that before you go off to war.'

Jez shook his head firmly. 'I don't want Cadi to know. She already thinks I'm jealous.'

'And you've good reason to be, if this is what's going on,' said Carrie. 'Why don't you at least sleep on it – see how you feel in the morning?'

Jez did agree to sleep on the matter, but he very much doubted he would change his mind by the morning. If he showed Cadi the letter, she would say that he had only done so because he thought there might be some truth in it, which wasn't the case at all – or at least not when it came to the kiss goodbye; he was certain that bit wasn't true, just like the bit about Cadi chasing Aled. If anything, it was the other way round, and he reckoned Daphne knew it, which was why she was trying to stir up trouble. No, he would keep this information to himself.

By the next day, little had happened to change Jez's mind. He said as much to his nan, asking her to keep the letter between themselves until he decided what to do for the best.

'As you wish, my dear. Just make sure you don't spend all your time worryin' over that letter.' Carrie tapped the side of her nose. 'As for Aled, you leave him to me – any funny business and I'll give him his marching orders.'

Kissing his nan farewell, Jez popped over to the Greyhound to bid Maria and Bill goodbye.

'Make sure you look after yourself, and don't go playin' the hero,' warned Maria. Standing on tiptoe, she kissed him on the cheek. 'We need you home.'

Bill gave him a firm handshake. 'Give 'em hell, Jez.'

With their goodbyes said, Jez and Cadi left for the station.

Making small talk as they walked, Jez tried his hardest to push the letter to the back of his mind. Glancing down, he saw the ring on Cadi's finger. With hindsight, he wished he'd proposed, but it was too late for that now.

As they approached the platform, he could see the train idling as passengers descended onto the platform. Keeping a tight hold of Cadi's hand, he cast an eye around them. 'Looks busy. I doubt I'll get a seat.'

'You will come back and see us after your training, won't you?' asked Cadi anxiously.

Jez placed his arms around her. 'Wild horses couldn't stop me!'

'And when you're settled somewhere, I'll come and visit you.'

Jez was staring over Cadi's shoulder. He couldn't say for certain, but he could have sworn he'd just seen Aled walking down the platform towards them. With the thought of Aled fast approaching and the letter springing to the forefront of his mind, he sank to one knee. Holding Cadi's hands in his, he looked up at her earnestly. 'I know I said it was a promise ring, but that's only because I thought you might run for the hills if I asked you to marry me. But Maria's always said that faint heart never won fair lady ...'

Cadi furrowed her brow. 'What on earth are you wittering on about?'

Seeing whom he assumed to be Aled drawing ever nearer, Jez blurted out his proposal. 'Cadi Williams, will you do me the honour of becoming my wife?' Kissing her hands, he looked up at her with such yearning that Cadi found herself nodding before the words left her lips.

'Of course I will.'

With a whoop of joy, he slid the ring onto her ring finger, whilst the people in their immediate vicinity broke into a round of applause. Getting back to his feet, he took Cadi in a tight embrace. Looking over her shoulder, Jez saw, with some satisfaction, that Aled, if indeed it was him, was walking away.

Lifting her up in his arms, he beamed at her. 'I can't wait to tell me nan.'

Laughing, Cadi pushed his hair back from his face, before sliding down between his arms. 'I can't wait to tell Poppy. She'll be that excited, I reckon she'll burst.' She remembered what Maria had said the previous evening. 'As for Maria, she'll be over the moon. She's always had a soft spot for you, and in truth she was quite disappointed when she learned that this was a promise ring rather than an engagement ring.' She grinned. 'I'm not going to say a word when I get home – I'll see how long it takes her to notice.'

Jez kissed the tip of her nose. 'What do you think your folks'll say?'

Cadi knew her father would most likely be thoroughly disappointed, but he would have to like it and lump it. She said as much to Jez, who pulled a face. 'When I get some proper leave, I reckon we should go and visit them, especially since I'm going to be their son-in-law.'

The guard blew his whistle, startling them both. 'I should've asked you weeks ago,' said Jez, 'cos we'd have had time for a proper celebration. But not to worry. I'll take you out for a slap-up meal when I come home.' Picking up his bag, he towed her by the hand to the train. Throwing his bags onto the train, he turned to face her. 'I don't half love you, Cadi Williams.'

She threw her arms around his neck. 'I love you too, Jeremy Thomas, so make sure you take care of yourself. And don't worry about your nan – I'll look after her for you.'

Taking her in his arms, Jez kissed Cadi with a passion she had never experienced before. Breaking free, he rested his forehead against hers. 'I'll write as soon as I'm able, and I'll telephone the first chance I get.'

'You better had,' said Cadi. Trying not to cry, she kissed him softly on the lips. 'Go on, Jez, get you gone before I start blubbing.'

Boarding the train, Jez walked down the carriages until he found one that was relatively empty. Taking a seat by the window, he waved to Cadi, who had followed him from the outside. He huffed on the window and drew a heart in the condensation. Grinning like a schoolgirl, Cadi blew him a kiss as the train slowly pulled away from the platform. Following the train until the platform ended, she continued to wave. Only when it was out of sight did she turn for home.

This morning she had been dreading saying goodbye to Jez, fearing what the future might bring, but it was with a spring in her step that she ascended the stairs to the concourse. She had come to Liverpool looking for adventure, and that's exactly what she'd got. But never for one moment did she expect to find herself a husband, and yet she'd done just that. And what a husband Jez was going to be!

As Cadi had predicted, the news of their engagement was received with great excitement. Poppy in particular wanted a blow-by-blow account of the proposal as well as a detailed description of the ring.

Flo had taken the news well, but warned Cadi not to get her hopes up when it came to her father.

'You know what he's like – a stubborn old fool to the end – so you must take his reaction with a pinch of salt.'

Maria was itching to get out her sewing machine, but as Cadi rightly pointed out, she would have to wait until they had seen her parents before arranging anything. 'I want to tell them when Jez is with me, so that they can actually meet their new son-in-law-to-be,' explained Cadi. 'Dad might give up the fight if he sees Jez with his own eyes.'

Bill placed the plates on the table. 'Why? Do you think the uniform will make a difference?'

'No, I want Jez with me because, no matter how many times I've told Dad I'm not coming home, it's like he doesn't believe me. But if he sees Jez, he won't have any other choice than to accept the truth.'

As they discussed the whys and wherefores, the phone began to ring. Instantly suspecting the worst, Cadi sprang to her feet. 'I bet it's Jez. I bet his train's broken down, or there's been an accident or …' She picked up the phone, gabbling, 'Greyhound pub, Cadi speaking.'

'Ah, the very woman.'

Her heart sank. 'Aled?'

'The one and only. How's tricks?'

'Not bad – you?'

'Same old, same old. When are you free?'

Searching for an excuse not to meet up, she voiced her thoughts. 'Difficult to say. I'm going to be too busy to do much, what with the B&B and the pub to run.'

She could hear the disappointment in his voice. 'Where's Maria?'

'She's still here, but Bill's got a job in the town hall, so we're a man down, as it were.'

'Oh.' Aled went quiet for a moment. 'I could always come to you?'

Cadi fell silent. She really didn't want Aled calling by, especially not now that she was a woman betrothed.

Sensing the awkward silence, Aled spoke cautiously. 'Cadi? Do you not want to see me?'

Feeling wretched, Cadi wondered whether she should tell him that she was engaged? But what if she did, and Aled asked her what that had to do with him calling by? She would both look and feel idiotic, for assuming he was only interested in her in a romantic way. There was nothing else for it – she would have to invite him over, then drop her recent engagement into conversation. That way, if Aled was only after her romantically, he would know she was off-limits; and if not, then it didn't matter. She smiled. 'Don't be silly. How about Sunday?'

He brightened. 'Splendid. Shall I come to you, or … ?'

No matter what his intentions, Cadi didn't particularly want him coming to the Greyhound. 'Have you heard of the Dockers' Umbrella?'

There was a stunned silence as Aled envisaged some sort of special umbrella used only by dockers. 'No?'

'It's what they call the overhead railway that runs along the docks. We could meet at Pier Head Station and go for some chips, then maybe a ride on the railway?'

'Splendid!' said Aled again. 'Shall I meet you there around eleven?'

'Yes, indeed. See you on Sunday.'

'Cheerio, Cadi.'

'Ta-ra, chuck.' Cadi replaced the receiver and smiled to herself. 'Ta-ra' was a real Scouse term, and it had fallen from her lips as though she'd been using it all her life. Retreating into the kitchen, she filled Maria and Bill in on her conversation. 'What do you think?'

Maria pulled a face. 'Can't see the harm,' she said, adding, 'Does Aled know about Jez popping the question?'

'No, I'll tell him on Sunday – not that I think he'll be particularly interested.'

'As long as you tell Jez, he's got no reason to worry. It's when you start hiding truths that people really get upset,' said Maria, wagging a finger, 'as well you know.'

Cadi knew that she was referring to them helping Izzy, and Maria was right. Keeping people in the dark only led to suspicion, and she had no intention of doing that to Jez.

As she approached Pier Head Station, Cadi was pleased to see that Aled was already waiting for her.

'You found it then?'

He looked up at the enormous railway on its bridge of stilts. 'Bit hard to miss!'

She pointed to a fish-and-chip shop across the way. 'We always go to Eddie's – he does the freshest fish with the crispiest batter.'

'Plenty of salt and vinegar,' said Aled authoritatively, 'that's the key to a good fish supper.'

As they stood in line for their dinner, Cadi noticed the looks of admiration Aled received from the others in the queue. 'If someone would've told me six months back that I'd waiting for fish and chips with you, I'd have thought them bonkers,' she said.

Aled laughed. 'You're not the only one. Funny how things turn out, isn't it?'

With their suppers wrapped in yesterday's issue of the *Echo*, they walked the short distance to the train station.

'Talking of how things work out, remember when I used to bleat on about how I was going to be this big career woman who shunned the very idea of marriage?' Holding her hand up, she wriggled her fingers.

Clasping her left hand, Aled stared at the ring. 'Bloomin' heck, you never said you was married! When did that happen?'

She smiled shyly. 'All right, so I'm not married, but I am engaged.'

The pair continued to talk as they ascended the steps. 'When did he pop the question? Only you never mentioned it in your letter?'

'The day he left – or rather, kind of ...' Cadi went on to explain the promise ring that changed into an engagement one.

The pair boarded the train and took a seat overlooking the docks. 'What did your parents say?'

Cadi opened the newspaper and took in the wonderful scent of salt and vinegar as it wafted upwards. 'Not told them yet. We're going to do that together, when Jez has some leave.' She looked up guiltily. 'I know we should've told them first, but Dad's been so difficult – he's only got himself to blame that he's the last to know.'

Aled popped a chip in his mouth and chewed thoughtfully. 'I understand what you're saying, but we are living in uncertain times. Surely a phone call or a letter wouldn't go amiss?'

But Cadi was sticking to her guns. 'When he heard you'd come to town, Dad was practically doing cartwheels, until I told him I knew all about his spiteful attempt to bring me home, he soon changed his tune then. I'm not having him belittle my engagement, and I'm pretty sure he will, because he doesn't seem to approve of anything I do.'

Aled looked at her mischievously. 'Well, you know the answer to that one: ditch Jez and marry me instead.' He laughed at the look of horror on Cadi's face. 'Calm down, chuck, I was only joking.'

Sagging with relief, Cadi shook her head. 'If my father heard you, he'd have marched us to the nearest registry office.'

Aled continued to smile whilst eating his supper, and Cadi couldn't help but notice how devilishly handsome her former acquaintance was. 'I must say I was rather hurt at the horrified look on your face when I suggested you marry me. Is the idea really that dreadful?'

Cadi turned her attention to her chips as she answered. 'It certainly would've been, at one time.'

He arched an eyebrow. 'And now?'

Cadi shrugged. 'Hypothetical, isn't it? But if you really pressed me for an answer, then I'd say you'd make some woman a wonderful husband.'

Aled's eyes twinkled as he laughed. 'You should become a politician, giving answers like that.'

She glanced up at him from under thick lashes. 'How's *Daphne*?' She said the other girl's name in withering tones.

Aled flashed her an impish grin, whilst wagging a chip in a reproving fashion. 'Now, now, play nicely!'

'Well, she was horrid about the Greyhound, and I don't think she particularly liked me much either – unless she's like that with all the girls, in which case I shouldn't imagine she's got many friends.'

Aled's grin broadened. 'I think she was a tad jealous.'

'A tad?' cried Cadi. 'She was positively green with envy.'

'When I told her I was going to stay at my friend's pub, I failed to mention that my friend was a woman, so you came as a bit of a surprise.' He glanced at Cadi in her green dress and court shoes. 'Daphne might have felt better about things, had you not been so stunningly beautiful.'

Cadi slapped his knee. 'Don't tease!'

He held a hand to his heart. 'I'm not teasing.' He winked at her, then carried on. 'If Daphne hadn't thought you a threat, she wouldn't have been so ...' He looked at the ceiling of the train as he tried to think of the correct word.

'Bitchy?' supplied Cadi.

He laughed. 'Succinct and to the point. But yes, that's as good a word as any.'

'Did you tell her she hadn't anything to worry about?' Cadi began, before adding, 'Hang on a mo, if you two aren't an item, then why is Daphne so jealous?'

Having finished his supper, Aled screwed the paper into a ball. 'Because she wants more than friendship.'

'And you?'

He shrugged. 'I wouldn't want to build her hopes up, only to dash them later on.'

Cadi eyed him curiously. 'What makes you so sure you will?'

'We've only known each other since joining up, and the only thing we've got in common is that we both come from farming families. And it's clear, from what Daphne's told me, that she very much wants to return to farming after the war – which is why I think she's set her sights on me. But I don't want to, or at least I don't think I do, so it would be wrong for me to get into a relationship that I think might be doomed from the start.'

Cadi was impressed. Aled was far more mature than she had given him credit for.

'Have you tried telling her how you feel?'

He nicked a chip from Cadi's open wrapper. 'Daphne's a bit like your dad – she only she hears what she wants to hear.'

'You mean she's persistent?'

Stretching his legs out, he crossed his feet. 'Don't get me wrong, she's not throwing herself at me. But it's obvious from our discussions, and the way she is around me – like when we were at the Greyhound – that she's keen. And she talks about the farm a lot, and has even said she wants a farmer for a husband.' Nudging Cadi's ankle with his feet, Aled chuckled, 'I'm no Einstein, but even I know what she's hinting at.'

'Do you find her attractive?'

He pushed himself upright. 'Of course. But it takes more than good looks to make a relationship work.' Seeing Cadi staring at him open-mouthed, he pulled a frown. 'What?'

'It's just ...' She shook her head. 'Nothing.' How could she tell Aled that if she had known he was like this, she would never have been so quick to dismiss him as a friend when they were younger.

It seemed that Aled had guessed her thoughts. 'Did I really come across as being that awful?'

Cadi opened her mouth to deny this, but changed her mind. As Maria said, the truth is better out than in. 'I'm afraid so.'

The mischievous grin returned. 'I guess covering you in muddy water wasn't my best chat-up line.'

'It was *not* muddy water, as well you know, seeing as you were the one doing the muck-spreading that day.'

He pulled an apologetic face. 'Yeah, but it sounds better than the truth, don't you think?'

She laughed. 'Probably would've smelled better too!' She tilted her head to one side as she gazed into his eyes. 'It's hard to look back at yourself as a child and justify the things you did or thought, because they were the thoughts of a child. Adults see things differently.' And she added to herself that, as an adult, she saw Aled very differently.

The train pulled to a halt and Cadi looked out of the window. 'We've been so busy chatting that we've missed the view.'

Gazing at Cadi, he smiled. 'I dunno about that.'

She rolled her eyes. 'Charmer. And if you talk like that to Daphne, you've only yourself to blame.'

'Why, does it work on you?'

'No, it does not, you cheeky swine!'

Aled watched the other passengers as they descended from the train. 'Good job we bought returns, isn't it?'

He winked. 'Or did you simply use that as an excuse to spend more time with me?'

Laughing, Cadi clapped her hands together. 'Now *that's* the Aled I remember.'

He grimaced ruefully. 'I wasn't very good at making friends, was I?'

She smiled kindly at him. 'I'd say it was six of one and half a dozen of the other.' Aware that they were in danger of missing the view once more, she looked pointedly out of the window. 'I don't want you to miss the view again – look, Aled, you can see for miles.'

Aled looked out over the Mersey. 'I know, I see it every time we go on a sortie.'

She clapped a hand to her head. 'How could I be so daft? There's me wanting to impress you with the view, when you've had the best one of all.'

'This is better, trust me.'

She knitted her eyebrows. 'How can that be?'

'Because when I'm sitting in the back of the plane, I'm hoping I get to see the view again, but here I can actually enjoy it.'

'Oh, Aled, I'm so sorry, I didn't think …'

He looked back over the Mersey. 'Don't worry about it. I'm glad I came up here with you – it reminds me what we're fighting for.'

Determined to keep the subject away from the war, she pointed out the dock where Jez used to work.

Aled eyed her curiously. 'What made him join up, do you think? Because he didn't have to, did he? Being in a reserved occupation.'

'It was the Blitz,' said Cadi. She turned her gaze to the other side of the carriage, which overlooked what was left of her beloved city. 'Jez wanted to do his bit, same as you. Why do you ask?'

'I'm always curious as to what drives people to sign on the dotted line.'

As the train reached its destination, they descended into the station below, before heading for a walk around the bit of the city that had survived the bombing.

'Last time I saw you, you hadn't been back home. Has that changed?' Cadi asked.

Aled pushed his hands into his pockets. 'Not as yet, but I will do, although I'm not sure when. I suppose I'm a bit like you. I'm not particularly looking forward to going home and spending my precious leave with a father who's barely speaking to me.'

'Has he not changed his mind?' said Cadi, who was surprised that Aled's father wouldn't be beaming with pride at his son's achievements.

'God, no, it was bad enough when they thought I was going to be a pilot. When he found out I was a rear-gunner, it reaffirmed his belief that I am a fool – he even said so.'

Cadi stared at him open-mouthed. How could any parent say something so horrid when their child was doing such a dangerous job? She said as much to him.

'Because he's angry and scared.'

'Not to mention thoughtless!' snapped Cadi. Hearing how Aled's father had spoken to his son had clearly got under her skin. 'My dad's just as bad. Throughout the whole of the Blitz not once did he come on the phone to forgive and forget. Heck, he didn't even phone to ask how I was – only Mam did that. Talk about pride coming before a fall.'

'It must be summat to do with them both being hardy Welshmen.'

'Stubborn old fools more like,' said Cadi bitterly.

Aled laughed. 'I can see that your father's going to get an earful when you see him next.'

'I know they're old-school – a different breed if you like – but this is war! You'd think they'd wind their necks in and jolly well grow up when their own children are in danger, especially when they've already lived through the first lot.'

'Maybe that's why they're being so stubborn, because they're desperate to get us home?'

Cadi relented a little. 'You'd think they'd see that we're only doing what hundreds of others have done before us, and would cut us some slack.'

As they continued on, Cadi told Aled of Jez's nan, Carrie, and how she'd taken the news.

'Ah, but that's different, because Carrie is a woman. You've only got to look at the way our mams have reacted to see that.'

'What is it with these men?' said Cadi, adding quickly, 'Not you and Jez, but the old folk.'

'Different generation, who are used to ruling the roost. They don't know how to cope when we rebel, so they fight fire with fire.'

Cadi heaved a sigh. 'So you're saying they'll never come round to our way of thinking?'

'We can always hope.' Aled glanced at his wristwatch. 'I've had a lovely time, but I'd best be getting back.'

'It's been lovely. I'm glad we met up.'

'Me too. Would it be too forward of me to ask if we can do it again?'

'I don't see why not – just let me know when you're free.'

Aled stood awkwardly for a moment, before waving Cadi goodbye and heading for the train. He'd wanted to give her a farewell peck on the cheek, or the very least a hug, but with Cadi being engaged, he knew that she was well and truly out of bounds – more was the pity.

As Cadi walked in the direction of home, she recalled Aled's conversation. If he was right, then her father might never change his mind about her and Jez. So she might as well tell him in a letter, let him get used to the idea and then go and visit.

When she got back to the Greyhound she was confronted by a curious Maria, who wanted to know how Aled had taken the news of Cadi's engagement. After reassuring her that he had taken the news in his stride, Cadi told Maria of Aled's suggestion that she should write to her parents.

'I think it's for the best,' agreed Maria. 'I dare say they'd be ever so upset if they heard it on the grapevine. And with Poppy and Aled both knowing the truth, word could easily slip out.'

'I didn't want to break it to them in such a manner, but I can see it does have its advantages. Not only will I not have to worry about them hearing the news second hand, but they'll have time to get used to the idea, and I won't have to suffer earache whilst they do.'

Cadi wrote and posted the letter that very same day, and when Jez rang to speak to her later that evening, she told him of her meeting with Aled and of her subsequent letter to her parents.

'You weren't as keen when I suggested it,' said Jez. 'What's changed your mind?'

'Talking to Aled. His father's just like mine, and I realised Aled was right. Dad'll never take the news well, so what's the point in wasting my time going there, only to be insulted, when I can tell him in a letter?'

Jez couldn't help but feel put out. The thought that Cadi was willing to listen to Aled rather than him wasn't a pleasant one.

'Sounds like you had a good old chinwag?'

'We did that,' admitted Cadi. 'I actually ended up feeling sorry for Daphne!' She went on to explain how the other woman doted on Aled.

Jez's cheeks burned hotly. It was a good job Cadi didn't know the truth. Thankfully, the conversation had turned from Aled and Daphne to Jez's time in the RAF.

'It's very intense, and there's always something new going on. It's a lot more fun than working down the docks.'

'Maybe I should think about joining,' joked Cadi.

There was a momentary pause before Jez spoke. 'Really?'

She leaned against the bar. 'No, not really.'

'But if you did, we might see more of each other – maybe even get posted to the same station.'

Cadi frowned. 'You really think I should sign up?'

Jez kicked himself for saying it, because he knew he was only doing so to get her away from Aled. 'It's up to you, but it would be nice if you did and we ended up at the same base.'

'I s'pose ...' She hesitated. 'But what about Maria? I couldn't leave her in the lurch.'

'Are you kidding? Nan'd take your place in a heartbeat – she loves working behind the bar, and Maria could do the laundry and heavier tasks.'

'Sounds like you've got it all worked out,' laughed Cadi. 'How long have you been thinking about this?'

Jez wanted to say ever since she mentioned herself and Aled being alone in Liverpool together, but he knew better than that. 'I haven't, but the more you think about it, the more it makes sense.'

Later that night, as she lay in her bed, Cadi mulled his words over. Slowly drifting into sleep, she saw herself standing beside a bomber, with Aled on one side in his bomb-aimer's uniform, and Jez on the other in his pilot's gear. Both were smiling at her, both wanting her to go with them to their separate planes.

A week had passed since Cadi's last conversation with Jez and she was making a fisherman's pie when Maria called her through to the bar. Covering the mouthpiece of the phone with her hand, Maria mouthed to Cadi, 'It's your mam,' adding as a warning, 'and she does *not* sound happy.'

Cadi rolled her eyes. 'I guess that means they got the letter.' Taking the handset from Maria, she took a deep breath. 'Hello, Mam. I take it you got my letter?'

Jill replied, her tone leaden, 'It's your dad.'

'I know,' sighed Cadi, 'because it always is. Why doesn't—'

Jill cut her daughter short. 'There's been a cave-in down the mine ...'

They were the words every mining family dreaded. Cadi steadied herself against the bar counter, tears already tracking their way down her cheeks. 'Is he all right?'

She could hear the hoarse emotion in her mother's voice. 'It's bad, Cadi. Arwel's in there with him.'

'No!' Cadi felt her knees give way, and Maria rushed across the bar to grab her. 'What about Dylan?'

'He's all right. He was near the mine entrance at the time, but he says Dad and Arwel were further down the tunnel when it collapsed.'

'I'm coming home. I'll get the first train I can.'

'God bless you, sweetheart, but there's no sense in rushing over. It's not as if you can do anything to help.'

'I can be there to support you.' She paused to gulp back the tears. 'I am *not* going to leave you on your own.'

'You're a good girl, Cadi.'

She smiled bravely. 'I'll see you soon. And, Mam?'

'Yes, dear?'

'I love you.'

'Love you too, sweetheart.'

Replacing the receiver, Cadi turned to Maria. 'My father and brother are trapped down one of the mines.'

Maria enveloped her friend in her arms. 'Oh, Cadi, I'm so sorry.'

Cadi's bottom lip quivered as she spoke. 'I told Mam I'd get there as soon as I could.'

Breaking their embrace, Maria headed for the door. 'You gather your things whilst I give Plevin's Taxis a shout.'

'Thanks, Maria. The sooner I leave, the quicker I'll get there,' said Cadi.

A few minutes later, Maria called up from below. 'Plevin's already outside waiting.'

'Ta. Can you give Jez's base a call and explain what's going on, please? Only I won't have time.'

'Consider it done.'

Whilst she was downstairs Cadi had held back the tears, but now she was on her own she let them flow. If her father was under the part of the tunnel that had collapsed, she knew there was no way he would be getting out of there alive – Arwel neither. Cramming a change of clothes into her bag, she fished her savings out of the jam jar on the windowsill and put them in her purse. Clattering downstairs, she wiped her tears away and took a couple of deep breaths before entering the bar. Deep in conversation, Maria waved Cadi over. 'It's Jez.'

Taking the handset from her, Cadi held back tears as Jez's voice, full of concern, came down the receiver. 'I'm so sorry. Give my best to your folks, and call if you need me.'

Her voice came out in a broken whisper as she fought to control her emotions. 'Thanks, Jez.'

'I wish I could go with you.'

She gave a grim smile of determination. 'I know, but don't worry – I'll be fine on my own.'

'Do you want me to tell Poppy and Izzy, or do they already know?'

'I should imagine Poppy's mam will've told her, but you can ring her if you like.'

'I'll do it now. Take care, my love.'

'Will do. Love you.'

She could hear the smile in his voice. 'Love you more.'

Unable to hold back the tears, Cadi quickly replaced the receiver and kissed Maria on the cheek. 'I'll phone as soon as I know what's what.'

The train journey seemed to take for ever and it was late in the day by the time Cadi arrived in Rhos. Heading straight for the mine, she soon found her mother, who was being supported by the Hardings.

Seeing her daughter, Jill rushed to take her in a tight embrace. 'Cadi! I'm so glad you're here.'

'Hitler himself couldn't've stopped me,' said Cadi.

Linking her arm through Cadi's, Jill walked her over to where the Hardings stood, anxiously watching the entrance to the mine.

Seeing Cadi approach, they turned to greet her, and Cadi asked the question uppermost in her thoughts. 'Any news?'

Mr Harding shook his head. 'I'm afraid not.'

Cadi's gaze gravitated towards a cart and the bodies that were lined up on the back of it. She pointed to the cart, her hand trembling. 'Wh – who ... ?'

Jill turned Cadi away. 'Don't ask, cariad, it's best not to know.'

Swallowing hard, Cadi fixed her gaze on the mine entrance. 'Have we any idea how far back it goes, or how many men are left in there?' She hesitated, almost too afraid to ask her next question. 'Have they found any survivors?'

Mr Harding pulled a grim face. 'Truth is, we don't know the extent of the collapse, but there's still a lot of folk unaccounted for. And in answer to your last question,' he sighed ruefully, 'no, not as yet.'

Jill ushered Cadi forward. 'We've tried calling out to see if we get any response, but so far we've not had any joy. Why don't you try, luv?'

Cadi called out to her father and brother, but her cries were met by a deathly silence.

For the next hour or so they took it in turns to call out to those trapped inside, but with nothing coming back they were beginning to give up hope until one of the men thought he'd heard a faint response.

Calling for silence from those outside the shaft, the man called again, and this time they all heard it.

Jill clutched her daughter's hand. 'I bet it's your father. He's been a miner all his life – he knows what to do, and the signs to watch out for.' She tightened her grip. 'He'll have Arwel with him, he'll …' She fell silent as the men moving the rocks began to get excited.

Cadi and Jill ran to the front. 'Have you found them? Have you found my boys?' cried Jill, her voice hoarse with emotion.

One of the men turned to face them. 'Please, Mrs Williams. We don't know what's what yet, so if you wouldn't mind standing back.'

As they backed away, Cadi turned to apologise for standing on someone's toes. Her jaw dropped. 'Aled!'

He smiled. 'You look surprised to see me.'

'I am. I thought you were in Speke.'

'Dad rang to tell me about the collapse and, seeing as the RAF still owes me that forty-eight, I used it to come here.'

'I see—' said Cadi, but her mother's cries cut her short.

'Arwel!' Sobbing with relief, Jill ran into the arms of her son, nearly knocking him for six in the process.

Leaving Aled, Cadi ran to join her mother. 'Thank God you're all right.' Craning over Arwel's shoulder, she tried to see if she could spot her father. 'Where's Dad – wasn't he with you?'

She felt Arwel sag slightly in her arms. 'I haven't seen or heard from Dad since before the collapse.'

Jill spoke softly. 'What happened?'

Arwel wiped the back of his hand across his forehead. 'It all happened so fast, I'm not really sure. I remember hearing a lot of shouting, and what sounded like thunder rumbling in the distance. I don't know whether Dad was one of them shouting or not, but I do remember him saying, a long time ago, that you should never run towards the sound, but away from it, because you'll not outrun a collapse. So I'm hoping that's what he's done.'

'He will have,' said Cadi knowledgeably. 'Dad's a miner to his bones, he'd not go against his own advice.'

'They've not found him yet,' said Jill encouragingly, 'so it only makes sense that he's down in the belly of the mine somewhere.' She paused. 'Did you hear anyone else whilst you were down there?'

Arwel averted his gaze to the floor. 'I tried calling out, but you can't hear anything, save people coughing or yelling for help.'

'It sounds as though there's a lot of survivors,' said Cadi optimistically. 'And the rescuers must have broken through most of the collapse, otherwise they'd not have got to you.'

Arwel didn't look so certain. 'A collapse doesn't follow a certain path, and it can trigger smaller collapses in other areas of the mine. It's possible it could've skipped over me – it all depends on the structure above you.'

Cadi paled, then started as Aled spoke from behind. 'Is there anything I can do to help?'

Arwel looked from Aled to Cadi. 'I thought … ?'

Cadi shook her head. 'Aled's only here because his dad told him about the collapse. I'm still with Jez, if that's what you're thinking.'

'I must admit—' Arwel began, before being cut off by the cries of the men behind them.

'You stay here with Mam,' Cadi instructed Arwel. 'Me and Aled'll go and see what's going on.'

Hurrying over, Cadi crossed the fingers on both hands, but the men who were being stretchered out obviously hadn't been as lucky as Arwel. Catching up to one of the injured men, she looked earnestly into his face. 'My dad's Dewi Williams. Do you know where he is?'

The man shook his head. 'Sorry, cariad, it's as black as a witch's hat down there.'

She went down the line of men, asking each of them in turn. It wasn't until she reached the man second from last that she got news of Dewi's whereabouts.

'As soon as we heard the rumblin' – and it were far off, mind you – Dewi threw his tools down and started runnin' towards the entrance of the mine. He were lookin' for Arwel.' The miner shook his head. 'We told him to stop, but he wasn't for listenin'.'

Cadi looked at the men responsible for carrying him out. 'Is the entrance cleared as far as these men?'

One of the miners adjusted the cap on his head. 'All we've done is clear a hole big enough to get through to those that've survived. It's possible someone could still be trapped, depending on whereabouts they are. That's why folk are still digging near the entrance, but we have to be careful, so we don't cause further collapses in trying to get this lot out.'

Cadi looked at Aled. 'What am I going to tell me mam and Arwel? He'll be devastated if he knows Dad ran into danger trying to protect him.'

Aled laid a reassuring hand on her shoulder. 'Just tell them they haven't found Dewi yet.'

Nodding, Cadi had turned to do exactly that when the man on the last stretcher called out to her feebly. 'Is that Cadi?'

She hastened to the side of the wounded man. 'Yes.' She looked down into his face, thick with soot, with only the whites of his eyes truly visible. 'Sorry, do I know you?'

Coughing into his hand, he shook his head, then winced. 'The name's Sam Mitchell. I was by your dad when the roof came down.'

Sinking down beside the stretcher, Cadi clasped his hand in hers. 'Have you spoken to him? Is he all right?'

He tilted his head to face her. 'When it first happened, no one knew up from down, so we focused on finding out who was who, and seeing if we could guess whereabouts we were in relation to the entrance.' He swallowed, then began coughing.

Standing up, Cadi looked around for someone to get him a drink, but it seemed Aled was one step ahead of her and was already hastening back with a cup of water. Cadi held it to the man's lips so that he might drink.

Thanking her for her assistance, he continued, 'I wasn't far from your dad, but neither of us could move. So we talked about our families – you know, to keep morale up – and he told me about you, and your pub,' he glanced at Aled, 'and your fiancé. Jez, is it?'

Cadi followed his gaze before turning back. 'That's right, my fiancé is Jez, but this is John Davies's boy, Aled.'

The man stifled a chuckle. 'That's right, the chosen one.' He smiled at Cadi. 'Your father was keen for me to pass on a message—'

Shaking her head fervently, Cadi cut him short. 'Not yet; if you do, it means he's unable to do it himself, and I'm not ready to give up on him yet.' Standing up, she strode over to the man who had stretchered Sam out of the mine. 'I need you to show me where you found Sam. He says my father wasn't far from him – they were certainly close enough to talk.'

The miner looked around him dubiously. 'Sorry, luv, but I can't take you in, it's far too dangerous.'

With a tear trickling down her cheek, Cadi felt her lips wobbling as she attempted to smile. 'You don't understand. My father asked Sam to pass a message on to me, which sounds as though he thought he wouldn't make it out. We've been at odds for ever such a long time, and I can't lose him, without even trying.'

Sighing heavily, the man took her by the hand. 'You've got five minutes, no more. You don't let go of me, and you come out when I tell you to: understand?'

Cadi nodded. 'Perfectly.' She turned to Aled. 'Tell Mam and Arwel I won't be long.'

Walking into the mine, Cadi blinked at the sheer depth of the darkness that engulfed her. As they moved on, the man stopped suddenly. 'It was by here; as you can tell, we've not got a lot further.'

Even with the light on his helmet, Cadi could barely see any difference. She called out into the darkness, hoping to hear a response, but all she could hear was the sound of men putting rubble into the carts to take away. The miner squeezed her hand in his. 'Try again.'

This time Cadi didn't just call out to her father, but spoke to him as though he could hear every word. 'Dad? It's me, Cadi. I can't see you, but I know you're in here somewhere. You needn't worry about Arwel – he's outside with Mam, waiting for you. Only we can't get you out if we don't know where you are, and I really need you, Dad. After all, what little girl doesn't want her daddy to walk her down the aisle?' She fell silent, expecting to hear only silence back, but was encouraged when there came the faintest of murmurings.

'Cariad?'

Cadi's heart skipped a beat. 'Dad? Is that you?'

With nothing coming back, the men began to dig in the area where the voice had come from. The miner took Cadi's hand. 'I think we should get you out of here.'

She pulled her hand from his grip and began tugging at the rocks, throwing them into the cart as though they were made of paper. 'Just two more minutes.'

The miner stepped forward. 'I know you're keen to find your father, but ...' His voice melted into silence as Cadi, seeing a hand poking through the rocks, dived onto the ground; holding it tightly in hers, she felt the hand grip her back.

'Dad!'

As more rocks were removed, Dewi's face became visible. 'Cadi, you came.'

Gripping his hand in hers, she kissed his knuckles. 'Of course I did.'

The miner knelt down beside Cadi. 'You've really got to go, so that we can do our job and get your father out of here.'

Nodding, Cadi wiped her hand across her father's brow. 'I'll see you on the outside.' With that being said, she followed the man out and beckoned her mother, brother and Aled over. 'They've found him, and he's alive.'

Jill sank to her knees. 'Thank God, thank God' were the only words she could manage, before breaking into sobs of joy.

Cadi pointed to a stretcher. 'That's him, Mam! It's got to be.'

Rushing over, Jill was the first to reach her husband's side. Holding his hand, she walked beside the stretcher, telling him how much she loved him, and that he needed to find a job that wasn't so dangerous.

Cadi joined her parents. 'Are you all right, Dad? Do you think you've broken anything?'

Dewi winced as he tried to move his fingers and toes. 'All seems to be in good working order, although my pride's taken a hell of a bashing, but I think that's probably a good thing.' He beckoned Cadi closer and held her hand. 'I'm sorry I've behaved like such an arse.

413

I was so caught up in wanting what I thought was best for you that I never stopped to think I might be wrong.'

Leaning back, Cadi smiled through shining tears. 'I don't care about any of that any more. I just want everything to go back to the way it was.'

Dewi nodded. 'No more interfering, I promise.' He glanced down at the ring on Cadi's finger. 'You must bring Jez home to meet the rest of the family.'

Cadi's heart gave a joyous leap. 'He'd love that – he's been ever so keen to see everyone.'

Dewi smiled weakly. 'And how's the B&B?'

Cadi waved a nonchalant hand. 'It's going really well, but I think we'll leave that for another time. First we need to get you some medical attention, because you were down that mine for a long time.'

Dewi began to shake his head, but Jill cut him off. 'Cadi's right, you need to get checked out like everyone else.'

Dewi looked towards the bodies lined up on the cart. 'I should be back there helping.'

Jill put out a hand to restrain him from trying to get up. 'Sorry, Dewi, but I'm not going to stand by and watch you go back down and risk your life all over again.'

'They're my *mates*,' Dewi said softly, 'I can't just leave them there ...'

'You're not fit, Dad,' said Arwel. 'You'd cause them more problems, going in like that.'

Unable to move properly, Dewi sank back onto the stretcher. 'I suppose you're right, but I'm coming back here first thing tomorrow.'

Bending down, Cadi kissed her father on the forehead. 'Now let's get you back—'

She stopped speaking as Dewi called out, 'Aled? As I live and breathe. Shouldn't you be in the arse-end of a plane somewhere?'

Aled laughed. 'Dad rang and told me what had happened, so I thought I'd come and lend a hand, seeing as I had a bit of time owing.'

Dewi smiled. 'You only get that sort of community spirit living in a village.'

Cadi was quick to correct her father. 'During the Blitz everyone came together, but I'll tell you all about it on the way to the hospital.'

It was much later when Dewi returned home. He had suffered two broken ribs, as well as a fracture to his forearm. Despite his injuries, it seemed he was keen to hear about Cadi's life in Liverpool, a topic that she was glad to talk about.

'I find it hard to look at you as anything other than my little Cadi,' admitted Dewi as he entered the small house, 'but with all you've had to tell me, it's clear to see you're a grown woman.'

Cadi placed the kettle on to boil. 'I've been through some tough experiences – a lot of them frightening – but I'd like to think I'm a better person for it.'

Dewi eyed his only daughter with deep affection. 'You and Poppy started a business and made it a roaring success. It may have taken me longer than it should have, but credit where it's due: you've done a grand job and I'm proud of you.'

Cadi blinked back the tears. She had been yearning for her father's approval for such a long time, and so to finally get it was quite overwhelming. 'Thanks, Dad, that means a lot, especially coming from you.'

'I mean every word of it. And the first chance we get, me and your mam'll come and see you at the Greyhound.'

Cadi beamed happily. 'There'll be a bed made up for you any time you're ready.'

Arwel placed his arm around his sister's shoulders. 'The perfect ending to a horrid day!'

Nodding through her tears, Jill leaned up to kiss her husband's cheek. 'I don't know what happened in there to change your mind.'

Dewi smiled grimly. 'When you're trapped with nothing but your own thoughts, things suddenly become very clear. And the idea that I might leave this earth without ever having said I was sorry was more than I could bear.'

'Which is why you asked Sam to pass on a message,' said Cadi, 'and that's why I knew I had to go and look for you myself.'

'Just as well you did,' admitted Dewi, 'else they might've found me too late.'

Cadi shuddered at the thought. 'After this cup of tea I'm going to go back to the mine and see if there's anything I can do to help.'

Jill went to object, but Dewi interrupted. 'She's a woman now, Jill. If Cadi wants to go and help, I don't see why she shouldn't.'

So it was with her father's approval that Cadi headed back to the mine, where she approached Aled, who was barrowing some of the rubble away.

'I've come to help.'

One of the workers looked up sharply. 'Sorry, love, but there's nowt here for you to do.'

Cadi nodded at a rubble-filled wheelbarrow. 'Why can't I do that?'

He raised his brow. 'Because it'd be far too heavy and you'd only do yourself an injury—'

He stopped abruptly as Cadi began throwing the contents of the barrow into the back of the trailer. 'Don't worry about me, *luv*, I move beer barrels as part of my living.'

With the barrow empty, she took it over to fill up with more rubble. Aled came jogging alongside her with an empty barrow of his own. 'You certainly showed him.'

Cadi spoke through pursed lips. 'Small-minded villagers, that's the problem round here – folk get set in their ways and they expect everyone else to follow suit.'

'You're certainly proving him wrong,' noted Aled, as Cadi picked up another rock and threw it into her barrow with comparative ease.

'Someone needs to!' She gave him a sidelong glance. 'You said your dad rang to tell you the news. Does that mean he's forgiven you for going into the RAF?'

Aled wrinkled the side of his nose. 'Don't know if I'd go that far. I think he rang me more out of panic than anything else, but I wasn't going to pass up the chance to smooth things over. And as I'm here for another day, I'm hoping I'll have time to do exactly that.'

'I hope so, but it shouldn't have taken a disaster to bring us all together.'

'It's often the way,' said Aled knowledgeably. Straightening his back, he wiped the sweat from his brow. 'I must admit I'm not used to this kind of work; running, jumping up and down on the spot, polishing the buttons on my jacket until they shine, yes, but not lifting ruddy great barrows of rocks.'

Cadi hefted another barrow-load over to the trailer. 'I remember the first time I tried lifting a beer barrel, I could barely budge it an inch – in fact it took three of us – but as time wore on, we got stronger and stronger until we could do it on our own.' She flexed her arms. 'You soon grow muscles.'

'So I see.'

She glanced up at a familiar tractor. 'Where's your dad? Our Alun too, come to that?'

Aled grimaced. 'They've taken one of the carts to the morgue.'

Her face fell. 'I think I'd rather shift rocks than do that. Poor Alun, I bet he'll know some of them – your dad too.'

Aled shrugged. 'Possibly, but someone's got to do it.'

The pair continued to work, but when the light faded too much for them to continue safely, the men called a halt. Organising themselves to reconvene the following day, they all went their separate ways.

'I know I said I'm strong,' confessed Cadi, 'but I feel as though my arms are about to drop off.'

'You and me both,' said Aled. 'Are you coming back tomorrow?'

She nodded. 'I want to make sure it's safe before any member of my family sets foot in there again. You?'

'Of course! I'll be down straight after breakfast.'

*

The next day they breakfasted early and the whole family headed for the mine, even Dewi, who insisted on supervising. The boys set about securing the shaft, whilst Cadi and Aled continued to help shift the rubble.

When most of the work was done, Cadi excused herself so that she might go and telephone Jez and Maria with the good news.

'That's fantastic, Cadi,' said Jez. 'Does Poppy know?'

'I believe her mam was going to tell her this morning, but I'll give her a ring later so that I can tell her about Dad.'

Jez was smiling as he spoke. 'I must say it's a relief hearing that your father has decided to accept our engagement.'

'Aled said you'd be pleased,' said Cadi absent-mindedly.

There was a brief pause before Jez's voice came enquiringly down the line. 'You've already phoned Aled?'

'No. Didn't I say? Aled's here, he—' She got no further, because Jez was already speaking.

'Why's he there? His family aren't miners!'

'No, but he's part of the community, so when his father rang—'

'He couldn't wait to get there,' said Jez bitterly.

Cadi was taken aback. Why would Jez speak as though the collapse was some kind of jolly for Aled? 'I wouldn't put it quite like that, but I s'pose if you mean it was a chance for him to make amends with his father, then you could say the same about me.'

Jez, however, thought differently. Daphne had written that letter making Cadi out to be the guilty party, but in Jez's eyes it was Aled who was guilty.

Thinking that he hadn't heard her, Cadi reiterated her words, adding, 'Like you've already said, Aled didn't *have* to come – his family aren't miners – so I think it was jolly nice of him to give up his forty-eight in order to help out.'

This was too much for Jez. 'You don't honestly believe he's there for his father, do you? Surely you can't be that naive?'

'Not *just* his father; obviously he's here to help with the rescue as well ...'

'He's there because of you,' said Jez briskly. 'If you weren't there, then he wouldn't be either – I'd lay money on it.'

Having thought Jez had given up his jealous notions, Cadi was annoyed to hear him making such wild assumptions.

'You can't say that! You don't know what goes on Aled's head.'

'Yes, I do,' snapped Jez. 'I knew it from the moment he stepped into the Greyhound, but you made out like I was being jealous, so I backed off. But even you must see that ringing someone most days and arranging to get posted so that you can be near them, then rushing halfway across the country so that you can spend the weekend with them, can only mean one thing.'

'Yes,' cried Cadi. 'It means my fiancé is paranoid!'

'*Paranoid?* Wouldn't you be, if you were me? As soon as I seen him at the station I *knew*—'

420

Cadi cut him off. 'Station? What station? What are you blithering on about?'

'I'll tell you what I'm *blithering* on about,' snapped Jez. 'The day I left for Prestwich I seen Aled on the platform. He was making a beeline in your direction, until he seen me going down on one knee. I had hoped that would put an end to his shenanigans, but apparently not.'

Cadi stood in stunned silence before speaking in low tones. 'I wondered why you'd changed your mind about the promise ring. I thought it was because you wanted to marry me, but it seems you only did it to warn Aled off.'

'Not that it worked,' said Jez sulkily, before his ears caught up with her words. 'Wait, no! I love you, Cadi, I'd never have asked you to marry me otherwise. I didn't do it *just* to warn Aled off.'

'You shouldn't have done it to warn anyone off,' said Cadi. 'An engagement ring is meant to be a symbol of an intended marriage, *not* a tag of ownership. Good God, I'm not a dog!'

'I never said you were,' spluttered Jez, but Cadi wasn't in the mood for listening.

'Don't bother, because right now I don't know whether I would believe a word that leaves your lips. So much for trust!' With tears forming, she replaced the handset of the telephone rather heavily before wiping her eyes, leaving the post office customers trying to pretend they had gone temporarily deaf.

Cadi stalked towards her old school. How could Jez be so underhand? She'd truly believed he loved her, yet it seemed he was treating her as though she were

421

some sort of trophy that needed guarding. As for Aled chasing her across the country? She shook her head. Jez had definitely got that bit wrong. She hesitated. *Had* Jez got that bit wrong? Aled had hinted that he liked her; and Maria had noticed something too. Surely Jez couldn't be right? To be sure, she left the school behind and headed for the mine, where she found Aled sweeping up.

'Can I have a word?'

He put the brush to one side and followed her away from potential eavesdroppers. Cadi turned to face him. 'I've just spoken to Jez, and I'm afraid things got a little heated because he made some wild accusations.' Taking a deep breath, she relayed the entirety of their conversation. 'I'm so sorry, I don't know what got into him, but I have to know …'

'If he's right?'

She nodded meekly. 'Not that it excuses his behaviour.'

Standing so that they were face-to-face, Aled placed his hands on her shoulders. 'Jez isn't making stuff up or imagining things. I *do* find you attractive, and if you weren't with him, then I'd definitely have made a move. As for following you up here? I'll not deny that my father and the disaster weren't the only reasons I came up.'

'And the platform? Did you see him proposing?'

'No, but I was there, and Jez must've seen me, but I didn't see either of you.'

'It still doesn't excuse his behaviour. I bet that's why he suggested I joined the WAAF.'

'Because of me?' said Aled, a smirk tweaking his lips.

'Yes, and it's not funny!'

'No, but it is a typically male thing to do,' said Aled truthfully. 'I don't know a single man, *including* myself, who wouldn't get defensive if they knew another man was interested in the woman they were courting. So why are you giving him such a hard time?'

Cadi hung her head in shame. 'Because I know I was in the wrong.' Feeling further explanation was needed, she continued, 'When I gave you that peck on the cheek and said I'd visit you in Lincoln, I only did it to annoy Daphne. It was the wrong thing to do, and I *knew* Jez would be annoyed – and rightfully so – should he find out what I'd done.'

Aled looked cross. 'So you used me to get at Daphne?'

Cadi nodded mutely. 'I'm sorry, Aled.'

He shook his head. 'I'm disappointed, because I rather hoped you meant it, but Daphne *was* being a major pain in the backside that weekend, so I suppose I can see why you retaliated. I only wish you'd chosen a different way to do it. How did you leave things with Jez?'

She pulled a guilty face. 'I put the phone down on him.'

'Oh dear. Looks like you've got some apologising to do.'

'What am I going to say? I can hardly tell him the truth – not after the way I've treated him.'

Aled shrugged. 'I'm afraid I can't help you with that one.'

Cadi peeked shyly at him. 'I know I've got no right to ask this, but can we let bygones be bygones?'

'Of course. We all makes mistakes,' he winked, 'even me.'

'Thanks, Aled, you're a gent.'

He grinned. 'I know.'

Thanking him again, Cadi bade him goodbye as she headed back to the post office. She would have to hope that Jez would accept her apologies.

When his voice came down the telephone, Cadi could hear that he was being guarded.

'I'm sorry, Jez, I shouldn't have stormed off the way I did. I've spoken to Aled and he said you were right and that he had been interested in me, and it was part of the reason why he came to Wales.'

There was a moment's silence before Jez spoke.

'So I wasn't being paranoid?'

'No, you weren't. I can't apologise enough.'

'You were right in one way, though,' said Jez. 'I should've trusted you.'

Cadi's cheeks bloomed. 'Can we agree to put the matter behind us and start afresh?'

She could hear that he was smiling. 'Of course we can.'

'Thanks, Jez.'

'I'll ring you when I get home.'

Placing the receiver back down, Cadi thanked her lucky stars that Jez had chosen to accept her apology. Although in the back of her mind she couldn't help thinking that if Jez knew she'd kissed Aled, albeit a peck on the cheek, he might not have been quite so forgiving.

Making his way back to the workers, Aled mused over Cadi's revelations. Up to this point he had hoped they could have some kind of future, should he bide his

424

time, but it was clear now that Cadi was in love with Jez. He turned his thoughts to Daphne: young, attractive and very keen on him. Was he being unfair in not giving the girl a chance? He smiled. There was only one way to find out.

Chapter Ten

September 1941

Several weeks had passed since Cadi's return to Liverpool, and Maria and Cadi were in the kitchen making scones.

'What time's Jez getting into the station?' said Maria as she cut the fruitless scones out with a pastry-cutter.

Cadi glanced up at the clock over the mantel. 'Two fifteen, so I'd best get a wriggle on. Thanks for letting me have the evening off.'

'My pleasure,' said Maria. She placed the scones on a baking tray. 'I must say I'm glad you managed to sort things out *before* he came home.'

'You're not the only one,' said Cadi, undoing her pinny. 'I'll bring him round to say hello before we go to his nan's.'

'No rush! He's going to be home for a week, so we've plenty of time.'

Cadi grabbed her mackintosh off the peg by the back door and headed off to meet her fiancé. She had the whole week planned out. They would visit the cinema, go for walks in Sefton Park and reminisce about times gone by, and she would cook him all his favourite meals.

Dashing up the steps to the station, Cadi gave a squeal of delight as she clapped eyes on Jez. 'You're home!'

Picking her up, he swung her round before setting her down. 'I certainly am. And guess what?'

'What?'

'I know you didn't like the idea of me flying a plane, so you'll be pleased to know that I've been selected to train as an engineer, so I shall have both feet firmly on the ground.'

Cadi smiled sheepishly. 'I *am* relieved, but it's not about me. How do you feel? Are you dreadfully disappointed?'

Jez laughed. 'Not at all. They took me up in one of their kites and reintroduced me to my breakfast!'

Cadi laughed out loud. 'Oh, poor Jez. Was it really that awful?'

'Worse. It seems flying isn't for everyone. First I got dizzy, then I got sick – not much of a man, eh?'

'Don't be silly,' scolded Cadi. 'I'm *glad* you didn't get through. Sorry, Jez, but the very thought of you up there made me feel quite ill.'

'That makes two of us,' chuckled Jez, placing his arm around her waist. 'So you're not disappointed?'

'Far from it. I'm delighted.'

'I didn't want to think I'd let you down ...'

'You could *never* let me down.'

As they left the station they chatted about Jez's training. Cadi listened eagerly. 'It sounds wonderful. I must admit I'm quite envious.'

He kissed the top of her head. 'You still thinking of joining up?'

Cadi shook her head. 'Whilst it sounds exciting, I'm happy where I am. The Greyhound is my home, and now the bombing's eased off' – she crossed her fingers – 'we're finally getting back a bit of normality.'

They reached his nan's and together they entered the jigger that led to the back yard. 'The front door's for weddings and funerals,' chuckled Jez, 'or at least that's what me nan's always told me.'

Hearing his voice, Carrie cried out with delight, 'Is that my Jez I can hear?'

Jez walked into the parlour and stood to attention, whilst ripping off a perfect salute. 'Reporting for supper, ma'am!'

His nan walked around him whilst he continued to stand to attention. 'Well, aren't you a bobby dazzler.'

'He certainly is,' enthused Cadi.

Jez hefted his bag into his hands. 'I'll go and put my stuff away – back in a mo.'

As he left the room, Carrie turned to Cadi. 'And how are you, my dear?' She lowered her voice. 'I must say I was delighted to hear that you and Jez had made it up. I told him not to be jealous, but when he read that letter, it tipped him over the edge.'

Cadi nodded slowly, not understanding which letter Carrie was referring to. 'We're fine now, thanks.'

'Good, because I'd hate to see that Daphne come between you.'

Cadi furrowed her brow. 'Daphne?'

'Have I got her name wrong? I'm referring to the young lady – and I use that term loosely – who told our Jez that you had the hots for Aled.'

Cadi stared open-mouthed. All she could think was that the old woman had got in a muddle. Rather than confuse things further, she patted Carrie's hands. 'All's well that ends well.'

When Jez re-entered the parlour, Cadi suggested that they make a pot of tea, so that she could voice her concerns to him in private.

'I think your nan's getting a bit confused.'

'Oh? What makes you say that?'

'She seems to think Daphne wrote you a letter …' She stopped speaking, because the look on Jez's face said it all.

Realising he'd been rumbled, Jez confessed, 'She did. I didn't tell you because I knew it was a pile of rot.'

Cadi tutted as she scooped the tea leaves into the pot. 'Honestly, Jez! If you'd told me she'd sent you a letter …' She hesitated. 'What did Daphne say exactly?'

Jez shrugged. 'She accused you of being after Aled, and said that I should keep an eye on the pair of you.'

Cadi's brow shot towards her hairline. 'She *what*?'

Jez nodded. 'I didn't believe it, of course. Aled was the one carrying a torch for you, not vice versa, which is why I chose to ignore it. Although having said that, it did unsettle me somewhat because it confirmed that Daphne knew how much Aled liked you.'

'Honestly, Jez, when did you get this letter?'

Jez's cheeks grew warm. 'The night before I left for Prestwich.'

'Yet you still proposed?'

He nodded fervently. 'Like I said, I knew Daphne was turning it all on its head.'

Cadi's tummy was beginning to turn somersaults. If Daphne had really wanted to set the cat amongst the pigeons, why hadn't she mentioned Cadi pecking Aled goodbye? 'Did she say anything else?'

'Nothing that was true.' He sighed irritably. 'She did try and make out that you'd kissed Aled goodbye, and that the pair of you had arranged to meet up in Lincoln. That's when I knew she was lying.' He looked at Cadi, who had gone very red. 'Cadi?'

She looked up. 'It wasn't a proper kiss, just a peck on the cheek.'

Jez leaned against the sink. 'Why would you even do that? The day before, you were sworn enemies. And whilst I know you'd put your differences behind you, I didn't think you'd got *that* close.'

'It was Daphne's fault,' sniffed Cadi. 'She said I stank of fags and stale ale, and that I was the chaff!'

His brow furrowed. 'You were what?'

Cadi relayed the conversation.

'Why did you care what Daphne thought?'

'You saw her, Jez, all glamorous in her fancy uniform and with her exciting job. I felt insignificant in comparison, made worse by her spiteful tongue.' Cadi's heart sank. If she was going to tell the truth, she might as well get it all out. 'Only Aled probably got hold of the wrong end of the stick.'

'I wonder why?' said Jez sarcastically.

'Please don't. I know how silly I've been.'

'But for your actions,' began Jez sternly, 'Daphne might never have written that letter, and I'd not have seen—'

Cadi looked up. 'I thought you said you didn't believe a word she'd said?'

'I didn't,' snapped Jez. 'I thought she was laying the blame on you instead of Aled. And I only thought that because I didn't believe for one minute that you would've done the things she'd accused you of. And I'm sorry, Cadi, but I have to ask myself why you did it? I know what you've said, but that doesn't make sense. If you ask me, you were doing it to show Daphne that you could have what she wanted.'

Cadi's jaw dropped. 'No! I don't want Aled, I've never wanted …'

Jez raised his eyebrows. 'I'm not saying you wanted him. I'm saying you did it to show Daphne that you were better than her, because you – a simple barmaid – could get what she, a driver in the WAAF, wanted most in this world.'

Cadi sank her head into her hands. 'I just wanted Daphne to rue her words.'

'You used Aled, which wasn't a nice thing to do,' said Jez plainly, adding, 'Does he know?'

Cadi nodded miserably. 'He was cross at first, but because he'd heard the things Daphne said, he forgave me.' She blinked shyly at him. 'The question is, will you?'

Jez placed his arms around her. 'We've both behaved rather immaturely.'

'You haven't,' sniffed Cadi.

'I joined the RAF to impress you.'

Cadi leaned back. 'You said you didn't.'

'Because I knew what you'd say! Why do you think I was so keen to become a pilot?'

'Because you thought it would be good?'

431

'No,' confessed Jez. 'Because it would be one in the eye for Aled.'

Cadi giggled. 'What a pair we are.' She paused. 'Do you think we're too young to be engaged?'

Carrie entered the kitchen, a shrewd smile on her lips. 'Forgive me for earwigging, but I believe I have the answer to that one.'

Cadi's face fell, as she felt certain the older woman was going to suggest they call it off.

'Relationships are hard work. It's not a case of falling in love and the rest takes care of itself – far from it. You have to make compromises, as well as take each other's feelings into account, be sure always to tell the truth and, above all else, learn to communicate. This is only one of the many arguments you'll have.' She smiled whimsically. 'Or lovers' tiffs, as they call them.'

Jez blew out his cheeks. 'You're not making it sound much fun.'

She laughed heartily. 'There will be plenty of fun to be had – you simply have to learn to take the rough with the smooth.'

'So you think we're ready?'

She nodded. 'Your first argument will always be the hardest, but you worked through it well, even forgiving each other and admitting your own faults. Carry on like that and you'll have many happy years together.'

It was the evening before Jez was due to leave and, as Maria closed the door behind the last customer, the air-raid siren sounded.

'Here we go again,' sighed Cadi as they trooped into the cellar. 'Has anyone remembered the cards?'

Carrie held them up. 'Me.'

'Good-o, that should help to while away the hours. Is the draughts board still down here?'

'It should be on top of one of the kegs,' said Bill.

'Found it,' cried Jez.

Closing the trapdoor behind them, they settled down, and Carrie began dealing out the cards. 'Gin rummy?'

'Why do we allus play gin rummy when I'm no good at it,' moaned Bill.

'That's why,' chuckled Carrie. 'Just be grateful I ain't got me purse with me.'

Her stomach jolted as the first bomb fell. She grimaced at the others. 'Not a false alarm then.'

Maria looked at the dust that was falling from the cellar roof. As the next bomb fell, the kegs vibrated. 'Close!' remarked Bill.

Maria cocked an ear.

'Did anyone hear that?'

'What?' said Bill.

'It sounded like someone walking round the bar.'

'Surely not,' gasped Carrie.

Maria got to her feet. 'I heard summat – I *know* I did.' She looked wildly around her. 'The till! I've only gone and left it up there.'

'Not *again*?' said Jez. He got to his feet. 'I'll get it.'

Bill shook his head. 'Don't be so bloody wet!' But he found himself talking to Jez's legs as they disappeared through the hatch.

They sat waiting for him to return, each hoping he would make it back before another bomb fell. Seeing Jez's legs reappear, Cadi breathed a sigh of relief. 'Thank God for—'

The last of her words were lost as the blast of the bomb took the very air from her lungs.

When Cadi came to, everywhere was dark. At first she forgot where she was, but as the memories came flooding back she began to panic.

'Jez? Maria? Bill … Carrie?'

She fell silent, hoping against hope that she would hear a response, but she was greeted by a deathly silence. She strained her eyes, trying in vain to see, but it was no use. As she coughed, brick dust and soot seemed to fill her mouth.

She tried to move, but something was lying across her legs. Grunting with effort, Cadi pushed it off. Crawling on her hands and knees, she felt about with her hands to make sure she wasn't going to hit her head on anything. It was as she was doing this that she discovered someone. She emitted a small scream as her fingers touched the cold flesh. She gave the person a gentle shake, but could tell by the feel of them that whoever it was had long gone. With tears streaming down her face, she tried to remember who had been in the cellar with her: Carrie, Maria, Bill and Jez. She gingerly felt down the arm, which was limp and cold.

Fearing the worst, Cadi began to sob as she continued feeling around, in the desperate hope that she would find someone else. Her mind flicked back to the time her father had been down the mine when it had caved in. This must have been exactly how he'd felt. Only he had Sam, whereas Cadi appeared to be on her own.

She reached out, and her groping fingers touched someone else. Frantic to hear the sound of another voice, Cadi shouted, 'Wake up!'

Maria stirred. 'What time is it?' Opening her eyes, she began to panic. 'Cadi? Is that you?'

'Yes. Do you remember what happened?'

Maria fell silent. 'Oh my God. The pub! Have you found the others?'

'Only one,' said Cadi. 'I think it was Auntie Carrie, but she was so cold, Maria – very cold.'

Maria's heart sank. 'We need to find the others and get her out of here. Give me your hand and we'll see if we can stand up.'

Holding hands, they tentatively tried standing, but it appeared that the roof of the cellar had caved in. Maria squinted at a tiny speck of light that pierced the darkness. 'I think I can see into the pub.'

A voice called down from above. 'Hello? Is anyone there?'

Maria and Cadi both called out to the unseen voice. 'Yes.'

'How many are there of you?'

'Five,' yelled Maria. 'Please hurry.'

Within seconds they could hear the sound of rubble being removed. After a few minutes Cadi and Maria blinked as a bright light pierced the cellar.

Holding Maria's hand tightly in her own, Cadi looked around the cellar, scared of what she might see. Bill was sitting on the floor, with the right-hand side of his face covered in blood. Carrie was still sitting in the same position, appearing relatively unharmed until Cadi looked into the old woman's eyes, which stared dully back. Cadi's bottom lip began to tremble as she turned her attention to finding Jez, who was lying at the bottom of the stairs, his face flecked with blood.

Releasing Maria's hand, Cadi flew over to him and began shaking him awake. Moaning, Jez eventually came to.

'Gawd, my head hurts.' He blinked around him. 'What happened?'

'The pub's been bombed,' said Cadi. 'Can you move?'

Grimacing, Jez got slowly to his feet. 'Where's Nan?'

Cadi's lip trembled. 'She's ...'

Seeing Carrie, Jez stumbled across the cellar. 'Nan?'

Cadi went after him. 'Jez, I don't think ...'

Holding his nan's hand, Jez sank to his knees and wept.

Having spent the rest of the night at Jez's house, Maria, Jez, Bill and Cadi went back to the Greyhound early the next morning to see if anything could be salvaged, but the building had been condemned.

'Sorry, luv,' said the warden, who was helping to clear the mess.

Maria shrugged. 'It's only bricks and mortar – some of us have lost a lot worse.' She looked at Jez. 'I'm so sorry.'

He grimaced. 'I know what you're thinking, because if Nan would've been at home, she'd still be alive. But that's not true, because one of us would've fetched her as soon as the siren sounded – only we'd never have made it back in time, and it would've been more than one life lost.'

He placed his arm around Cadi's shoulders. 'What now?'

Cadi's lip trembled and she wiped the tears away before they fell. 'I'd better ring my folks and tell them what's happened.'

'I meant, what are you going to do? The Greyhound wasn't just your home – it was your job too.'

Cadi grimaced. 'Oh, that. That's easy. I've thought about nothing else all night. I'm going to join the services.'

Jez's brow shot upwards. 'Are you sure?'

Cadi nodded firmly. 'Never been more certain of anything in my life. I'm going to make the Germans pay for what they did, and I'll not do that serving egg and chips.' She buried her face in Jez's shoulder. 'I hate them, Jez, and I've never hated anyone in my life. I won't be half the woman I think I am if I stand by and do nothing.'

Jez kissed the top of her head. 'If that's what you want, then you have my full support. In the meantime, don't worry about where to stay, because I saw the landlord earlier and he said you're all welcome to stay at Nan's until you sort summat else.'

Cadi didn't need to mull it over. 'I'll go down to the recruiting office as soon as it's open.' She turned to Maria. 'Do you fancy joining me?'

Maria shook her head. 'My place is here with Bill. With a bit of luck, another pub might come up for grabs, and when it does, we'll make sure we're first in line.'

Having been allowed extra leave on compassionate grounds, Jez had been able to bury his nan before leaving Liverpool. The funeral had been attended by all the locals who once frequented the Greyhound, as well as many friends and neighbours, proving how well loved Carrie was. As soon as the funeral was over, Jez and Cadi hastened to the station so that he might catch his train on time.

'I can't believe she's gone,' sniffed Cadi.

He gave her a grim smile. 'Me neither. Life's sure going to be different without Nan around.'

Cadi's lip trembled. 'I'm really going to miss her.'

Jez squeezed her in his arms. 'She was one hell of a woman.'

Cadi looked up at him. 'Are you going to be all right?'

Leaning down, he kissed her softly. 'I will be, with you by my side.'

'Only I'm miles away,' sniffed Cadi.

Jez brushed his lips against hers. 'If we're lucky, you might get posted to the same base as me.'

Cadi melted into his kiss, before replying softly, 'Oh, I do hope so.'

Seeing the porter closing the carriage doors, Jez picked up his kitbag and swung it over his shoulder. 'Time to say goodbye.'

Cadi wrapped her arms around his waist. 'I'm going to miss you so much.'

He brushed his lips against hers. 'I'll …' He hesitated; he had been about to say that he would ring the pub when he got back to base, but realised this was no longer possible. 'I'll write as soon as I'm back.'

Burying her face in his chest, Cadi nodded. 'I'll let you know what's what as soon as I get my papers.' Looking up, she blinked the tears away. 'I love you so much.'

Kissing her gently, Jez smiled as he pulled away. 'I know you do.'

She jabbed him playfully in the ribs. 'Don't tease!'

Pulling her close, he kissed her again. 'I love you too, and have done since the first day I clapped eyes on you.'

'So it *was* love at first sight,' mused Cadi. 'Poppy said it was.'

'As soon as I saw you jumping on Eric's back to save your pal, I knew you were the girl for me. You're one in a million, Cadi, and you're all mine!'

She giggled softly. 'We've certainly had our fair share of excitement.'

Jez kissed her for the last time, before walking her over to the train, keeping her hand in his until he was aboard. Closing the door, he slid the window down and leaned out. 'Life with you will never be boring, and I wouldn't have it any other way.'

Tears brimming in her eyes, Cadi waved to him as she followed the train down the platform. 'Me neither.' With the train moving too fast for her to keep up, she stood and waved. 'I love you, Jeremy Thomas!'

He just managed to shout the words 'I love you more, Cadi Williams!' before the train, and Jez, were lost from sight.

READ ON
FOR BONUS
CONTENT

Dear Reader,

Cities have always been a great attraction, offering opportunities, excitement and a social life to match no other, so it's no wonder they attract young people dreaming of a bright future. But what happens if you live in a rural community during a time when opportunities are hard to come by, especially if you're a woman?

These are the sort of questions that incite me to write. Eager to learn more, I began researching what life was like for those living in small villages, such as the mining communities. It was whilst perusing the internet that I came across a leaflet advertising the Rose Queen Carnival. Staring at the young girl whose photograph adorned the front page, I started to imagine how excited she would have been, and how special she must have felt, only to be disappointed when her day came to an end. I was so intrigued with this unknown's life, I knew I had to invent a character that I could follow, and so created Cadi Williams: a young woman yearning for a faster pace of life, with the independence and freedom that city life brings. Sadly, for women like Cadi, the life of a village girl holds no such opportunities.

It's hard for us to imagine that war was seen as an opportunity. But to women like Cadi and her best friend Poppy, it was the only way out. Knowing that Cadi's father would object, the girls hatch a plan to visit Cadi's aunt in Liverpool so that they can join up without being discovered.

Once in Liverpool, Cadi believes the world is her oyster but, as we all know, life just isn't like that. And when the services refuse to take the girls, so strong is Cadi's desire to be independent, that she unknowingly leads Poppy into a dark world, full of danger. With the girls out of their depth, it seems their adventure is over before it's begun.

I simply loved writing this story and, with the girls' lives taking so many different twists and turns, it's now become the first in a trilogy!

I hope you enjoy reading it as much as I enjoyed writing it.

Much love *Holly Flynn xxx*

STRAWBERRY UN-DAIQUIRI

Strawberry picking is one of my favourite things to do come the summer months and I enjoy using them in all kinds of different recipes. However, this was the first time I've used them in a drink – though it certainly won't be the last. Delicious!

INGREDIENTS
2 cups fresh or frozen strawberries

1/8 cup lime juice

1/8 cup lemon juice

1/4 cup crushed ice

1 tbsp lemon zest

2 tsp caster sugar

1 tbsp freeze-dried strawberries (for garnish)

METHOD
1. Pour the lemon and lime juices into a blender along with the caster sugar, and blend until smooth.

2. Add the 2 cups of strawberries and the ice, a few at a time, blending until smooth.

3. Pour into chilled glasses, decorate with the freeze-dried strawberries, and enjoy!

Turn the page for an exclusive
extract from the brand new
Katie Flynn novel

THE
WINTER
ROSE

KATIE
FLYNN

**COMING OCTOBER 2022
AVAILABLE TO PRE-ORDER NOW**

CHAPTER ONE

Bill indicated to the approaching train, as it crawled into the platform. 'Looks like this one's yours, queen,' he winked at Cadi, who wore a hesitant smile. 'Second thoughts?'

She paused briefly before shaking her head. 'No, but I'll admit I'm finding the whole thing a tad daunting now it's arrived. Though I suppose that's only natural when I'm starting a new job in a place I've never been to before.'

Maria smiled. 'You've done it before, only you were a lot younger, so if anything, this should be easier.'

Cadi arched her brow. 'I had Poppy with me then though, and it's much easier doing things with a friend by your side.'

'True,' conceded Maria, 'but I've a feeling you're going to come up trumps. You usually do.'

They watched as the passengers descended onto the platform.

Cadi looked down at the rail pass she had been issued. It may have sounded silly to anyone else but, to Cadi, the pass itself had made her feel important – like she was a part of something big, which she supposed she was. The WAAF was a huge organisation, taking on thousands of women each week. She drew a deep breath. She was going to be a small fish in a very big pond, but Maria was right: Cadi had left home a long time ago. If anything, she should count herself lucky; for many of the women joining, this would be their first experience living away from friends and family. Cadi pocketed the rail pass and picked up her small suitcase.

'I'm going to get myself a window seat before they're all taken,' she said, looking at Maria, who was blinking furiously in an attempt to stop tears forming. 'I know you don't like goodbyes, so I'll not make this any harder than it is.' Leaning forward, Cadi kissed Bill briefly on

the cheek before setting her suitcase back down and pulling Maria into a tight embrace. She hugged her friend tightly as she said, 'Thank you, Maria, not just for coming to see me off, but for everything. Had you not decided to take a chance on me, I daresay I'd not be half the woman I am today.'

Sniffing loudly, Maria stepped back from their embrace to fish a handkerchief from her handbag, and waved a dismissive hand. 'None of that, or you'll have me blubbing like a good 'un.' A wobbly smile tweaked her lips. 'I hope you know how incredibly proud I am of you – Poppy, too, come to that.'

Standing behind his wife, Bill placed his hands on her shoulders. 'She's always bragging about "her girls"; anyone'd swear she was your mam!'

Cadi took a handkerchief from her jacket pocket and absent-mindedly dabbed her eyes. 'She is! Or at least she's my Liverpool mam.' She glanced at the train, which was filling up with passengers. 'I hate to go, but I really must dash.'

Bill winked at Cadi. 'Ta-ra, queen. Keep in touch.'

Nodding, Cadi picked up her suitcase and hurried off before she could change her mind.

As she boarded the train she made a beeline for the first carriage with a window seat. Stowing her bag on the rack above her, she sat down and scanned the platform for a sign of her friends. She soon spotted Maria pointing her out to Bill, whilst frantically waving, and it caused her to smile. Waving back, Cadi heard the rail guard shout something before placing his whistle to his lips and blowing hard whilst flourishing his flag. She felt her stomach lurch as the train's whistle blew its response and began pulling out of the station. With Maria and Bill no longer visible, she settled back into her seat and smiled at a girl who had entered the carriage without her noticing.

The girl smiled back. 'Was that your mam and dad?'

'No, that was my old employer, Maria, and her husband, Bill,' replied Cadi.

The girl, whom Cadi assumed to be in her late teens, looked impressed. 'Blimey! I wish I'd had a boss like that – mine couldn't

wait to see the back of me!'

Cadi eyed the outspoken girl curiously. She seemed pleasant enough, with a cheery smile, and kind blue eyes. Intrigued to hear more, Cadi spoke the question uppermost in her thoughts. 'Where did you work?'

The girl rolled her eyes. 'Behind the jewellery counter in Blacklers…'

Having seen Blacklers – or what was left of it after the May blitz – Cadi grimaced. 'Before the bombing, or after they'd moved?'

'Both.'

Cadi furrowed her brow. 'You'd think your boss would be a bit more charitable; it's not easy upping sticks and moving elsewhere, especially to the premises you're in now, which aren't nearly as grand as the one on Great Charlotte Street.'

'I think that was part of the problem,' confessed the girl. 'You see, in the old place, I only worked in the restaurant, but when we moved, the position to serve the customers on the jewellery counter came up and me mam said I was to go for it, because it pays a little bit more and it's a lot fancier than serving sarnies for a living.' The girl shrugged. 'It just wasn't for me, though. I am what I am and I can't talk the same as the toffs, nor would I want to.' Pinching her nose, she put on a haughty voice, 'And Hyacinth thought I was far too common!'

'Oh,' said Cadi knowingly, 'she was one of them! Thinks she's as good as the customers that come in to buy the fancy jewellery, even though she couldn't afford to do so herself.'

The girl stared at Cadi open-mouthed. 'Nail on the bloomin' head!' She thrust a hand toward Cadi. 'I'm Kitty Hall.'

Cadi shook the girl's hand. 'Pleased to meet you, Kitty. I'm Cadi Williams.'

Beaming, Kitty fished out a small paper bag, which she offered up to Cadi. 'Everton mint?'

Thanking Kitty, Cadi took one of the sweets, peeled the paper off it, then stowed it into her cheek. She glanced at the small satchel that Kitty had placed on her knee. 'Where are you off?'

Kitty patted her bag. 'Seein' as I can't get me old job back I decided to cut my losses and leave Blacklers in favour of the WAAF.' She sucked her sweet thoughtfully before continuing, 'They're sending me to somewhere called RAF Innsworth to do my initial training. How about you?'

'Snap!' said Cadi, much to Kitty's surprise and delight. 'Only I'm not leaving Blacklers, of course.'

Kitty nodded thoughtfully. 'With an employer like that lady on the platform, I'm surprised you wanted to leave at all.'

Cadi told Kitty all about her work in the Greyhound and the subsequent bombing. 'The Belmont's lovely, but it's not home – or not to me, at any rate,' finished Cadi.

Kitty gave a knowing smile. 'Bit like me with Blacklers – only I didn't live there of course,' she rested her elbow against the arm of the chair. 'It sounds like you'd invested a lot of yourself into the Greyhound. It can't have been easy losing your job and your home like that.'

Cadi nodded. 'The Greyhound meant everything to me. It may sound silly, but I think I took the bombing personally.'

'I can see why. My auntie's place got bombed during the Christmas Blitz and she wasn't that bothered because it wasn't hers – she only rented it. She cared about her personal possessions, photographs, pictures, stuff like that, but not so much the place itself.'

'That's the difference,' said Cadi. 'The Greyhound was something I put my heart and soul into, and I know I could do the same with the Belmont, but quite frankly I don't see why I should have to start again when I shouldn't have lost the Greyhound in the first place. Not only that, but I've got friends in the WAAF, and of course my fiancé Jez is in the RAF. So I guess it feels like this is the right time for me to move on, as well as get my revenge on Jerry, of course...'

Kitty's eyes were full of admiration for Cadi. 'I don't think I would've been brave enough to leave home at sixteen, like what you did. Blimey, I'm a little nervous to do it now and I'm going to be twenty in a few months' time.'

Cadi sucked on her sweet thoughtfully. 'Have you any siblings?'

Kitty shook her head. 'Only child, why?'

'Just wondered if you'd ever shared a room before. When I lived with my family in Rhos, I used to share a room with three brothers. Imagine having to do that, with no privacy save for a curtain to divide the room up.' She smiled as she recalled the small bedroom. 'You share a room with three miners and believe you me, you can't wait to get out from there.'

Kitty laughed. 'I can imagine it can't have been very pleasant.'

'I love them dearly, but a girl needs her privacy – *especially* when she gets to a certain age.'

Kitty gazed at the fields that stood bleak after the autumn harvest. 'I've been trying to imagine what it's going to be like sharing a room with so many other women, but it's hard to envisage,' she said, as her cheeks turned pink. 'I don't want to come across as naïve, sheltered or prudish, but what do you suppose happens about things like getting changed for bed?'

Cadi nodded wisely. 'I'm guessing you're a little shy?'

'When it comes to stripping off in a room full of complete strangers, then yes, I suppose I am…,' she hesitated. 'Aren't you?'

Cadi, having never given the matter any thought, considered this before answering. 'I don't think so. I shared a room with Maria, Poppy and Izzy at one time, but maybe that's different because we all know each other?'

Kitty mulled this over before replying. 'I wasn't overly shy when we used to get changed for PE in school but, having said that, I did keep my vest on.'

Cadi coughed on a chuckle. 'True…' Smiling fondly at her new friend, she continued, 'I think you'll have to cross that bridge when you come to it. There's usually a way around these things and I daresay you won't be the only one who's cautious about undressing in a room full of strangers.'

With the matter settled, Kitty steered the topic round to something new. 'Any ideas what you want to do in the WAAF?'

Cadi shrugged. 'Poppy and Izzy are both in the MT – that's short for Motor Transport – and it sounds rather fun. They get to go all over

the country, so I suppose I'd like to do something like that. You?'

Kitty nodded. 'I'm hoping to work in the cookhouse. It's what I enjoy doing, and I'm good at it.' She smiled fondly into the distance. 'In Blacklers we only had the finest produce, but we had to be pretty thrifty with it. They used to tell us that every currant counts, and you couldn't afford to waste a single one. I enjoyed serving lots of people a hearty meal from little ingredients – it was challenging, but that's what I liked about it.'

'I don't think you'll have any difficulties getting into the cookhouse,' said Cadi. 'They'd be mad to turn someone with your experience down.'

Kitty didn't look so sure. 'Square peg, round hole, that's what my father always says.'

Cadi frowned. 'Sorry?'

'Dad reckons the army enjoys placing people where they don't belong, to test them out type of thing.'

Cadi's frown deepened. 'But that's silly. Surely you give people the jobs to which they are best suited?'

'Let's hope so, because I wasn't any good at flogging jewellery – although I can't see there'd be much call for that in the WAAF.'

Cadi laughed. 'I jolly well hope not.' As she looked out of the widow, she felt a pang of envy towards Kitty, who knew exactly what she wanted from the WAAF. The more Cadi thought about it, the only thing she was 'qualified' to do was make meals and change beds and, whilst she might not mind doing that in the B&B, she didn't much fancy the thought of doing it for hundreds of people. She wondered what she'd be like at driving. Poppy said it was easy enough and they gave you good instruction. Cadi smiled wistfully as she imagined herself sitting in a black Daimler, with Churchill in the back. She was pulling up to a set of traffic lights and the dreadful Daphne was coming towards her, behind the wheel of a dirty great lorry. When Daphne's eyes met Cadi's she could see the other woman was positively spitting feathers as she compared their vehicles. When Cadi drifted back out of her daydream, she was surprised to find a smile creeping up her cheeks. Was she really still affected by the other

woman's actions? A vision of Daphne, smiling in blissful ignorance to the trouble she had created, formed in her mind. *I'm angry*, Cadi thought to herself, *because Daphne was never held accountable for her actions*. Daphne had indeed been the cause of the chaos, by blowing things out of proportion, but there had been at least one shred of truth in her letter. Cadi had pecked Aled on the cheek when he had gone to leave the Greyhound. She had only done it to annoy Daphne, which, as it turned out, had worked a treat, but that was where it ended – or at least it had for Cadi. Not for Daphne, though, who chose to use it as a weapon against Cadi. Cadi cursed herself inwardly. Was she angry at Daphne for telling tales, or herself for being so silly in the first place? Cadi had often questioned whether Daphne would have sent the letter had Cadi not implied that she liked Aled.

And therein the trouble lies, thought Cadi bitterly. *You don't know, because you never got the chance to confront Daphne*. Cadi knew that it was better to let the matter lie, but if she were to bump into Daphne she would definitely tell the other woman exactly what she thought of her behaviour, whilst hopefully getting an answer or two along the way.

By the time Cadi and Kitty arrived at their destination station, both girls were relieved to learn that they wouldn't be boarding another train.

Kitty was eyeing the length of the platform as the train drew into the station. 'I wonder where we go from here?' she said curiously. Spotting a man in RAF uniform, she pointed him out to Cadi. 'Do you think he's here for us?'

Cadi pulled her suitcase down from its rack. 'I suppose so, but I guess there's only one way to find out. Are you ready?'

Kitty swung her satchel over her shoulder. 'As I'll ever be.'

KATIE
FLYNN

If you want to continue to hear from the
Flynn family, and to receive the latest news about
new Katie Flynn books and competitions,
sign up to the Katie Flynn newsletter.

Join today by visiting
www.penguin.co.uk/katieflynnnewsletter

Find Katie Flynn on Facebook
www.facebook.com/katieflynn458